THE GOLD MINE

a novel of lean turnaround

by

Freddy Ballé & Michael Ballé

Published by the Lean Enterprise Institute
lean.org

Lean Enterprise Institute

© Copyright 2005 Lean Enterprise Institute, Inc. All rights reserved.
Lean Enterprise Institute and the leaper image are registered trademarks
of Lean Enterprise Institute, Inc.

Design by Off-Piste Design
Library of Congress Control Number: 2004117725
Ballé, Freddy and Michael
The Gold Mine: a novel of lean turnaround/Freddy Ballé and Michael Ballé
ISBN: 978-0-9743225-6-8

Lean Enterprise Institute, Inc.
215 First Street, Suite 300
Cambridge, MA 02142 USA
(t) 617-871-2900 • (f) 617-871-2999 • lean.org

For Catherine and Florence

FOREWORD

Today the effectiveness of lean thinking has been well established. Companies from myriad industries in every corner of the world have proved that the principles are well founded. By posting record profits, while laying the basis for further growth, these companies, led by Toyota, reveal the promise of lean. Yet while these leaders appear enthusiastic and confident, for many others the reality of practicing lean management is a daunting challenge. Much of the technical basis for a lean transformation has been codified in an accessible manner, yet beyond the mechanics, managers often find the basic reasoning of the approach counterintuitive. The necessary behavioral changes are stubbornly challenging, and often lead to doubts that undermine the prospective leader and team.

Freddy and Michael Ballé's book, *The Gold Mine*, serves to remove these doubts. Readers of this story will find in the all-too-human details of one lean turnaround a helpful reminder that this process takes more than technical prowess. More important, they will be inspired to use their natural talents to lead others to improve.

Over the last 20 years of implementing lean systems, from my position on the board of GKN Automotive, then later at the helm of the Kaizen Institute, and currently as an advisor to McKinsey & Co., I have had the chance to work with many interesting and exciting people. While professional ethics should prevent me from having preferred clients, principles sometimes bow to reality. Having known and worked with Freddy for more than 10 years, I can say that he stands out as a remarkable combination of knowledge, drive, insight, and impact.

Working at the upper levels of the automotive industry is not for the faint-hearted. Freddy has always accepted the challenge of making change in an environment of unforgiving and unremitting pressure for results. He is legendary for the sophistication and intensity of his management of the budget process. But Freddy has never lost sight of his roots: the shop-floor, ground-up approach so critical to lean thinking. Exposing himself to the challenge of serving Toyota, he acquired a detailed knowledge of the specifics of the Toyota Production System that I believe is unequaled in senior management. Characteristically for Freddy and uncharacteristically for a senior manager, he used that knowledge as a means to instruct, challenge, and lead his managers through the lean transformation.

Together with his son, Michael, who has pursued his own successful consulting career, Freddy could have written an authoritative work on the technical aspects of lean implementation in the automotive components industry. Or they could have written what I suspect would be the definitive work on performance management for lean (which I hope that the success of this book will encourage them to do). Instead they chose to write the novel you now have in your hands.

This story is primarily about people, about how people's minds have ideas about making things, and about how those ideas change based on their own perceptions, interests, and capabilities. This focus teaches lean at the point of use: the intersection of where we think, feel, and act. The authors have not lost sight of the fact that the tools and systems of lean are merely a codification of answers to specific questions that individuals have asked as they try to apply the basic principles.

The story is constructed like *Alice in Wonderland*. You can read and appreciate it as a simple piece of human drama, with a series of quirky and engaging characters, with twists and turns that will challenge and amuse you. You also can look below the surface to see a well-constructed framework that introduces and applies all of the tools of lean. Look even closer and you will see the basic beliefs on behavior, leadership, and problem solving that are the hidden aspects of a lean transformation.

The best thing about this book may be that you don't have to *study* it. Instead, sit back, read, and enjoy it, quite possibly using it for group reading with your colleagues. I guarantee that you will find that the lessons, turns of phrase, and pithy explanations will guide you on your own lean journey.

– Peter Willats

Chapter One

PROFIT IS KING, BUT CASH RULES

First came the phone call. "Mike?" said Charlene. "Is Phil with you?" There was an edge to her voice, a hint of panic. "Haven't seen him," I answered. "Is anything wrong?"

"I hope not. He phoned saying he would drop by your place in the evening, but I haven't heard from him since." It was already past 11 p.m. by my watch, reason enough to be worried — but not quite that worried. I tried to get her to talk some more, but she just asked me to ring if Philip came around. I put the phone down, puzzled. Philip Jenkinson is a close friend. We go all the way back to senior high, and we'd had a drink only a few weeks ago. He was the successful one. He'd made it big in the world. He'd made it rich. I knew he had been under a lot of work pressure lately, but beyond the usual signs of executive stress, he seemed perfectly fine. I worried he may have had an accident.

The front doorbell rang. A disgruntled cab driver was trying to steer a drunken Philip, who was swaying and blabbering. "This your friend?" grunted the cabby. We lugged Phil inside and dropped him on the couch. He was not only deeply under the influence, but shivering badly, and soaked from the driving rain. I paid the driver, added a tip, and watched him retreat into the filthy night. Philip was already snoring. Feeling like a snitch, I phoned Charlene, remained vague on the details, and told her not to worry, I'd drive her husband back to her in the morning. I could hear the kids bickering in the background and was surprised that they were still up at this time, unusual on a weekday, but after all, it was none of my business.

1

I pulled the drenched coat off Philip, battled with his boots, and left him to sleep it off spread-eagled on the sofa. He looked strangely childish, mumbling in his drunken stupor, an echo of the gangling teenager he'd been in our youth, and, not for the first time, I wondered why on earth he'd retained the nerd-like haircut-and-glasses look of his teens. He even had pens sticking out of his shirt pocket! He was a big man, tall, blond, with strong features marred somewhat by pockmarks. A good face, though, and a good man, I reminded myself, irritated. Not particularly subtle or refined, he'd been a good friend over the years — terribly sharp in his own one-dimensional way. Slightly on the boring side, he rarely drank, never smoked, and, aside from a weakness for flashy cars and a compulsion to work, had no particular vices to speak of. What, I wondered, had got him into this dreadful state?

The morning broke bright, cheerful, and noticeably warmer than the past few days. It had been raining continuously for the past week, and I hoped that spring was finally here to stay. I love northern California, but do I hate this late-season rain! I kicked Phil awake and shoved a pot of black coffee, a half-pint of beer, and a raw egg in his face, a fail-proof hangover recipe from our wilder days. He guzzled the beer, drank the coffee, balked at the egg, and finally sat up, slumped on the sofa. I sat down, carefully sipping from my own mug.

"Want to talk about it?"

A shake of the head. Painful, obviously.

"Family trouble?"

He looked up, blearily surprised.

"Nope. Work trouble."

I blinked. Work trouble? How could that be? Philip was a success story. He'd gone to Berkeley, gotten a Ph.D. in physics and ended up developing some high-tech gizmo, which he then patented. On the back of that he and a partner had successfully started a small manufacturing operation on the West Coast. I was studying for my doctorate in the United Kingdom at the time and didn't know much about it, until the mysterious currents of modern life brought us both to the same town. Two years ago, Phil and his partner bought an established company, with the aim of integrating the new technology into the existing product line. When I got a job with a good college, Sarah (ex-girlfriend) and I stayed with Phil and Charlene before finding a place of our own in the area. He pulled in more money in a month than I did in a year with my measly university salary, and his constant talk about IPOs and share prices would have bored me to bits if I hadn't been slightly, ah, jealous.

Work trouble? What kind of work trouble can get you dead drunk and crashed out on a friend's couch?

"Bad?"

"Worse." He held a second cup of coffee, his eyes red and vague, the lines of his face showing stark in the morning light. He ran a hand over his face. "I can't cope anymore. I don't know where to start. It's just too much!"

"Tell me."

"You wouldn't understand," he shrugged, and then continued all the same. "If we don't do something real fast, we will be bankrupt in a few months. Everything we own is mortgaged. The banks won't give us another dime. And we've tried everything we can think of. There's just no way."

As I understood it, Phil and his partner Matthew had gambled that they could buy an ailing company in their industry for a bargain price, turn it around with their new technology, and basically make a killing. With what they could raise of their own money and a lot of bank debt, they closed the deal, and, after an initial burst of enthusiasm, the two seemed to settle in to the sober realities of running a company. But I had never realized things had been this hard. I guess everyone was suffering in this latest economic downturn — entrepreneurs more than the rest, barring laid-off workers.

"Too much," he whispered again, with true desperation. An academic myself, I found it difficult to grasp both the scope of his problems and why it should be so tragic, but I was well aware that for some people, business was more important than family, life, and the universe wrapped together. I knew. My father was one of those people, and I'd grown up with these sorts of issues, or rather, in spite of them.

"I've looked at the figures from every angle. If we don't find a way to get some cash in real quick, we're about to lose all we have. All of it!"

"Come on, it's only money!"

"I knew you wouldn't understand," he said with a sulk. "See, the banks are calling our loans, we've mortgaged everything we own, and at the moment, we can barely pay the interest on the money we borrowed. If they don't extend the credit line, we can't pay wages, we can't pay suppliers, and that's that. We fold!"

"Oh, hell," he moaned. "I've got to get home. Oh boy!" He put his face in his hands, raking his hair with his fingers. The only thing that went through my mind was that I'd better think of something before driving him back in that state to Charlene.

"Well, there's one thing we can do, although I'm going to regret this," I ventured. He looked at me, not quite listening. "We could go and talk to Dad."

My father was the only person I knew who might be able to help Phil, but, as we drove down to the bay, I was having second thoughts. My Dad was retired now, and spent most of his time fiddling with his boat at the Bay Yacht Club. In his heyday he'd been a successful executive in the automotive supplier industry. He'd joined the navy right out of high school, and used the G.I. bill to get a degree in industrial engineering when he got out. Then, oddly enough, he found a job in Britain working for British Leyland. This was around the time of the merger between Austin Morris and Leyland — back in the days, that is, when the United Kingdom still had a domestically owned auto industry. This is where he met my Mom, and my brother and I grew up in the Midlands, until Dad got a big job back in the United States with a Detroit-based automotive supplier.

The move was horrendous. All of a sudden, I lost all my friends and found myself in a company of strangers. I didn't speak like them, I didn't dress like them. Brother, I didn't even like them — and they hated me back (to be fair, I think it was even worse for my younger brother). At the time, the cool kids equally shunned Phil for his nerdish and complete interest in science, not to mention his hand-me-down clothes. Somehow we got to be friends, two ugly ducklings in a pond, and stayed friends even while I went back to Britain to go to university and eventually to complete my Ph.D. in psychology.

My father had had an unusual career, distinguished by the fact that he'd caught on to the Japanese industrial offensive early on. While most of his colleagues ignored or belittled these new manufacturing techniques, he'd become obsessed. In my teenage years, all he seemed to talk about were barbaric-sounding words such as kanban and kaizen. He went as far as learning the language (approximately), and made a number of trips to Japan, in particular to visit Toyota. Not surprisingly, this had not made him very popular with many of his colleagues, particularly since he insisted on lecturing them on the shortcomings of Western managers. The British resented his American bluntness, and the Americans just ignored him. Some considered him a crank, others a downright pain. As a result, he had moved through a number of companies, turning operations around and then losing the inevitable political battles. Ultimately he would be forced to leave, joining yet another company for yet another fight.

In the end, he became vice president of operations for a large automotive supplier. All went well for a while, until his boss retired, and my father realized he wouldn't be considered for the top job because the board was looking for a younger man. Disgruntled, he retired in a huff, and still tells anyone willing to listen that since he left the company has gone down the tubes (true, but whether there is a cause-and-effect link, I can't say). Eventually my parents decided to settle down near my brother and me in sunny northern California, and found a house in the hills within easy driving distance of where I now live.

Dad had been a workaholic all his life, and I thought he'd go on working as a consultant. Once again he surprised us. As soon as he retired he walked away from industry without looking back. Being a man of passions, he now poured all his energies into his first love: boats. He'd always had an old tub moored or docked somewhere, but with all the moving around my Dad hadn't had much time to devote to his sailing. On top of which, I think he was deeply disappointed that neither my brother nor I shared his enthusiasm for getting wet and cold and sick just for kicks. He'd bought a lovely wooden 40-foot ketch and spent most of his time tinkering with it, talking endlessly to anyone who'd listen about his navy days. In no time he became something-or-other at the Bay Yacht Club and seemed to spend more time there than at home, to the unspoken relief of my mother, who enjoyed having the house, and the day, to herself.

As we drove, I explained all this to Phil, who was listening distractedly. He'd just been on the phone to his dearly beloved, and the earful he got was not mixing well with last night's drinks, adding to the sour look on his face. In the end, I think he just felt too ill to argue, and wasn't quite up to going home.

"Don't step over there, the varnish is not dry yet!" growled Dad as I was about to step aboard. "Hi, Dad," I answered wryly, after nodding to the florid, red-faced man who lounged in the cockpit with a mug in his hand. My father, his back to us, was working careful strokes on the roof of the cabin. His friend wore a navy blue shirt and pressed chinos, very much the postcard yachtsman. He gilded the lily by wearing a ridiculous sailor's cap at a rakish angle, giving him a vaguely piratical air. He was soaking up the morning sun and smiling contentedly, in total contrast to my father, who was on hands and knees in his working clothes, a torn gray sweatshirt and stained jeans, sporting his usual scowl.

"Hop on, hop on, don't mind him. You know what he's like!" said Long John Silver with an expansive gesture toward Dad. We clambered on board gingerly, and I sat down on the deck while Philip looked around bewildered, trying to find some place on the ship that could accommodate his bulk.

"Harry, this one here is my son. Boys, meet Harry," Dad said, flashing us an evil-tempered look as he carefully dipped his paintbrush into the pot.

"Harry," nodded Philip politely, "Mr. Woods." Dad turned around and stared at him, his two pale eyes and beak of a nose (family trait, I'm afraid) giving him the hawkish look which made every one feel an instinctive urge to straighten up and salute. I'd managed to shake the intimidation off over the years, and laughed quietly when I saw Philip squirm uncomfortably.

"Hi there, Philip," said Dad. "These rascals used to steal my whiskey and think I didn't notice," he said to Harry, turning back to his work. I never knew that he did. Philip laughed out loud, remembering our foraging in my Dad's office, and the years fell from his face, finally making him look more his age.

"You're Bobby's kid," said Harry, squinting at me. "I'll be damned. I could tell. Same nose," he added with a smirk, draining his mug.

"Well, what brings you boys out here?" asked my father, his back resolutely turned on us again, carefully applying the varnish on the ancient, venerable wood of the boat's cabin.

"It's like this, Dad. Phil has problems with his business, and I thought you could talk it over with him and maybe help him out."

"Well, why don't you let Philip tell me his troubles then?"

I sat back, held my breath, and let Phil haltingly begin his story. "Do you remember, Mr. Woods, the last time we talked, I told you I had developed a patent for a new technology in the high-voltage business, which applied, among other things, to industrial circuit breakers? Well, I found a partner, and we set up a small factory. It did quite well, and two years ago we bought up one of our competitors, which was filing for Chapter 11 bankruptcy."

"What was wrong with it?" interrupted Harry.

"Too expensive," Phil answered with a shrug. "Antiquated technology, inefficient operations, plenty of deadwood in management. At the time we were getting more orders than we could handle and we needed the extra capacity. There was a lot that could be used in the old plant, which had some highly qualified workers. We thought we could turn the business around."

"So you started streamlining," pursued Harry, fishing a metal flask out of his pants pocket and looking uncertainly at his empty cup. "But it wasn't as easy as you thought and ..."

"Let the man finish!" exclaimed Dad. I wondered who this Harry character was. He was obviously enjoying himself. Though his sailing costume and his gut made him look a bit like Falstaff, the keenness of his eyes signaled a deeper wisdom. With a loud sigh he heaved himself up and clambered into the cabin to pour another cup. "Coffee, anyone?"

"Not for me, thanks," continued Phil. "Yes, we did okay at first. My partner Matt has a law background, so he managed to negotiate the departure of the management team, which really helped with costs. We made do with the remaining people, but eventually we ran into a number of difficulties.

"Matt had secured a bank loan for a big portion off the purchase price, which made it possible for us to buy it, but left us with regular payments to fulfill the loan. As we had guessed, the company had orders, but they weren't being fulfilled. So, we got the veterans together and asked them what was going on. They told us that management had invested so little in the shop floor over the years that machines were often down, and productivity suffered from a lack of simple tools and many other glitches. They were right, and for a year we worked very hard at cleaning up operations, while setting up our new technology. We also worked with consultants to improve production flows on the shop floor."

He took a breath, which turned into a sigh. "And it worked," he said, "for a while, but then ..." he shook his head, still at a loss.

"Cash problems?" asked Harry, spiking his coffee refill from a silver hip flask.

"Yeah. We just seem to be running out of money all the time. And the bankers have just told us they won't extend our credit. We're having huge problems paying the interest on our loans, we're so late in paying some of our suppliers that they've put us on COD, and naturally we're having trouble finding the money to pay wages." As he talked, he leaned forward, his hands absently pulling his hair.

"What's wrong with your outfit?" pursued Harry. "Products aren't profitable?"

"It isn't so much that. The products are profitable — when we are able to produce them consistently and on time. But materials are expensive and we never seem to be able to make things as effectively as we could. It's really frustrating. We could do a lot more business, but that would mean investing in additional capacity, and new materials, which, of course, would require more cash.

"We figure that we would be making a healthy profit on the products if we just had simple standard costs: no extra costs for overtime, or extra materials, or the million unexpected fees that crop up everywhere. If we weren't constantly incurring these penalties, then we figure that we'd be consistently profitable."

"What are you doing about overhead?" Harry asked.

"We've cut all that we could. I don't see what else we can do to reduce our fixed costs."

"And what about working capital?"

"We've done all we could on that front. When we took over, we focused on receivables, and made customers pay on time. Now we're the ones who are delaying payment to vendors, and they are threatening to cut us off."

"Which leaves inventory," said Dad, turning around and settling in the cockpit, cleaning his brush with a rag.

"Inventory is high," agreed Phil. "We tried to get it under control, but then we couldn't make deliveries. At first we weren't too worried when we bought the company, because they had very reasonable average inventories ..."

This made my father guffaw, but he didn't say more.

"Then we found out that the average didn't actually mean much. We discovered they held far too much stock of some parts, and were out of others. Since different parts go into different end items, they had constant production stoppages from missing parts, which they then compensated for by working on other orders, thus creating in-process inventories. We've been fairly successful in reducing the missing parts problem, but the trouble is that in doing so we found it very hard to reduce the existing inventory of overstocked parts. They usually were long lead time parts, mostly from low-cost countries, and we had to increase the inventories of the parts missing the most. In the end, our inventory kept increasing, and we didn't know how to get it down without damaging delivery."

"Which contributes to your cash-flow problem," concluded Harry, nodding wisely. "Increased orders also drove up the cash outlay needed to build the product, which compounded the inventory problem, along with having to pay for the wages and equipment, and, eventually, the pile of cash you started with just melted away."

Phil said nothing, and just sat there looking miserable.

"Happens all the time," said Harry. "I used to be in purchasing. I've seen more than one supplier go through this, and then go bust. The industrial game is not very complex, but it's tough. Basically it's about economies of scale. The more you repeat a sale, the less it costs you. Double your volume and your cost goes down by about 10%, which is why everyone is always trying to get bigger. The theory is that as long as you can leverage the capital to grow, you're okay."

I looked to Dad for confirmation, but he'd gone back to his work, struggling to get a second can of varnish opened. The whole scene was a bit surreal. We were getting an economics lecture on the deck of his beautiful yacht, on this glorious, balmy morning. It dawned on me for the first time that Dad might have good reason to spend so much of his time down here. The air was clean and fresh from the night's rain, the water peaceful. Phil, though, was listening intently, chin in hand, oblivious to the scenery. I saw that he had removed a notebook from his jacket (since he was a kid he always carried a notebook with him) and was jotting down notes.

"But there's a catch," Harry continued. "Several catches actually. First, economies of scale only work if you're always selling the same product. Diversity is costly, and doubling your diversity usually brings on a cost hike of the same 10% or more. Trouble is, most customers of industrial goods want customization. So although you're dealing with the same core product or technology, you're not actually selling the same product, and the economies of scale don't materialize. Your costs grow with volume." He let the point sink in and shook the remains of his mug over the rail.

"Second, the larger you grow, the more coordination is needed, which means more overhead, and so the cost-per-sale economies of scale have to be balanced against an increase of management costs. This is why only 20% of mergers and acquisitions are financially successful. You might double your volume by taking on a similar firm and the market that goes with it, but if you can't lose one of the management structures altogether, you've not gained much. You had a good go at it, from what you're saying, but beyond the obvious, getting rid of administrative costs is a lot harder than it seems. By and large, businesses need their systems just to operate, even if these systems are inefficient," he said, taking a swig from his flask. "Right?"

Phil nodded glumly.

"And then comes the clincher. The more you sell, the more you have to finance the cost of the goods you sell, if, as you say, the material content of your product is high. To add insult to injury, supposing that you've worked your way successfully through all that, you soon find out that the only way to guarantee delivery is to keep a very high inventory in order to cover vendor and customer variation."

"Yeah, you've got it," agreed Phil, pulling his glasses back on the bridge of his nose. "We thought taking over this company would let us leverage our technological edge. And we've handled the coordination cost well enough, mind you. We've reduced overhead quite drastically, after initially putting a lot of money into improving shop-floor equipment and operations, which had been totally neglected. We've also worked hard at reducing lost production because of missing parts. We've had some results from these actions, in terms of getting products out to customers, but it's not nearly enough and our cash situation is catastrophic, all the more so since we had already leveraged our first company quite badly to get enough cash for this deal."

"Since you seem to know all about it," I asked Harry hopefully, "isn't there anything Phil can do to get out of this mess?"

He looked at me doubtfully.

"Hard to say," he answered with a frown. "Generally speaking, there are three ways to turn around an industrial firm quickly when you're facing a cash crunch.

"First, you have to drop any nonprofitable activity and stop throwing good money after bad. You need to invest all the cash you can muster up in the profitable stuff, or that with the greatest potential in the market.

"Second, squeeze suppliers. Used to be my job; and,

"Third, improve shop-floor operations. Now, I don't know much about that — your Dad's the expert in that regard."

He shook his head. "Unfortunately, I don't see what they can do. Not on the financial front anyhow. Why do you think so many new businesses fail each year? They go through this cycle and collapse," said Harry, fiddling with his flask. "I've seen enough of it to know why it happens, and how, but it doesn't mean I know how to fix it. Your problem is on the operations side. Bob might have some ideas about that," he added thoughtfully, tossing the ball my father's way.

"Not likely!" protested Dad.

"Why not?"

Dad fixed his steely-eyed eagle stare on me for a long, uncomfortable silence. Finally he opened his arms in a helpless gesture. "There are so many reasons, I wouldn't know where to start."

"Like what?" I pushed. Silence.

"Well, I'd have to go to his factory, for starters," he answered irritably. "And I swore I'd never set foot in another plant as long as I live."

"What am I going to do?" Philip gasped, and, to our dismay, we realized he was hunched up over himself, on the verge of sobbing. Overhead, a seagull gave its high-pitched cry.

Chapter Two

GOLD IN THE FLOW

My Dad's not that bad. Really. Once you get over his abrupt communication style, that is. We ended up locking the boat, walking Harry back to the Yacht Club, and piling into my derelict car. As we drove to Phil's plant, he talked incessantly about his business and technology to my father, who seemed to follow, although it was all Greek to me. Dad spoke little and mainly listened, which, for all his faults, he is rather good at. "Aw, call me Bob," he interrupted at one time as Phil was plodding on with "Mr. Woods." I concentrated on the driving, trying to follow Phil's directions as we entered the no-man's land of the industrial estates, a desolate land of corrugated iron, security fences, and ugly gray buildings. Finally we turned into a driveway and parked in front of a large, off-white building looking like a great big plastic box with a glass front.

It didn't look like much more than a couple of glorified warehouses, but the lawn was mowed, the signs neat, and my friend's company IEV (standing for "Industrial Extreme Vacuum") logo was proudly displayed, with a tacky bolt of lightning coming off the letters.

"Matt's away," Phil said as he ushered us through the glass doors into the lobby, "but I can introduce you to Dave Koslowsky, our production manager."

"I'd rather not meet anyone," answered Dad, bluntly. "Let's see your shop floor."

Phil led us through a corridor of large windowpanes overlooking spacious, open-plan offices where people were busily working in their cubbyholes. At the end of the corridor, a heavy door opened on the plant itself, and I realized I had never actually been in a factory, no matter how much I heard about it at home. It was overwhelming — the people, the machinery, the noise. I could not make heads or tails of it, but I could see my Dad taking it all in with a sigh. He knew what he was looking at, and looking for.

Phil led us straight to a central display, right in front of us, where several products were showcased along with the major parts going into them.

"This is the vacuum core," he explained, holding up a white ceramic capsule, roughly the size of a large beer can. "The new technology we developed enables us to pack more punch into a smaller and better core," he continued, pointing for contrast to a much larger capsule resembling a fat mineral water bottle. "The new ones have better efficiency, have fewer failures, and last longer. They are in great demand for new applications, but many of the current market installations are tied up with the old technology.

"And this is the completed product," he said, patting a squat, ugly, metal box, the size of a jumbo filing cabinet, with an instrument panel. "Inside the cabinet, you find these breaker mechanisms, one for each circuit," he said, showing a variety of capsules embedded into mechanical and electrical contraptions of various shapes. "These are what actually do the job of breaking the circuit, to prevent electrical overloads in high-power industrial applications like factories and power plants.

"We manufacture the mechanisms and the cabinets, and fit them with the control panels our customers send to us. The new technology allows us to build smaller mechanisms, so, in simple terms we can put in more breakers to protect more circuits in one cabinet. There's an increasing demand for that.

"Basically, we build the cabinets in one part of the plant, while we assemble the mechanism that fits around the cores in another. Then we install a purchased circuit board in the cabinet, fit the mechanisms in, wire the whole thing together with a control panel provided by our customers to their specifications and, *voilà*, a completed product. An outrageous oversimplification, of course, but, that's basically what we do."

"These new vacuum cores are what you manufacture at the other plant?" inquired Dad.

"Yes. But we still manufacture some of the old cores here. You see, the new cores need much higher oven temperatures and they rely on different composite materials. This is what my original research focused on."

"Why not just sell the cores?" cut in Dad, clearly avoiding a lecture from Phil on the properties of matter at high temperatures.

"Well — good question," answered Phil, frowning. "We've certainly considered that. It turns out that although the new cores are clearly an improvement, we couldn't sell as many as we'd expected. Because they have different parameters than the old vacuum cores, they're complicated to design into mechanisms. And so our customers or their vendors tend to have trouble building mechanisms for my new cores. In the end we were even contemplating building a manufacturing capability from scratch, but then this opportunity came up.

"What we finally did is modify their existing mechanism design to work better with our new core, and we made additional savings on the way. So we're now building the entire breaker box, which our customers can integrate with their other electrical equipment. Indeed, that's where the real markup is. That's why we bought this plant. We wanted to be on the higher-value part of the food chain."

"Hmm, other than the cores, the parts don't cost that much, but are more labor-intensive to manufacture and assemble. Right?" Dad asked.

"This is what we found out," Phil agreed ruefully. "We were not prepared to run a factory of this size. We did not realize all that it entails. Making the vacuum cores is a highly technical process, but can be done with just a few expert operators. There are very few steps involved and very few parts to buy from outside vendors. Making the complete product is another matter.

"Anyway, we sell four types of completed breaker boxes in the market. Our highest runner is the STR model. It uses our new core, which is very compact, meaning we can fit four mechanisms, to protect four circuits, in a slim cabinet. It's by far the best performing device on the market, and Matt says we can sell as many of these as we can produce. But I'm not so sure. STRs don't adapt well to old plants and are meant for high-power applications, so the market is mostly limited to new power plants.

"Then we have two additional products using our new technology. The QST-1 and QST-2 both use the Q core, which can handle slightly less power. The QST-1 uses four mechanisms while the QST-2 uses three. Finally, we still manufacture the DG product using the old D core and a single mechanism," he added, pointing to a large metal cabinet. "These are mostly replacement items for existing power plants, and managing the high-power requirement with the old technology requires a much larger cabinet."

"I don't know much about equipment," mumbled Dad. "Are any of these industry-standard items?"

"Not quite," Phil answered with a shrug. "The cores and mechanisms are standard in terms of the job they perform, but each customer order requires some customization, mostly in the interfaces with the circuit board and the instrument panel on the front of the cabinet. Plus the cabinets themselves. Customers all seem to want to specify cabinets that will fit neatly in the intended installation. We don't manufacture circuit boards or panels, and often the customer specifies the design and even the vendor. So we have to integrate the mechanisms, the circuit board, and the instrument panel within a confined space in the cabinet. That's what all the designers you saw in the office are working on: costing and customizing orders."

"Right," Dad muttered, looking doubtful.

"The complete device is assembled in four steps, after we make the core," Phil continued, pointing to a diagram of the assembly process. "First, we assemble the mechanism, which is mostly mechanical parts including a small motor to move the core back in position if the circuit is broken. It's like a hand-held drill motor — we actually use the same vendor. Then we fit the core into the mechanism, which is a pretty delicate operation with a lot of adjustment. Next we wire up the completed mechanism at the end of the assembly line and send it to electrical testing. Once the mechanisms pass the test — and we often have to change out parts — they are fitted into the cabinet and wired to the circuit board and instrument panel, again with a good bit of adjustment.

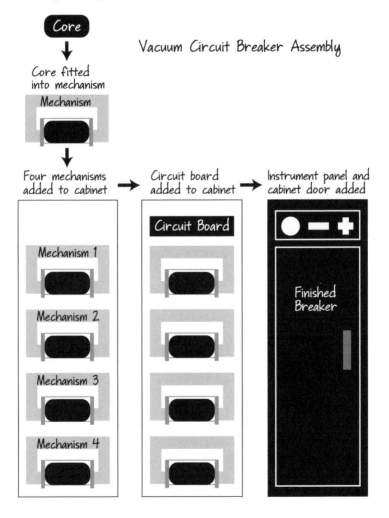

Vacuum Circuit Breaker Assembly

"At this stage ..."

"Never mind the rest, son. Just show me the plant," said Dad.

Phil stood for a second in mid-explanation, closed his mouth, and muttered, "This way, please."

I followed them both, trying to keep my usual irritation with Dad's appalling manners under control. The plant was a large, bustling place, with tubes and wires running along the ceiling and down columns, and people milling about among racks of odd-looking parts and machinery. It smelled of large empty places, oil, and metal dust. A loud banging could be heard rhythmically. It felt like walking through a gigantic garage — not the type of place in which to spend the best part of your daylight hours!

To Phil's credit, the place seemed rather clean, albeit painted in a grubby, off-white greenish color. Alleys were clearly marked on the floor, and I managed to more or less stay out of the way of the speeding forklifts, honking away as they rounded corners. Phil took us around to a huge glass-walled side of the building. Through the tinted glass wall, we could see a clinically white environment, which looked more like a lab than a production facility.

"This is where the old cores are manufactured. We need to dress up in protective clothing to go in there. The cores are very vulnerable to dust contamination."

"Don't bother," Dad cut in. "I see you hold entire racks of these capsules."

"Technological time," Phil answered with the hint of a smile. "Not all of it is inventory. The cores need to cool down for at least 24 hours before being safe to use."

"Well, that's still 24 hours of cash sitting there," replied Dad dryly.

"You mean, you have to incur the cash outlay to buy the material, but you can only use it after a certain time?" I asked, feeling like an idiot.

"That's right, Mickey," said Dad, using my childhood nickname.

"And that's the whole trouble. You've got to buy materials upfront, and then you've got to pay for labor, and finally you get a check back from a customer after a sale. All this while you've been financing your own production — so the longer it takes to get the cash back from the customer, the costlier it is for you."

"And in their case, the materials themselves are expensive."

"Which compounds the problem, correct."

"But doesn't every business face the same problem?" Phil asked.

"Of course, but not necessarily in the same way. A supermarket, for instance, gets the cash out of the shopper's pocket way before it pays its suppliers. In essence, the company gets cash from goods it hasn't paid for yet — not a bad way to run a business," he added with a grin. "Yes, everyone deals with the same type of issues. The trick is resolving them, and there is no one set of answers. It all depends on your customers and your markets."

"In that area over there, we have all the cabinet-making equipment — sheet-metal cutting, punching, bending, and assembly," Phil continued, pointing at a confusing area of machines, boxes, and people. "This is where we make the metal parts for the cabinets. And, yeah," he added, giving Dad a sidewise glance, "this is the inventory." We walked by a large room lined with racks of wire-mesh crates filled with all sorts of metal plates. "We know about this," he went on. "We call it 'the wall,' but we haven't found a way to reduce it without penalizing production."

Dad said nothing, just shook his head.

"Now, over there," Phil continued, "is our big innovation. We have three parallel lines specialized by products. The first line assembles the STR mechanism, incorporating the capsule. The second, deals with both variants of QST, and the third is a DG line, but it doesn't run full time."

"Two shifts or one?" asked Dad.

"One. We work from 8 a.m. to noon, with an hour lunch break, and then from 1 p.m. to 5 p.m. And, of course, a short mid-morning and midday break. We're looking into moving to two shifts, but we don't have enough people as it is, and it would be a serious investment to hire some more qualified operators."

"But would you have the business to sustain two shifts?"

"Matt claims so," Phil answered dubiously. "We currently have quite a backlog, so I guess we could. On STR I think we could. But given our current cash situation, it's not even in the cards. We just couldn't pay a second working shift."

On each production line, operators were working bent over their tables, assembling a variety of rigs, which, I guessed, somehow would transform themselves into completed products in the end.

"At the end of the lines, we send the assembled mechanism and capsule over to that electrical testing area over there," showed Phil, pointing toward a partitioned cubicle with a number of racks filled with mechanisms waiting in front of it. "Testing is actually quite sophisticated, and we use high voltages in there, so it has to be kept clear of the rest for security purposes. It needs special equipment that we couldn't include in the lines."

Dad turned away and exclaimed, "What the heck is this monster?"

"I'm sorry?" asked Phil, perplexed.

"This conveyor. Just look at that!"

A row of cabinets was hanging by hooks from a massive superstructure, fixed to the ceiling, like carcasses in a butcher shop. Operators worked at different assembly stations, fitting mechanisms into the cabinets, and then pushing the cabinets to the next station to add cabling or the circuit board or the instrument panel, while a number of cabinets waited patiently between the stations.

"Ah, that's where the major components are assembled into the cabinet to make the finished circuit breaker, as you can see. The cabinets are supported from the ceiling by the conveyor to allow the operators to walk all the way around the cabinet as they work. The wiring in particular is a bit of a pain and requires assembler access from many points, including the bottom. At the end, they fit the control panel, wire it up, and lock the breaker."

"Doesn't it move?" asked Dad, staring quizzically at the ceiling.

"Well, not automatically," Phil continued. "It's not a conveyer in the usual sense, just a way to keep the cabinets at working height and to allow access. It has no built-in pace. When the operator is finished, he pushes the cabinet ahead to the queue before the next station."

"And all of your products end up going down this same line?"

"Yes," Phil acknowledged, "which is why we often get pile-ups upstream as the different fabrication operations feed the one line. But in any case, we are now finished with assembly. You can see where the fully stuffed cabinets are lowered to the ground and onto pallets, then picked up by forklifts and taken to the final testing area. When they pass the test, which may require more changing of parts, they are taken by forklift to the packing area for crating and then to shipping."

He guided us around the packing area and up a long aisle running the length of the plant, past endless floor-to-ceiling racks of boxes with components, until we finally reached the shipping dock. A few men were stretch-wrapping the finished circuit breakers in their crates while, further off, other employees were unloading a truck on the dock, moving piles of cardboard boxes through what looked like an airplane crash site.

"Yeah, I know," said Phil, rubbing a hand on his face. "It still looks a mess, but it used to be much worse. Anyhow, that's about it. If you come back over here," he said, walking us back toward the door to the offices, "we have an actual map of the plant's layout." (*See inside front cover for map of plant layout.*)

"Okay, Mr. Woods, what do you think of it?"

"Well, son," said my father looking at the plant's hustle and bustle, "I can see your inventory. But where is your factory?"

"Ouch," said Philip, downcast.

"Look at it like this," Dad pressed. "You've got three big piles of inventory with a little manufacturing in between. You've got a heap of vacuum cores over there by your glass box, mountains of metal parts across the aisle, racks of assembled mechanisms right after testing, and

I don't know how many of your cabinets queuing on the conveyor. What do you expect? This place is storing and moving around a lot of stuff, with very little useful action."

"What makes you say that?" I asked Dad. All I could see was a beehive of activity. It was just what I expected of a plant and, even though I had never set foot in a factory before, there didn't seemed to be much wrong with it. After I got used to the din, it was a far cry from the "dark satanic mill" Phil and my father had led me to expect.

"Well, let me put it this way," started Dad, which was a sure sign Phil was in for a serious put down. "I don't know much about your industry, so I try to look at your operations as if I was a potential customer."

"Eye of the customer, yeah, we've done that with the consultants," interrupted Phil, attracting the glint of Dad's stare.

"Consultants, hah. Well, here it is. Let's assume I don't understand anything about your process itself. I'll worry about two things:
- the quality of the product and
- the inefficiencies I see, because I know that somehow, all of your inefficiencies will be reflected in your price."

"Our quality's not too bad," Phil ventured. "We've had only five customer complaints over the past month from about 1,000 units sold: five defects per 1,000 ..."

"Five per 1,000! That's outrageously high!" cut in Dad. "Never mind now, that's not what I'm looking for at this stage. I want to see how quality is built into your product."

Phil looked at him, puzzled, reaching instinctively for his notebook.

"Well, look at your process. I'm sure that mistakes and defects must happen here and there. But I haven't seen any. Which means that there is no system to identify nonconforming parts. In other words, whenever a defective part appears, I have no guarantee that it will not find its way back into the product somehow."

"But our people are trained to spot and isolate defects!"

"Hey, you asked me, son. And if I were a potential customer, I'd be worried. You guys can tell me whatever you want, but I don't see any system in place making sure that defects are systematically identified at each step of the process, and separated from good parts. Nor am I sure that anyone is asking why these defects show up when they do. That tells me you don't control your quality."

"But what about our testing? You've seen our testing procedures, and they're very rigorous!"

Dad seemed to weigh Phil for a moment and replied, "All well and good, but testing doesn't tell me how quality is built into the product, or, more to the point, how *nonquality* is built into the product. See, any defect that turns up on one of your products has in fact been put there. It is the result of work, albeit bad work. You need to understand this. Do you track how many defective parts are found at each testing phase?"

"I don't know," Phil mumbled, "but I'm sure that Dave would. Let me go and find out."

"Forget it. I told you I don't want to talk to anybody," Dad said crossly. "Anyhow, that's not the point. The point is that I am troubled about quality in your production process. Five defects per 1,000 in the customer's products are terribly high in my book. That's about how often airlines lose your luggage. You happy with that?"

"What about inefficiency?" I asked, to get Phil off the hook.

"Right. Well, look at it this way. Anything that does not directly add value to the product is inefficient, correct? So when I walk through operations I always look at people first and foremost. I count:
  – line operators actually working on a product,
  – operators waiting,
  – operators moving parts around, and
  – operators just walking around, or talking, or, like these guys over there, asking questions of the supervisor.

"The ratio of operators who are actually adding value to the product to total operators gives me a good feel for how efficient the process is."

Phil just stared at Dad and then started looking around, counting silently. I'm not good at numbers, but I could see that for every operator we saw actually doing some work, there were two or three people just doing something else.

"That's not entirely fair, Dad," I ventured. "It's not because they aren't working on the product that they're not working!"

"I never said that," Dad replied flatly. "I'm sure all these folks are doing their job. That's precisely my point. Look at this lady over there searching through a pile of parts for the one item that she needs next. Clearly she's working — but her efforts aren't adding any value to the product. What I'm saying is that you need to figure out a better system. In particular, you need to distinguish motion from work."

"Work is adding value to the product, and motion is everything else, is that right?" asked Phil.

"Correct. At the end of the day, improving operations means transforming motion into work."

Phil opened his mouth, but then said nothing again. He stood there, taking in the shop floor, pushed his glasses back on his nose, and looked distraught.

"Now, the second thing to look at is inventory," continued Dad, relentless. "Same principle applies. Every part out there that is not being worked on is a sign of inefficiency. We've paid for that stuff, and it's not being transformed into value. It's just sitting around gathering dust. That's inefficiency."

"Okay, okay, Mr. Woods," Phil conceded, "I get your point, but you don't understand. What you see is —"

"I don't have to understand, son. All I know is that all these inefficiencies somehow translate into cost. And if I'm a customer, I know that if you plan to stay in business all these inefficiencies will eventually be reflected in your price — and mine."

"But we've come so far."

Dad just shrugged and started walking away.

"Come on, Dad, don't be like that. I, for one, would at least like to know what Phil's been doing with this plant."

My father gave me his irritated stare, but relented with a sigh. "All right, let's hear it."

"It might not look like much to you," started Phil, "but you should have seen it when we took over. There were piles of inventory surrounding every workstation. I mean heaps!"

"I can imagine," mumbled Dad, nodding wearily.

"When we took over the plant, it was organized in five shops:
— mechanical assembly of the mechanism frame,
— fitting of the motors and the capsules to the frame,
— electrical wiring,
— testing, and
— final assembly of the mechanisms, the circuit board, and the instrument panel into the cabinet.

"Each shop dealt with all the products. The first shop would do mechanical assembly for all mechanisms. Then they would move to the mechanical fitting shop to get the motor fitted, then to electrical wiring, then back to fitting for the capsule, then to wiring again, then to testing, and finally to the final assembly line.

"Inventories were sky high in each shop! We had some consultants come in, and they got us to separate our products into families, which came down to the four I've mentioned. Because of all the customization we do, it wasn't clear to us that product lines existed at all!

"Then they broke the shops and created the lines we saw. It was a revolution, let me tell you! We initially halved the inventory! Halved it, I tell you," Phil repeated excitedly. "And the same for lead time. It was amazing, you should have seen the stuff lying around before. Not that we're particularly good now, but back then, it was just horrendous."

"What I don't understand," I asked, "is why final assembly was not split into lines as well?"

"We had endless arguments about that. The end of the matter is that we can't afford another two lines."

"I can see," I continued, "that with the old layout you would have had parts being moved around a lot."

"Yeah, talk about motion!"

"So, if you've already solved the problem, what's the panic?" asked Dad coolly. Phil's face fell as if he'd doused with cold water.

"It's not enough!" he cried. "That's the problem! You said it yourself, there's still too much inventory around this place. Too much inefficiency, and we don't know where to go from here."

"Well," answered my father after an awkward silence, "the usual: waste reduction."

"Waste?" I asked.

"To be efficient, the trick is to maximize value — the work that the customer really thinks is worth paying for. In any operation, you've got a value-creating element, like tightening a bolt, a necessary element, like getting the bolt to the operator, and then a whole load of waste. Most people don't even see it. You can basically split waste into seven types, as Toyota does:

　　– overproduction, by producing ahead of what is needed;
　　– operators waiting, imposed by an inefficient work sequence;
　　– excess transport, which means the work flow is neither direct nor smooth;
　　– overprocessing parts, more than they require;
　　– unnecessary inventory, in excess of immediate needs;
　　– unnecessary operator motions, which don't contribute to value; and,
　　– defects, which create rework and more waste.

"So get your consultants to work and systematically reduce the waste!"

"No offense, sir, but we know all that," Phil said carefully. "The trouble is that we've reached the limits of our consultants. They don't seem to get any more results than what you've seen, and they tell us that it's because of too much resistance to change, and anyhow that's no longer the issue."

"How do you mean, not the issue?" asked Dad, bristling.

"We're running out of time," Phil answered with a hint of desperation in his voice. "Whatever we do in continuous improvement is going to take ages and it won't solve the business problem — we're against the wall!" he almost screamed.

My father sighed and shook his head in this exasperating, seen-it-all-before manner he has, and said in a quieter tone, "Come on, nothing's ever that desperate. But maybe we should continue this discussion out of earshot rather than right in the middle of the shop floor. Let's get a cup of coffee."

I looked around and, indeed, many people were looking at us with a mixture of curiosity and defiance. The company had already changed hands and been reorganized, so God knows what they were thinking of their strange visitors. Another sale perhaps? With Dad dressed like a house painter, stains and all, not likely, I thought with a chuckle. Phil took us back to the engineering area, past an acre of cubicles and ushered us into a large pleasant office with bay windows overlooking the parking lot. He sat us at a round conference table, and went back out to ask someone for coffee.

"Can you help?" I asked Dad, but he just shrugged, mulling over his thoughts and looking grim.

"Okay, Philip. What's the problem then?"

"As I've told you earlier, we're out of cash!"

"I understand that," Dad said with exaggerated patience. "But what's the business problem? Why are you out of cash when your products seem to be selling?"

"Well, we have two issues," Phil said. "First, we still carry far too much inventory, which eats at our cash flow. Second, we're not covering our fixed costs, no matter how much we've already cut overhead. We just can't find a way to get more output from the money we've invested in this factory, given the capabilities — and customers — that we have."

"So you have a market for this?"

"Yeah, plenty, especially the new stuff. We have about a month's backlog of orders on the STR and some on the QST. Matt thinks that if we get the price down just a bit, we could easily double our sales volume. But at this stage, we would never find financing for additional capacity. It would require more factory space, more people, and more equipment. We just don't have the cash."

"Suppose you could magically produce your backlog overnight, would that help?"

"Well, sure. These customers pay promptly, so if we could catch up on late deliveries without increasing our parts inventories, we'd be improving our cash position."

"Well, there's your solution, son. Reduce the waste to produce more with the same facilities, since the market demand is there."

Phil looked back, mystified.

"Oh, heck, it isn't that hard to make money in industry," said Dad animatedly. "Your company thinks in terms of fixed costs and variable costs, right?"

"Variable costs are the costs which can be attributed directly to the product, like materials and direct labor, aren't they?" I asked, vaguely remembering a business course back in college. "And fixed costs are all the other costs related to running the plant itself."

"Correct, Philip is a fixed cost," Dad answered with a wink. "The trick to running a profitable operation is to find ways of increasing production without increasing fixed costs if the demand is there; and reducing fixed costs if you have to reduce production because demand falls."

"But wouldn't that be treating fixed costs as variable?" asked Phil.

"Not quite. It just means that you have to be ready to close down entire parts of the plant, or product lines, if they're not profitable. Like Harry told you this morning. Fixed costs are not fixed by an act of the Almighty. They're called fixed costs because they can't be related to each single product. It doesn't mean they can't be reduced. You could still close down half your shop and relocate to a cheaper building or something like that. But that's not the issue anyhow since the demand is there. Your problem is to find a way to increase production without increasing your fixed costs, right?"

"Yes, absolutely. But how can that be done?"

"By reducing waste in the product flow, of course!"

"I'm sorry I'm being so slow, sir, but I don't get it," complained Phil as Dad made a show of looking at his watch. He would be missing lunch with his cronies soon, I figured.

"Right. Let me put it another way. Suppose that you could move from one shift to two shifts. You follow? 6 a.m. to 2:30 p.m. and 3 p.m. to 11:30 p.m. You'd be doubling your output without increasing any of your fixed costs, right?"

"Assuming people would agree to it, we'd need more people to staff the second shift," Phil reasoned.

"Direct labor is a variable cost."

"Well, not quite in this process. Each of these operators is both trained and skilled. We couldn't find people on the street just like that. And anyhow, we can barely pay those we have on the payroll now, there's no way we could hire any more," said Phil.

"Well, you've figured it out yourself. Your challenge," said Dad, "is to staff a second shift without hiring any more people. This is assuming, of course, that you could sell everything that second shift would produce."

"But we'd have to double our productivity! And we'd run the risk of further increasing our inventory!"

"That's what I meant. Get rid of the waste in the process!"

Phil looked at my Dad thoughtfully, digesting this. "Can it be done?"

"Double productivity? Yes. Quickly? No."

Phil pulled off his glasses and started polishing them on his shirt, shaking his head in a mixture of dismay and irritation. Not that I blamed him. My Dad has the same effect on me. He looked at Phil and continued, "But a 20% increase right away, maybe. As far as I understand, you wouldn't want to double your lines anyway. It's only the STR product that is a potential high runner."

"You're saying that if we improve productivity on the three lines we could pull enough people out to staff one second shift for just the STR line?"

"Well," said Dad, "all you need is five or six operators. Surely if you improve productivity in the entire area, you should be able to liberate enough people. It doesn't solve your problem because you still have to move all the additional STR mechanisms through the final assembly conveyor to get paid. But if you can do that, then you've got something."

"We might be able to do that," Phil said, thoughtfully. "Right now the conveyor is not operating at full capacity, we've got an inventory of QST mechanisms, and we're chronically short of STRs. As a result we're not utilizing our people fully, and we keep hearing from the veterans about how the conveyor used to produce far more output when they were only doing the DGs," muttered Phil, the cogs in his mind spinning wildly. "Wow."

"Listen, son," said Dad, "when the Toyota people first showed us their continuous improvement system, all they talked about was 'waste reduction.' I didn't understand it anymore than you, so I asked them what the strategy was. Simple, they said. First we thought that:

Price = Cost + Profit

"But then we realized that:

Profit = Price − Cost."

"It's the same thing!" I blurted out.

Dad corrected me patiently: "Hmm, it took me three years to get it. We used to produce and tote up the cost to whatever it amounted to, slam a 20% margin on it and try to find customers for our junk at that price. When the market turned around on us, we found that we had to sell at market price, and adjust our margins to what was left once the cost was taken out. So if we wanted to keep selling and make a profit, we had to find ways to pull costs down — without affecting quality. This meant reducing the waste in existing operations. That's your current situation."

Phil looked uncertainly at both of us in turn.

"Can you help us?" he finally asked my father.

"I just did," was the grumpy reply.

"No, yes, I mean, help us really. Help us to do it. Help us to get the waste out of the system!"

"Sorry, son, I don't do that anymore."

He stood up abruptly and gave me a nod toward the door. "Well, it's been nice talking to you boys, but I'm expected at the Yacht Club for lunch, and the day isn't getting any younger. Mickey, you're driving me back."

In the end, we all drove back together. Phil had enough tact to sit in the back of the car in gloomy misery and keep quiet, so we drove in silence, my Dad and I having, as usual, nothing much to say to each other once the lot of daily news had been chewed through. We dropped Dad at the Yacht Club, and Phil persuaded me (bullied me, really) to drive him home to Charlene and the kids and stay for lunch. I knew he wanted to talk, and I guessed he probably wanted to discuss my father, which made me uneasy.

Don't get me wrong. Phil is a good friend. Only a few months ago, when my girlfriend Sarah ditched me, Charlene and Phil had proved a staunch support as I moped through the usual sad palaver of denial, anger, and despair. Now I felt one good turn deserved another. Of course, the cure seemed to promise at least a small dose of pain all around. My Dad probably had answers for Phil; after all, he had been turning companies around all his life. Yet he had also been embittered by the endless political battles, particularly at the end, and had largely closed that chapter of his life. Phil had yet to show that my father's direct approach was helping him see the situation in a fresh light. It struck me that bringing them together was my doing, and that there was much more at stake to lose than the possible benefits of this arrangement. At the end of the day, my relationship with my father had never been an easy one, and we had learned to keep our distance. I was not sure I wanted to get involved in this.

As it turned out, Charlene forced my hand. Phil's mood had lifted considerably. He raved about Dad during lunch, adding to my unease, and I could see he was already making plans in his mind. Yet, instead of running back to the office, he had the good sense to stay home and enjoy the sunshine. As he was playing with the kids in the garden, Charlene cornered me in the kitchen. She is a forceful woman with a cultivated Southern drawl. Quite pretty, in an all-American blond way, and hard as nails. She's always been very friendly, but I've never felt entirely comfortable around her.

Phil, by contrast, had a good head for physics, and an instinct for the effects of heat on exotic materials, but not much else. He was a large, friendly, happy-go-lucky character and had struggled to get interested in making products as opposed to research. From a humble background himself, he couldn't resist the lure of the success that being a self-made man would provide, and I often wondered about his occasional hankering for gaudy success symbols. His bias for showy sports cars, for instance, I found in rather poor taste. Philip and Charlene seemed at times a study of contrasts, yet their marriage had held together through 13 years and three children. As I was rummaging through the fridge for a soda, she got straight to the point:

"Can you help him?"

I hesitated, but she just stood there, her arms crossed, her face set.

"I don't know. Personally, I don't have a clue about what's going on in the factory."

"But your dad does."

"I think so. The trouble is that he has walked away from all this and doesn't want to get drawn back in."

We faced each other as she stood defiantly in front of me, hugging her sweater to herself. I shifted my weight uncomfortably from foot to foot.

"How long have you two been friends?"

Ouch.

"Like, forever. Charly, you know that."

"Well, in all this time, Phil's always been there for you, no? Cover for your stupid pranks, get you out trouble, cope with your moods and break-ups and what not!"

"Yes," I agreed curtly. "What's your point?"

"It's payback time, Mike. You've got to help him on this one. This is serious. We've always been there when you've fretted through papers and politics, right? Well this is it for us. Make or break. And Phil's breaking, and I don't want to be there and watch it happen and do nothing. So you'd better help him make this work."

It felt as if she had slapped me. I needed time to digest this, but she was on a roll.

"Listen, I know it's not easy with your father, I'm aware of the baggage and all. But he's your father. If you ask him, he'll do it."

"You don't know what you're asking."

"I think I do, Mike. More to the point, I think you do too."

I drove home but then continued on to my parents, as they were getting ready for dinner. Dinner in a very loose sense. Since it was just the two of them living in that big house on the hill, they'd dropped any attempt at sitting down at the dining-room table. They mostly drifted toward the kitchen roughly at the same time to make themselves a snack before going back to the sitting room and their home cinema. My mother had always been a movie buff and for some time now she'd become a DVD film critic for a number of clubs and even a magazine. So every night was movie night. They had bought one of those large-screen TVs and she watched every film, whether a children's story or a horror sci-fi extravaganza, taking notes with the same thorough concentration. Dad usually fell asleep halfway through.

Before I could speak, my father said, "The answer is 'No.'"

"Dad, it's Phil we're talking about. Remember? This is not a business deal, this is about helping out my best friend!"

He looked at me quizzically, and then sat his martini glass on the kitchen bar. He poured one for me, refilled his own, took a sip, and then held his hands behind his head, leaning against the kitchen cupboards.

"C'mon, Dad. You won't have to do much. Just talk to him, that's all."

"Do you remember I always say it's not about the process, it's about the people?"

I nodded. I had heard it enough times. That's one thing we'd always agreed upon — I'm a psychologist, after all!

"Well, I don't know how to say it nicely, son, but Philip's not up to it. He's cracking under the pressure."

"What do you expect? He was a physics student, a lab rat, before he got into all this entrepreneurial nonsense. But he's bright, right? He'll get it. We've got to help him."

"We?" repeated Dad with an amused grin. "We, is it? All right, here's what I propose. I don't want to deal with the drama. I don't want to argue and explain and cajole and do all the people stuff. I'm done with having to convince every man, woman, and dog of the most obvious common-sense moves. And make no mistake, whatever I say out there, they'll fight it. It's human nature. People need to disagree to understand. But I've had my fill of it, so no more. I'll talk to him, but you come along and hold his hand. If and when he goes to pieces you deal with it, and we'll finally see if all your psychobabble is any use in real life. Deal?"

I balked a bit, I guess. I was on a sabbatical, so I was pretty free with my time, but that didn't mean a vacation. I was in the midst of writing a book and not doing too well. I just couldn't see myself spending my time baby-sitting Phil or driving Dad to the factory for kick-ass sessions. Still, Phil was my friend, and it was my idea.

"Well?"

"Deal, Dad."

Great! I thought, and then suddenly realized what I might be getting into. Could we help Phil out? I hadn't the faintest idea.

"Hey, Mike, long time no see!"

I never did take to Matthew. He had a cheesy smile and slick trappings: whiter-than-white shirt, pressed chinos, a soft paunch, and golf-course tan. "Mr. Woods? Phil tells me you can double our STR production without further investment? That would really save our butts!"

"Hold your horses, son. I'm not going to double anything. You're going to do the work here. No pain, no gain. Anyhow, can you really sell more of that stuff if it comes off the line?"

A flicker of uncertainty broke over Matt's plastic smile, and I remembered that my Dad's style had an occasional benefit.

"For sure," Matt said, snapping back to sales mode. "Our current contract calls for us to be shipping about twice the number of STR that we are now, so we're paying late-delivery penalties. We argued about stopping everything else and producing only those to catch up on the backlog, but we don't want to screw up the deals with our other customers either. Right now the market is booming. All sorts of global industrial players are pitching for energy markets." He flashed his smile on Phil, adding, "You build them, I'll sell them."

Phil just shrugged, and we looked at each other uncertainly. We'd bumped into Matt in the plant's lobby earlier as he was dashing to yet another "important meeting." I'd met Matt on and off over the past couple of years, and always wondered how Phil ever ended up going into partnership with the guy. He looked too much like a con man to me. To give credit where it's due, he had always been fair to Phil. Sure he'd exploited Phil's patents, but he'd also made them both rich in the process. In any case, Phil never understood why I didn't take to Matt, whom he considered a real friend, so he probably deserved more credit than I gave him. But I couldn't stand his manner any more than Phil's taste in cars.

"I'll let you guys get on with the important work," said Matt with an unctuous grin. "I'm off to race a customer check to the bank and keep us open one more week! See ya."

"Was he serious?" I asked Phil as he walked us past reception and toward his office.

"Matt? Yeah, it's been like that for the past month or so. But I don't worry too much; he's really good at getting money out of people. He's had plenty of experience since we started this racket. He keeps the business afloat day-to-day, and I'm more of a long-term worrier. Here, come on in."

He ushered us into the room and, as we went in, a young Hispanic woman in an expensive suit stood up from the conference table and walked to my Dad, hand outstretched.

"Hi, I'm Amaranta Cruz," she announced with a toothy, engaging smile and a firm handshake. "I know you don't want an audience, Mr. Woods, but I'm the HR manager here, so I thought I'd take an interest. Also it will give me the opportunity to learn more about what the company actually does for a living," she added with an impish smile.

Phil and I shared a glance, expecting my Dad to bite her head off, but to our mutual surprise the old man smiled politely as he shook her hand. "Call me Bob. Pleasure to have you on board, Ms. Cruz."

"Call me Amy," she answered. She was a petite woman with roundish features and a surprisingly deep, smooth voice, like a radio announcer. She gave the impression of being filled to the brim with the kind of cheerful energy I am repeatedly told we should all radiate, but in her case it came across as a naturally sunny disposition rather than neurotic positive thinking, and it did lift some of the gloom Phil seemed to lug around with him these days.

"Good," Phil said. "I've asked Amy to prepare a more formal presentation of the company to give you to have a better idea of what we —"

"Can't stand presentations, son, just bring along your notebook, and we can hit the shop floor."

"Ah. Fine," said Phil, taken aback. "Let's go. I've asked Dave, the production manager, to join us too, but he can catch up when —"

"One last thing to get clear before we go anywhere, Philip," said my father with his best scowl. "Down there it's my way or no way. Period. I don't particularly want to do this, and I certainly don't want to deal with any politics, resistance, or plain stupid questions. Is that clear?"

"Yes, sir," answered Phil uneasily. I could swear Amy was biting her lip to hide an amused grin.

"All right then. Let's go!"

"Okay, Philip," said Dad as we entered the plant. "What you have to tell yourself is that this is a gold mine. There's gold in these people's hands. Our job is to find it. You follow?"

"Gold," repeated Phil uncertainly.

"The problem," continued my father, "is that so much happens in a factory that it becomes very difficult to see where value is actually created. As we saw yesterday, most of what people do out here may be necessary, but it does not add value to the product. So where will we find the gold?"

"Where they build the products?" I guessed.

"Correct. That's where value is created. Products are built up part by part, so, in fact, value flows through the factory. The first thing to get clear is to identify the various streams value flows through."

"Product lines, right?" asked Phil.

"Yep. In your case, you've split the flow into three streams, but that's not all. Think of all the tiny rivulets that move parts into these main streams. Sooner or later we will need to map these value streams in order to see where we are creating value and where we aren't. But we need to take other steps first. Where should we begin our walk?"

"At the start, I guess," muttered Phil, "with frame assembly."

"Wrong," countered Dad. "Is that where the gold is? I don't think so."

We stood there looking at each other like guilty kids.

"Of course," exclaimed Amy unexpectedly. "Finished products. That's the gold, right? I mean when we've panned it out of the river and all, right?"

"There's hope for you yet," said Dad with a brief smile. "You're right. Finished products tell us exactly what comes out of this place in both quantities and variety. So let's move it, to shipping."

So we trundled through the factory with Amy looking like the cat that's got the cream, and Phil obviously trying to make sense of all this gold-mine talk as we dodged forklifts and passed racks of inventories.

"What have we got here?" Dad asked when we arrived at the loading dock, where crates were packed haphazardly around the place.

"A bit of everything," admitted Phil ruefully.

"Yep. Not much of a gold miner who doesn't keep different kinds of nuggets separate!"

"I'm sure the guys in charge of shipping know what is where, though," Phil said, looking around.

Dad just shrugged, and pressed ahead.

"I'd like to understand your shipping schedule. How often do you make deliveries?" asked Dad.

"We're shipping one truck a week to each of our customers. At the moment, things are relatively simple. We're delivering STR breakers to our biggest customer, which is a global energy group. We're rather late on our deliveries and, needless to say, they're not happy."

"I bet."

"Yeah." Phil shrugged a bit and added, "They claim that the

missing breakers slow their own manufacturing of electrical panels. I'm not so sure about that, but they are on our backs to deliver faster — which we can't."

"How much more do they want?"

"We're shipping 50 a week in one truck. They would like to double that, to 100 a week. Which is clearly impossible, as we tried to tell them."

"Double, heh," chuckled Dad.

Phil ticked off the other items on his fingers. "QST-1s go to another customer, and we're shipping 60 a week. We're shipping 50 QST-2s a week to a different plant. Mature energy stations comprise the major market for the DGs; and we ship about 20 a week, give or take."

"Well, son, that's the first good news I've heard since we got here."

"How?" asked Phil, puzzled.

"We'll deal with this later," said Dad. "All right, for the moment, we can assume that all the gold eventually arrives here. Now, remember, the key to operating a successful gold mine is optimizing how fast the nuggets are pulled out of the stream and sold to customers, correct?"

We all nodded.

"So, what we need to do now is walk back through the stream and figure out how the gold flows through it, and what kind of rocks might be holding it back. Rocks would be ..."

"Waste!" answered Phil immediately. "The inefficiencies we talked about yesterday."

"And how will we see them?"

"I'll be damned," cried Phil, rubbing his chin. "Inventory, right? If the gold gets held up in the flow, if we see an inventory pile-up, it's because there's a rock in there somewhere."

"You got it. And how do we find the rocks? We pick a stream, and walk backwards. Then we track the key steps and count the inventories. Waste rarely appears to the naked eye, which is precisely why you don't know how to improve your production system beyond your current state. But we can see inventory — and assume that some sort of waste hides beneath every accumulation."

"Is all inventory a sign of waste?" asked Amy.

"Mostly," answered my father, stopping to turn to her. "Inventory can be divided into three broad categories:

– raw materials,

– work-in-process, which we will call WIP, and

– finished goods.

"And these serve several key purposes. You have buffer stock to deal with changes in customer demand, and safety stock to guard against problems in your process or your supplier's process.

"Everything that is not currently being worked on is wasteful inventory. Which means the company has paid for it because it has been bought, but has not yet sold because it's still here. This lot costs serious money," he concluded, waving his hand around.

"So what kind of streams do we have ending up here?" he asked Phil, pointing at the packaged boxes.

"Essentially, four product types: STR, QST-1, QST-2, and DG. Although it's a bit more complicated than that, since each item is often customized to fit the customer's requirements."

"Does each of these products come off a different stream?"

"Mostly, yes," answered Phil uneasily. "Although I've done some checking since we talked yesterday. All the products go through the same final assembly line, of course. But the subassembly areas further upstream are separate. STRs clearly come from the STR line, because the demand is high. The second line produces both QST variants. I thought the third line was dedicated to DGs, but I've found out that since the demand on those is sometimes sluggish, Dave uses the third line to catch up on STRs or QSTs. So it's not as clear-cut as I thought. Thankfully, most of our operators can handle any of these products without too many hiccups."

"Have you thought about dropping the DG product line altogether?" asked Dad. "Remember what Harry told you. The first sound principle of business is abandonment. If a product has no future, let it drop!"

"But it's still profitable!" Phil protested.

"Maybe, but it also consumes valuable resources. Wouldn't you be better off producing more STRs with the same line?"

Phil pushed his glasses back on his nose, thinking.

"Listen," said Dad. "Make three lists: A, B, C. Then draw a chart with two columns. Is the product profitable? And is there a growing market for it? So it's easy:

A list: the product makes money and there's a growing demand — make some more.

B list: the product is not profitable and the demand for it is shrinking — abandon it quick, avoid sunk costs.

C list: question marks. Either the market is growing, but there's not much money in it, and you must find some way of making it more profitable. Or, the product is making money, but the market doesn't want it anymore — abandon!"

"Works with people too," Amy suggested cynically.

"That it does, Ms. Cruz," agreed Dad. "That it does."

"But, you're saying to shut down the capsule production in this factory entirely!" exclaimed Phil, distraught.

"That's exactly what I'm saying. What d'you need that drag for in here? You could forget about the whole thing, build the vacuum capsules in your other plant, and focus here on building the circuit breakers. Maybe, if we can make enough space, we can move the new capsule operation here and sell the other plant. More cash!"

"But, but … ," stammered Phil.

"Relax!" Dad said, though Phil looked anything but. "I'm not saying do it tomorrow. It was just a thought. You're going to have to figure that one out on your own. For the moment, let's focus on the STR stream, where you need to focus your commercial effort. In order to improve your cash situation, you have to be able to deliver more products without increasing your costs."

"Is there a formal way to define value streams?" asked Amy.

"Sure," said Dad. "The so-called experts consider it to be all of the actions required to bring a product from concept to launch and from order to delivery — both value-adding and nonvalue-adding, mind you. But really, it's just a family of products that go roughly through the same processes, or products that can be manufactured with the same basic operations, but have different components, or different settings. What we want to do here is pick a stream, and see how the value flows through it. So, Philip, you're going to take us back through the STR stream, and at each step show us the work in process, and then take us to where it came from. Got that?"

Phil nodded.

"Now, as we do that, we're going to count the inventory we see at each step, to try to figure out where the rocks lay hidden. Chances are we're going to find inventory all over the place: before a step, at the step, after the step, and everywhere in between. To avoid confusion, we'll count all the inventory between one step and the next as belonging to the upstream step, you follow?"

"I think so," nodded Phil. "All the finished goods beyond the packaging area get counted at packaging. But these completed units over there, which are waiting to be packaged, will be counted as final inspection or test inventory because that's the previous step. Is that what you mean?"

"Yep. Let's go. How many STR crates do you see?"

"There are three rows with 10 in each for a total of 30," replied Phil.

"Thirty? And I thought you had cash-flow problems," Dad rubbed it in, with his mordant wit.

"You don't understand. They're probably about to be shipped to the customers," Phil said defensively.

"Sure, son, sure. And is that all there is? What about this lot over there?"

"Different product. The labels are a different color."

"Are you certain?"

Phil shrugged and moved across the hall to another stack of boxes, shaking his head. A few seconds later he came back slightly embarrassed.

"You're right. Six more crates over there are STR. Different customer."

"So that's 36 finished products waiting to be delivered," said Dad.

Phil nodded unhappily. "Yeah, we only send a truck once a week."

"Okay, where do they come from?"

"Over there, packing. We have a lot of five being stretch-wrapped and put into crates. So that's five more for packing, I guess."

"Forty-one finished products," Dad said, adding it up.

"That's a lot of cash, huh boss?" asked Amy in mock innocence.

Phil didn't respond, but Dad grinned wryly. "Never tire of pointing this out, Ms. Cruz. These production guys, they get so used to this mess, they forget. Do you see why I'm calling it gold?"

"Because the products have value?" she asked.

"Because each product represents cash in the customer's pocket that should be in yours. These products are already sold. The hard part is done. They should already be at the customer — and his cash should be here. That's why it's gold!"

Lord, does my Dad irritate me when he lectures like that. Phil just moved on.

"From there," he continued, "they come from final inspection, which is this area over there. And don't tell me, I know this end of the process is a mess."

"Those four there next to the test equipment are going through final inspection?" asked Dad.

"Yeah. And they come off the conveyor here."

"Philip, there are at least 30 cabinets hanging on this conveyor!"

"Not all of them are STRs," Phil replied. "Look, I count 20 STRs.

45

That's about two days' production. On average, we produce 10 STRs a day. The other cabinets are a mix of QST-1, QST-2, and a couple of DGs. We should really be doing nothing but STRs the whole day until we catch up, but the STR mechanism assembly can't keep up."

"Whatever, son, but that's still a lot of inventory on this conveyor! I count 65 STRs which are finished or almost finished but not yet delivered to your customers. It all adds up," he pressed. "Now lets follow the path of your key component, the mechanism. "

"How many parts fit in each of these racks on wheels?" I asked, wondering at the big moving shelves that held the mechanisms.

"Twenty," answered Phil. "Those are the mechanisms that go into the cabinets. For the STR model, you have to count four mechanisms per unit. Then we get to testing, which is where these racks with the assembled mechanisms come from."

"Hey," I muttered getting into the game, "you've got at least four racks of 20 each there ..."

"Yeah, well," Phil said, giving me a look, "each of the assemblers wants enough mechanisms for at least a day's worth of production as they start the shift."

"Never mind the explanations, son, just count them," snapped Dad. "Mickey's right. I count 20 racks holding a total of 80 mechanisms there. Plus two in the testing booth, so that's 82. I guess we've got a bottleneck there."

Phil looked puzzled. "Only two mechanisms in testing? This booth is supposed to take at least six at a time. What the hell ..."

"Later, Philip, later. Don't get distracted," cut in Dad.

"Hey," I chipped in just to rub it in, "what about those two full racks over there?"

"Yep. You're right, two more racks of mechanisms lying about."

"Yes," agreed Phil gloomily. "I count another 34 STR mechanisms."

"Well, I tally 114 finished mechanisms between testing and final assembly," Dad said. "Let's move on to the mechanism assembly line."

"What's a bottleneck?" I wondered out loud as we walked to the enclosed testing area.

"Operations is not my forte," Amy answered with a wave of her hand, as we trailed behind the experts, "but I gather that a bottleneck is a slow step in the process. Because the work is not as fast as downstream needs, work-in-process gets stuck there and accumulates."

"Like when the express lane moves from two lanes to one, it creates a traffic jam although there are the same number of cars trying to get through," I reasoned.

"Something like that. I think bottlenecks are a sign of inefficiency. Production people certainly go on and on about them. 'Where are the bottlenecks? Have the bottlenecks moved? Can we get rid of the bottlenecks?' Dave and Phil keep arguing about them, but it doesn't seem to help all that much."

"How did you end up working with this lot anyhow?" I asked.

"Oh, you know how it is. I was HR manager with a dotcom. You can imagine how that ended up. When Matt and Phil took over, they got rid of most of the old team, except for Dave and the engineering head. I was curious about real industry, you know, like making things. So I got the job."

"Tense, eh?"

"You mean the financial situation and all?" she asked with a smile. "Man, after working with a start-up in a bubble economy, this place is as stable as can be. Almost humdrum."

Phil finished counting the assembled mechanisms on a half-empty rack and announced, "Eight."

"Plus one being assembled," answered Dad. "Nine."

"And seven at assembly," said Phil.

"Four at wiring — is that what you call it?"

"Motor wiring, yes."

"Six at motor assembly, before that?" asked Dad, looking around. "And five at mechanical assembly."

"Yeah, but it's not consistent, since we have four STR mechanisms per finished breaker. We can't mix finished units and mechanisms, right?" Phil asked.

"Fine, let's focus on the mechanisms for the moment, since you think the final conveyor is not a capacity constraint. Let's see what this mechanism line looks like. Dad reached for Phil's notebook and drew a chart:

Mechanisms By Process Step

Mechanical assembly	Motor assembly	Motor wiring	Capsule assembly	Capsule wiring	Testing	Finished mechanisms	Total
5	6	4	7	9	2	114	147

Phil looked at the numbers and rubbed his cheek. "That's 114 finished STR mechanisms? But we're late in delivery! I don't understand."

"Philip, you've got a break in the flow. What do you expect?"

"But it's not always like that," Phil said, poring over the numbers as if they were one of his science experiments. "It's not really a bottleneck, because at the end of the day, most of this is gone. In fact, sometimes the guys at final assembly complain that they're out of mechanisms to install in the cabinets."

"An inventory pile-up is not necessarily a bottleneck. It can be a place where the flow of materials gets temporarily redirected, for one. But we'll worry about this later." Dad was clearly in his element. "Okay, let's tally up. You use four mechanisms in one STR. In this part of the stream, we hold 147 mechanisms, which translates into how many STRs?"

"About 36," Phil replied.

"And what happens if you break it down by stages?"

"I get it!" said Phil. "We could build 28 STRs right away out of the 116 mechanisms waiting for assembly at the conveyor. And then we could build eight additional STRs from the 33 mechanisms in the flow."

Dad nodded. "That's 36 STRs worth of mechanisms in work-in-progress before final assembly — more than half of what you ship in a week. If we add this to the 20 or so STR cabinets we saw on the conveyor, the four in final testing, and the 41 at packaging and in the crates, it adds up to 101 in total.

Mechanical assembly (4 per STR)	Finished mechanisms (4 per STR)	Conveyor final assembly	Final testing	Crating	Packaged STRs	Total
33/4=8	114/4=28	20	4	5	36	101

"Altogether, you've got two weeks' worth of STRs in your process, just from the beginning of mechanism assembly. Yet all the manufacturing steps together require only a couple of hours." Dad paused, then added, "Now, do you see the gold in the stream?"

"At the cost of these things? Are you kidding?" answered Phil grimly. "So what can we do?"

"Right now?" said Dad with a mischievous look. "Nothing."

"What do you mean, nothing?"

"Patience, now. One thing at a time."

"Yeah, easily said, patience! And where the hell is Dave anyhow? He's supposed to run this show!"

Dad suddenly stopped and looked at Phil. "Son, you have to start making choices."

"Like what?"

"Well, you need a strategy!"

"Just like that?" Phil asked doubtfully.

Dad glowered at him.

Okay," relented Phil. "Our main problem right now is to catch up on the STR deliveries. We'd need to shift from 50 a week to 100. The STR is a fairly new product, and orders have consistently been as high as 100 per week. We just have never been able to produce and deliver more than 50."

"What's stopping you then?"

"Ah," hesitated Phil, looking dubiously at my father, "to start with, we could never produce that many mechanisms. Each STR takes four STR mechanisms, and, at the moment, we produce 40 a day, if that."

"So, all you have to do is double that, right?" Dad asked. "With 80 mechanisms a day, you could build 20 STRs a day, which would give you your weekly 100, correct?"

"Yes, but —"

"And could your final assembly cope with this?"

"I don't know," said Phil, trying to keep up. "They tell me that when this place was producing DGs at full capacity, the conveyor was churning out 50 finished units a day. Now we're down to about 30 to 40 breakers a day. The DG breakers are easier to assemble, but I guess we should be able to get back into gear at close to 50 a day."

"I don't know what they tell you, but you have a heck of a lot of finished mechanisms waiting there to be assembled."

"Yeah," agreed Phil worriedly. "But that could also be for scheduling reasons. Dave has been building other products, so the STR mechanisms pile up. I'm pretty sure that we've got extra capacity on the conveyor. The problem has always been to produce enough mechanisms. Although after what we've seen today ..."

"If that's what you think, then you've got your strategy, son. You want to double your STR production without increasing fixed costs. That's all there is to it," suggested my Dad as if it was the most obvious thing in the world.

"Ah, yeah, but ..."

"Listen," Dad continued, "I think that half your problem is with that blasted conveyor. But that's not the easiest place to start. The only question here is which part of the process we start with."

"Yes, sir," said Phil, playing with his glasses, looking somewhat overwhelmed.

"Well, you've got to start this turnaround somewhere, haven't you? Or would you rather start with mechanism assembly then? We're going to have to deal with the conveyor sooner or later."

"Mechanism assembly is good," Phil said. "We have a real bottleneck there. If we can't increase the number of STR mechanisms, we will never catch up on the breaker backlog. And we've done all that work with the consultants to set up specialized product lines, so I understand what's going on."

"Fine. Up to you. Ideally we'd start working closest to the customer — say, in final assembly or packaging — and then work our way back through the process, but we need an area you already understand well and where we can have spectacular results quickly. So, if mechanism assembly fits the bill, go for it."

"But we've already tried everything we could to increase mechanism production," Phil moaned. "I just don't see —"

"Now that we've visualized the stream, and where the gold gets held up in the process," interrupted Dad, disregarding Phil's lament, "we need to count how many gold diggers you need."

"You mean the people, right?"

"Yes, direct labor to start with."

"That's easy, for STR mechanism assembly we've got:

Mechanical assembly	Motor assembly	Motor wiring	Capsule assembly	Capsule wiring	Testing	Finished mechanisms	Total
5	6	4	7	9	2	114	147
1 operator	1 operator	1 operator	1 operator	1 operator	1 operator		6 operators

"And these six people are supposed to produce and pack how many mechanisms a day?" queried Dad.

"Forty. But we're lucky if we make 36 or 37. We have a schedule of 10 STRs a day on average. We need four mechanisms in each of them."

"So you have six operators working directly with the STR mechanism value stream, what you call the STR line, from mechanical assembly to testing."

"We've got a total of six operators and 147 mechanisms in WIP, out of which 114 are on racks waiting to go into the final product."

"Have you got any notion of how much scrap you produce?" Dad pressed on.

"I told you, we have a bad unit every 200 breakers or so."

"That's defects discovered at customers! I'm more interested in how many internal defects the line produces at this stage, as discovered at testing, for instance."

"I wouldn't know," answered Phil. "Where the hell is Dave?"

"All right, this is how it goes. On this segment of the value stream, we get 40 parts per day with six people and 33 mechanisms in WIP, plus the finished mechanisms:

Finished mechanisms inventory	114
Mechanisms WIP inventory	33
Productivity (40 parts/person/day)	6.6
Quality	?

"If you want to sell more STR breakers without increasing your fixed costs, you must focus on these three key numbers. You have to increase productivity, improve quality, and decrease inventory. That's it."

"What about lead time, and all of this? The consultants kept going on about production lead time," Phil said.

"Well, think about it. What's the lead time for a product in this current process? How long does it take it from start to finish?"

"We'd have to follow a product throughout the entire flow to know, wouldn't we?"

"Not necessarily. You're assuming 40 mechanisms a day, right?"

"More or less."

"And we find 33 parts in WIP and 114 more finished mechanisms. That's a total of 147 STR mechanisms waiting at the mechanism assembly stage. Dividing by four mechanisms per STR, that's 36 potential STRs. So how long does it take a mechanism to reach the final assembler's hands?"

Phil and I stared at each other, completely at a loss, while Amy was muttering to herself, tugging on a rebellious lock freed from the short bob over her left ear.

"Wait a minute!" she cried. "I think I've got it."

We stared at her.

"Something like four days? Right?" she answered excitedly. "It's like that high school problem of how many people die per year?"

"What?" Phil and I said together, totally confused.

"You know, there are, say, 250 million Americans and the average life expectancy is probably about 75 years. How many people go every year?"

"About four million," answered my Dad right away with a grin, "250 million divided by 75, very smart!"

How on earth does he do that? I can't multiply to save my life, let alone divide 250 million by 75. As far as I am concerned there are three kinds of people — those who can count and those who can't.

"Same problem," she said with a smug smile. "We have a stock of 147 mechanisms, which get consumed at the rate of 40 per day. That means 3.7 days, or 30 working hours, for a piece entering mechanism assembly to reach the final assembly line — neat!"

Nobody says "neat" anymore, I thought, slightly peeved.

"The consultants measured 34 hours with the parts timer if my memory serves me well," mused Phil, frowning. "And all because it gets stuck in inventory. No wonder we get a backlog and our customers are always screaming! I'd never thought about it this way," he continued, writing on his pad:

$$\text{Lead Time} = \frac{\text{Total WIP}}{\text{Production Rate}}$$

"If I do the consultant's value-adding ratio calculation, it takes about 45 minutes to build one STR mechanism completely from scratch, and 30 hours to get it from start to use. That comes out to … 2.5% value-adding efficiency. On a simple line like this! How can we … ?"

"How did you compute that, son?" Dad asked, raising an eyebrow.

"Ah, value-adding time divided by total lead time, " answered Phil a bit uncertainly. "That's how the consultants calculated the process's efficiency."

"Consultants!" snorted my father. "This kind of number doesn't mean a thing. It's neither overall efficiency nor total value-added time. And it only deals with mechanism assembly. Really, just what does this number tell you? Listen: don't bother too much about ratios which tell you there's something wrong, but don't show you how to fix it!"

"Still!" Phil persisted, "2.5% efficiency!" He always was impressed by statistics, I remembered. Even meaningless ones.

"Don't lose focus here," growled Dad. "My point was that, to start with, all you need to consider about a process is:

– parts produced per operator per day,

– internal scrap percentage, and

– in-process inventory.

"You can worry about finer details later. Now, at least, you can set some meaningful objectives."

"How's that?" I wondered.

"I see," agreed Phil, nodding thoughtfully and writing in his notebook. "Like 10% improvement in productivity, 50% reduction in inventory, and so on."

"Something like that, Philip. But where do you get these figures?"

Phil looked nonplussed for a second: "That's what the consultants always used to tell us. Go for 50% improvement in lead time, which will give us something like 10% productivity improvement and 50% inventory reduction."

"And I can just see how well these goals have been met," said Dad, sarcastically. "Let's get back to the real work. How do you set an objective anyhow?" he continued, grilling Phil with the patented Woods' glare.

"I know that one," Amy answered cheerfully. "Objectives have to be SMART, which means Simple, Measurable, Achievable, Realistic and ..."

"Time-constrained," Dad finished with a sigh. "You must have an MBA. Tell me, what the heck does this alphabet soup mumbo-jumbo mean in practice? Real life, real people, real problems."

"I'm probably way off base here, Dad," I ventured. "But wouldn't their objective be to work without waste, as you said earlier?"

"Darn right!" he said, looking unexpectedly pleased. "That's the objective. You look at what they do, imagine how it could be done if flowing without a hitch, and than establish that as the objective. Make things work! None of this pulling figures out of a hat?"

"But what then? What if they get there?" Phil asked.

"Aha!" said Dad with a wicked glint in his eye. "That's when you use the 'Oh No!' method. Taiichi Ohno, the production manager who developed just-in-time at Toyota, had this simple method to improve productivity. When people with, say, a resource of 100 worked without problems to achieve a certain production, he'd come in and pull 10% of the resources away, expecting them to achieve the same level of production with only 90% of the resources. So of course they ran into all sorts of problems, which they then had to solve. When finally they'd achieved the new goal, he would come round again and say, 'Fine, I'll now take 10% more resource away.' They all screamed, apparently, and so it came to be known as the 'Oh No!' method."

"Clever pun."

"Probably an apocryphal story," agreed Dad, "but it makes the point."

"Is that what we're supposed to do?" asked Phil worriedly.

"Overall, yes, that's the idea. As it relates to this simple bit of process here, we have a better way to estimate what the ideal number of operators should be for a given production target. But do you get the point about objectives?"

"I think so," answered Phil. "Before we start fiddling with the process itself, our first step should be to set ourselves aggressive improvement objectives in terms of WIP, productivity, and quality."

"Correct," grumbled Dad. "So, what should be our WIP objective on the line?"

"Zero inventory!" I quipped. "Isn't that what the fuss is all about?" They all glared at me. Brother, do they take this stuff seriously.

"Right," said my father. "We're going to have to get a closer look at the line."

So we all walked back to the STR process, and Dad went straight to each of the operators, shook their hands, and talked to each of them quietly. Phil, Amy, and I stood like nincompoops when a large black woman stomped toward us from a tiny office by the side of the line.

"Oh, hello, Gloria," said Phil uncertainly.

"What's going on, Mr. Jenkinson?" she asked in a rather peremptory tone.

"Nothing much, we're just —"

"Training," said Dad authoritatively, coming back from talking to the operators. "My name is Bob Woods, and I'm training these folks here in line efficiency," he said, embracing us in a wide-armed gesture.

"This is Gloria Pritchard," introduced Phil. "She's the supervisor for the three mechanism assembly lines, and she knows more about building them than we ever will. It's okay, Gloria. We're looking at the production efficiencies again."

She eyed us diffidently. To her credit, I would not have known what to make of our little group. My Dad was wearing the same used jeans and gray sweatshirt he seemed to live in since retirement and not looking much like a corporate trainer. As for the HR manager's presence on the shop floor, even as an academic I could see how that could get people worried. Gloria seemed about to say something, but thought the better of it and left us, saying, "Well, I'll be back at my desk. Yell if you need anything."

"Thanks, Gloria," answered Phil, looking relieved.

"No overall product manager, I gather?" asked Dad.

Phil looked confused again.

"Managing the entire value stream? From order to delivery?" Phil considered the question, and said, "No. We have people responsible for the design part of each product, one for STR, and one for QST-1 and QST-2. Dave still takes care of DG, but only for the design part. On the shop floor, Gloria handles this part, and Jake Rogers over there is supervisor for the final assembly."

We stared at the row of desks where each operator was busy working, surrounded by parts and small shelves with varied-colored containers. While we were pondering this question, Amy piped in.

"One thing for certain," mused Amy. "We can see all the wastes Phil was telling me about this morning. Look," she said, pulling back the sheets and reading from his notes:

"First, *overproduction*. Obviously, if we have this massive stack of finished mechanisms at the end of the line of what, about 80, we're producing too much stuff for the next step.

"Second, *waiting*. Look, the second operator seems to be looking for something. He's looking for a missing part. And now he's calling his supervisor.

"Third, *transport*. They have to move the parts from working station to working station. But while the stations are aligned, the work doesn't seem to flow easily. Look, this lady is picking up four parts from the previous station — and they look heavy!

"Fourth, *processing*. I wouldn't know about overprocessing pieces. But part of it must be a design issue. We're looking for inefficient operations in assembly. Is anyone working at an unnecessarily high quality standard? One that is unrelated to the functional quality of the mechanism?"

Phil shrugged.

"Okay, fifth, *inventory*. They obviously all have more components and WIP than their immediate needs.

"Sixth, *motion*. I don't know if that counts, but a minute ago, I saw one of the operators go away and come back with a container of components."

"Do they do their own supplying?" asked Dad. "If they do, it doesn't contribute to adding value, does it? And then it goes further than that. Look at how they work and ask yourself if all their motions are absolutely necessary."

"And seventh," Amy continued, "I don't know about *rework*, but —"

"There's rework, all right," agreed Phil. "That's why we need well-trained workers. They really have to know what to do with those mechanisms. Gloria also helps out, she knows the assembly inside out."

"There you go, Phil, all your seven deadly wastes," she said with a shake of the head.

"Hey, how come you can see all of that?" Phil asked.

"Are you kidding? I paid my way through college by working in a fast food joint. If we'd been organized the way these guys are, I tell you, the Golden Arches would've gone bust a long time ago!"

"Of course!" exclaimed Phil suddenly, snapping his fingers, "single-piece flow! If the flow went as smoothly as possible through the stream, we should only handle one piece at a time. And so we have a target of one piece per operator: six parts plus whatever we put in finished parts inventory!"

"Correct," agreed Dad. "Good thinking. And you should listen more to your HR manager here. Long time in the fast-food industry?"

"Too long. I made it to manager, but the work pressure got to be too much. I couldn't do that and continue my studies. So I stuck to the less demanding environment: my HR degree," she added with a wry grin.

"Must've taught you a few things about working in a structured environment, though?" Dad asked.

"No joke. The dotcom job was a ball after that. These guys were so, you know, fluffy."

Fluffy?

"Essentially, you're right, Philip," said Dad, returning to his lecture voice. "At the moment, each operator holds from four to nine products on or around his or her station. As Ms. Cruz just pointed out, this has a number of consequences.

"First, long lead times. Remember that WIP accumulation directly impacts lead time.

"Second, you have to wonder why they don't move parts in a smooth continuous flow. Chances are that their jobs are not equally distributed. Balancing the work between them will be difficult as long as they each hold inventory to compensate for such imbalances.

"Then, as Amy pointed out, they have to move the products from bench to bench, which is wasteful and dangerous, both to the person and the product."

Dad paused for emphasis, then went on. "There is also a quality problem. If, say, the guy doing the final wiring finds a problem with the previous assembly, it is very difficult to figure out what created the problem, because of the time lag between the defect's cause and its identification. You can't just turn to the person upstream and say, 'Hey, watch it, if you do it like this, I get problems!' The defect is hidden in the inventory. Anything can happen when it is not clearly identifiable.

"And finally, not a problem you'll be having on this line since you only do STRs, but imagine that you shift production from one type to another, as on your last line. Every time you do so, you have to move out all that WIP, or keep it there and get very confused."

"So single-piece-flow is the answer?" wondered Phil.

"In an ideal case, it is. If they could just move one item at a time, most of these problems would disappear. The number of items would be equal to the number of operators on the line, so you would reduce WIP, and in doing so, lead time. Then you could place the workstations right next to each other since they wouldn't need to park all this inventory, which would also improve communications. Then if operators encounter a problem, they can discuss it right then and there. Finally, they would be better able to balance their work to smooth the flow and prevent in-process inventory to build up again. You can't always do it, of course, and sometimes you've got processes like metal stamping that run at entirely different rates. But that's what you should aim for."

"But I thought we had single-piece flow," complained Phil. "That's what the consultants told us, and that's why we broke up the old shop organization to move to this line here!"

"Aw, heck, Philip," said Dad irritably. "Just look at this line. What do you see?"

"Continuous flow?" ventured Phil.

"Flow, sure, but not continuous. Look at it in detail. Each operator is working with at least five parts in front of him or her."

"I see it," chipped in Amy. "They place the parts in a neat row in front of them and then they work at them in sequence, before moving the five parts together to the next station."

"Yes, you're right," said Phil. "Why do they do that?"

"Well, it probably makes them feel comfortable, since they've always got a buffer of parts to work on. But think of how this affects your lead time," Dad answered. "Look," he said, scribbling an explanation, "you said earlier that the mechanisms take about 45 minutes of total operator time to assemble, right? So the lead time for a single mechanism is —"

"Forty-five minutes."

"Yes. 45 minutes. Now this breaks down into six equal steps of, say, eight minutes. If you're moving mechanisms by batches of five each, every time you do eight minutes of work on one, the other four are waiting there. So the total lead time for one mechanism is going to be five times eight minutes at each step —"

"Forty minutes," said Amy.

"Forty minutes, multiplied by six steps, gives you 240 minutes' lead time to get the first complete mechanism. So what you do have is flow of a sort. The first product in is the first product out. But this is not single-piece flow," Dad chided.

"Four hours' lead time rather than the 45 minutes needed if we just move one piece at a time, I see," agreed Phil, looking at Dad's sketches. "Actually, the consultants kept going on about this in theory, but they never managed to make it work. At first they had set the workstations right next to the other, which wasn't workable. So Dave and the operators spread out the line to give themselves some room."

"Some consultants," fumed Dad. "As to the how, we'll get to it soon enough. It's not that hard, but we'll need stopwatches."

"Stopwatches?" repeated Phil uncertainly. I frowned, remembering all the horrors described in social psychology classes of the Fordist hell where the operator is sweating it out under the glare of the white-coated productivity expert, the dreaded stopwatch in his hand, evoking Chaplin's vision of *Modern Times*.

"What do you expect?" Dad grumbled. "It's all about lead time and working cycles, so we'd better have a precise idea of how the parts flow through the stream. Stopwatches."

Phil shook his head, looking resigned.

"Anyhow, we've resolved part of our objectives question. We now know we want to reduce WIP inventory to one part per person. As junior here pointed out ..."

I hate it when he calls me that.

"Although absolutely zero work-in-process inventory isn't physically possible, our quality objective should indeed be zero defects. And the last thing we need to sort out is our productivity objective, and not to pull a number out of a hat. We need stopwatches to figure it out. Oh well, enough for today. You find the gear, and we'll have a look at all that tomorrow," Dad concluded, glancing at his watch.

"May I ask a question?" ventured Amy, as we were walking out of the plant.

"Sure, Ms. Cruz, go ahead."

"I missed your talk yesterday, but from what Phil told me, I understand that you can help us reduce the costs in our manufacturing processes so we can improve our cash position."

"That's correct. It's what we're doing."

She looked at Dad uncertainly before saying: "That's what I don't understand. I haven't once heard you mention costs."

Dad nodded, "So?"

"Well, in any other company, all they do is root around for 'cost reduction.' You know, cut the cookies kind of thing. You're not going to do that?"

Unexpectedly, it made my father laugh.

"Not as yet, Ms. Cruz, not just yet."

"That's what I don't get."

"I'll have to backtrack a bit," said Dad, just as I was about to get out into the open and make my escape. We stood by the reception desk while the sun was shining outside, and the real world beckoned.

"As I mentioned yesterday, any industrial strategy should be about reducing costs so as to make a profit while selling at market price. But there's a catch. What happens if you just 'cut costs' without knowing exactly what you're doing?"

"You may also limit your production," answered Philip. "That's what the previous owners did to this place. They squeezed every kind of cost to the point where the operators had to share the same tools, machines were not maintained, and, in short, nothing worked. When we took over, we had to start by mending the roof which had a massive leak in it!"

"Exactly," said Dad. "Before worrying about costs, what is the first way to get cash in?"

"Cook more of the burgers for the hungry customers in line," Amy said, quick as ever. "I'm with you. If you don't deliver, you can be as cost-effective as you want, and still no money comes in. We got that drilled into us back in the fast-food days."

"Yep, the best way to cut costs is simply to close the place down," agreed Dad. "Which, incidentally, some people do. I know of a factory that was turned into a 'cost center' by its corporate management. The factory's management bonuses were linked to how much costs they cut — so cost cutting they did. So delivery was shot to hell and quality problems went through the roof. One year down the line, in the same month, they lost their two major customers, and had to close down the entire shop. So it does happen.

"What we want to do is cost saving, not cost cutting. To do so we've got to have our priorities right. First, delivery. If we don't deliver, we don't get paid. This is what we're doing here. The immediate problem is to deliver 100 whatchamacallit breakers per week."

"STRs," confirmed Phil. "We need to double shipments from 50 to 100 STRs a week. You're right, that's our urgent concern."

"The problem," said Dad, "is that guaranteeing delivery on time in full in an operation that runs like yours means holding a high inventory of WIP and components to cover for all the internal problems and inefficiencies."

"Suppliers too," added Phil. "When we took over, the place was a mess, but they had customer orders. So we spent all the cash we had making sure that parts were on hand from our suppliers to make the products, which, in the process, pushed our inventories sky high, and got us in the present jam."

"Precisely. Still, you were right to think about suppliers," Dad said. "First worry about delivery, and then try to figure out what happens to inventory. The first time we worked with Toyota as part of their supplier development program, they had us increase inventories everywhere we had delivery problems! We couldn't believe it! Imagine the worldwide champions of 'zero inventory' asking us to increase in-process stocks. The difference is, of course, that those were called inventory buffers. But customer satisfaction comes first, always, which means first take care of delivery. Then, once we had that under control, they helped us to reduce inventory back to its lowest possible point.

"But second, you must work on inventory. As soon as you can guarantee delivery on time in full, then you worry about reducing the inventory you've had to let go of. I warn you that as we increase delivery of STR breakers, we'll also increase WIP inventories at first. Then we'll find ways of reducing those."

"How?"

"A variety of ways, but essentially you work with buffer stocks of parts, which you learn to replenish, and then work at reducing this buffer by attacking the underlying causes."

"But what about costs?" Phil pressed.

"Just the same. At first, some costs may look like they'll go up, particularly transport costs. But don't sweat it. By reducing the inventories intelligently, we'll get rid of many of the process' structural inefficiencies. It won't affect 'costs' as such, but it will directly impact productivity and so —"

"Cash," muttered Phil.

"Correct, cash. Now, once we've got the inventory in control, we can worry about 'costs,' because we'll know exactly which cost to save. And we will know which not to touch because they're important to the whole system. Inventory is the key, not in itself, but as the best indicator of the effectiveness of your processes, like the speedometer needle in your car. The needle does tell a story, but simply moving the needle in the hopes that your car will go faster wouldn't make much sense, would it? Well, that's what many companies do when they launch cost-cutting campaigns blindly. Remember, we want cost savings, not cost cuttings. Oh well, enough of that. We're off. Philip, get us these stopwatches for tomorrow, will you?"

Chapter Three

TAKT TIME

I called Phil later that night. "My Dad phoned. They're organizing a regatta at the Yacht Club over the weekend so he won't be able to make it tomorrow. It will have to wait til Monday."

"Damn. I'm sorry to hear it."

"He sure sounds excited about it though."

"Does he think we have a chance of making a difference?"

"How should I know? But he sounds fairly positive, and he knows his stuff."

"Great. Ah, listen ... ," he said, and then hesitated. "You're a doctor, right?"

"It depends. What's on your mind?"

"I told you I sleep badly, right?"

"You're under a tremendous amount of stress, you know that. What's troubling you?"

"Ah, I didn't tell you, but it got worse. I had a bit of an accident a couple of weeks ago. I woke up in the middle of the night with terrible chest pains, and my heart racing like mad. I couldn't move my arm, and it was all stiff and tingling. To make a long story short, Charlene drove me to the hospital where they thought I was having a heart attack. But later they told me they couldn't see anything wrong with me. They said I suffered from anxiety. It was an anxiety attack. They said I should see a shrink." It all came out in a sudden rush, almost like a confession.

"Hey, you know I'm not that kind of doctor," I told him.

"Yeah, but with you a psychologist, and all, what do you think?"

"Do you smoke?"

"Of course not!"

"Do you drink?"

"Apart from, um, well, no, not regularly."

"Do you exercise?"

"I still run every morning."

"Is there a history of heart problems in your family?"

"Not that I am aware of. My folks are still in good health."

I knew the answers to these questions, of course, but it was part of the routine. I hated having to play "psychologist" with any of my friends. I had gone into experimental research precisely because I had been very uncomfortable with clinical work. And with friends, it's worse. Much worse.

"Well then, the chances that there would be something wrong with your heart are slim. But please don't take my word for it. Take the time to have a proper checkup. If there's something wrong, they'll find it!"

"Yeah. What about the shrink thing?"

I sighed. "I think you should focus on your real problems. Beyond your company, is there anything else? I don't know, how are things with Charlene?"

He hesitated a moment, before admitting, "Not so good. We seem to argue a lot. She says I'm irritable and moody. I find her, well, you know."

"It does sound like you're packing a lot of stress. How about hot and cold sweats?"

"It happens," he answered defensively.

"Recurring thoughts of failure? Fear of injury or of accidents? Lack of sleep?"

"Yes, yes. You made your point. So shrink it is?"

"I didn't say that. If you feel it will do some good to talk to someone, go ahead. It won't solve the problem, though it might help you to face it. Fix the problem, Phil. You can do it. Sort that business out. Take vitamins. Agree to whatever your wife says or wants. Doctor's orders. You'll be fine."

He laughed. "Thanks, man. You're right. I'll get by."

"No problemo."

I sat staring at the room around me for a while. As I was talking to
him, I had been describing the very same symptoms of anguish that
grab me from time to time. I thought it odd he'd seen me through
some of these anxiety spells without ever realizing what they were.
Praised be innocence! A silvery reflection of moonlight drew bright
patterns in the darkened room, by the bay windows. After the break-
up, I had rented the top floor of a small apartment building right in the
middle of a barrio. It was conveniently close to the university. I liked
the Latino bustle around the place and didn't have to fear for the rust
pile I called a car. I had fallen in love immediately with the unexpected
bay windows the architect had used to save wall space. On a fog-free
day, you can even glimpse the ocean from here, if you try hard enough.
I realized with a shock that six months down the line, I still hadn't
gotten around to furnishing the place after hurricane Sarah had blown
through my life. The living room was empty except the old-fashioned
leather sofa, which she'd left behind, too cumbersome to move, and a
trestle table on which I kept my computer. Messy piles of paper and
books were glistening eerily in the pale moonlight.

I had thought that taking a sabbatical would help. I had been asked
to write a textbook on "casual irrationality," which encompassed
experimental cognitive psychology and some developmental psychology.
It was my big break. The book had a fighting chance of being picked up
as a text by several universities, and then the royalties would start to roll
in. I had already published my share of technical papers for professional
journals, and while nobody ever made a penny on them, the potential of
a book for the student market was something else altogether. Somehow,
I hadn't been able to get the work done with classes, students, and the
rest. But the isolation the sabbatical offered didn't seem to help, and
writing was just as slow and painful as ever.

To some extent, these factory jaunts with my Dad and Phil were a welcome relief. Something real. I thought about Phil and his entrepreneurial dreams, of my own academic ambitions, of Sarah chasing after the perfect relationship, and back to my work on irrationality and the rather disconcerting human penchant for wishful thinking. I had learned from working with schizophrenics that the fact that I couldn't share their delusions did not make them less real to them, just as I didn't believe in ghosts, but I believed in people who did. But my recent work made me all the more aware of the extent to which we all do that, sane or insane alike. The world is our wishing well, and we are wired to feel that if we believe in something strongly enough, surely it must be true, like finding gold mines in industrial waste.

"Good morning," said Phil brightly, ushering us into his office. "Come in, I want you to meet Dave Koslowsky. I've told you about Dave, he's our production guy here."

"Mornin'" said Dave blandly. He was a thickset man of fifty-something, with a mane of curly gray hair, a short pug nose, and the ruddy cheekbones of someone who spent a lot of time outdoors. He wore a plaid shirt and an ugly beige jacket, which made me think of duck hunting. You could sense the tension in his raised shoulders and in his fists tightly balled in his pockets. He looked high-strung, and I wondered what the matter was. My father must have sensed it too, because he tensed immediately, standing very straight, with his arms stiffly crossed.

"Phil got me to buy stopwatches," rasped Dave. "Are you going to time the operators while they work?"

"That's right!" answered Dad with his usual tact.

"Not in my plant, you're not!" snapped back Dave, swinging toward us as if he was going to shoulder his way into a crowd. Phil's jaw dropped, aghast, and Amy threw me a warning look. She had seen this coming.

"I don't have time for this," shot back Dad, turning around immediately and heading for the door.

"Wait, Dad, wait. Let's talk this through," I said calmly. To my surprise, he stopped and turned around, facing Koslowsky, who was glaring at him.

"What on earth is the matter with you, Dave?" exploded Phil. He'd gone all red in the face, whether from anger, surprise, embarrassment, or all three together.

"Come on, Phil," Dave argued, "We work with these people! We can't just walk in there and stand over them as they work with a timer in our hands. Think! They're going to blow up in our face!"

"There's no easy way to do it," said Dad grimly. "Just get them together and tell them that we're conducting a study, and not to worry about us, that's all. Don't you run morning meetings in this place?"

"Of course we do. And what do I tell them? That no one's is going to be fired as a result. I've been through these streamlining efforts before, and there's only one ending for operators, and they know it." Dave looked at my father defiantly.

"Who the heck are you? The union representative?" asked Dad.

"Take it easy, Dad."

"I'm the production manager, that's who I am. And I don't know who you are, but I don't want to deal with a revolution down there. And that's exactly what you clowns are about to face if you waltz in there with stopwatches and time studies. It's all been done before."

"Fine then. I'm done here," said my father acidly. But he didn't move. "It's your call, Philip," he finally added.

"Come on, Dave," Phil said, almost plaintively. "You know the situation we're in. We need Mr. Woods' advice. You can say what you want, but you haven't solved any of those problems we talked about yet." That must have hurt, because Dave's face clouded even further.

"Fire me if you want, Mr. Jenkinson, but I'm not having people walking around my shop floor with stopwatches without warning or any preparation. I'll do it myself if you ask me to, but not like that."

"We had a deal, Philip, I warned you I am not taking any of this any longer. So long. Mike, you're driving me home," Dad said as he walked to the door. I followed him as a loud argument erupted between Phil and Dave. I had witnessed my share of professional quarrels in my time, but nothing in the university had prepared me for the intensity of this confrontation, which, as usual, made me really mad at my father. Dammit, couldn't he ever deal with other people like a civilized human being instead of doing this John Wayne number on them?

"Wait!"

Amy was running after us across the courtyard as we were about to get into my car. "Just a word. Please."

"Ms. Cruz," Dad said evenly, still walking. Eventually, as we reached the car, he turned around to face her.

"I'm very sorry, sir," she said. "I know you said you didn't want to get involved, but you must understand. David has been working here for so long. It's all very difficult, especially now. We do need and value your help. We really do."

"Yeah, Dad, come on. Let's talk this over."

"What do you suggest?" he relented. Amy gave a sigh of relief, and one of her quick, open smiles. I liked her, she had a way with people. Even with my cursed father.

"David will calm down. I think that what he really objects to is our dealing directly with his workforce. But if you told us what to do, I'm sure he'd be the first to agree to do it himself. Really, he always has in the past."

I could see Dad was uncertain. He'd gotten interested, regardless of his pretense at aloofness. Besides, I didn't know much about industrial practices, but I did see the logic of the production guy's argument. I would have been very uneasy standing in front of an operator with a stopwatch in my hand, and I knew enough about observing people in experimental situations from the cog-sci lab.

Phil then rushed out of the building to join us as Dad was toying with his car door.

"I'm truly sorry, Bob," he sputtered "I don't know what got into Dave."

"I'll tell you what's the matter," Dad said. "They probably have some sort of negotiated piece-rate or standard times, or whatever. He's got a deal going with the workers about what the timings should be. Heck! Is the place unionized?"

"Not as such, but, yeah, Dave's in charge of the relations with shop floor employees, and we've got to be careful. These employees are very skilled, and we really don't want to lose them."

"What about you, then?" said Dad, turning his ire against Amy. "Aren't you supposed to be HR manager or something!"

"I am," she answered serenely, "and Dave and I will have a serious conversation about this. A serious *polite* conversation," she said in a rather matronly tone of voice. Dad just glared at her, and I expected more sparks to fly, but she just smiled sweetly. Then he spoke.

"Aw, okay. You're right, I was out of line. He has a valid point, and I probably would have reacted the same way in his shoes."

I looked up at Dad, astonished. An admission of imperfection? Hear, hear.

"But I have no patience for any of this anymore. I've spent my entire life dealing with people throwing in my face why we shouldn't do this, or couldn't do that, or, anyway ... ," his voice trailed away, and he looked really bitter for an instant, and old. I thought I could glimpse defeat on my father's face, something I had rarely seen before. "Don't expect me to get back in there when I'm not wanted, though."

Phil's face fell. I knew he was looking for some argument that could convince Dad, but, thankfully, he stayed quiet. Dad raked his hand through his sparse white hair, and harrumphed loudly in our uneasy silence. I thought of how silly we probably looked, arguing in the middle of the parking lot.

"Okay, we'll try it this way for a while. I'm not going back — but," he said, forestalling Phil's explosion, "we can still talk about it. I'll be at the Yacht Club tomorrow, and if you want to join me there, I'll tell you how to go about it, and you do what you can back at your plant. We'll see how this goes, and if it doesn't, well there's nothing much more I can do for you."

Phil brightened up immediately, repeatedly pushing his glasses back on the bridge of his nose, in that annoying manner he has when he gets excited or anxious.

"That's fine, Bob. Yes, truly fine. Thanks a lot. We can do that," he answered with obvious relief. I could swear Amy had winked at me, and I bit my lip to keep from grinning.

"All right," said Dad after gathering his thoughts. "To start with, how do you get on with this Gloria woman we met yesterday?"

"The shop supervisor? Pretty well, I guess."

Amy laughed out loud. "They're all terrified of her. She's the one who really runs the place down there, but why do you ask?"

"You said she was real good at assembling that stuff?"

"Yes," confirmed Phil, "that's how she got the supervisor job. Why?"

"Well, we still need to establish the ideal number of people we want on your blasted line, and I need some numbers!" Dad answered grumpily. "Real numbers, not garbage from a vague study from God knows when!"

"I can talk to her," chipped in Amy. "She's all right, really."

"Okay," said my father dubiously, "I want you to ask her how long it would take her to assemble an STR mechanism from start to finish, testing included. That's in one go, no breaks, with all the material there and everything."

Amy nodded as she wrote it down on her pad.

"Better still, if she'd agree to have you time her as she assembles one, maybe after the end of the shift. You could take the times for each segment of work, you see?"

"I have it," confirmed Amy.

"Okay, Ms. Cruz, you do that, and you guys can come down to the Yacht Club tomorrow for lunch and we'll talk about it."

"We'll be there," answered Phil.

My Dad's battered old pick-up was already parked at the Yacht Club when I arrived. I wondered what he saw in that wreck, but then realized there probably was a sentimental streak in the old man I had not thought about before. It was my mother who was keen on the brand new plush sedans. I guessed he was already at work on the *Felicity* (silly name, but it came with the boat, and some sailors think it's bad luck to rechristen a ship), so I lounged around for a while in the pleasant shadow of the pine trees bordering the Club's parking area. A few moments later, Phil's bright orange vintage Porsche roared in, closely followed by Amy's snazzy little red convertible.

Her smart business suit drew some stares from the local boys loitering around a half-painted skiff as she gave me a wide wave and cheerful smile. Although she smiled easily, she had in fact a rather serious face. Phil hardly saw me as he walked past toward the Yacht Club's entrance, staring at his shoes with the downcast gait of a man shouldering his load of trouble.

The Club was a two-story building overlooking the pier, with its back to a fragrant hill of ponderosas. The top floor was arranged as a bar-cum-restaurant with a wide porch on the second floor and an open deck overlooking the harbor. I could spot my Dad's boat at the end of the pier, and she did look a beauty. The place itself was fun, full of varnished wood and polished brass in a fake 1920s style. There wasn't much action on a weekday apart from a few locals and a party of tourists, and Dad had found a pleasant table in the shade where he was already absently sipping a cup of coffee.

"Forty-two minutes," announced Amy resolutely when she sat down, slamming her pad on the table, which made Dad grin.

"How did it go?" asked Phil.

"Fine. She prepared all the parts first, and I timed her as she assembled the whole thing in 42 minutes, including testing. But she said it usually takes a lot longer because something always goes wrong."

"Did she mind?"

"Being timed? No, she asked what it was for, though, and whether people should worry about their jobs again. You know, after going through the sale and all."

"What did you tell her?" worried Phil.

"Nothing," she shrugged. "I said I'd ask you, but that I didn't think it was in the cards. We'd better work out a communication strategy, though, and quick!"

"Yep, especially if you want to split the work into two shifts. People will have to get used to the idea, and realize we're not cutting heads," emphasized Dad.

"You're right," nodded Phil glumly. "More work."

"No sweat, boss," said Amy brightly. "We can do it. The time itself break downs like this:
— Twelve minutes to assemble the mechanism,
— four minutes to fit the motor,
— six minutes to wire the motor,
— seven minutes to fit the vacuum core capsule,
— four minutes to do the wiring, and
— nine minutes for testing.

"Fitting the vacuum core gave Gloria trouble. She had to jiggle it a bit and then be careful of the settings. She said it's a delicate operation, and sometimes it falls in place by itself and is fine, but other times you have to actually rework the attachments."

"I can see there is a huge imbalance between the first and second step," mused Phil, picking up the pad.

"Never mind about that for the moment," Dad cut in. "That's just one case, it doesn't mean much. Maybe that's her own way of working, and it could be that the guy who does it every day on the line is much faster. Sooner or later, we're going to have to take times, you follow?"

"Okay, yes. I get your point," confirmed Phil.

"All right, so our problem at this stage is figuring out what should be the appropriate number of people on this line, correct?"

We all nodded like a bunch of Sunday school kids.

"Now what's the critical element here?"

"How fast they work?" I asked.

Shake of head.

"How balanced are the working stations?" suggested Phil.

"Nope, think about it!"

"How many we want to produce each day!" proposed Amy with sudden insight.

"Top of the class, miss. It's all about *takt time*."

We all exchanged glances, expecting Dad to define this new word. Instead he continued his lecture. "What do your customers do with these breakers anyhow?"

"They assemble them into larger pieces of equipment with other modules, like large stationary cupboards, which then go into power plants, ships, and the like," Phil said.

"How many of these STR breakers do they require in a month?"

"For STR breakers they have two big projects running in parallel, one late as I understand it. Our original order was for 400 STR circuit breakers a month, but we said from the start we couldn't provide that, so at the moment we are delivering 200 a month."

"How frequent are the shipments?" Dad asked.

"We are supposed to deliver 50 STR breakers in weekly shipments."

"Twenty working days in a month?"

"Barring accidents and rushes, yeah. We often do overtime to catch up with the backlog, which costs us a pretty penny."

"Never mind. Now your customer would like 200 of your circuit breakers a month, which means 10 per day, correct?

"So in terms of mechanisms, we're talking 40 a day, correct?"

"Right. Four STR mechanisms per breaker."

"Which means that if your customer consumes these parts with clock-like regularity, you should be delivering one completed STR every 45 minutes, and delivering a mechanism every 11 minutes and 30 seconds to your own final assembly."

"How do you make that out?" Phil puzzled.

"Let's imagine a perfectly smooth flow," said Dad. "The gold flows through the value stream and produces a nugget at regular intervals, do you see it?"

"It's science fiction," said Phil with a smile, "but I can see it."

"You work eight hours day, not including lunch, so that's 480 minutes. Let's account for two 10-minute breaks, which gives us 460 daily working minutes. Your gold-mine stream should pop a nugget out every 460 divided by 40, or 11.5 minutes, you follow?"

"Mmm …" frowned Phil. "Better make that 15-minute breaks. You're saying that a perfectly smooth flow should produce a mechanism every, let's see, 450 divided by 40, every 11 minutes something?"

"So, 11.25 minutes," said Amy, her calculator in hand.

"What I'm saying, Philip," said my father slowly, "is that if your customer is running a smooth operation, he should be consuming one of your STRs every 45 minutes. So if you want to avoid overproducing, you have to deliver precisely one STR every 45 minutes to finished goods. If you're faster, you'll create inventory, and if you're slower, your customer will have to wait for you, right? To do so, you've got to produce four STR mechanisms every 45 minutes, which comes down to one mechanism every 11.25 minutes."

"Hypothetically, I see what you mean," said Phil. "In reality, it's a different matter. We don't even know when to ship him the things."

"What you're saying, really," said Amy thoughtfully, "is delivery first, no more, no less."

"That's correct. And to do that, you need a rhythm, a pacemaker. That's what takt time is all about. It gives the rhythm to the entire factory."

$$\text{Takt Time} = \frac{\text{Available Daily Production Time}}{\text{Daily Customer Demand}}$$

Phil wrote this down dutifully, noting out loud, "It's the reverse of the production rate."

"Mathematically, yes," Dad said, considering this. "But the perspective is completely different. Suppose that you have to produce 40 parts per day, which, in our case, is 40 parts per 450 minutes. This means that we should be producing 0.0888 mechanisms per minute. And this doesn't make any sense. So what happens is that people think of production rates in averages for the whole day. For instance, we could produce 30 mechanisms in the first four hours of the day, and due to whatever failure, 10 in the afternoon. We'd still be producing 40 parts a day."

"I see," said Amy thoughtfully. "In aiming to churn a product out every 11.25 minutes, we have much less leeway. You always have a sense of where you stand in relation to daily demand."

"That's the idea. Furthermore, in traditional operations the production rate can be decided by the production manager. If I want to utilize my equipment fully, for instance, I might decide that I really can produce 50 parts a day. If I do that, I increase my utilization rate considerably."

"But you'd have 50 extra products at the end of the week!" I remarked.

"So what? I can store them and use the extra day to produce something else. How is that a problem?" asked Amy.

"Inventory!" sighed Phil. "In fact, that's what Dave keeps doing with the DG breakers. Since most of the demand we get on those is for maintenance, it tends to come in spurts. He tends to do long runs and then store them!"

"Exactly," noted Dad. "Overproduction, which results in excess inventory, comes from making too many products, either before the customer wants them, or in excess of their demands. Takt time is all about producing what the customer consumes, no more, no less."

"But what happens if the customer suddenly wants more?" asked Amy. "Say, 50 a day?"

"Takt time goes down to nine minutes," calculated Phil. "It might, but if we're producing one mechanism every 11.25 minutes, how are we suddenly going to produce one every nine minutes? Magic?"

"That's the rub. Figure it out," challenged Dad.

We mulled it over in silence for a while.

"Gloria assembles one STR mechanism in 42 minutes," said Amy.

"Correct."

"So, how many Glorias should we need to produce one mechanism every 11.25 minutes?"

"Forty-two divided by 11.25 is 3.73," answered Phil.

"Can't have 0.73 of a person," I scoffed.

"Right, so four."

"And every nine minutes?" asked Dad.

"That's 4.6! But we need a complete person, so that makes five," said Phil. "So we'd need four with a takt time of 11 minutes, and five with a takt time of nine!"

"Essentially, you've got it," said my father with a satisfied smile. "There is a direct relationship between the takt time and the number of people you've got working on the line. Remember that they're not each building the whole product, they're organized along a production line."

"Right. So we have a relationship between the takt time, the number of operators, and ... ," Phil paused, and Amy finished his thought.

"The time it takes to do the work!"

"That's it," said Dad. "This is called the product's work content. And in your case, the mechanism work content is 42 minutes, because that's what it took Gloria to build one from start to finish by herself. Actually, if we had timed each of the operators on their specialized jobs, we'd have a slightly smaller work content, because of the specialization effect."

"You mean they complete their work more quickly because they have a smaller job to do and are more familiar with it?" asked Phil.

"Yes, mostly, but we'll worry about operator cycles later. Let's stay focused on the relationship. It takes 42 minutes of work content to come up with a tested mechanism. You need to produce one every 11 minutes. So how many people do you need on that line?"

"Blast, no more than four. And we've got six! Ahh," muttered Phil disgustedly.

"Forty-two divided by 11 is 3.8," confirmed Amy, as she motioned Phil to write down:

$$\text{Number of Operators} = \frac{\text{Total Work Content}}{\text{Takt Time}}$$

"Hold your horses, son, we'll get to why you have six operators working on the line, rather than four, in a minute. The important point is that we can have a SMART objective, as Amy would say, for that line: from six to four people. Never mind how for the moment."

"In a perfect world, it should be feasible," agreed Phil.

"Which is precisely how to set an objective: so that it is a stretch, but not unrealistic."

"That's a huge productivity hike!" stammered Amy.

"Difficult, but not unrealistic."

"However," pointed out Phil, suddenly excited, "if we can achieve this on each of the three assembly lines, we liberate a total of six people! That's enough to start a second shift for the STR line!"

"That's the idea," confirmed Dad smugly.

"Holy smoke!"

"Take it easy, son, we're not there yet."

"But do you really think we can do it?"

"Do I think it can be done?" said Dad carefully. "Yes. However, do I think you can do it? I haven't got a clue. Considering my first contact with your production manager, I wouldn't place any bets yet."

Good old Dad, kick a man when he's down. I sensed that Dave would pay for the welcome he'd given us, sooner or later.

"But that's not the issue yet in any case. What we have to understand first is why you use six operators on that line rather than four."

"Oh," complained Phil, deflated.

"Because they're not as good as Gloria?" Amy suggested.

"That could be true, but I don't believe that's the reason."

"Because the system is inefficient?" I chipped in.

"Yes, but in what ways?"

I shrugged. What did I know about factories anyhow?

"Think about it the other way round," he pursued. "Six people producing 40 parts a day —"

"Or less!" grumbled Phil.

"Or less, means a total working time on each product of 66 minutes, which is 24 minutes more than Gloria used."

"That's almost 30%!"

"An average of four extra minutes per person per product," calculated Amy. "That's not that much."

"Especially considering the line's not particularly balanced if the way Gloria worked is anything to go by," added Phil.

"Will you let go of that for the moment, Philip," Dad chided. "We'll come back to balancing later. What we're saying is that there's more time spent building the product than absolutely necessary, at least by Gloria's standard. What could it be? Let's say they're not slow. Let's go by what Mike said, that it's the system. What can happen?"

"Oh, I don't know!" exclaimed Phil, throwing up his hands in frustration. "Anything can happen: a missing part, something doesn't fit, going to the toilet even."

"Precisely. Variation," said Dad.

"You mean it could be anything?"

"Not quite anything. My Toyota mentor talked about three types of waste. There's *muda*, we already spoke of, nonvalue-added work, but there's also *muri*: overburden."

Phil simply said, "Huh?"

"Muri is all the unreasonable work that management imposes on workers because of poor organization, such as carrying heavy weights, moving things around, dangerous tasks, etc. It's pushing a person or a machine beyond its natural limits. Unreasonable work is nearly always a cause of variation," Dad explained, adding, "Finally there's *mura*, unevenness."

"What do you mean by that?"

"Variation per se, but not in the work itself. Rather, it's in the scheduling. Mura is variation imposed on the process by fluctuations in the production scheduling. It means that in order to absorb the peaks of demand, we always need extra capacity on hand — which is wasted when we're in a production valley."

"*Muda, mura, muri*," repeated Amy. "It covers a multitude of sins!"

"Sure, but at this stage we don't know what or where. All we know is that there is a discrepancy between what could be in an ideal situation and what is actually happening. In my experience, there are far more causes of variation in a process than we can see, which is why you can't seem to find the bottleneck, or the line imbalances to account for the in-process inventory pile-ups."

"Hmm, it would also explain while pile-ups never occur twice at the same place!"

"Precisely. From Amy's numbers we can see that the process is not wildly unbalanced, which it would be in a tighter flow sequence like the final assembly. But we can also see it's not running smoothly. At this stage, all this gives us is our second objective. To go from six operators to four."

"I still find it hard to believe that variation in the process could account for a difference from six to four operators," muttered Phil stubbornly.

"Not just variation," Dad corrected. "All the types of waste we've discussed! Look at it from another angle. Rework, for instance. We've got our inventory objective, one part per operator, and we've figured out our productivity objective. Now what about quality?"

"You said it earlier," I said. "Zero defects."

"Zero internal defects, correct. What do you think about that, Philip?" asked my father with a twinkle in his eye.

"Can't be done!" said Amy.

"It's a target!" said Phil. "We have to strive toward it but it cannot be achieved. Something is bound to go wrong somewhere."

"The term as we've learned it is a mistranslation," stated Dad with a grin. "The original concept is 'zero defects *accepted.*' At each step of the process, the operator has been trained to identify defective work from upstream, and to refuse it. In effect, if the operator accepts defective work from upstream, adds his or her own work to it and passes it downstream, he or she is actually taking on the responsibility for the defect.

"I agree that 'zero defect' seems unachievable as an absolute, but that's besides the point," Dad continued. "Toyota teaches the principle of *jidoka*, or built-in quality. The key concept is to make sure that when a defect occurs, for whatever reason, it is stopped as early as possible in the value flow upstream."

"The further downstream, closer to finished goods, it is finally caught, the more it costs!" exclaimed Phil, writing down:

Zero Defects Accepted

"The worst being when the defect reaches the customer and is spotted there. We might not even know about it. For one customer who complains, nine simply walk away, so they say," added Amy in a mock-wise tone.

"Not in our business. Oh they tell us about it," said Phil with a rueful smile. "But they can easily ruin our reputation in the market and then we're dead."

"I know, Dad, I know. Like Henry Ford used to say, the two things that don't appear on a company's balance sheet are its people and its reputation," I chimed in.

"Do I ever say that? Still, you're all missing the point. It's not zero defects at the customer. You need to have zero defects accepted at each stage of the process. This means the operator refuses to work with defective components, materials, or to do any rework."

"No rework?" asked Phil incredulously. "But then we'd bin one part in four!"

"Precisely, where do you think all that variation comes from?" Dad replied. "I didn't say throw the parts away, I just said the operators on the line don't do the rework, and don't accept anything that they consider to be not good enough."

"That'll make an interesting change," whistled Amy.

"Why should they have to cope with all the crap the company can throw into the process? Why should they be the ones to deal with poor designs, incompetent vendors, and shoddy work?" ranted Dad, getting quite worked up about it.

"So that really is our quality objective: zero defects in the process." Phil was working hard on taking this in.

"That's it, son. No shirking that one!"

"And you know how to help us get there?" asked Phil, eyeing my father dubiously, for once not letting himself be intimidated by the bristling glare.

"I can give you a few tips along the way, yep."

"So this is what it comes down to," said Amy, scribbling on her pad, all business now:

	Now	Objective
Parts per day	About 40	40
WIP inventory	33	4
People	6	4
Quality defects	?	0

"You can't be serious," Phil cut in. "You're saying our objective is to reduce WIP by, huh, 90% and people by 30%. Amy, that's just nuts. It's unrealistic."

Dad ignored Phil. "Well, Ms. Cruz, I couldn't have said it better. There's your objective. Are you all extremely clear on that point? Do you see the gold you're hunting in the stream?"

"Single-piece flow. No scrap from station to station. And two operators less, for the same production," she answered with a challenging smile. "Deal. Where do we start?"

"Easy," answered Dad with a knowing smile. "Red bins!"

"Red bins?" muttered Amy and Phil in unison.

"Yep, and simple Pareto charts. So far, you still don't believe that variation in your process is causing so much havoc. I'd kick off with a simple action: the red bins. You're going to find red plastic bins, and set them at each work station with one simple instruction to the operators: no rework. If they don't like something about the part they're holding, whether a mechanism from the previous station or a component, they put it in the red bin and that's that."

"But if we do that, the line will grind to a standstill!" Phil protested.

"Maybe, maybe not," Dad answered. "Since they carry enough inventory, they can just grab the next product and work on that instead."

"Okay," said Phil uncertainly.

"Listen, son, you said you'd do what I said. Remember? I can help you only if you let me help you, so don't argue and just do it!"

Now, that sounded more like my father.

"What happens to the stuff in the red bins?" asked Amy.

"Let's say that you stay there for a while to see how it goes. Who knows what can happen. From the look of it they might throw out their entire shop and your precious Dave will have a fit. Work it out with Gloria. Have her create a notebook and write down the cause for chucking each part, and ask her to do the rework jobs herself. For now, when she's reworked a part, she can simply place it back in the station's in-tray with the rest of the inventory. We'll see later about how to do the same without in-process inventory."

I got a call from Phil the very next evening. "Mike? Hi. Listen, I've been running your dad's red bin system all day — do you think I could talk to him about it?"

"I don't know. I'll ask him."

"Why don't you boys come out here?" was my father's response when I called. "And pick up some Chinese takeout on the way, will ya?"

"Hi guys!" waved my Mom from the large settee where she was intently watching some new movie release. "Bob's out on the porch and the beers are in the fridge!"

My parents had been real lucky in finding this house when they came back from the Great Lakes. It was situated right by a celebrity resort in the hills, so although they lived in a fairly urban area, all we could see around was empty brush and tall, looming eucalyptus trees, which smelled sweetly in the cooling air. Dad was lounging on the porch, watching the last glimmer of the sunset reflected in the pool. Phil and I settled down with the impromptu meal and drinks, as I recalled how lucky my parents had been with their timing, with Dad retiring right before the Internet bubble burst. He'd paid for the house and the boat in full and was in fact pretty relaxed about the ups and downs of their pension funds. With everything to prove in my own professional career, I envied him that peace of mind.

"Twenty percent!" Phil was repeating, shaking his head and waving his bottle around. "Twenty percent rework in your red bins! In one day."

"Slow down, son, 20% of what?"

"Of all parts produced! We started this morning, and we tallied the results up this evening. Of the 35 mechanisms assembled from the start to the end of testing, eight of them needed reworking at some stage of the process.

"Four after the first wiring, although we haven't figured out why yet. It was amazing! Right at the start, we explained the red bin system to the operators, and they all caught on right away. We'd only just started, when the woman fitting the motors had hers almost full! It turns out many of the motors we get from the suppliers have problems and sometimes she fiddles with them herself. And then ..."

He just waved his beer some more, not knowing how to describe the obvious chaos on the production line.

"How did Dave take it?" I wondered.

"Oh, man, he went ballistic! The real treat is that if each of these eight parts had been right the first time, the line would have produced 43 parts today. Dave realized that having the rework done on line by the operators probably hid this kind of waste every day. He was beside himself. I tell you, you should have seen it. I thought the man would fall apart. Thank God for Amy. After the first hour, she spent almost half her time holding his hand. We won't get many arguments from him now."

"Can't really blame him for what he doesn't know," said Dad, which I thought was fair-minded of him after the other day's drama. "Having said that, this is his job, the core of it. Operators should only do value-added work. It's management responsibility to make sure of that and to get rid of the waste."

"I know, I know, I've been thinking hard about this muda, mura, and muri thing. We're not even close, are we? And then, what really pissed me off is that I realized that Dave's just doing his best, and so are the operators. Let's face it, it means we have pretty shoddy designs!"

"You figured that out, eh?" chided Dad.

I caught Phil's hurt look in the penumbra. One can think whatever one wants of him, but one thing for sure — he's not dumb.

"Yeah. The problem is that I took it up with Gary Pellman, the product engineering director, and he didn't even want to hear about it."

"Who's that?"

"When we took over the company, Matt fired the entire

management structure, except for Dave and this guy, Gary Pellman, whom he knew from before. He's the guy in charge of our product engineers. He handles the customization part of our products to customer specifics. He's a pretty big guy in the business because of his experience of what customers want. And touchy, too."

"Designers, prima donnas, the lot of them," Dad grumbled.

"Well, that's what I wanted to talk to you about, Mr. Woods. What do I do? Tomorrow I'm going back to the plant and I have to tell the operations people something."

"Relax. You're not telling them anything they haven't known for a long time. Remember they've dealt with these sorts of problems for years. Just make sure Ms. Cruz is ready to listen to a lot of 'I've been saying so forever but no one ever cared!'"

"I can see that, but it doesn't solve the problem, does it?"

"I guess not. What would?"

"To start with," Dad said, "get an engineer to work directly with the operators and find out why there's so much rework on the mechanisms."

"I can deal with the vendor side, but there's something we must be able to do with our own designs! Jeez, 20%!" said Phil.

"You didn't expect it, did you?"

"To be honest, no. We have so few defectives at the end of the process."

"Okay, think about it this way: there are several ways to measure quality." Dad held out his fingers and ticked them off. "First, you do a final inspection and count the defectives at the end of the process, plus the unfortunate cases which slip through and get to the customers. This gives you a percentage of defects: so many defectives out of so many produced. In your case, you mentioned something in the order of five per 1,000. This tells you how good your product is, but it doesn't say much about the process, though, or where your real problems are.

"Second, the next stage is to count internal scrap, or all the parts you've got to throw away or rework in the process. As you've seen, that can be surprisingly high in the kind of assembly that depends heavily on the know-how of the operators. Still, supposing a product has two defects, you're probably only going to spot one.

"To be more precise, you can start identifying all the obvious things that go wrong at each stage of the assembly. Let's call them defect opportunities. In this way, you can catch the mistakes and count the types of defects as they occur. Counting defects per million opportunities will give you a fairly accurate picture of how good your process is.

"Now, quality can't be inspected into a product, they say, but it sure as heck can be inspected out! The first thing to do is to continue with the red bin system, and train the operators to recognize what exactly is wrong with the product they're working on."

"I figured that much, and we've already talked with Gloria and Amy about setting this up," Phil said.

"Second step," Dad went on, "is getting people to link the defects with the way the work is done upstream. Usually, operators have no clear notion of what good — or bad — work means. No one's ever told them. They just figure it out on their own. So you need to help them figure this out. Try these questions:

How do they know they are doing the job right?

How do they know they are not creating problems down the line?

What do they do when they encounter a problem?"

"As in bin it, or call Gloria rather than deal with it themselves?"

"Yes, but that one's tricky. So you really need to work your way carefully through it. In the Toyota Production System, they set up a big board called an andon so that if the operator has a problem, a lighted number comes up and the supervisor can rush to the spot."

"I've heard the operators can actually stop the line if they find nonquality," Phil noted.

"Well, that's what people say, but it's not exactly the case. Whenever an operator has a problem, he calls for help by pulling a cord or pushing a button. Then a line manager comes running to see what can be done about it right away. If the problem is not resolved within one work cycle, the process will actually stop rather than produce nonquality. However, the operator did not actually stop the line. All he did was call for help. The line stops if management's help is not quick enough or good enough. The pressure is on management as well as operators. It's all about zero defects accepted. If you take it as seriously as they do, you end up doing stuff like that."

"It's quite a big responsibility for an operator isn't it?" I wondered, quite curious about the motivational angle

"Indeed. That's a big part of the system. There's more pressure for operators, but there's also more responsibility and opportunity to resolve the problem for good. There's also a lot more responsibility for front-line management. We'll have to discuss all that a lot more when we get to standardized work and such. But for the moment, let's concentrate on inspecting nonquality out of the product and making it the responsibility of every operator! Plus remember that all we're setting up is still only after-the-fact quality control. It's not true built-in quality, so we'll have to come back to this topic later on."

Phil set down his bottle and pushed his glasses back. "I think I understand what you're saying. We're going to have to create a more permanent system for dealing with the problems that the red bin system spots."

"Correct. You must work with the operators to understand the details of the defect opportunities — where they're most likely to encounter one — and how this problem affects the rest of the line. It'll be interesting, anyhow, to get them to discuss it among themselves."

"But what about the design angle? I'm convinced that something must be done to improve our basic designs. We can't just rely on the operators' skills to compensate for design problems, can we?"

Dad let out a loud sigh, and grabbed himself another beer. He probably had a few battle scars to show on this issue.

"No argument there, Philip. Someone's going to have to clean up the product design. The question is 'who?' and how are you going to get them to do it?"

"Shouldn't it be Pellman's job?"

"He'll just tell you that he's too busy with the backlog of customer modifications, that he hasn't got time for anything else, and that all his guys are fully loaded. Let production deal with their quality problems."

"Close enough to what he already said," admitted Phil. "And unfortunately, probably true too!"

"Quite likely," agreed Dad.

"Hang on a second," said Phil, thinking out loud. "There's this younger engineer, Josh. A bit of a hot rod, and he's chaffing under Gary's authority."

"He any good?"

"I think so. He's quick off the mark, and customers like him. Ambitious too. He's been telling us he needs more challenges." Phil thought for a second. "What about letting him work on the entire STR flow, with a specific brief to work with the operators and improve the generic designs so that there is less room for mistakes and rework?"

"Makes sense to me, if he's up to it," Dad said. "You can give him the responsibility for the entire process, delivery, quality as well. Now ideally, he would report to you and Matt. But in this case, you probably shouldn't push it. For now, leave him under your engineering guy. From what I've seen, you can probably handle the turf problem with Dave."

"Dave? No sweat. He's got his temper, but he's okay. We usually manage to turn him around. No, it's more a problem of convincing Matt and Gary," he grumbled. "I hate that!" he cried out suddenly. "I'm a scientist for heaven's sake. I hate all this people business and politics."

"Well, son, in the end, it's all about people," said Dad after letting the moment pass.

"Yeah. I don't have to like it, though."

"No you don't. I never did!"

They sat there for a while in companionable misery, nursing their beers, reliving their turf wars, the veteran and the rookie, and I felt a sudden unexpected flare of jealousy. Is that what my Dad missed in his sons? The fact that both my screenwriter brother and I had chosen careers as far away from business as possible?

"Fine!" exclaimed Phil after a while. "What's the point of being the boss if I can't do what I like? I'll talk to Matt and convince him to give Josh the job, and we'll see if he's as good as he thinks he is. I'll get him to work with the operators and improve the designs of these damned mechanisms. What happens next?"

"Well, do you agree now that the variation could be causing far more inefficiency in the process?"

"Are you kidding? I have seen the light," Phil joked. "I am converted!"

"The next step is to redesign your line so you can liberate two of the operators, but I don't think we're going to tackle it tonight. For the moment focus on improving the quality in the process."

Thank God for that, I thought. Such a pleasant evening.

That Sunday morning, my father was back at work with the varnish on the *Felicity*'s deck, working the portside roof. I arrived a bit late, and had been waylaid by Harry for an amiable chat as I stepped out of my car. As I reached the end of the wooden pier, I walked in on a rather surreal scene. Dad was on his hands and knees applying a coat of varnish with the concentration a Swiss watchmaker reserves for the most delicate springs. Phil was sitting in the cockpit, hunched over the pad on his knees taking furious notes. And Amy, who had swapped her executive look for jeans shorts and a white tank top, was lounging on the deck, wearing oversized sunglasses, idly kicking her feet in the air. She didn't fit any of the "California girls" canons of beauty, being short and somewhat well rounded, but I noticed a rather lovely pair of legs. And then I realized I was staring! I quickly fumbled my way on board, and parked myself in the cockpit, across from Phil, who gave me a distracted nod.

"I'll say it once again, Philip, don't do any of this until you've timed each operator's cycle at least 20 times!"

"But that would be 200 minutes, sir. Three hours for each?"

"Okay, then, but at least 10 times. No argument, you need some statistical validity to any number you use or people won't buy them. Never even mention the timing you got off Gloria, it's not relevant to them. Got that?"

"I guess so."

"The operator cycle is the time it takes an operator to do the work, right?" asked Amy.

"Yes, but you have to be more specific. An operator cycle has to be measured from fixed point to fixed point. Mickey! Mind where you put your feet, I've got my brushes over there!"

Yeah, Dad. Good day to you too.

"Look, suppose I'm an operator on the line, and my job is to paint. Here, I dip my brush in the pot, apply the varnish, check that it looks good, and then dip again. It's a cycle. Now, if you take your watch out, you can measure how long it takes me to paint a strip."

"Wait," she said, trying it. "It's not easy."

"Exactly. The hard part is to have a precise starting point and ending point. Say you start the cycle when I dip the brush in the paint. You can now measure from that point to the next time I dip my brush."

"Sure."

"Okay? Now watch this," said Dad, straightening up. He made a face as his knee joints protested, and scrambled down to where I had almost messed up his precious pots, and started cleaning his brush. Then, he returned to his workstation by the porthole.

"Are you still timing me?" he asked with a chuckle.

"No, I —"

"Precisely, you got tricked. I said from fixed point to fixed point!"

"Damn!" she muttered under her breath.

"My very thoughts, Ms. Cruz. Don't you worry, it's a very common mistake, and I've seen more than one plant manager do exactly the same thing. But see here, if the operator has to regularly move away to clean his brush, that is part of the cycle, correct?"

"Variation!" muttered Phil as if he was having an epiphany.

"Variation. A cycle has to be measured from fixed point to fixed point. The lower point will give you what the 'normal' job is, and the high point, what it takes to do the job if you have to go and fish for supplies, the equipment doesn't work, or whatever. All this time, gold is not flowing through the stream!"

"And your boat is not getting painted!" I quipped, just to be part of the conversation.

"Exactly. How do you expect me to get any work done if I spend my time yammering away with you youngsters?"

"Wow! I had never thought about it that way. You're right, our processes are full of variation!" Phil said.

"Listen to the man!"

"So for each operator, we measure a working cycle of, say, 10 measures. Then what?" Amy asked, keeping her eye on the ball.

"Then you draw this graph, showing both minimal and maximal times for the cycle. Hand me your pad, Philip!" My father sketched.

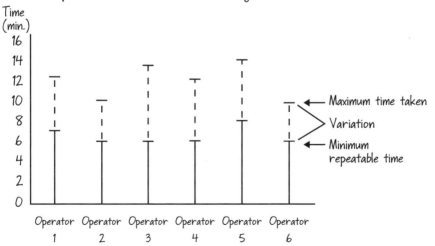

Operator Balance Chart with Cycle Time Variation

"It's a balance chart," he added with a wink to Phil.

"I knew balancing had to come in somewhere," muttered my friend in reply.

"And then what?" continued Amy. "We average the times for each operator?"

"No!" answered Dad emphatically. "No averages! Averages don't mean a thing. You just keep with minimal and maximal, or if you want to be clever about it, minimal plus variation, call it 'delta.'"

"Why no average?" wondered Phil. "Everything we do is based on averages."

"And that's plain stupid," said Dad tactfully. "Averages don't mean much in the real world. Look here, the minimal tells you the best that the operator does in normal conditions. What the maximum tells you is the worst variation he or she has to deal with in doing this job. What would the average tell you is real? Do me a favor, spare me averages."

I could almost hear Phil chewing this one over. Amy came down to sit next to him, studying the graph in his hands carefully.

"But surely," she said carefully, "from all we've been saying, the operator's average cycle time should equal the takt time, no?"

"Think about it!" shot back Dad. "Here, Mickey, can you pass me another pot of varnish?"

"Aha!" exclaimed Phil, straightening up. "You're absolutely right. It's not the average; it's the minimal cycle time that should equal the takt time! No variation!"

"That's right. Now what you do is take that graph, and draw the line for the takt time on it."

"It shows you two things. First whether the minimal times for each operator are more or less identical, meaning that the line is balanced; second, how those minimal times compare to the takt time, and finally what kind of variation we have in each operator's cycle. When you take the measurements, you try to spot at least two main sources of variation for each operator, such as frequent rework, or going for parts or whatever."

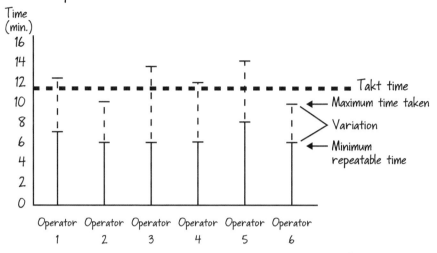

Operator Balance Chart with Takt Time

"Hey, but if I do this with Gloria's timings," said Amy," I find that most of the operations are well below takt time!"

"As I said," repeated Dad looking up from his work. "Don't use Gloria's timings. They don't mean anything to the people currently doing the job. But in principle, yes, you're correct."

"And this is how we can improve productivity!"

"Yep. It's not that hard," explained Dad. "What you now have to do is to decompose every operator cycle into basic movements. Every operation has its own natural cycle. Imagine we're doing a number of operations in a sequence where work content exceeds takt time. What do you do?"

"Obviously we have a problem," I pointed out, "because your operator has not finished his work!"

"That's right. That's the problem."

"I get it!" exclaimed Phil. "You pass on the job to the next operator!"

"But it's not completed," I protested. "It would not make sense to pass an almost dry brush to someone else!"

"On a tight sequence, it would," said Dad. "See, the big mental change you need to bring about on your production cell is that the operator should not think in terms of doing a 'job' from start to finish, but a set of operations within a standard time — the takt time."

"It's because I was thinking 'job' that I ignored it when you went away and did something else," suggested Amy.

"Exactly. We don't want to think job, we want to think flow. Remember, the gold has to flow smoothly through the process. So, two consequences:

First, you break down 'jobs' such as fitting or wiring into component operations, with each operator doing a takt time amount of work regardless of whether it is fitting or wiring or some combination, and then passing the buck onward.

Second, you get rid of all possible causes of interruption of this set of operations, such as rework, resupply, and so forth!"

"It's simple, but not easy. Dave is not going to like that!" muttered Phil, pushing his glasses back in deep concentration.

"What matters is the flow, not the job," Dad repeated.

"And since the cycles are lower than the takt time, we'll get to combine jobs and hence save people on the line, right?"

"Bright lady!" said Dad with a grin. "You should give her a raise!"

"Give me a raise, Boss," she said, nudging Phil with her elbow. He lifted his eyes to heaven in a "why me?" gesture.

"I get the theory," he said, "but how do we know which parts of the operation to remove?"

"Well, you take your graph, draw the takt time, and fill the first station up to the takt time, then the second, then the third until you get to the last one where some elements of the operation are bound to be left over.

"You can't cut people in half. Even if you're left with work that requires a tenth of the takt time for the last operation, you still need a whole guy there, with nothing to do for most of the cycle," said Dad. "That's why you need continuous improvement to reduce the operator work cycles, and then get rid of the little bit of time left over. This is what they call *kaizen*!"

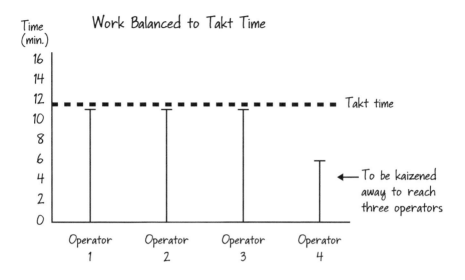

Phil took a deep breath. "Hold on there," he pleaded. "This is going too fast for me."

"It looks that way," nodded Dad. "Let's stick to balancing the line, and we'll discuss kaizen later. But it's a key historical point. Taiichi Ohno realized that no operator likes to be seen doing nothing, even if the line is completely unbalanced. As long as the operator has inventory, he can start working on another piece."

"I get it, this is where it links to WIP inventory," said Phil, trying to keep up.

"That's right. Now Ohno imposed one-piece flow, where no inventories were allowed between operations. Because of the imbalances in the lines in the amount of work for each operator, some guys would be doing nothing while others were working to catch up. These guys would find themselves other jobs to fiddle with, until, as legend has it, Ohno ordered them to stand still with their arms up in the air if they did not have a piece to work on!"

"No kidding?" I muttered.

"Well, that's the story. In any case, that's supposedly when he realized that a tenth of an operator still requires the physical presence of one entire person. And that's why it doesn't make much sense when people talk about percentage productivity improvements across a complex sequence of operations. You're much better off talking about the number of people. So, what we now have to do is:

– take some measurements,
– identify causes of variation,
– break down jobs into elementary operations, and
– combine and balance operations according to takt time."

"That it?" countered Amy.

"You got it, but be careful with your communication!" admonished Dad, waving his brush in the air. "You've got to tell people what you're doing and why. In particular, you've got to be very clear about the fact that those who are pulled out of the process are not fired, but will start a second line!"

"Yeah," agreed Phil, rubbing his chin, "as well as work like crazy at getting rid of causes of variations, such as supplying the stations and so forth ..."

"Absolutely!"

"Still, following this logic," Phil continued, "I'm missing the link with keeping the inventory to a single piece in one-piece flow. Don't operators have an incentive to build up inventory no matter what?"

"Ah," said my father, putting down his brush, "there's a neat trick to that one. Turn common sense upside down. The idea is to move from push to pull."

"Push and pull. I've heard that before. I had a business professor who kept talking about it," said Amy. "But I never figured out what he meant."

"Well, it's because professors think like professors, not Japanese farmers," answered Dad, with a sarcastic nod in my direction. "In the early days, Toyota workers still had small lots of land they would tend after work. All these techniques were conceived by very practical people. We overcomplicate them in trying to understand them. It's actually very simple. Look," he said, sitting down next to me in the cockpit, and simulating an operation.

"I have a stockpile of materials, I build my product, and I *push* it on the next guy. It's a push system. As long as I've got my pile of material, I just keep doing my job, and moving the stuff along. Who cares what happens to it downstream?"

"From what you were saying the other night," I pointed out, "you don't even know whether you're doing the job right. You're just moving it along."

"Exactly. Pretty simple. I take the material, assemble my product, and push it through the door."

"But what about *pull* then?"

"Aha! That's the neat trick. Now, between each operator's stations I'll mark a special space with room for only one component. It can be a plastic tray, or a square chalked on the desk, it doesn't matter. All that counts is that there be room for only one finished product. From that point on, the operating rule is very simple:

– If the square is empty, I build a new product.

– If the square is full, I stop working."

"And as long as the square is full I do nothing?" asked Phil.

"That's it. Arms in the air!"

"But wouldn't you be wasting an operator's time?" I asked.

"Not really, think about it. If the operator starts a new product, he or she is just building up —"

"Inventory!" exclaimed Amy.

"Correct," said Dad. "That's how inventory piles up. Now in a normal production system you don't actually see that, because of all the variation which hides this type of inefficiency, but, in fact, in most production chains, about half as many people are working as are just moving around."

"Which is what you were looking for the first day we visited the plant. Who adds value, and who just moves around," I recalled. "I do pay attention!" I griped when Dad gave me a surprised look.

"Mike's right," he answered, amused. "We're pulling because the empty square is a pull system. We only build what the downstream link has just consumed, and that's the basis of the entire pull system."

"Just like that?" mused Phil. "That simple?"

"Well, the truth is that it's simple on a production cell, but generalizing it to the entire factory is somewhat trickier."

"But how does the whole plant know when to pull?" asked Amy, still working it out.

"Excellent question, although in your case it's rather simple. What's the takt time? 11.25 minutes. They have to pull every 11.25 minutes, yes? Okay, that's 40 parts a day, because customer demand is how we calculated the takt time in the first place."

"Now," continued Dad. "Remember those big racks on wheels you carry the mechanisms in?"

"Yeah. They hold 20 pieces each."

"Well, set up two of those after testing, and tell the operators they have to fill up these two racks by the end of the day. No more, no less."

"At a rhythm of a good mechanism every 11 minutes," Amy added. "I get it."

"But that creates an inventory pileup!" countered Phil.

"It does to start with, but if we can keep it down to 40 parts it's already better than the 100 or so you've got between testing and final assembly right now. Don't worry more about this for now; we'll get back to it. To start with, focus on a very simple pull system. The operators have two 20-piece racks to fill, one in the morning, one in the afternoon, and they can only work if the downstream square is empty and there is space on the rack. If not, they wait."

"Okay. I see it. What happens while they wait?"

"To them, nothing. They just wait. But let's hope management gets off their butts and figures out why they're waiting!"

"That means Gloria, right?" Phil asked.

"And Dave, and you. Remember, Gloria's already going to be busy dealing with all the rework."

"Ah! Rework!" cried Amy. "How is that possible if they can only work one piece at a time. Won't pulling rework out of the system completely throw off the flow?"

"Not quite," Dad growled in response. "I just don't want you guys to get mixed up. What you need to do is establish a separate place for rework, such as another bin. Now, when an operator comes across a part that needs rework, he or she puts it in the rework tray. Right?"

"And then stops working because there's no inventory upstream."

"Yes, and then stops working at first. The supervisor takes the part away and does the rework off line at a rework bench. Now, when the rework is done, chances are that the operator is working anew on another part," Dad explained.

Phil puzzled this over, then suggested, as if testing a theory, "If she then takes the reworked part back, according to your one-part-per-square rule, it will block the work upstream, because the upstream square will remain full if you introduce another part in the flow."

"Exactly, that's why the reworked piece must be placed back into the rework tray. It will stay there until the problem appears again."

"And then the operator can swap the new part which needs rework with the one which has been reworked," Amy concluded, "which should not disrupt the flow."

"That's it. Simple, but not always easy."

"You bet," agreed Phil, scratching his head and trying to write it all down.

"That's looking good," agreed Dad, looking over Phil's shoulder. "All right, boys and girls, the day is not getting younger and my boat is not getting painted. So that's all for today, folks. You figure it out and come back to me with questions. Now, get!"

"Mike?" said the voice on the phone a few days later. "It's Amy."

"Hi, what's up?"

"Listen, can we talk to you guys?"

She meant Dad.

"It's been a bad day, and we're a bit in a mess," she said, sounding weary over the line. "Phil's real unhappy, and I think it would really help if he could talk this over. Me too, I guess."

"I'll see what my father's up to. I'm working right now, but maybe you could come to my place. It would make it easier for me."

"Sure! Phil knows where it is?"

"He does." I smiled to myself, imagining how much he hated leaving his car in this neighborhood.

"We'll be over then. See ya!"

"I'll get my Dad to come over," I agreed, hanging up and wondering what the panic was all about.

"I didn't know you lived in a barrio," she said shortly afterward, as she followed Phil in. "I grew up in a place just like this."

"Do you miss it?"

"What? The catcalls and everything else? Not in a lifetime. I've spent my entire youth getting out."

"Ah, well, I quite like it. People are friendly, and it's close to the university, and, 'Hi, Phil, come in.'"

"I warned you Mike's taste in decoration was minimalist, to say the least," Phil kidded as Amy took in the bare room, and finally settled in the couch next to him.

"What this place needs is a feminine touch," groused Dad, coming out of the kitchen with a steaming mug of coffee and parking himself on the desk chair.

"What you see here is precisely the outcome of a feminine touch," I glowered back, surprised at the sudden anger in my voice. I moved a pile of books out of the way and sat down against a wall.

"Yeah, yeah," he answered dismissively. "So what's been happening?"

"It started this morning when a vendor made quite a fuss about being paid on the spot for a delivery," said Phil, looking profoundly discouraged.

"Which started a rumor that the place was folding — again," continued Amy.

"Then, at the management meeting, I told Gary about giving Josh the responsibility for stabilizing the design of the STR products."

"Without discussing it previously with his Human Resources manager," cut in Amy dryly.

"Yeah, so sue me!" answered Phil with uncharacteristic petulance. "Dammit, you want my job, you can have it!"

"Take it easy, son," Dad intervened quietly. "How did that go?"

"Oh, about as well as expected. Gary screamed bloody murder about not having been consulted, and decisions made behind his back, respecting the chain of command, and more of the same old stuff. Matt started agreeing with him and proposed to forget the whole thing, so I had to put my foot down!"

"Which he did," Amy added with a half-smile.

"God, do I hate all of that. And then Dave!"

"Hang on," said Dad. "What have you done about Joshua?"

"Oh, it'll happen. It will be messy, but the kid's all excited about it. I'm not sure he's understood the challenge yet, but I'll make sure he works with the operators. The trouble is that Dave screwed up."

"He went straight to Gloria," Amy explained, "with a new mechanism line arrangement combining the fitting and wiring jobs. Not surprisingly, she chewed his ass off saying it wasn't possible, not with the kind of production rates he was expecting, and then I had to come down to see what was happening and she gave me a piece of her mind about abusing her trust. A real mess."

"Was it your idea, Philip?" wondered Dad. "Did you tell Dave to redesign the line?"

"Of course not," Phil answered irritably. "I just explained to him what we had discussed, and he went out there and played the Lone Ranger! The thing is, I should have anticipated it. It's typical of Dave. He always wants to sort everything out by himself."

"So now the operators are dead set against everything, and I had to go assure them again that we weren't about to fire anybody, and that if we did, we'd have told them about it by now. But they weren't having any of it," reported Amy.

"Why do people have to be so, so ... change-resistant!" whined Phil.

"In what way?" asked Dad, testily.

"Well, no one seems to want to change anything, right? Hell, they don't even want to move their workstations 50 centimeters to the left!"

"Don't give me that!" Dad replied impatiently. "I've done more flow-and-layout redesign workshops than I can remember, and we moved everything around: robots, presses, you name it. The first time we worked with real masters in this field, they just walked into the plant for a visit. It was late at night. They start looking at what we've done, and then they ask if there's a night maintenance crew. Sure we say, we run three shifts. So call them in, they say. And they shoved machines around until 3 a.m., and were still there at five to explain to the operators how the new flow worked. Don't reason it, son. Just do it!"

Looking uncertain, Phil sat there shaking his head.

"You just don't get it, do you?" snapped Dad with a sudden flash of annoyance. "It's about the people! It's not about machines, or organization, or even money. It's about *people.* Don't you *get it*?"

They stared at him, and so did I. What was he saying?

"Ask Mike, he's the psychologist!"

"Ah, well," I fumbled, "of course it's all about people."

"People are not machines," ranted Dad. "They have thoughts and feelings, and they know their stuff. You have to work with people, not against them. The money is only the tallying sheet, a way to keep the score of how smart people can be if they work together! Jeez!"

He took a sip from his mug, shaking his head in frustration. We continued to stare at him, chastised. It was not the kind of talk I expected from the man, and I was truly curious.

"What do you mean, Dad? In specifics?"

"Think about it. It's not because an operator's working environment is limited to his or her workstation that their mind is. They're the experts, you see. The experts in their narrow, specialized universe, but the experts all the same. The fitting guy is an expert at fitting. So when you come along and tell him he's going to have to do it differently, of course he thinks you're full of crap. He thinks he knows better, and he's right. That's what he does eight hours per day, fitting. He knows more about fitting than we ever will."

"He can still get it wrong, though?" asked Phil.

"Of course he can. He has to work within a set system. And he may not understand the whole process or the whole design. For instance, he may know how to set your capsules exactly in the right way for the circuit breaker to work, but he may not know why. You will, because you've designed the capsule. So you guys are going to have to talk!"

"You're right, Mr. Woods," agreed Amy, biting her lower lip as she does when she's working something out. "Communication 101."

"Forget communication!" Dad answered with his usual disregard for what others are saying. "Leadership. It's all a leadership problem. You can't just tell people how to work; they're not robots. You can't communicate either because half the time, management is not credible, no offense, Ms. Cruz, but most management talk is full of bull, especially coming from HR. Have them work the problem out by themselves! Look, I hate to say I told you so, but if you had let me handle this my way from the start, things would have been rather easier."

Phil sighed loudly, took off his glasses, and rubbed his eyes. "Right, so what do we do now? Is there a way to salvage this?"

"We start right from the start, the way we should have," answered Dad after thinking about it.

"Amy?" he asked. "You've run group sessions when you were in the fast-food business?"

"All the time."

"All right, the important thing here is that operators, and especially Gloria, discover for themselves the impact that variation has on their performance. Everyone wants to produce good parts and achieve daily objectives. What we have to show them is how the system stops them from succeeding."

"I see what you mean," Amy said. "I have to set up a small group with Gloria and a couple of experienced guys and have them time their working cycles themselves."

"Yes. And you have to insist on the 10 measures, so that they agree that the minimal working cycle is real, not some management device to increase productivity. They'll say, 'Okay, sometimes it takes us half an hour to do this because we've encountered a difficulty, but mostly, we can do it in seven minutes.' They'll trust their own measurements.

"Then we have to explain to them how we're going to take away all the causes of variation from work," she continued.

"Which means we have to solve their problems as well," Phil cut in, "like who supplies the material and so on."

"And they'll come to realize some jobs can be combined," said Amy.

"And we'll tell them about the one-piece flow system," Phil added. "Okay."

"Never lose track of the fact that fundamentally we're trading higher expectations for more responsibility," added my father. "So you have to work with them to implement this system, not just throw it in their faces!"

"But what about the line redesign itself? Do we let the operators decide on their own?" Phil looked a bit dubious about this.

"Yeah, what about these U-shaped cells the consultants used to rave about?"

"You mean a perfect U-form with precisely four feet across the U?" asked Dad with an amused grin.

"Yeah, that one. They couldn't implement them or explain to us how we could, but they said that's how it should be!"

"They couldn't implement them because they could not control the WIP inventory in the process, and so people always need more room," Dad explained. "As to the U-shape, that's a design commonly associated with Toyota, and which doesn't really apply to your case."

"Why?" asked Amy, ever curious.

"In your case, you've got both straight manual assembly, without any fancy machines or equipment, and rather large working content, so you might as well keep operators in the same side-by-side, one-per-station configuration.

"But suppose you've got a much lower working content total, say a few minutes, and that you have to use heavy equipment like robots or welders. Then the parts will move through the process, but so will the people. What you then want is a layout that minimizes the walking they do. For instance, if one operator does it all, the most effective design would be the U-cell. She can then do a full circuit for each product. Now, if the takt time decreases, you need to staff two operators on the same cell.

"The idea is that each operator does a short circuit within the cell. For instance, they can do the start and the finish of the product, and then steps in the middle. Remember, we've done away with the notion of 'job,' so especially in operations, which, unlike yours demand no special skills, you can cut it any way you want. The four feet is just the right distance so that they can turn around and work on both sides of the cell without taking more than one step. That's all."

"We're back to this idea of breaking up the notion of doing a 'job' on a product, and seeing it as a sequence of elementary operations," said Phil, mulling it over.

"Yep. In some cases, with machines to load and unload, for instance, I'll have operators cycling the opposite way to the product."

"How's that?"

"Well, if you follow the product around, and you have to load it and unload it from a machine, what do you do in the meantime while the machine is performing its task?"

"I get your point. You wait."

"Exactly. Wait. Now, suppose you have one more product in WIP just before every step in the process. If you cycle opposite to the product, what you do is start by unloading the machine, position the part in the next machine, then start the machining cycle. Right?" Dad looked around to make sure everyone was following along.

"Then, you move one station upstream, pick up the product which has been unloaded by the next machine upstream, and load it in the one you just emptied. In effect, machines are mostly faster than people so it isn't much of a problem. This is why Toyota insists so much on self-unloading machines. Do you see it? As the products progress in added-value, let's say clockwise, your operator will move counter-clockwise, unload machine three and load machine three, then walk back to two, unload the product from two and load it into three and start three, and then move back to one, unload one, load two, start two, and finally unload four into the finished parts bin and start the cell again."

"I see what you're saying," said Phil. "Doesn't it apply to us then?"

"Not at this stage. Continuous side-by-side operations would be fine. As long as the two operators are on the same side so they can be supplied from the front. Just remember, the important part is to have just one square between stations and only one piece allowed. If there's a jam, the operators wait. You can see the imbalance!"

"Bob?" asked Amy. "Could we backtrack a bit? There's something I missed. You mentioned that in the U-cell, if the takt time diminishes, we want to move from one operator to two. How does that work?"

My Dad sighed heavily. "Are you sure you want to get into that right now? It might confuse you more than help ..."

She was sure.

"That's a totally different concept. Let's adjust your assumption that the total working content on your product is, what?"

"Forty-two minutes."

"Right. Your customer demand is 40 per day, so we're dividing 40 into the 450 available minutes for a takt time of 11.25 minutes. Now, suppose the customer demand climbs to 60. The takt time will be faster, like 7.5 minutes. Total working content hasn't changed but —"

"Ah, yes, the required number of operators on the line will. 42 divided by 7.5 is ... 5.6 operators, that is six operators with one with a lighter load, right?"

"Correct. So if demand varies from 40 parts a day to 60 parts a day, you should be able to change your line organization from four operators on that cell to six. Lean cells are organized to be able to do that. The trick is to create standardized work so you have specific working standards for each level of takt time. Obviously, the amount of work per operator changes with the takt."

"But then, why do you think we should start a second shift with the extra operators, instead of simply increasing production on the existing line?" asked Phil puzzled.

"You're the one who was all gung-ho for a second shift, son. Actually I'd much prefer increasing production on this line. If your guys would be happy to do so, go for it. But we're talking about people, not robots, darn it. Remember the 'Oh No!' method. If Amy here gets it right with the operators, she'll manage to convince them to try to do the same work with four people instead of six. Will they be able to?"

"At first, no!" Amy answered with a twinkle in her dark eyes. "They tried to do that to us at the fast-food joint, but no one removed the waste and variation from the process so the gold could flow."

"Exactly. So?"

"So my job will be to put pressure on everyone in this plant to resolve the operators' problems. Great. Think about it for a second. Can you see me going to talk to the quality guys and tell them to get cracking?" said Amy.

Phil made a wry face.

"The point is that if you simply try to increase production on that line with your current setup, it's going to blow up on you. There's no people logic to it. So, to start with, the easiest bet to increase productivity is to maintain the same level of production and try to pull people out, which forces everybody to resolve the problems and get the parts flowing through the line."

"But what about the flexibility we were talking about?" Phil asked.

"That kind of flexibility is for later. In order to be able to work with shifts of four or five or six operators, you need to have resolved all their problems first. And you need to have standard work for all levels of production. You'll get there someday, but first learn to stand, and then learn to fly, son. Nature's rule, not mine."

"I take your point, but that's a brilliant concept!"

"It is. One person for 10 parts, 10 people for 100. Spectacular when you see it working. But you're a far cry from this right now."

"Fine, I've got my workshop more or less clear in my mind," said Amy, biting her lip. "What should I pay particular attention to?"

Dad thought that over before answering.

"First, avoid management interference. Make sure that Dave and Phil are not hanging around when you work with the operators, but, second, and this is really important, have Dave and Phil back when you present the new layout, and make them commit immediately and publicly to the changes."

"I can take care of that," agreed Phil with a decisive nod.

"Second, make sure they understand the deal. Delivery comes first, so, no matter what, they're going to fill a rack of 20 mechanisms every four hours, and try to do so as smoothly as possible. In exchange, you'll get the entire company working for the operators to solve their problems so that they can achieve this. You've got to lay it on thick about this deal because they're so used to coping with all the usual crap they won't believe you. Now, Philip," he said pointing at Phil with his mug. "This is your make-or-break chance. Management is committing to free operators to do their job. Which means freeing them from anything other than adding direct value. In turn, it means putting the whole shop at their service, as opposed to the other way round, as per usual. They're going to test you on this, so you'd better deliver. Can you do it?"

"We'll see," said Phil thoughtfully. "Anyhow, I'll give it my best."

"Beware: that will mean putting a heck of a lot of pressure on people who are used to lording it over production, such as purchasing, quality, and engineering. You get the picture?"

"I do," he said, sounding cautiously confident.

"Third, you have to make sure their material supply is designed properly."

"You mean how they store their components?" asked Phil.

"Yeah, and how they get supplied."

"If we follow the logic through, everything should be delivered to their workstations so the operators never need to search for parts."

"Absolutely. In industries with much lower work content and lower takt times, racks with rollers are installed in arm's reach of the operators to hold parts in small containers. On the lower rack sits the box the operator takes the components from. On the upper rack, the empty box is placed, to be picked up by the logistics operator.

"But in your case, the easiest thing to start with is shelves on the workstation with a double bin system. Place one bin in front from which they pull components. Behind it is a second at the back, which is full. When an operator empties the first bin, he places the empty one for refilling on the top of the shelves, and pulls the second one in place. The guy who does the replenishing, and it must be somebody with clear responsibility for this job, even the supervisor, will then come back and place the full bin behind the one they are using. Right?"

"Yes, one in use, one full, and someone assigned to do the replenishment. Okay!"

"But will all these containers fit at the station?" asked Amy, which unexpectedly made my father laugh, and she bristled immediately.

"No, no, I'm not laughing at you. It's a very good question. It's just that it took me a very long time to get that very same point. You have no idea how hard it was for us veterans of mass production to understand all this just-in-time garbage. I really do feel for Dave; I've been through it.

"So there we were, part of the Toyota supplier program, and they keep telling us to cut back on inventory, reduce inventory, less WIP inventory, and no matter what they do, they always want further inventory reduction. Then one day, I let it rip. 'What is it with you people and inventory?' I asked the Toyota consultant. 'I know it's costly and it eats cash and so on, but not that much!' 'Inventory is more trouble than you think,' he says.

"'Great, how?' I wonder. And then he tells me. 'See, it's like this. We want an operator to be able to build several different models at the same workstation for flexibility, okay?' Okay. 'We want the operator to have all the components he needs so that there is less unnecessary motion, okay?' Okay. 'Well, since we also want a small workstation to limit unnecessary movement, that means really small boxes to fit it all, so — reduce inventories!'"

He laughed some more, remembering. "That's when I realized I was still thinking like a run-it-by-the-numbers manager, whereas they were reasoning like Japanese peasants. You know, everything visual, practical. Everything in its place. It was a real 'aha!' moment. So there's your answer. Yes, it means a lot of containers, so you'll just have to get some smaller boxes!"

"But that'll play hell with logistics!" protested Phil. "The smaller the box, the more often it has to be refilled. The store guys are not going to like it either."

"Remember what I first said. Customer satisfaction always comes first, so you start by worrying about delivery, then you worry about reducing inventory, and only then will we rationalize costs. Yes, the just-in-time system involves moving parts around in small boxes all the time. Which does not mean more people to do it, but better organization. Just accept it for the moment. The truth of the matter is that you have plenty of resource wasting away on your hands all over the plant, but you don't see it yet. Don't worry, in the end we'll do more with less. For the moment, concentrate on smaller boxes."

"Dave's going to blow a fuse!" Phil said, shaking his head in dismay.

"Well, isn't that precisely what you manufacture? Fuses?" shot back my father, laughing loudly at his own feeble joke.

Chapter Four

STANDARDIZE WORK

We'd agreed to get together on Friday evening at the Yacht Club and see how the week had gone. I got a phone call from Amy saying they were getting away early, and it was still bright and hot when we got to the bay. As we arrived on the pier we found my Dad rummaging in the bottom of his boat. He'd opened the aft coffers of the *Felicity*, and had spread his junk all over the deck, making the dock look like a garbage dump in a four-yard radius around his boat. As we wondered what to do, he threw an empty paint can on a pile of junk in the middle of the mess. In the end, I recognized the huge blue plastic bag of the dinghy, and sat on that. Amy joined me, surprisingly cool and fresh in the afternoon heat, while Phil sat awkwardly on the ground. My Dad scrambled up from the boat and sat on an upturned metal bucket.

"I've got to put a coat of paint in the hold," he muttered, "which I hate. So it's the right opportunity for a spring cleaning. Don't mind the mess. How did it go?"

"Real good," she said, looking pleased. "They were surprisingly interested in the experiment, and they actually timed each other!"

I already knew things had gone well because I'd had Phil on the phone telling me that the financial crisis was improving slightly as one of their backers had agreed to extend his credit for a bit longer. But they needed to show some improvement fast, he'd said.

"Did you pull people out?"

"We did. We got the idea of the two shifts across and it turns out that some time ago the entire plant worked two shifts. Some of the veterans took to the idea, saying they liked the early shift because it leaves them with some time to do odd jobs at home. You never can tell. Anyhow, they'll ask around to see how to organize things. It seems that moving the starting time to 6 a.m. is less of a problem than I'd thought, for the operators at any rate. Thank God the engineers are not immediately concerned!"

"Who did you pull out?"

"Two of the old-timers. Amy suggested in the meantime they could help us with stabilizing the process and getting the other lines to do the same."

"Good call," said Dad, looking impressed. "People tend to take away the worst performers, which is stupid, because if you do, they'll never learn. Pulling out the veterans to use as a core team for the new shift is smart."

"See, told you so," she smirked at Phil.

"Yeah, okay. The other interesting development is that Josh has been getting on the rework case. He's done an analysis of our rework problems and found that our motor supplier has made a small change to his design, which we weren't aware of. A third of the rework is due to settings issues with the new design. It also turned out that the motor fitter had noticed, tried to tell us about it, but no one had listened."

"Not surprising!"

"Sad, but true. In any case, Josh is talking to the supplier, to either get the old design back, or, alternatively, he'll look at modifying our mechanism. He's been brimming with ideas about how to simplify the mechanism from the assembly point of view."

"That's good, but you'd better make sure that doesn't harm the performance of your gizmo at the customer."

"I know, I'm doing all the checking since I had to pull Josh completely from Pellman's authority, which is another crisis in the making, but we'll cross that bridge when we get there."

"So, what results have you got?"

Amy pulled her pad. "At the end of today we did 32 mechanisms with four operators. We had six WIP and six rework."

	Before	Now
Parts per day	About 40	32
Inventory	35	6
People	6	4
Quality	?	6 rework

"No increase of problems at the testing stage?" asked Dad.

"No, everything seems fine."

"You'd better check," Dad said firmly. "Every time you touch the process you've got to double check on quality."

"Okay, I'll look into that," said Phil. "But with 32 mechanisms produced today, we're going backwards from our goal of 80!"

"Hey, with only four operators!" snapped back Amy. "It's still a productivity improvement. And it's a miracle that we managed to get the line started," she grumbled. "But if we stabilize, we'll get there. The flow is much better, and we can see how many problems they encounter, because at some times, they're all working in unison, and at others, one's working but everybody else is stuck. The interesting side effect is that when they get stuck, they're all curious about what happens downstream. In one case, we found that the guy who does the motor wiring was creating difficulties every second part for the capsule assembler from the way he placed the wires, but they'd never talked about it."

"Hmm, that's encouraging."

"Yes, patience, son, patience," patronized Dad. "Go on, Amy."

"One thing I wanted to talk to you about, sir. When we took the times — and we did do 10 measures for each station — Gloria was not far off the minimum total working content, which is 39 minutes."

"So you should be fine with four operators," I pointed out.

"In theory yes, but there are still massive variations in the working cycles. Anyhow, when we did the measures, we ran into trouble because you said to split each job into elementary operations."

"And?"

"They don't always assemble the mechanism in the same way, so it's difficult to measure."

"Ha! Spot on, well done, Amy, well done," interrupted Dad with a guffaw.

"Well done what?" she asked perplexed.

"You've hit the nail right on the head, so to speak. You're right on the stabilization issue, and it's all about people again."

"All right," said Dad, warming to this topic. "Now, what's a good operator?"

"A guy who works well?"

"Yes, yes, but what does that mean in practice?"

We looked at him, confused.

"Someone who gives us no trouble, who doesn't create any defects?" said Phil uncertainly.

"Here," said Dad. "Watch."

He bent over and picked up miscellaneous objects from the mess at his feet: a screwdriver, a small pot of glue, a file, and a plastic object of unidentified purpose. He arranged them in a circle at his feet and then started turning them one after the other, in random order.

"Every task can be broken down into elementary subtasks. To cook some pasta, I need to boil some water, add some salt, add some oil, boil the pasta, stir it so it doesn't get stuck together, drain the pasta in the colander, and then serve." He punctuated each action with twisting one of the objects in front of him.

"Now what is quality work?"

"Work that you do well."

"No. Not if you've forgotten anything!" Amy said suddenly. "Doing it well means doing each of the subtasks without forgetting one. Each subtask can itself be broken down into elementary tasks and so on."

"You got it!" said Dad, pleased with his star student. "A worker who works well is one who does not forget any of the subtasks on the way. The problem is that we all have limited shelf space in our heads, and if the list is long, it's easy to forget one. Particularly in a mess or a panic. Next, what is an efficient operator?"

That drew another blank. Dad continued to twist each object, now in the same sequence.

"One who always does the tasks in the same order!" I exclaimed.

"Correct. If I do each task always in the same order, I'll be a lot quicker. And there is less risk that I'll forget a task. So if one of the objects is missing as I come to work," he said, taking the screwdriver away, "it's easy to forget turning the screwdriver since it isn't there. Bingo, I create a defect. Now, if I'm always working in the same sequence, I'll notice the screwdriver is missing, and deal with it. What else?"

"You're right," I said. "You know how distracted I can be." He raised his eyes theatrically. "Well, before leaving the house, I run a sequenced check to make sure I've turned off the stove, the electricity, brought my wallet and key, and so on, the kind of thing I tend to forget. It works."

"The order you were using doesn't make much sense," suggested Philip, pointing at the tools spread at our feet. "You could work your task in a circle, which would be a more logical sequence."

"Indeed, if I work always in the same order, I can realize that my sequence could be optimized. It's like getting up in the morning, washing hands and face, going to the toilet, and then realizing you've got to wash your hands all over again. By attempting to work in a sequence, you can improve your effectiveness."

"You can also add steps to the sequence," I thought aloud. "I agree that we have limited shelf space in our heads. What tends to happen when you teach people is that each new volume you add to the shelf pushes an old one off the edge, so we gain knowledge, but we also lose some. Now, knowledge stored as a sequence rather than independent steps will be memorized as a single volume. So you can add more knowledge to the shelf."

My father looked at me quizzically. "I hadn't thought of that, but you're right. The sequence is not just the key to single-piece flow, it is also the basis of multicompetence. It figures. You're right, Mike, that does make sense."

I'm right? No way!

"You're saying that in order to stabilize the process we have to talk the operators into always working in the same order?" asked Phil.

"Yes, and that's precisely the supervisor's job," replied Dad. "And I'm not just talking about operators, it applies to any repetitive work in your company short of artistic creation."

"And even there," I pointed out, "the artist's own technique comes from doing things repetitively a great number of times, when knowing to apply what coat of paint next makes a difference!"

"Stay with the logic," said my father. "Point one," counting on his fingers, "productivity comes from ..."

"Reducing the variations in the operators' cycles," answered Phil dutifully.

"So, point two, in order to do that we have to ..."

"Take away all the tasks which don't add direct value and disturb the operators' cycles," chipped in Amy.

"Yes, and three?" he asked, holding a third finger out. "Three?"

"Ah! Getting the operators to always work in the same sequence!" she exclaimed brightly.

"Absolutely. The secret to single-piece flow is reducing the variation in the working cycle. I told you that the secret to reducing the variation in the working cycle is standardized work. Always perform the same operations in the same sequence. Based on a uniform takt time and a standard inventory, of course, but we'll get to that."

"But you said yourself people are not machines. How do you expect them to always follow the same sequence?" I asked.

"That's the challenge. That's precisely why it's a people issue, we're going to have to convince them that this is the right way to work."

"Sounds like the navy!"

"Sounds like any front-line operation," pointed Phil. "Follow procedure, right?"

"Correct. But you're not in the navy, or the army. You're in a factory, and you're going to have to make your people understand about standardized work."

"And I can tell whose job that's going to be," said Amy, suddenly deflated.

"Good guess. Now, standardized work is the key to keep waste from creeping back into the process, and it's such a fundamental notion that we're going to have to involve people deeply in it.

"So, standardized work involves a takt time, a sequence of operations, and ..."

"Inventory?" suggested Phil.

"Yes, required inventory, what else?"

"How about," I thought with sudden insight, "the key points you've got to be especially careful of? You know, what you called defect opportunities."

"Correct. Good thinking. Now pay attention," Dad said. "We also have to highlight every point in the process where we find safety issues for the operators. Engineers tend to dismiss such concerns too easily. Safety issues are part of standardized work."

"No joke!" exclaimed Amy. "That's incredibly precise! Who has that kind of rigor?"

"In the Toyota system," explained my father, "establishing and implementing standardized work is a large part of the supervisor's job. That's in addition to training new operators to the standard sequence, and anticipating potential problems which could throw a wrench in the works."

"And we're supposed to implement that back at the plant? No way," Phil said.

"Not right away, don't worry," Dad reassured Phil. "Standardized work is not a paper rule you force people to comply with. It's a way of working. It's like on this ship. There are no three ways to make certain basic operations, like a cleat knot. One knot, one way to do it, and that's that. If only for safety reasons. In this way, I can see at a glance if all the knots are done correctly and that's one less worry.

"You can't impose standardized work on someone. They'll only resent you and ignore the standard the moment your back is turned. You've got to involve them into understanding this is the proper way to work. It is about people, do you follow?"

"Okay," Phil seemed to agree. "So how do I do that?"

"I seem to remember," said Dad quietly, "seeing large 5S posters in your plant when we visited. Have you been conducting 5S initiatives?"

"Not us," answered Phil. "The previous lot. In fact, they had a huge 5S drive before they sold the place, to make it look more attractive. It continued for a while, but we found it very difficult to keep alive. It must have died a natural death by now."

"5S?" asked Amy.

"Some other Japanese gimmick. Let me see, 'sort and eliminate,'" said Phil.

"*Seiri*," confirmed Dad.

"Order."

"*Seiton.*"

"Clean."

"*Seiso.*"

"Maintain."

"*Seiketsu.*"

"And discipline."

"*Shitsuke.*"

"That's right: seiri, seiton, seiso, seiketsu, and shitsuke. I understand the first three, eliminate, order, and clean, but every one seems rather vague about 'maintain' and 'discipline.'"

"That's not very surprising," agreed my father. "To most people, 5S means 'clean your room.'"

"That's how I've always understood it," agreed Phil.

"The first S, seiri, is fairly obvious," Dad continued. "It's what I'm doing now," he said, waving his hand at the mess. "Every working environment naturally accumulates junk. And that also goes for desks and computer systems," he added pointedly to Amy, who nodded thoughtfully. "Every now and then, one has to go through the pile and sort it, eliminating everything useless along the way, like I am doing now with all this mess. It's not easy, we have to fight the pack rat in all of us."

"Mom thinks you could start with the garage," I quipped. Dad just glared, and continued. "Most people bitch about throwing things away, but, by and large, they agree that it's a good thing. In a way, seiri can also be done at the highest level, as with unsuccessful product lines or activities."

"DG circuit breakers," grimaced Phil.

"Or people, yes. But on the shop floor, managers often miss the most important point of seiri. It's not just about throwing out junk. It's about decision making."

"I don't follow," muttered Phil.

"Well, it sounds silly, but asking an operator whether she really needs this old bit of iron pipe is about more than just clearing out junk. Maybe she does, and she uses it for something, which we'd better worry about because we've missed a problem in the process. I remember finding old potatoes on a line once. It turned out they were using a special sort of glue, which only adhered properly if applied with a cut potato. All the 'official' methods were too cumbersome to use effectively, so the operators had found their own 'unofficial' fix. Secondly, maybe she doesn't need the tube, and throwing it away is actually making a choice, taking responsibility for her working environment."

"You're making this sound as if it's a big management thing," said Amy. "It's no more than basic housekeeping."

"Yes. But the fundamental point is that the operators start taking responsibility for the housekeeping of their work universe: their workstations. The simple act of throwing old junk away is already both a choice and a commitment."

"I need to think about this," said Phil, frowning.

"The second stage is seiton, order," continued my father. "Once I've sorted all this junk out, I need to find a place for each thing, which, shipside is both a headache and a vital necessity. Because you always need the pliers in an emergency, you can't afford to look for them in a panic. So you'd better know exactly where they are! The first thing I notice in a skipper is whether he keeps his boat in order or whether it's all in a mess."

"As with a kitchen," agreed Phil, who occasionally cooked as a hobby.

"Exactly. Now seiton is very important for the operator, because you'll discover that nothing has been set up to help him or her keep the station in order: no racks, no shelves, nothing. Well, seiton needs management intervention. We're talking really small things like shelves, but in the operator's universe."

"You're so right!" exclaimed Amy. "During the workshop, they kept complaining about stuff like that."

"Of course they do. Operators spend all their working lives at their workstations. And it's also a good test of management commitment. They're used to seeing management be all talk and no walk, so when you work on seiton with them, they'll expect to see some changes soon. If not you lose all credibility."

"In a sense, you keep drawing them in, right?" I supposed. "First you get them involved with making choices about what to keep and what to throw, and then you establish a working agreement by coming up with some goodies that they've asked for? Smart."

"At the end of the day," Dad nodded, "we have to help them help us with our products, so it's a good deal for all. The aim of seiton is to organize tools and parts for the greatest ease of use. It shouldn't cost much anyhow. So start with a small budget, and see where you go. Remember that small things count in the operator's universe."

"I had never looked at it that way," confessed Phil. "What about 'clean' then?"

"Seiso is where most confusion starts. Seiso is not fundamentally about cleaning your room, or having a neat and tidy factory. It's mostly about maintenance."

"How so?" Phil was curiously rapt.

"Well, why do you think the navy is so hot about spit and polish? In the old days they used to scrub, wash, and sand decks every day. Why?"

"Obsessive, compulsive, anal-retentive behavior of military types," I suggested with a grin.

"Save it, Junior. Cleaning parts is in fact the best way to look for cracks and anticipate future failures. Remember, my main concern when I'm out there at sea is which part is going to break first. Usually, breakage happens in the worst conditions, when everything is under the strain of heavy seas and weather. If something breaks, then I could be in serious trouble. So in quiet times, I clean and polish, and replace all stressed parts. Cleaning is essentially about checking and maintenance."

"Which also works with people!" Amy said with another of her intuitive leaps. We looked at her.

"She's darn right," said Dad. "Think about it. After worrying about equipment, I worry about people: which human part will fail first. People are notoriously bad at the discipline of maintenance, so by asking to keep the equipment in order, you can also see who gets to it cheerfully, and who drags their feet and does it sullenly.

"A disaffected crew is an accident waiting to happen. The point is that ongoing maintenance is about more than keeping your room tidy. It's a management tool. The same goes for the argument that some people are naturally neater than others. The issue here is professional behavior at the workplace."

"I can see now why I never really understood the value of 5S," said

Phil. "I really thought it was a matter of tidiness, no more. This is why I never could get the hang of the last two Ss, I guess."

"Probably. Seiketsu, 'maintain,' is about regularly conducting the three preceding Ss. For instance, after a cruise, the ship must be cleaned from end to end. After cooking a meal, the kitchen must be put back in order."

"Not fun," acknowledged Phil.

"Not fun for the amateur, but essential for the professional, if you think of a grand chef. How do you think she would want her kitchen? Seiketsu is about setting up routines and precise times for order and maintenance. Once at the end of every shift? Before taking a break? Whatever. The important thing is to work on a number of set clean-up tasks so they become automatic."

"Always in the same sequence?" I suggested.

"Of course. This is actually how we're going to introduce the notion to the operators. Building the 5S discipline is a practical way of introducing standardized work, because we can quite easily suggest standardized cleanup sheets, which is something people will be familiar with."

"And you also lock them into their commitment to take responsibility for their workstation!"

"That's right. Responsibility is not a command, it's a feeling. You can't order anyone to take responsibility; you must talk them into accepting ownership of responsibility. It's quite tricky, because at the same time, you don't want to create mini-fiefdoms, you want to retain overall control, which is why 5S is such a powerful tool."

"Still," commented Amy, "you need someone to supervise the whole thing. If not, we're back to being dependent on 'tidy' people."

"Which is what the fifth S, shitsuke, is about: discipline," Dad went on. "Making sure the daily 5S discipline is kept up is purely a management problem. In my plants, it used to be part of the responsibility of the team leader, but it also includes any auditing system you can devise. Whatever the mechanism, the point is to make sure 5S is maintained day in, day out, rain or shine."

"I'll confess I had never conceived of 5S as a key management job," admitted Phil, pushing back his glasses several times.

"It's at the heart of the matter. In the glory days of learning about lean production back in the 1980s, we worked with a Japanese consultancy that made us do two years of 5S before even touching any other subject. Of course, we groaned and moaned, but we did it. You're lucky I'm not insisting on the same experience for you! They took us all the way through to standardized work sheets as part of 5S, and when they popped the layout transformation and single-piece flow, it all happened as if it was perfectly natural. Later we tried to short-cut the 5S step in other plants, having only understood the significance of the first three Ss. Of course we fell flat on our face. It took me years to grasp the significance of 5S."

"Standardized work!" exclaimed Phil.

"Not just that."

"Employee involvement!" said Amy. "It gets the operators on board with the changes from the start!"

"That's right. This was one of the hardest lessons to learn. We came from the old, die-hard, Taylorist school of designing the work for the operator, and then making sure they did it the way it had been planned by the experts. Sort of the way Dave went about it with the line redesign."

Dad stretched his legs, completely at home on his overturned bucket. White stubble on his chin, his thin hair stirring in the breeze, wearing his grease-stained work clothes, he looked like a subject from a Dorothea Lange Depression-era photo who had somehow wandered into a Winslow Homer painting. He looked around the bay for a moment and continued.

"Of course we knew all about human-relations stuff, and theory X and Y, and being nice to each other and all that crap, but as far as we could see, the Japanese guys we were trying to copy weren't into any of this touchy-feely stuff. They had engineers telling operators what to do just like us. It took us years to realize the engineers could actually talk to the operators, because the operators felt involved and had many valuable contributions to make. In essence, the operators understood what the engineers tried to do with the process and helped them rather than hindered them, because they realized it meant an improvement in working conditions."

"What this comes down to," said Amy with a petulant look, "is that I am going to have to do this 5S with them until we reach the production target, right?"

"And produce standardized work sheets," agreed my father.

"But shouldn't that be Gloria's job, from what you said, the supervisor?"

"Ultimately, yes, but we've got to start somewhere quick."

"Amen to that," said Phil.

"And that's not the half of it," sighed Dad. "But I'd better get this mess cleared out before it gets dark," he grunted, getting up from his old bucket. "What I suggest is that you come back tomorrow in the morning, and we can continue this discussion. Tomorrow, we talk about kaizen!"

"Won't Charlene mind if you start spending your weekends on work?" I probed Phil as we walked back to the cars.

"She's used to it by now," was the terse reply, and I could draw nothing more out of him.

Chapter Five

IT'S ALL ABOUT THE PEOPLE

When I arrived at the Yacht Club the next morning, the parking lot was almost full. I found a spot at the end of the gravel, almost on the grass, and walked right into Amy, who was standing next to her car, looking over at the bay thoughtfully.

"Hi there," I said. "Bit of blues?"

She turned toward me, startled, and bestowed upon me one of her glorious smiles. She'd been so deep in thought she hadn't heard me coming. The harbor was buzzing with activity with long graceful sailboats being ferried all over the place. "Regatta day tomorrow," I ventured.

"What? Oh, the sailboats. Yeah."

"So, what are you thinking so hard about? No more lessons?"

"Quite the contrary, actually," she said with a frown. "I'm still digesting that workshop with the operators. It was like opening Pandora's box. You have no idea what they have to say about management. It was good, in a way, that they should speak freely, but, boy, do we look like idiots!"

"Isn't that what HR is supposed to do? Talk to people?"

"Or look like idiots? Sure," she answered in a dismissive tone. "But we also do the hiring and firing. In general, the word out there is whatever you do, don't talk to HR. Can't blame them. I wouldn't talk to HR myself," she added with her mischievous smile.

"So, it's good that they're talking to you."

"Yes, no question about it. But also hard to figure. See, your dad hardly seems to be of the 'communicate' school."

"You think?" I noted with mock surprise.

"In business classes, we were taught to distinguish between the Taylorist approach: one best way, operators work for their paycheck, the organization is like a machine, and so on."

"Sounds like what my Dad is saying, all right."

"Ah, but see, the other approach is the Human Relations movement, the company as a social environment, theory Y versus theory X. If we see the operators as self-motivated and responsible, they'll behave as such, but if we manage them by fear they'll do the least possible."

"I see your point. Dad is also saying, in his own way, that the operator's workstation is their universe and management must build responsibility and trust in that domain."

"Yes, his whole point about 5S being an involvement tool. I can see the merit of it. I just find it puzzling the way his outlook cuts across the established perspectives."

"You shouldn't take any of these theories too seriously. Doctor's orders," I chided her. "The one thing you learn as a psychologist is that what works works, and leave it at that."

"You might have a point there," she said, rewarding me with another of her smiles. "Let's go and find out what else your dad intends to add to my 'To Do' list!"

We found my father already in earnest conversation with Phil in a corner of the bar. The Yacht Club had turned into a hive of young, healthy, tanned people in the bright synthetic colors of sailing gear. Some just swapped loud stories around hefty breakfasts, others were milling around purposefully with sail bags and various other mysterious implements. The place had lost any trace of its quaint look as a watering hole for ancient mariners, and had transmogrified into an MTV clip.

"You're late," commented Dad in lieu of welcome. Amy and I

exchanged a glance. "Follow me, I want to show you something."

We made our way through the sailing crowd into the building and down the stairs. I'd never been to the first floor of the Yacht Club, which opened onto the water. We crossed a large, empty meeting room, with many incomprehensible charts pegged onto whiteboards; even the walls themselves were covered with chalk drawings. My father led us to a smaller side room. Holding a finger to his lips, he opened the door, waved to someone inside, and motioned us to stand by the door quietly. Inside, five or six young crew members were sprawled on plastic chairs around a video screen where an older fellow, deeply tanned and with the leathery skin of one who spends most of his time in the ocean's glare, was commenting on operations. I realized we were watching a video shot on board a racing sailboat, during maneuvers.

"Jack, what happens to you there?" asked the older man.

"Yeah, I messed up, dude."

"Watch the time!" The timer was running on the side of the image where, presumably, Jack was taped from the back, obviously struggling to unclasp a line from somewhere.

"These clips!" muttered Jack, "they're too tight. It's just a pain to get them on or off the cable."

"Fine. We'll change them. Next, Christie, watch the way you pass the bag forward. If you do it that way, Dev has to slide back at least five feet to have a secure hold on it."

Dad motioned us to leave, and we closed the door quietly. We returned upstairs and settled at a table on the porch, which was just liberated by one of the crews. A fresh breeze was blowing, and it felt nice and lazy to be sitting on the veranda watching all the unusual activity down there.

"Big J class regatta tomorrow. Those white boats over there," he pointed for Amy. "All the crews race the same type of boat, so it makes it more interesting."

"Is that a kaizen workshop we just saw?" asked Amy, once more a step ahead intuiting the heart of the matter.

"Well, you're keeping your eye on the ball, miss! Yes, you could say it was."

"They were debriefing training maneuvers, right?" asked Phil.

"Yes, but what were they specifically looking for?"

"Hitches, problems, things that went wrong," I suggested.

"Standardized work!" muttered Phil, eyes widening.

"Beyond that," corrected Dad. "Continuous improvement. Obviously, in racing conditions, a maneuver not only has to be standard, but also as fast as possible. So they were looking for all causes of variability, like those clamps, in order to improve their timing."

"But not just that," mused Amy, still thinking on her HR track. "The older guy was also using the session to get them to work and think as a team."

"Very good. You noticed that he made them focus on how they interacted, and the precise coordination between tasks. This guy is the skipper. He used to be an Olympic sailor, and he takes the cup here every second year. He is really good."

"So the point here is to reduce variability in the maneuver by standardizing it, which increases team coordination?" I asked.

"Aren't you supposed to be the psychologist on this team? Whatever do they teach you in college these days, I wonder!"

"Thanks, Dad, I love you too."

"It's the other way round. Few crews perform as well as this one, because few have both the same *esprit de corps* and precise coordination. What the skipper is doing is getting his crew to take ownership of their stations. If a bit of equipment doesn't suit them, they either change it or find a better way to use it. In building their involvement he gets ..."

"Their personal commitment to getting the maneuvers just right during the race!" Amy blurted out. "Yes, they're not just working for him, but for themselves also."

"And their teammates," added my father with a nod.

"Are you saying that kaizen is yet another tool to build employee involvement?" asked Phil.

"Kaizen — that's continuous improvement, right?" I checked.

"Wasn't it the idea from the start, this kaizen — continuous improvement?" asked Amy with a frown. "I seem to remember that the whole theory was that, in the West, we were very good at large-leap improvements."

"Like technology, what we did with the new vacuum cores," chipped in Phil.

"But not with small, everyday improvement, and, as a result, the outcomes of the large leaps would deteriorate over time. The Japanese approach, we were taught, was that 10 small steps of 10% were easier than one large step of 100%."

"I like that!" smiled my father. "But that wasn't exactly the trouble. The truth of the matter is that operators' suggestions rarely contribute significantly to cost savings. Which is partly why we must remain vigilant to communicate the 'zero investment' rule of kaizen."

"Zero investment?" asked Phil, who'd started taking notes again.

"Well, zero investment in management terms. Small stuff. The point is to fight the knee-jerk 'big machine' mentality that reacts to every problem by installing more expensive and less flexible new technology. People invariably ask for more equipment, more automation, more of everything for that matter, before they get their brain in gear and figure out how to improve work through better organization."

"But what's the point then, if you feel the suggestions are not that useful?" I asked, puzzled.

"Wait a minute," said Phil, frowning with concentration. "It's not that they're not useful, but that they are not a significant source of cost savings. However, if we keep focused on the fact that the operator's universe is his or her workstation, just as it is for sailors' maneuvers, these small improvements can do wonders to ease the job, and to improve its working content."

"That's right, Philip, 10 times 10%," confirmed Dad. "Don't underestimate the impact of small, detailed contributions. But you're right, don't look for the big bonanza in operator suggestions. It's not there because such finds are usually out of their world, more to do with engineering or design of the total process. However, every good idea helps in the long run."

"As well as involving operators in committing to a standard — and so takt time!" concluded Amy.

"Absolutely. Do you recall how we balanced the line to the takt time?" asked Dad.

"Total working content divided by takt time gives the right number of operators," Amy answered immediately.

"Which worked fine with Gloria's total work content of 42 minutes. But what happens if you use the minimum work content you measured with the team, what was it?"

"Thirty-nine minutes."

"With a takt time of 11.25 minutes you get 3.47 operators."

"So, we need kaizen to lower the total working content!"

"Yep. A lot of nonsense has been said about kaizen over the years, but at the end of the day, you have a very practical goal in mind, which is reducing the line total working content in order to reduce the number of operators at equivalent takt time.

"Now, what you do, " continued my father, "is first to try to run the line with only three operators, asking the team leader to chip in when they fall behind, and see what happens. In doing so, you create a pressure to improve. Then you go back to the graph we used to measure working cycles, remember? We wrote down the sequence of key operations, and timed them, with at least 10 measures, 20 if we can."

"I got it," said Phil, turning the pages of his notebook.

"Good. Then we ask the operators to do a more detailed study of their work cycle, and we stack the operations like so, like a layered cake. In some cases, it can be by five-second slices. In your case it's going to be in minutes."

"We've already done that!" exclaimed Amy. "When we balanced the line."

"Same thing, but more detailed," answered my father. "Once you've got the stacks about right — which assumes we've done enough 5S so the operators have learned to keep to the same working sequence — we can work on each of the items to see what can be eliminated or simplified."

"The operators have to do that?" asked Amy.

"Of course. They need coaching and supervision, but it's essentially their job and knowledge. The best way is to use video, or to ask a team leader from one line to run the kaizen workshop for another line. The aim of a kaizen workshop is to modify the working environment in order to produce a new standardized work chart with a lower working content."

"Let me check the logic once more," said Amy. "We produce gold nuggets regularly at takt time through pulling one piece at a time through the flow, right?"

"Correct."

"To do this, we must get rid of the variations in the operators' working cycle to get it as close as possible to the minimum working content."

"Go on."

"Then we stabilize the working cycle through standardized work, which represents the sequence of basic operations of the minimal working content."

"That's right."

"And now, we try to reduce this minimal working content through kaizen, in order to further reduce the number of people on the line?"

"At the same takt time, yes."

"How realistic is that?" asked Phil, writing it down.

"The first 20% is easy as pie," affirmed Dad. "Then it gets trickier. But don't make the usual mistake. Don't lose your focus. We know the gold is in the process, and we can also say how much. But until we can guarantee that the operators can work within takt time, we haven't achieved any solid gain. 5S and kaizen are the tools to painstakingly sift the gold out of the process. In that sense, all that was said about small continuous improvement is true, but its goal is far more specific: takt time based on customer demand."

"Lord, but it's an ant's work!" grumbled Philip.

"It's digging for gold, son. No one said it would be easy. Think about prospectors panning sand in rivers for hours on end for one single nugget. Anybody can talk about it, but walking the walk requires determination, obstinacy, and patience," Dad added grimly.

"However," Amy pointed out, "this is our job. We're talking about adding real value here. And we must get the employees to do it themselves — it sounds like a genuine HR mission!"

"That's the spirit!" said my father approvingly. "This is real HR work. Which, I might add, few of your colleagues I've met have been willing to undertake."

"What I don't understand is why you keep saying there are no cost reductions in kaizen activities," I wondered. "If you do find the patience to keep on chipping at working content, eventually, you should get some serious savings?"

"Over the years, yes," Dad agreed. "But it's far from immediate, and the gains come from cost saving, not cost cutting. Remember how I mentioned the alleged 'Oh No!' method of productivity improvement? Toyota kept growing, but Ohno's attitude was that growth should be funded by savings before investment. How long is a piece of string? Sooner or later you do need capital investment, but not until you've squeezed all you can out of all you've got. Keep in mind that when he started, right after the war, the Japanese economy had been reduced to rubble and everything was scarce. Ohno figured he needed experienced workers to start new lines with new products. So whenever a line was up and running, say, producing 150 parts a day with 100% resource, he'd come round and take away 10% of the people to put them on a new line. Now, of course the takt time hadn't changed, so the working content for each of the remaining operators increased considerably. As a result, they spent their evenings doing kaizen like crazy to get the working content back down to where it had been. For Toyota, this was a real productivity gain. They were producing the same amount with 90% of the original resource."

"As opposed to producing 170 parts with 100% resource, which is easier to achieve, but would be overproduction since the takt time hasn't changed," noted Phil.

"Yep, and then you can use the resource you've saved to start a new production line. Now if you keep doing that for 30 years, as Toyota had done before we even started taking them seriously, it's bound to make a considerable difference. So yes, Mike, you're right, over the long term, you can definitely save costs with kaizen. I don't like to stress that point, though, because most of the managers I know tend to expect immediate, obvious 'cost' results, and that's really not the way it works."

"Delivery first," said Phil, pushing his glasses back excitedly. "Deliver, reduce nonquality costs and rework, increase productivity and reduce inventory, and you're really saving costs!"

"The 'Oh No!' method," I chuckled. "Must have been a popular guy!"

"I wonder what they'll call us if we do the same?" Amy asked with a cheeky smile.

"Right, I can think of a number of names," said Phil, "none of them polite. But we really must get cracking on this kaizen thing. Do you feel up to running the workshops, Amy?"

"Hey, you know me," she said. "I'm ready for anything. But there's more to it than workshops, I believe," she added thoughtfully. "In the fast-food joint, we also had to do a lot more stuff, like a daily five-minute meeting at the start of each shift —"

"Five-minute meeting?" asked Dad, sounding surprised.

"Every shift," she confirmed. "The shift supervisor took the team through whatever problems had happened in the previous shift, and talked about what to do to make sure it didn't happen in the next one. We had a whiteboard to write all the 'to do' things on, like change the light bulb in the restroom, that sort of thing. It was really good because we could solve problems as they appeared."

"I'm amazed!" said my father. "In fact, we're going to do exactly the same things. But first, I need to talk to you more about the team leader. Not now," he said, putting his hands in the air. "I need to go and help with the admin for tomorrow. Today is training and the actual regatta is tomorrow. If you want, you can pop over tomorrow morning and we'll discuss the team leader role."

"Tomorrow's Sunday, Dad," I moaned. "Can't we give it a rest?"

"As you wish," he shrugged.

"Tomorrow's fine!" jumped in Phil, obviously anxious to satisfy my Dad's every whim. "What about you, Amy?"

"Haven't got anything better to do," she added with cheerful resignation. Or was that heavy irony? I couldn't tell.

"That's settled then," said Dad. "Get here early."

Even at this ungodly hour, it was pandemonium when I arrived: cars, crowds, white sailboats sparkling in the early morning sun. I managed to park, and spotted my father's truck in a tight squeeze of cars right by the main building, but I couldn't see Phil's orange pumpkin anywhere. The place was milling with people when I walked in, but I saw Amy right away, tucked in a corner of the porch in a deck chair, sunning herself and engrossed in a book, impervious to the mayhem around her.

"Whatcha reading?"

"Hey, Mike," she said, showing me the cover of the hardback she held in her hands.

"*One Hundred Years of Solitude*," I whistled. "Heavy stuff."

"Hmm. Slow reading. Your dad is down there somewhere with the organizers."

"You're reading this in English?" I cried, finding a seat close to her.

"Yeah?" she lifted her sunglasses on her forehead and eyed me suspiciously. "So?"

"In English?" I repeated dumbly. "One of the greatest classics of the Spanish language? Didn't you tell me your parents came from Mexico?" I stammered, feeling suddenly way, way out of line. She didn't seem to mind and gave me one of her big smiles.

"Oh, *si Señor!*" she answered with an outrageous Mexican accent. "My *padres*, they work in the fields, *Señor*. I can speak Spanish pretty well, but reading is easier in English."

I said nothing, with my foot in my mouth.

"My boyfriend is crazy about Latin American literature," she explained with a shrug, flapping the book open and closed again. "I couldn't care less, but he's into the roots trip, and heritage, and so on. So I try to be supportive and read some of it. I'm not too sure I like it anyhow," she said with a grimace. "And yes," she added smiling softly, "my parents are from Mexico and pick salads in Monterey. I got a scholarship, got a degree, got a job, so I help them as much as I can, but as far as national identity goes, I'm just another ugly American."

Boyfriend, right.

"I wouldn't say ugly," I mumbled.

"And it's got a character with my name in it, no? So I had to read it."

"Amaranta? I remember."

"Yeah, Amaranta. It's not really my kind of reading. I'll tell you, I'm not a big reader."

"I liked it," I said defensively.

"You would, you're an intellectual!"

"It's a classic!" I replied, vaguely outraged. "I still remember how each character has some extraordinary feature, you know, like that sorcerer Melquiades."

"Yes, and the madness of José Arcadio Buendia."

"The sorrow of Aureliano," I countered.

"The beauty of Remedios." she answered, warming to the game.

"The passions of Amaranta."

"Yes, *las passiones de Amaranta*," she repeated, staring at me with a soft, slow smile.

An angel passed. A legion of angels passed and I felt myself blush, mesmerized by her dark, dark eyes.

"Whatcha reading?" asked Phil, as he managed to push a scavenged chair through the crowd and sit with us, chasing the moment away.

"There you are!" shouted Dad from further away, waving a wad of Yacht Club papers and signaling us to join him. "Come on in, they're about finished briefing the crews for the race," he said, leading us in the big room on the Club's ground floor, which was full of sailors and gear.

"Watch!"

What was there to see? The crews were filing back to their boats to get out of harbor in time to be well positioned at the starting line, and the worthies of the racing committee were arguing among themselves sotto voce. As the room emptied, I realized one of the crews was lingering behind, near the chart detailing the regatta's course. It was the same crew we had seen before, analyzing their performance on video. Their skipper looked older than I had thought at first, with deep lines running through his face and sparse hair. They stood around him at the board while he detailed each of the maneuvers he expected them to make over the course. For instance, he insisted that since the beat leg was short, they had to be prepared to take the spinnaker down almost as soon as it was up, which meant paying attention to the jib sheets over the pole.

"What are they doing?" murmured Phil to my father.

"The first task of a team leader. He is taking them through the race step-by-step, making sure that they know what to expect when."

"Ah, so they make their moves within the proper allotted time?" said Amy.

"Takt time!" emphasized Dad. "Most crews have problems with timing their maneuvers, they never start soon enough, so are usually in a complete panic when the mark comes up, which is how most accidents happen on the water."

After making sure everyone understood the day's course, the skipper asked each of the crew members if they had a specific point to remind their colleagues before setting out, which led to some banter between the number one and the woman who had to pass him the shoot back, referring, I guess, to the incident they were commenting on yesterday. It was all good-natured but the messages were going through. Then they broke up and walked past us, chattering along with obvious good humor.

"This is like the meetings I was telling you about, in the fast-food business. What to look out for and what you're supposed to do in the shift," said Amy frowning. "The supervisors at the plant conduct morning meetings at the factory, but it is nothing like this!"

"To start with, there's a lot more people. A supervisor usually covers a number of lines, and all the operators attend," answered Phil thoughtfully, as my Dad went to the skipper and they exchanged pleasantries.

"Yes, and it's a lot more about management messages being relayed. Nothing is said about takt time or practical problems," sighed Amy. "I guess we've missed the point once more."

"Come on, kids, I'm taking a launch to the first marker. I'm supposed to make sure none of the boats touch it as they tack around it," said Dad, clapping his hands. He picked up a battered pair of binoculars, a walkie-talkie, handed me a plastic folder to carry, and we were off.

I could feel the buzz in the air as we walked down the pier to the old-fashioned launch my father picked. Boats were being towed out of harbor, with a great deal of sails fluttering, people yelling, and the usual bedlam of getting everyone on the line on time. Being part of all this bustle was more fun than I'd expected. Dad was clearly enjoying himself as he maneuvered his old tug between the yachts, casually waving to the people we crossed. The ocean was dead calm, and there was just enough wind to power the sails, but, Dad explained, the Jays were very light and could move at impressive speeds with very little wind on smooth water. Amy had settled across a bench, next to me. She wore her hair tied in a bright scarf with a long black strand falling over her forehead, and her oversized sunglasses made her look very much the movie star. Phil was actually grinning from ear to ear, which lifted years of concern from his face. We left the harbor, and headed for the distant mass of ships of all sorts getting in place for the race around huge inflatable orange buoys. Dad steered the launch toward one of the garish markers, which looked like it would fill the boat, got up close, and dropped an anchor right before it. At the sound of a horn, we looked back at the frenetic activity on the starting line, and then settled as comfortably as we could to soak up some sun.

"Are you saying a team leader is like the captain of a ship?" asked Phil in the quiet that followed.

"More like a skipper, an important nuance," answered my father.

We looked at him, not quite sure of what he meant.

"A captain is God on board, he or she makes the strategic decisions, which may lead to life or death of the crew. A skipper, particularly on small crafts like this, doesn't have such an exalted position. He or she is part of the crew to start with, and makes tactical choices about the race. Strategy is set by the course itself."

"I'm not sure I understand," said Phil.

"Well, let's say a captain would be the traditional supervisor, whereas the skipper is a team leader. If someone is ill or fails at the job, the skipper will never think twice before taking the post for the duration. A captain, or, God forbid, a supervisor would never do that. They'd find someone else to fill in, or live without a body in the breach. To take another military example, think about all the war movies you've seen. A patrol is led by a lieutenant, who is usually a young know-nothing straight out of officer training, and a sergeant who is part of the team but runs the day-to-day show, both bully and mommy."

We nodded, visualizing the clichés of endless Hollywood wars.

"Captains are needed at the very top, certainly, but every hierarchy tends to fill up with staff officers with far too much authority and not enough responsibility. The team leader has no hierarchical rank. He or she is part of the team itself, and the job is to make sure production happens at takt time. Team leaders are sergeants, not officers. They are part of each production cell, sometimes on the line itself. They're paid 5% more. They get a slightly bigger bonus but they're not, I repeat not, managers."

"But how many do you need?"

"Oh, I'd say one for every five to seven operators."

"That's a hell of an increased expense," muttered Phil with a frown. "Doesn't it just increase your fixed costs?"

Dad just laughed. "Right on, son, right on. Of course it would if you'd just hired team leaders, but the point is you can't do that. They have to come from the ranks. In fact, you create the team leader post through productivity improvements in the cell. As soon as you can extract someone through the kaizen work, the most experienced operator takes the team leader role!"

"Here they come!" I cried.

We could hear orders being barked from the first boat, distant still, but the sound carried clearly over the water. The pack was following like hounds behind a hare. As the Jays approached, we could see the first skipper holding the tiller and yelling orders and insults at his crew, who were scurrying all over the deck, preparing to deploy the shoot once they'd come round the mark.

"Sure sounds like he knows what he's doing!" said Amy.

"Him?" huffed Dad. "He knows how to make a good start and then how to be a pain with protests to the race committee. He never wins, and it's always someone else's fault. Watch, here comes Marty."

The first boat passed the mark with less than a foot to spare, and Dad checked like a hawk that they didn't touch the buoy. As they passed, we could see the tangle of people and ropes as they rushed to raise the spinnaker and lower the jib. The number one was screaming about something stuck in the pole, but the skipper was yelling something else to someone else, and they passed the mark still unraveling the mess. A couple of boats back, we recognized the crew we'd watched in the morning. The skipper wasn't steering but standing in the hatch, quietly surveying both the water and his deck. He waved as he passed us, and Dad waved back. None of the crew even saw us, they were so focused on their individual tasks. They rounded the buoy with room to spare and had the shoot up before they were even out of the beat. We heard it pop open with a snap, and watched the boat move two places up in what seemed like a leap, a sudden surge of speed.

"See the difference?" Dad exclaimed. "The first guy is full of bull and bluster. He is the thinking head, and he treats each of the crewmates as an extension of his limbs. So he gives the orders, and they follow them as well as they can. This, in effect, is how old-fashioned supervisors manage their shop floors. Did you see what happened? There was a problem with the spinnaker's sheet and the pole. The number one was out of the beat, but still the skipper was concentrating on another operation at the winch, probably something to do with putting more pressure on the jib to avoid the buoy, as they were too close to be safe. In a plant, supervisors keep shifting workers and load around to keep producing even if there are problems in the process. Since, once things are set, the only possible decision is who gets priority and who doesn't, supervisors use their own notions of which orders are important and push these through, at the expense of all else."

"Dave still tends to do that," agreed Phil.

"Not exactly delivery first, or takt time thinking, is it?"

Phil said nothing. "What about the other skipper, Marty?" asked Amy, intrigued.

"Remember, he's planned it all from the start with his team. The crew knows exactly who's doing what and when. Have you seen how focused they all were? They're looking for signals from each other to coordinate the maneuver."

"I see," I interrupted. "It doesn't have to all go through the skipper.

No need for the information to move through a central coordinator."

"Who becomes a bottleneck," added Phil.

"Indeed. Now, Marty is still running the show. But basically he looks around and tries to anticipate what could go wrong and — watch him!"

We watched as the boat was barreling downwind, swaying slightly under the immense yellow canopy of the light weather shoot. Marty had sprung out of his hole, and was helping the number one pass the jib sheet over the spinnaker pole.

"When he sees something's not right, he acts upon it before there is a problem, not as it blows up in their face. Because the crew is so focused on their tasks, they can't be asked to keep an eye out for whatever imponderable is going to come their way. That's the skipper's job," Dad explained. "The team leader's job is to make sure his crew mates are in a good position to do their job, and to anticipate any problems they might encounter, and resolve those for them."

"As well as training them and getting them to kaizen their maneuvers," Amy suggested.

"Let me summarize," answered Phil, writing it all down, and exposing his precious notebook to wind and spray.

"First the team leader communicates the takt time and discusses the production for the shift with the operators."

"Yes. In most cases, we set up a daily production analysis board with hourly target/actual good parts produced," Dad sketched on a scrap of paper from his waterproof folder. "Like so, we have the takt time, the hourly objectives, hour by hour, the number of good parts produced, and comments explaining the difference between objective and actual.

"The operators meet for five minutes around this board, standing up so the meeting is quick, and discuss the difficulties they encountered the previous day and how to resolve them. First and foremost safety issues, if any, then all other problems that were encountered in the previous shift and that might crop up again this shift.

Production Analysis Board			
Hour	Plan	Good parts	Comments
1			
2			
3			
4			
5			
6			
7			
8			

$$\frac{\text{Good parts}}{\text{Number of operators} \times \text{hours}} =$$

"Second, the team leader makes sure that all working conditions are normal and anticipates potential problems."

"Third, the team leader takes the responsibility for 5S and on-the-job training to make sure that all operators can perform their standardized work within a given beat, a takt time," concluded Phil.

"The team leader must always make sure that standardized work is respected and that the kanban works, never lose track of that. The team leader also collects the shift's information about quality problems and does the rework," added my father.

"No joke. It's just like managing a shift in a fast-food restaurant, you guys!" said Amy, catching her balance on my arm as a passing speeder's wake rocked the launch. "That's exactly what we were supposed to do. Run the team, make sure every one does what they should do, organize the cleanup at the end of the shift, and do the paperwork for the shift."

"Yeah, you'd still need people to take care of the interfaces," said Phil dubiously.

"And encourage kaizen. That's what the supervisors are there for," Dad added. "And the production manager does the production planning and scheduling. In any case, are you clear about the team leader role?"

Phil answered:

"– Five-minute meetings at the start of the shift about the day's production target and the problems encountered the day or shift before,

– making sure standardized work is applied,

– making sure the schedule or production instructions are working,

– dealing with rework and quality problems,

– making sure 5S is maintained, and

– doing the line's admin like the required data gathering."

"That team leader!" I quipped. "He's got to be superman!"

"What do you mean?" asked Phil with a frown.

"Well, think about of all these things he's got to do. Or she. Amy, what do you think?"

"I can foresee difficulties," she answered carefully. "Certainly, we'd need a lot more training than we're doing now."

"You do it step-by-step," replied Dad. "You don't have to do all at once. Start with the five-minute meeting to discuss with the team what the team leader from the previous shift has passed on. Then ask the team leaders to coordinate the 5S at the end of the shift, and the rest will fall in place as you go."

"And the supervisor?"

"The supervisor does roughly the same thing, next level up. It's more to do with keeping the logistics working, such as the regular pickups and so on, and looking out for potential problems, which the team won't be seeing because they're busy working," proposed Amy.

"Partly, but don't forget the standardized work. The supervisor's role is also maintaining the standardized work at all levels: in operations, logistics, everywhere."

"So the supervisor manages kaizen, right?"

"Yes, and on-the-job training," explained Dad.

"It's hard to visualize this team leader role in practice," said Phil.

Dad rubbed his face, making his wispy white hair stand in spikes.

"Well, as you will see, I hope, in your plant, the team leader is *not* a manager, but a *lead* worker who makes sure the team runs smoothly and delivers. Get it?"

"Yeah. I can see it. I doubt we could implement this, but I can see it. Sort of."

Dad brought us back ashore in the pause between the two legs of the race, and then returned to his observation post, chattering on the radio, without a backward glance. I was slightly disconcerted about how familiar he seemed with this Yacht Club environment, as if he'd done this all his life. Is this what he really wanted all along? We made our way to the sun deck by the bar, and ordered sandwiches and beers. In the distance, we could see the shining sails jockeying for position at the line for the new start. I collapsed in a low seat. "So, how are you coping with my Dad?" I asked.

"Same as I remember him," answered Phil with a wry grin. "Blunt, and to the point."

"Yeah. You can take the man out of the navy, but never the navy out the man."

"Listen to you wimps," jibed Amy. "I think he's charming." She fluttered her eyelids.

"To you, he is," Phil muttered. "You've got him under a spell."

"That's macho bull," she snapped back. "I'm just the only one fast enough to catch what he's saying. Right first time!"

"Yeah, well, you didn't have to grow up answering 'Aye, aye, sir!' at breakfast!"

"Whatever," answered Phil, rubbing his face tiredly. "He does make me feel like a moron most of the time. How come we're not taught all this stuff? It sounds really obvious when your dad tells it."

"It took him a lifetime to learn, though, and he never got any thanks for it."

"We get taught all this touchy-feely stuff in management courses," said Amy morosely, "but then it's all hardball the moment you start work. Nobody cares about people, they're just numbers on the P&L. Your dad might not be very considerate in the way he goes about it, but at least he takes people seriously."

"I know, you're right. I guess I'm biased. All those years later I still find him irritating as hell."

"He's your father, what do you expect? Hey, you're the shrink, man."

"I know, I know. I must say, your discussion about running teams really made me think."

"How's that?"

"Well, Amy, how were you taught to motivate people?"

"Professionally? Carrot and stick, mostly," she shot back. "The carrot is the paycheck, and the stick is being fired. Although that's not at all what we were taught in college. It was all about values and social environment then. But I've seen very little of that in the business world."

"Don't say that!" argued Phil. "I really believe respect and trust are the basis of a healthy working relationship."

"And you're so blind to office politics I could kick you," she fired back. "Sometimes you're just on another planet! How can you be so oblivious to what happens!"

He glared back, clearly uncomfortable.

"Your dad's angle about involvement is really good, though. Hard to explain, but I'm starting to have a feel for it. It's not about carrot and stick, it's about, I don't know, ownership."

"*Esprit de corps* he calls it, fighting spirit, but I'm not quite sure what he means by that. Something about making people feel special, part of something, and keeping them under pressure. Motivation is really not my area. I work a lot more on reasoning and logic, but I was thinking about it earlier on. Let's assume that people respond to stress."

"Is that true?"

"Well, not just negative stress, but also positive stress like interest, or ambition. If they're under too little stress, they don't care, so it's very hard to motivate them to do something. But if they're under too much stress, they panic. They freeze, or they get angry and do completely irrational things."

"It makes sense. Every involvement technique your dad has been mentioning is about handling the stress curve," said Amy. "On the one hand, there is pressure to keep to the takt time, and all the securities are taken away, which increases the stress. But on the other hand, there is all this work with the operators, about 5S and kaizen, which helps them gain some control over their environment, which should be reassuring."

"Yes, and demonstrates management commitment. So management is looking at how you work, which is stressful, but management is interested in resolving problems, which is reassuring."

"But it's also about ownership," she insisted. "You know, if I'm just there to push a button, I'm not likely to get very involved. But if I invest in thinking about my workstation, in cleaning it and studying it, it's like these guys and their boats. They get interested. Work matters. What I think is brilliant with what your dad is telling us is ways to develop the operator within his or her sphere. See, it doesn't matter if all the guy does is punch holes all day long, as long as we give him the credit of becoming a hole-punching master!"

"O master of the hole-punch!"

"I mean it," she said with an earnest frown. "Think about it. Operators are just as smart as you and me, but don't get the same breaks."

I couldn't help being impressed again by how sharp she was, and suddenly remembered: "My Dad says that, in Japan, you can find masters of everything. I remember a film in which there was a master of the noodle soup. He was a bum, but cooks from all over the country came to learn about the art of making noodle soup."

"Just so. A master of the hole-punching. A master of the bolt-tightening and so on. You can laugh, but it gives a completely new dimension to these jobs."

"We're not laughing. You're very convincing."

"At least I've convinced myself," she said, crossing her arms with a pout. Which did make us laugh.

"Actually, there's been some research on that topic. Some people have been testing what makes people happy on their job, and find that you've got to reach a balanced point between the challenges of the tasks you must do and your proficiency at them. Too much challenge, and you're overstressed and anxious —"

"That's me!" said Phil, raising his drink.

"Not enough stress, and you're bored and listless. The other point is that people need to hold to a theory that explains reasonably well what is happening to them. As long as it works, they're happy. And guess what this theory is called in psychological research?"

"Go on."

"Flow. I kid you not!"

"Get out."

"I swear! It's close enough, though, with what Dad's saying," I plodded on. "I remember that when I started studying psychology, we'd had yet another argument about something or other, but he made an interesting point. He said one of his gurus had taught him he should be producing people before producing parts."

"Producing people before producing parts?" repeated Phil.

"Yeah, that came as a big revelation to him at the time. It links back to this team leader role. He argued that management's job was developing people, who would then add value to the product. What we argued about was that he then believed in 'producing' people quite literally. You know his style. Do this, don't do that, don't argue just do it!" I said, mimicking Dad's voice.

"That's him, all right," laughed Phil. "Which is exactly what we've been doing to our own guys with 5S and kaizen."

"And what your dad's been doing to us!" pointed out Amy.

"Fine, then. Here's a toast to producing people!" proposed Phil, raising his glass.

"And to Mike's dad!" added Amy. So we drank to my father's health and enjoyed the sunshine and each other's company.

Chapter Six

LEVEL TO PULL

I didn't hear from either Amy or Phil for a couple of weeks, until Phil turned up unexpectedly at my door one evening.

"Got a beer?" he asked as I let him in.

"In the fridge," I snapped, returning impatiently to my desk, annoyed at the distraction as I was finally getting some writing done.

"How's the book going?" he asked, tossing me a can.

"The usual. I'm a slow writer," I answered wearily. "What about you guys? Dad was asking if I'd heard from you lately."

"It's a mess!" moaned Phil. "A real mess."

"Any worse than it was a month ago?"

"Better. We're actually keeping the wolves at bay. Our strongest backer is reassured to see we've got things moving in the plant. But I now have a different set of problems on my plate: my crew."

"What happened? The second-shift idea didn't work?"

"We didn't go for that in the end. The people problems actually surfaced with Gloria, the area supervisor. She had been a champion of the 5S initiative in the bad old days, so when we pulled it out again, and she saw we were serious, she went back to it with a vengeance. With Amy conducting flow-and-layout workshops with the two other lines, these two have the subassembly area totally straightened out, and they managed to pack a fourth line in there, doing STRs, just by throwing junk out, reducing the space between stations, and fixing stuff to build the extra stations. With a minimal investment, we're up and running with two STR lines in the day's production."

"That's good, right?"

"You bet, we're making 80 STR mechanisms a day in a good day, with practically no increase in fixed costs. My productivity is up 20% at 10 parts per person per day on all four lines."

"What's the problem then?"

"People, I told you. Amy and Gloria have banded together, and they're running the area like one of your dad's fighting ships. The final assembly guys downstream are not coping, and although they're doing all the overtime they can, the inventory is piling up between the subassembly area and final assembly."

"Well, just let Amy loose on them to do the same thing!"

"Not that easy. Gloria and Amy cornered Jake Rogers, the supervisor of the final assembly, to talk about single-piece flow. He's an old coot close to retirement and really set in his ways. Imagine how that went! Dave refuses to get involved and, in any case, he and Rogers have been pals for years. Dave felt so humiliated by Amy's success with mechanism assembly that he's completely backed off production issues and is now limiting himself to scheduling and planning. And, oh, yes, to get some of his luster back, he decided to clean up the mess in the materials store, so more 5S, but in Dave's style."

"Not too much people involvement, right?"

"Understatement. Not that I care, those slobs deserved it, but it's started another fire in the plant. And of course, it feels like fixing one problem just creates another. The problem now is Gary Pellman, the engineering manager. It started with Joshua, working on the STR products. He now has a pile of ideas to improve the product, and, as you can imagine, he's firmly at Amy's beck and call."

"I can imagine."

"Pellman is starting to feel the pressure, and Amy can be a bit abrasive at times. So he's starting to say that she's getting too big for her britches, and, while she plays hero on the shop floor getting in Dave's way, the real HR work, such as annual appraisals and the like, is not getting done."

"Where does Matt stand on all of this?"

"Matt listens to Pellman. But there's also this other guy, Kevin Morgan, who deals with logistics and purchasing for the two plants. I've gone to see him with more of the red bin results, and it hasn't gone well. He's a new guy, someone we hired to manage the integrated logistics of the two factories, a supply-chain manager. Pellman knew him from before. Oh well, in the end Matt and I have always agreed that he takes care of sales and finance while I handle engineering and production, so … it's just a bit tense, that's all."

He sighed and took a long sip of beer. He really looked as though he hadn't slept in the past month.

"No, what's the matter is that our real problems are starting to surface," he said with another loud sigh. "It's been tough for the final assembly guys, but we've more or less doubled our production in STR breakers, right?"

I nodded encouragingly.

"So, we've caught up with most of our backlog of orders, and, miraculously, the customer has actually paid us straight up on delivery, which has eased the cash crisis for another month."

"That's good."

"And Matt has other customers lined up to buy more STRs."

"Splendid, so what's the problem?"

"The problem is that I now find out that the design customizations required by the customers for the new contracts are stuck in engineering and won't be ready for us to start the new production once we're done with the backlog!"

"Huh?"

"You see, traditionally, engineering is always telling production that they do the smart part of the job by customizing complex products for difficult customers. Production is always the bad guy because they can never ship the damn things in time. What I'm finding out is that engineering takes forever to get the designs right, and production is slow because they have to cope with all sorts of design screw-ups."

"Like the rework issues Joshua is working on."

"Yes! And that was the tip of the iceberg. We've found on the line that operators sometimes have to drill holes to pass wires because they're not on the drawings, things like that."

"So what about, was it, Pellman?"

"Oh, he's blustering around, acting tough. He wants Josh stopped. He wants Amy toned down, he wants ..."

"And what do you think?"

"Well, when I say it like this, it's quite obvious, right? Only —"

"Only?"

Shrink mode tonight: whatever the patient says, rephrase as a question.

"Only, Mike, you know I'm not good with this kind of stuff," he said in muted appeal. "You know I never could cope with conflict. Not at home, not at school! I'm at a loss. Should I ask Amy to tone it down?"

"What are your feelings about this?" I asked. "What's your priority?"

"Priority is clear: we need to turn around this business."

"So?"

"Yeah, I know. Keep pushing."

We sat there for a while, guzzling our beers, and I could almost feel the tension emanating from him, the constant grind of his mental cogs, and the resulting anxiety.

"You know, Phil, I suspect my Dad was right about one thing."

"He was right about plenty. What in particular?"

"Well, you won't like this, but I think you're still trying to deal with your mess as if it was a technical problem. Move this machine here, change this design there, which it is to some extent, but ..."

"What?"

"It's all about people, that's all. You're having a leadership problem, not just a production or business problem. Matt's a businessman. He's always out there chasing new deals. He's not interested in minding the store, and, by default, you're saddled with it. Now, you don't want to take a strong leadership role because that's not your style and you hate conflict.

154

We both know that. But unless I'm wrong, nature abhors a vacuum —"

"Yeah, that I agree with. A vacuum is something I do know about," he joked weakly.

"Listen to what you're saying. Amy is ambitious and pushy and terribly bright. Now that she's found what she does well, she's pushed poor Dave out of the way. I suspect that the guy who actually ran the place was this Gary Pellman. He's an old hand, knows the ropes, and runs the high-status part of the company, the engineering. So he's top dog. But suddenly, you start pulling the rug from under his feet, with this guy Joshua to start with —"

"It's even worse," cut in Phil. "I've started floating the idea that engineering should be organized along value streams, like production, with a value-stream manager running the entire chain, from sales to engineering to production to delivery for each product family."

"There you go. Where does that leave Pellman?"

"He knows an awful lot about the product, our market, and our customers."

"I didn't ask that. Where does that leave him in terms of power?"

Phil started to say something and stopped. He finished his drink in silence, mulling it all over.

Why is it so easy to see our friends' problems while being blind to our own? The more I thought about it, the more I became convinced that Phil was grappling with a leadership role he wasn't ready for. Dad had been right on this one from the start.

As a psychologist, I know that people prefer comfort to being told how to solve their problems. Yes, your head hurts from a sunburn, gee, that must be very painful. But telling them to stop driving in the sun in their open-top convertible doesn't help them feel better. They tend to know the solution in the first place, yet don't apply it for any number of personal reasons.

Dad had never empathized with a soul in his life. He saw the world as a set of problems and solutions, period. A true engineer. His take on people was that if you were not part of the solution, you were part of the problem. I had chosen a profession where real problems are largely ignored and the idea is to help people feel better about themselves, regardless of how objectively useless they are. The more screwed up, the more they need help. Which makes sense, right?

In getting involved in Phil's case, I was starting to appreciate my Dad's contrary attitude. Phil's company problems were real, and could be solved. But solving them demanded more grit than one would expect, especially for Phil who, in the end, had never reconciled himself with being an entrepreneur, much less a manager. He still saw himself as a scientist who'd got a lucky break and now had thrust upon him a leadership role he had neither asked for nor wished for. Now it looked as though he was going to have work for all that money after all.

"They did what?" yelled Dad over the phone when we called him a bit later on to apprise him of recent developments.

"A fourth line, I understand, with one shift per day."

"So they've got two parallel lines producing the same STR mechanisms?"

"I gather so."

"Tell Philip that's plain stupid."

"I guess you'd better explain that to him directly, here he is."

"No, hold that. Tell them to meet us for lunch tomorrow at the Pacific Mall."

"At the mall?"

"You heard me. 'Night, Junior."

At the mall? Phil and I looked at each other perplexed. What now?

Amy was not pleased. She'd gotten a piece of Dad's mind when she expected high praise, and now sulked while he walked us through the shelves of a supermarket. He was shopping for cleaning supplies, and telling Phil why doubling the lines wasn't such a hot idea.

"You've doubled your daily production, correct?"

"Yeah, we're now going for 20 STRs a day."

"The market is absorbing that?"

"Currently, we're still catching up on our backlog of orders. We were late on our deliveries, so the customer is pleased to see two trucks a week come in, although sooner or later they'll start piling up on their premises. But if I manage to straighten out some issues with the engineering department, we should have new orders which can absorb our new capacity."

"Okay, so what happens to the STR mechanism takt time?"

"It halves, I guess, down to something like five and a half minutes."

"So, Ms. Cruz, what does that mean?"

"I know, I figured it out. We should have a single line working at the lower takt time with more operators on it," she answered testily.

"Exactly."

Amy was clearly under pressure, and not so smiley as usual. It seemed that all her best efforts were appreciated on a general level, but drew her nothing but criticism on specifics. I could see she needed a pat on the back, some recognition for all her hard work.

"What I don't understand, sir, is why two parallel lines are such a problem. We're producing at takt time!"

"Well, why isn't one line possible then?"

"People like their jobs the way they are. They feel silly when you break down operations into smaller and smaller chunks," Amy explained. "Do you know what I mean?"

"I sure do. The blasted craftsman mentality. You're in business, you know! The best way to avoid mistakes and to standardize work is to get operator cycles under one minute. One minute, mind you! So if your takt time permits you to go down to five minutes, that's all benefit! The operators will make fewer mistakes and you'll increase productivity even further!"

"I take your point," she finally answered. "But you're not the one who gets to tell Gloria we'll have to change everything around again, and break down the jobs into smaller and smaller units!"

"No one said it'd be easy," said Dad. "But I have another reason for insisting on one line rather than two parallel ones, which will become clear later. It's all to do with the supermarket problem."

"Is that why we're here?" I muttered.

We passed through the checkout where my father paid for his odds and ends. The cashier gave us a strange look. How many people does it take to buy a can of paint? Then, while we were still standing there, he asked us: "What do you see?"

I was reassured to see that Phil and Amy looked as befuddled as I felt. I saw people lining up at checkout stands. Some kids near the registers were helping customers pack their stuff into grocery bags, which was smart. They didn't do that at my local store and it always took forever to both pay and collect the groceries, which made you wait twice as long in the line. More flow stuff, I figured.

"Imagine this is a factory."

"The register is final assembly, is that what you mean?" asked Phil.

"If you like. What do you see?"

They looked and looked until Amy cried:

"Pull! They're pulling from a wide array of components all through the factory, is that it?"

"Yep, and?"

"Shelves," she said, like her old self again. "Fixed quantities of boxes in the shelf space. It has to get replenished somehow."

"Very good. But why does this matter?"

"I don't know," she muttered, chewing on her lower lip. "You've got people moving around helping themselves, bringing it to final assembly. You've got stocks at fixed locations on the shelves."

"What's your issue with the final assembly conveyor?"

"Oh, please, don't remind me of that jerk, Jake Rogers. Do you know he called me 'girl'?"

"Never mind that now, figure out the problem."

She glared at him in a way that would have made me take a step back, but good ol' Dad stared right back with his pale eyes, never even batting an eyelid.

"All right," he said after a while. "Let's take another approach. Philip, what's your main problem?"

"Flow?" proposed Phil uncertainly.

"Gold, right? How the gold gets stuck in the value stream, got it?"

"I'm with you."

"So where does it get held up?"

"Same three points you saw right away. I've got a pile of inventory with the capsules themselves, then with assembled mechanisms, and in the conveyor and finished goods."

"Why there?"

"Breaks in the flow, you said?"

"With the conveyor, it's easy," pointed out Amy. "Dave keeps scheduling long runs of finished units, so they accumulate. For instance, if he does an entire day with QSTs, we're piling up STR mechanisms which don't get consumed by the conveyor — a day's production of STRs can go up to 80, so it piles up really quickly. And I get laughed at seeing how my process improvement has in fact increased inventory."

"Face it, it has," said my father without much tact. "The question is why does Dave do this. Why just do QSTs for a day?"

"Precisely because we're not a supermarket," said Phil, a bit combatively. "We get monthly orders from customers, and we schedule them weekly. At the top of his capacity, Jake can assemble 50 breakers a day. So if he's got to deliver 100 STR, 50 QST-1, 50 other QST-2, and 20 DG breakers, he's going to run STR all day on Monday and Tuesday, QST-1 on Wednesday, QST-2 on Thursday, and DG on Friday."

"Why does he do that?"

"I guess mostly because we've always done it like this. His guys can do the same assembly throughout the day. They find it easier to repeat the same assembly. There's less risk of error."

"They're correct, of course, but what's the upshot?" asked Dad, trying to pull the answer from us.

"While he's doing final assembly of QSTs or DGs on the conveyor, STR mechanisms just accumulate in front of assembly!" exclaimed Amy.

"Yep, you're pushing all these mechanisms on him, and he has no use for them until it's planned, so they just stack up."

"And he's slow. On some days we've moved two operators from the DG mechanism assembly to the conveyor to increase his output, but he's still well beneath the 50 finished units a day we need!"

"That's another issue. Stick with the problem, Ms. Cruz. You're pushing STR mechanism on him, and it accumulates. How does that relate to what you see here?"

"It doesn't. It's stupid," she said with irritation. "It's as if the cashier said to that customer over there, 'Sorry I can't check out your items. I'll first check out all the people with butter, and then I'll take care of all those with bread.'" She suddenly went dead quiet as my Dad started laughing quietly.

"Come on," he said, "there must be a coffee shop in this place."

"That's just it," said Dad, sipping his coffee. "We're running our plants like the Soviets used to run their economy. Because it's easier for the producer, you can buy only sugar on certain days, so you'd better stock up on sugar. Another day, detergent, and so on. Long runs, high inventory! We have this big central planning machine which coordinates it all, the blasted MRP —"

"MRP?" I interrupted.

"Material Requirements Planning system," Dad explained. "Where was I? Complaining about having too much of some parts and not enough of others."

"You mean we have to convince Jake to schedule the final assembly differently?" Phil asked.

"That's it, Philip. Remember our friend Taiichi Ohno? Legend has it that he had an epiphany when he heard about U.S. supermarkets. In a supermarket, customers help themselves to what they want with a wide array of choices and without needing any help from a salesperson. And, the store replenishes the shelves frequently to replace what has just been bought. I'm not sure he ever stepped into a real American supermarket, but he clearly saw the two main implications."

"The customer comes and picks up exactly what he needs."

"And?"

"Like with the hamburgers!" exclaimed Amy. "You only produce to replenish what has been picked up. At lunch time, for instance, when we had a lot of people at the counter," she explained excitedly, "we had set rows of fresh burgers, one per type, like cheeseburger, double burger, chicken sandwich, etc. Each of these rows could only contain seven burgers. Whenever a customer asked for a cheeseburger, for instance, he'd be given one from the bottom of the row, and we'd know we'd have to produce one more in the top of the row to replace it."

"Okay, that's a great parallel. In fact, you've got two kinds of pull. One is replenishment, for instance for the standard burgers, like the basic cheeseburger that are high demand. For these you keep a small inventory, and whenever one is consumed, you produce another. Because people are asking for these all the time, they don't have time to get stale on the shelf. Also, the inventory covers for spikes in demand, like when five people ask for a basic cheeseburger at the same time, and you can't make them all at once."

"Exactly!" exclaimed Amy excitedly. "That's just what happens."

"Now, you also have your special items, like cheeseburgers with no pickles, which you can't keep in the buffer, because they are ordered infrequently and might go stale. If you had an inventory of those —"

"It would be overproduction!" interjected Phil, with an "aha!" look on his face.

"Precisely. So you need to work hard at building the extras on demand, which is of course ideal."

"But since we have only so many people making the burgers at the one time," continued Amy, "we're going to be either swamped with demand of one-off orders, or, on the contrary, with time on our hands. Variation."

"Mura," said Phil, who really looked as though he was enjoying this variation idea.

"Yep," agreed Dad, "unevenness. So the way you work this is that you use your buffer. You build to order as long as the special orders come in, and the rest of the time you work at replenishing the buffer of high-runners, which levels your workload. Ohno brought two key ideas back to Toyota about how to organize his plant like a supermarket. First, the downstream customer comes and helps himself from a supermarket of parts presented by the upstream supplier; and second, the supplier only produces what has just been consumed, whether in replenishment pull or sequential pull if we produce to order."

"Pull system!"

"Yep, the idea is always to minimize lead time. Now think about how our plants are run. We come up with a weekly production schedule, whether manually or from some MRP, then we send production instructions to each of the links."

"The STR mechanism line gets a daily order saying, 'Produce 80,' and so does every other line," Amy said.

"Like the Soviet economy. Now you produce your 80 mechanisms, and you try to push them onto the conveyor, which is busy making QST-1 breakers. So they accumulate. Next day, you produce 80 more, but he's now busy doing QST-2, so now you've got a 160 pile-up of mechanisms."

"At the cost of these capsules, I'd rather not total up the dollar value! It'll make me sick," muttered Phil.

"Aha, but three days later, the conveyor suddenly starts producing STR breakers like there's no tomorrow, and eats up your inventory real quick. It's like a party of school kids at your burger joint who all ask for grilled chicken sandwiches at once."

"They completely empty the stock, and then all we can do is produce more one-by-one, which takes ages."

"And that's what Jake is currently doing at final assembly by 'ordering' a big batch of STRs," concluded Phil.

"Correct. With your current setup, the only way you can deliver large orders at a single go from final assembly is —"

"By carrying huge inventory in your shelves!" I exclaimed, pleased I could catch on.

"Exactly. Which is why you have so much gold piling up in the value stream before the final assembly conveyor."

"You're saying that we are going to have to mix and match the orders going onto the conveyor to avoid the inventory build-up of mechanisms?" Phil exclaimed. "Yikes! That's not going to be an easy one."

"No joke!" said Amy with a dark look.

"Yep," said my father, making a face at the watered-down coffee. The rundown mall coffee shop was filling up with a motley crowd of families and workmen, surrounding us with their noise and chatter, but Dad just continued, undisturbed.

"In TPS, they call it *heijunka*, which translates as leveling."

"How is it done?"

"Well, it really depends on customer demand. At the moment, what does your demand look like?"

"With the catch up in STRs? We're trying to produce 100 STRs a week, about 55 QST-1s, about 50 QST-2s, and no more than 20 DGs in a week."

"What about your conveyor? What's its daily capacity?"

"If we push it, we can build 50 finished units a day on that thing," Phil replied.

Dad scribbled on a napkin and asked, "So the conveyor runs like this:

Monday: 50 STR.

Tuesday: 50 STR.

Wednesday: 50 QST-1.

Thursday: five QST-1 and 45 QST-2.

Friday: five QST-2 and 20 DG, with Friday taking on the backlog you've accumulated during the week because of various problems slowing or stopping the line."

"It's usually much worse than that," said Phil. "We tend to start slipping by Wednesday and often work all day Friday, plus overtime, but that's about how we plan it."

"Since an STR takes four mechanisms, we're stockpiling 80 STR mechanisms a day from Wednesday to Friday," pointed out Amy. "That's 240 WIP of mechanisms! Not counting the other mechanism types."

"Sure, your conveyor is consuming 200 mechanisms on Monday, while you push only 80 out of mechanism assembly, so you need a stock of 120 at least on Monday morning. Final assembly takes another 200 on Tuesday, and you produced only 80 again. So to keep from starving final assembly your Monday morning stock needs to be 240 parts, which is exactly what you churn out from Wednesday to Friday."

"In fact," Amy broke in, "the conveyor operators encounter more problems than we do, so they actually don't complete the whole 50 units on Monday, which gives mechanisms some leeway," she muttered. "And we can also do overtime with mechanisms."

"Slow down," Dad said, holding up his hand. "These details are critical, but let's focus on one important principle. Barring variation, at the moment, you're still pushing your production onto the conveyor. It should be the other way round. The conveyor's schedule should trigger how much you produce, like the supermarket."

"I understand the principle," muttered Phil, "at least, I think I do. But how do we actually schedule the conveyor?"

"Customer demand," Dad answered. "Figure it out."

"Okay, we've got our weekly plan, which we can get from our monthly plan," mused Phil.

"Takt time!" Amy exclaimed with another intuitive leap.

"Demand always comes back to takt time, right?"

Dad just smiled and grabbed another napkin. "Look at it this way:

Product	Weekly demand	Daily demand	Takt time based on 450 min./day
STR	100	20	22.5 min.
QST–1	55	11	40.9 min.
QST–2	50	10	45 min.
DG	20	4	112.5 min.
Total	225	45	10 min.

Basically, from these numbers, it's apparent that you've got to get one completed unit off the conveyor every 10 minutes to satisfy your overall demand."

"Yeah, that totals up to 45 a day, and 225 a week. I'm happy with that," said Phil.

"Now, let's imagine a schedule with 10-minute slots:

Time	10 min.	10 min.	10 min.	10 min.	10 min.	10 min.	10 min.	10 min.	10 min.	10 min.	10 min.
Conveyor											

"What's the longest takt item we have?"

"DGs, of course," answered Amy. "We've got to come up with one of those every 112 minutes."

"Okay, so let's schedule them in the 100-minute time slot:

Time	10 min.	10 min.	10 min.	10 min.	10 min.	10 min.	10 min.	10 min.	10 min.	10 min.	10 min.
Conveyor										DG	

"Now, what's the next slowest?"

"QST-2, one every 45 minutes."

"Fine, here:

Time	10 min.	10 min.	10 min.	10 min.	10 min.	10 min.	10 min.	10 min.	10 min.	10 min.	10 min.
Conveyor				QST-2				QST-2	DG		

"I get it!" exclaimed Amy. "Now we can slot in the QST-1 every 41 minutes."

Time	10 min.	10 min.	10 min.	10 min.	10 min.	10 min.	10 min.	10 min.	10 min.	10 min.	10 min.
Conveyor			QST-1	QST-2			QST-1	QST-2		DG	

"And the rest will be STRs!" Phil announced.

Time	10 min.	10 min.	10 min.	10 min.	10 min.	10 min.	10 min.	10 min.	10 min.	10 min.	10 min.
Conveyor	STR	STR	QST-1	QST-2	STR	STR	QST-1	QST-2	STR	DG	STR

"Something like this," agreed Dad, "but you can level your build sequence even further if you want to:

Time	10 min.	10 min.	10 min.	10 min.	10 min.	10 min.	10 min.	10 min.	10 min.	10 min.	10 min.
Conveyor	STR	QST-1	STR	QST-2	STR	QST-1	STR	QST-2	STR	DG	STR

"And so on. The idea is to have the most leveled sequence possible, within the takt time by product. This way we have an STR available every 20 minutes."

"Good God!" swore Phil, rubbing his face. "This is going to take some thinking about."

"I don't know," said Amy. "It's pretty straightforward. You just level the flow of finished units, so you can pull steadily on the mechanism parts. It would help with your mountain of cabinet parts coming off the stamping press too!"

"Fine. Do you feel up to going to Jake with something like this?" Phil said peevishly.

"Uh-oh. Not me. Your turn," she replied.

"Aren't we assuming there won't be any variations in our weekly schedule?" asked Philip.

"Good point," answered Dad. "Yes, we are banking on the fact that since you've got customer orders at least a few weeks in advance, volume is stable over the period, so you're only leveling mix. Actually, the entire takt time device is a leveling tool. We take a level average as a north star, and try to stick as close to it as we can."

Phil was scribbling furious notes, looking doubtful. Amy was tugging at her hair, thinking furiously. I was trying to read the future in the coffee dregs at the bottom of my cup.

"Take it one step at a time," sighed Dad. "At the moment you're filling up these god-awful 20-part racks for the mechanisms, right?"

"That's what you said we should do," Amy complained. "What's wrong with them?"

"Inventory, of course," he snapped back. "But let's keep it like that. Try to get this Jake character to at least level his production enough to make the right mix of each type every day: 20 STR, 11 QST-1, 10 QST-2, 4 DG, for a total of 45. If he produces 20 STR breakers each day, you need to hold 80 mechanisms ready for him. That's four racks, or one day of production in mechanism assembly, and that's not too bad compared with the 12 racks you have right now."

"If he does the 20 STR breakers in one go, he's going to gobble up the 80 mechanisms in, what, three or four hours," calculated Phil, thinking out loud. "It means he needs an inventory of 80, while we produce the 80 for the next day? Right?"

"That's how it works. Overall you will have a maximum of 80 mechanisms in the flow," nodded Dad.

"Now, what you're saying is that if he further levels production to make one STR every 20 minutes throughout the day, we have the time to make the four mechanisms needed," Phil continued. "So we won't have more than one rack of four mechanisms in inventory in final assembly."

"That's the idea," agreed Dad, ordering another round of coffees. "A real one, please!" he growled at the waitress, who simply ignored him.

"And in this way, we can produce only what he consumes. The supermarket," continued Phil. "It's brilliant."

"Easy to say," chipped in Amy, uncertainly. "But the practicalities are daunting."

"Never mind that for the moment," said Dad. "Moving from producing every part every week to every part every day is already a huge leap forward, and it will have a dramatic impact on your WIP. The important thing to understand is that the inventory you hold between your processes can't be reduced unless you understand the link between the customer's behavior and the supplier's constraints. The inventory is created by the differences in flow between the two processes. If you level the final assembly, you can pull constantly on the supplying process without needing too much inventory."

"Yeah," doubted Amy. "As long as you've got neither variation nor downtime. This means being incredibly precise in our capacity to produce finished units at takt time."

"It is in any case," growled Dad. "But you just don't see it. Variation is hidden in uncontrolled inventory. Now, obviously, we do need some buffers in the system until you can do it properly, but if you can't tackle this issue, you will absolutely continue to carry the amount of inventory you've got at the moment. It's physics."

"No it's not," retorted Phil. "I've learned my lesson. It's all about people. Now we're going to have to make them see the light. Oh boy!"

Which earned a sudden clap of full-throated laughter from Amy.

"Okay," said Phil finally, flicking back through the pages of his notebook. "I hear what you're saying. I also understand why you object to Amy and Gloria's solution of a parallel line for STR mechanism assembly, although I must point out that you did say it was easier to improve productivity by pulling people out of an existing line than by getting the same amount of people to produce more."

Dad glared at him, but kept his composure.

"What you're now saying is that reducing the variation in the operator's cycle is not enough. We also need to level the mix at the conveyor?"

"Yes, heijunka. Correct. Mechanism inventory will go down by leveling final assembly alone. But then you need to deal with implications further upstream with stamping as well, where you probably have batches and lot sizes which need to be looked at, as well as the purchased parts inventory which needs to be resized and delivered to the line according to takt time!"

"*And* do some work on the operator cycles," Amy added, "because right now the conveyor is *not* coping with the extra STR production."

"Okay. You can do that."

"No, I can't, unless you square it with that jerk, Jake Rogers."

"Okay, okay!" repeated Phil irritably, taking a deep breath. "I'll see what I can do. My point is that we should know how to do that, and we have people from the DG mechanism who could help."

"Go on, son, you're doing fine," said Dad somewhat patronizingly.

"The point I wanted to get at," said Phil slowly, "is takt time. If I understand you correctly, that's the key, okay?"

"Sure is," grunted Dad.

"So, if we assume a completely stable daily demand of 20 STRs, 11 QST-1s, 10 QST-2s, and four DGs, that's 45 finished units to produce each day, right? So takt time is 450 minutes divided by 45. That's 10 minutes."

"Let's say that if all goes well you can produce this in a normal day," agreed Dad.

"Now, there are four mechanisms per STR breaker and QST-1, three per QST-2 breaker, and one per DG breaker. This means that if we were flowing perfectly, we have to come up with four STR mechanisms every 22 minutes, four QST-1s and three QST-2s every 21 minutes, and one DG mechanism every couple of hours."

"An exotic," agreed Dad.

"Now, you're also suggesting it makes sense to actually have only two mechanism lines working at a five-minute takt time, one producing STR mechanisms, and the other producing both QST-1 and QST-2?"

"We've been through this before! Of course it would," said Dad impatiently. "By shortening the takt time and the operators' cycle, you're also giving yourself a lot of room for further improvement."

Amy rolled her eyes, but kept quiet.

"I've got four operators on one STR mechanism line," said Phil, "four on the other, four on the QST mechanism line, and five on the DG/QST line. That's a total of 17 people. If I assume a working content of 40 minutes for both the STR mechanism and the QST, although the latter has a simpler design, I need eight people working on a single STR line."

"Assuming they'll agree to work shorter operations," Amy reminded him.

"Yeah. And I need to produce 74 QST mechanisms a day, so a takt time of, say, six minutes. So seven people for a QST line should do it as well."

"Now," continued Phil, "I don't actually need a line for the DG. All I need is one guy who builds the mechanism from start to finish four times a day."

"What you need is to get rid of the whole DG product line," retorted my father.

"I'm working on it, okay? But it's not that easy. We've made commitments. Anyhow, that's one guy. So I still have two people left who can be assigned to the final assembly line to beef it up if they have trouble keeping up."

"If it works, this is what it looks like, from when we started," said Amy, drawing a matrix:

		Before	After
STR mechanism	Parts	40/day	80/day
	People	6	8
QST-1, QST-2 and DG mechanisms	Parts	70/day	78/day
	People	12	7 + 1

"Well, we're certainly boosting direct productivity."

"That's not the point, Philip. Don't lose your focus. The issue is that you have delivered more STRs to customers for cash without increasing your costs. That's the whole point: getting cash in."

"Yes, as well as avoiding late-delivery penalties so we collect all the cash we were expecting."

"Your next challenge is not so much productivity but the inventories between the processes, although the conveyor line has to be able to deliver the finished units. Which means drawing a final assembly plan which levels the flow."

"Wait a minute," said Amy as my father was waving for the check. "I understand all this theory, but I need to be clear on how to apply it for real. You're saying that if I move to two lines as opposed to four, I'll have productivity gains because the operator cycle will be that much shorter, and so it will be easier to reduce variation, correct?"

"Yep. However, if you feel that there'll be too much resistance, this can wait until you've done more kaizen."

What? Give from the old man? Pinch me.

"Now, you're also saying," completed Phil, "that we need to smooth the build sequence on the conveyor line by alternating models. This will smooth the pull of mechanisms from the market and will reduce the in-process inventory."

"But, in practice," jumped in Amy, "how do we implement the supermarket logic? You keep saying you dislike the racks. What do you suggest instead?"

"I don't know, you tell me."

They both looked at him thoughtfully.

"Come on, Amy, you were on the right track. You compared the cashier with the conveyor final assembly line. What does that mean for the product?"

"The product is the consumer's basket! Yes, of course. And you've got infinite variety since no two baskets are the same."

"And?"

"Well, let's consider that each operator on the conveyor is a shopper. And they receive a supply of mechanisms, ideally, in containers with just the number of mechanisms necessary for one breaker. That'd mean four for an STR."

"Special containers?"

"She's right, Philip. You need to start thinking about dedicated, small containers, each with the right number of mechanisms. Imagine a plastic box with a partition for each mechanism."

"What about the cost of it?"

My father just shrugged.

"Logistics is going to freak."

"Go on, Amy."

"If we follow through, the boxes should be placed on shelves right next to the operators working at the conveyor, so that when they need the mechanisms for the next unit they just go and take them from a supermarket aisle."

"Excellent, that's exactly right," Dad said, with the pleased smile of a doting uncle. "Alongside all the other parts they need to assemble the finished unit on the conveyor."

"But how? I mean, in practice?"

"Rollers, Amy. Rollers. Imagine racks with rollers. Flow racks. The mechanism lines must assemble and pack them by boxes of four."

"Or three according to the product," interjected Phil.

"Or three, and when they've finished a box they put it on a rolling channel that feeds right into the conveyor area, so that the conveyor operators can pick and choose what they need according to their program."

"Wow. And all parts should arrive to them like this?"

"Indeed. They can either arrive directly, because the cell is right there behind them, or be placed in the rack by logistics from a shop. In this case, since we want to reduce the mechanism inventory, I'd recommend having a direct link from the mechanism assembly to the conveyor, so we eliminate stocks and movement."

"That means moving the mechanism lines again!" she exclaimed.

"So?" asked Dad superciliously.

"Oh, nothing. Kaizen-time again, I guess."

"But it's brilliant," added Phil suddenly. "It flows. I get your point. Of course!"

"Think about the gold, Philip. Think about the gold."

"Awesome."

"Okay, gentlemen," said Amy forcefully, "let's get to it."

"Hey, we need to think about this first," blurted out Phil, and then looked around so guiltily for fear of procrastination that we all laughed.

I was away for a couple of weeks on a research project on the East Coast, and rang Phil on the evening of my return. I had not expected to get so involved with the high drama at the factory, and now here I was impatient to find out how events were shaping up.

"Full, all-out war, brother, I'm telling you!"

"What do you mean?"

"Well, the conveyor supervisor, Jake Rogers, said there was no way he was going to hear how to run his assembly line from a girl."

"No kidding?"

"For real. We were putting his people under tremendous pressure already and that crackpot idea of alternating types of breakers on the conveyor line would never work. We'd have endless quality problems and so on. Repetition was what made the job easier for the operators and that was that."

"He probably has a point."

"No doubt, but considering the inventory it creates upstream, a very expensive point. In any case, I'm sure the guys would adapt eventually since they already assemble all four types of breakers. So I pushed for a compromise, but no give!"

"So, what happened?"

"I told Jake it would be that way, or else."

"You threatened to fire him?" I asked, astounded.

"Yeah. He immediately asked what kind of package I would be offering for him to leave without a fuss."

"What?"

"Hey, life is full of surprises. So I passed the hot potato to Matt, and adios Jake Rogers. He was gone by the end of the week."

"But I thought you were strapped for cash."

"Yeah, well, Matt negotiated some sort of deal which spreads the money we're coughing up over some time. The guy was close to retiring, and I think he'd really had enough. Or had other plans. Hell, who knows?"

"What did you do then?"

"Listen to this," he answered gleefully. "Gloria and Amy picked a new team leader, one of the operators on the final assembly line."

"You didn't! Someone from the ranks without a fancy education?"

"You bet. One of the things we are learning is that some people catch on to these new methods quickly and really want to make it happen. That's what's important and Gloria and Amy knew whom to pick right away. So Ester Ramirez, the new supervisor, has already wrangled a compromise out of the final assembly team, and they're doing what your dad suggested. They are making every product every day, although they are still all bunched together."

"Meaning?"

"20 STRs in a row, then 11 QST-1s, then 10 QST-2s, then the DGs."

"And does that help with the inventory?"

"Are you kidding? It's spectacular. Mechanism WIP has visibly fallen. Not as much as if we could completely level final assembly, but it's still day and night. The good thing is that we now have a new STR-X product coming online, and I think this makes some room to absorb it."

"Amy must be pleased!"

"Yeah. You know how she is, she's pushing the design guys to straighten out rework problems on the new QST line. We're still up to our necks, but I think it's looking good. She asked about you, by the way."

"About me?" What do you know?

"No reckoning for some people's tastes," he snickered.

"Get lost! In fact, I'm phoning to tell you my Dad is inviting Charlene and you to dinner Saturday night. He's got one of his cronies coming, a business school professor who specialized in lean production and all this just-in-time stuff, and he thought you'd be interested to meet him and talk things over."

"Interested?" answered Phil excitedly. "You bet I am. Let me see if Charly has anything planned. I'd love to come."

"Good, I'll tell Dad."

"And, ah, do you want me to bring Amy along?" he chuckled.

Dad's invitation had surprised me, and I did expect a lot of shop talk. Indeed, as I arrived, Phil was already in an animated discussion with a small rotund man with the thick, square glasses, tweed jacket, and the general manner of an academic. Stephen MacAllister was a business school professor somewhere in Michigan, and a specialist in what he called lean production. I had always thought of these ideas and phrases to be elements of what Dad called the Toyota Production System — but apparently here in the States, these principles, pioneered by Toyota after World War II, and which, in all fairness, had roots in the work of Henry Ford and others, fell under the term of lean production.

Dad had met Stephen during his first visit to Japan as part of a study group, and they had stayed friends ever since. MacAllister had researched just-in-time systems from an academic perspective while my Dad was conducting his own field work. They'd exchanged views and tips for most of their careers and, put together, probably knew more about lean production than anyone in their right mind would ever wish to. Steve accepted consultancy assignments on occasion, which had brought him to town. He usually came to dinner when he was around, to the dismay of my mother, who had to cope with endless discussions about production systems. Since Stephen was coming tonight, Dad thought that it would be a good opportunity to introduce him to Phil, which led to our impromptu dinner party.

"Do you remember the first time we went to Japan?" asked Steve, comfortably ensconced in his armchair, swirling his brandy. He was bald, paunchy, and tweedy — definitely an academic (I'm nothing like that, I swear). Unexpectedly, we had managed to go through a pleasant dinner without even touching upon production systems. As it happened, my mother and Charlene got on like a house on fire, and most of the dinner conversation revolved around the plight of women in the workplace, and then moved on animatedly to Mother's film critique business. Charly certainly seemed in better spirits, and Phil seemed quite relaxed with her, so I surmised things were better between the two of them.

After we finished our desserts, mother and Charlene drifted off to the TV room, discussing some new Middle Eastern movie about women under the veil. It was time for the veterans to reminisce.

"Glory days!" Dad agreed with a fond smile.

"You remember those French engineers, who upon seeing kanban cards for the first time told us that 'these Japanese were not very smart: they could have computerized their kanban card system in no time!'"

"Be fair, Steve, we didn't know any better either."

"You're right. Those were the days!"

"D'you remember when I first got confronted with this lean approach?" reminisced my father, pouring himself a generous ration of the brandy Stephen had brought.

"Yes," laughed MacAllister. "They might want to hear this."

"I first got exposed to the Toyota system when I was running a parts plant for a large automotive supplier. Toyota and GM were operating a joint venture around here, and headquarters had decided we should supply them. As a result, they chose my site as a pilot, and I was to become part of the Toyota Supplier Development program.

"Now, the first thing the Toyota advisers say as they walk into my plant is that my parts bins are too large. They want them cut in half! 'Why on earth would you want to make the parts bin smaller?' I protested. 'It will only mean someone will have to do the trip twice to move the same amount of parts, correct?'

"And then they tell me to create a dedicated spot on our shipping bay, and that we should deliver finished parts to it every two hours, although they would only come and pick up the shipment once every two weeks! 'D'you want me to pretend you're picking parts up every two hours although you're only coming every other day?' I asked.

"'Yes,' they said. Furthermore, since I was going to produce two parts on the line reserved for them, they wanted me to work harder at reducing my tool changeover times. For more production? 'Oh no,' they say, 'to do more changeovers!' At this point I was ready to kick the whole bunch of raving loonies out of my plant."

"I can see why you sympathized with poor Dave," I laughed.

"Correct me if I'm wrong," asked Phil studiously. "But I think I understand the bit about more tool changes. That's what you've been telling us, it's about leveling, right? More tool changeovers means running the parts in smaller amounts more frequently."

"Smaller batches," agreed Steve, nodding wisely.

"Except that you can do that on your conveyor without having the hassle of changing tools, which is a real pain as you'll discover when you get to reducing batch sizes on your presses!" grumbled Dad.

"But I still don't understand how that makes you more efficient overall," I wondered. "Why would smaller batches lead you to eliminate waste?"

"Ah," sighed MacAllister. "Deep question. The classic Toyota analogy is the lake and the rocks. Inventory, they say, is the level of water in the lake. The rocks are the inefficiencies. When the water is high, it hides the rocks, so you can function at a high level of inventory with many inefficiencies. But it's wasteful. Not cost-effective. If you reduce the water in the lake, however, the rocks will start to surface and you will need to solve these problems to continue producing — to sail your boat safely. In doing so, you're getting more and more efficient because you're eliminating waste."

"I've heard this before," agreed Phil, "but it sounds really theoretical. I mean, I see the point, but, in practice ..."

"Um, yes, well," muttered the professor, quite professorially. "It is central to understanding lean though. You see, most people are so impressed with the image of a conveyor line that they miss Ford's real achievement. When he started building cars, every part off a machine had to be reworked by a fitter to be assembled with other parts. Through strenuous work on technology, Ford eliminated the need for fitters, which opened the way for the assembly line."

"Standardization of parts," explained Phil, back on his favorite subject. "But how does that relate to smaller batches?"

"Indeed. The point is, you see, that Ford's so-called mass-production system is not incompatible with lean at all — it's just a special case. You work flow with a single product and dedicated machines. One model, one color, no options, and so on. Ford's personal dream was the perfect car for farmers, no frills."

"They can have any car they like as long as it's a black Model T."

"Absolutely correct. Now, Toyota, in its early days, did not have this luxury. So they took Ford's assembly system, and developed the general case, taking variety into account," noted MacAllister.

"I'm sorry," complained Phil, shaking his head. "I still don't follow you. Mike's right. How does this relate to waste reduction?"

"All right, here it is, this is the secret of the TPS masters. Do you have a piece of paper?" asked MacAllister as he looked around.

I had to laugh at Phil's dismayed expression when he realized he had not carried the ubiquitous notebook to the dinner table, and, out of the greatness of my heart, I went to fetch pen and paper in the kitchen.

"Thanks, Mike. Let me remember how it goes," continued MacAllister. "Imagine you have one single machine that produces three products, like squares, circles, and triangles."

"Listen up," said Dad. "You'll never understand pull if you don't get this. This is the first thing my own sensei taught me along with the lake and the rocks, and for some reason, few people ever hear about it."

Phil stared intently at MacAllister's pad, eager to discover the hidden secrets of the lean masters.

"Now, these three parts always have to be delivered together. Imagine that you're supplying an OEM, and the three parts go into the same vehicle, but they come from one single machine, not three separate dedicated machines. Unfortunately, with a long changeover time, you're batching, like this:

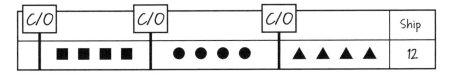

"At the end of the day, you're shipping all 12 parts, in four sets of square, circle, and then triangle. In order to ship, you need to hold 12 parts in stock. Now how can we reduce the stock?"

"That's easy!" exclaimed Phil. "Reduce the batch size."

"All right, let's double the changeovers:

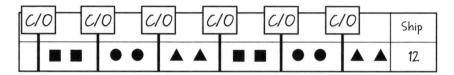

"That's all well and good, but we've not reduced the inventory," said MacAllister.

"What do you mean?" I asked, puzzled. I thought I had figured out that if you reduce the batch size, you reduce the stock.

"We haven't reduced inventory. We're still holding 12 parts in order to ship."

"Damn," swore Phil with sudden insight. "Of course. To reduce the parts we hold, we also have to double the deliveries."

"Exactly," MacAllister replied, "so let's do it."

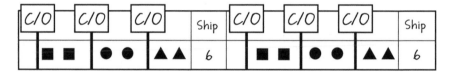

"All the way to single-piece flow," pursued Phil excitedly. "But I have to double the deliveries again if I want to see the benefit?"

"Yes," said MacAllister, who again drew:

	Ship		Ship		Ship		Ship
■ ● ▲	3	■ ● ▲	3	■ ● ▲	3	■ ● ▲	3

"But do you see the implications?"

"Of course, this is why even though you had only a weekly shipment to Toyota, they asked you to simulate regular pulls. This is the only way to reduce the WIP stock. Brilliant."

"There's more to it than that!" exclaimed MacAllister, red-cheeked and bright-eyed. Boy, was he into his own argument. "Don't you see it? What would happen if you were back to your long batches, but still increased the shipments? Watch, we start with:

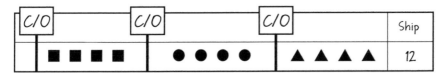

C/O	C/O	C/O	Ship
■ ■ ■ ■	● ● ● ●	▲ ▲ ▲ ▲	12

"So let's double the shipments, and include a buffer of stocked parts to be able to complete the shipments without having produced the exact demand:

	C/O		Ship	C/O		Ship
Produce	■ ■ ■ ■	● ●		● ●	▲ ▲ ▲ ▲	
Buffer	▲ ▲		6	■ ■		6

"What you're saying is that if I still produce with batches of four, but hold two in stock, I can still ship two sets of square, circle, and triangle in the morning, and two more sets in the afternoon?" cried Phil, bewildered.

"Yes, yes, look, in the morning, you're producing two squares more than you need for shipping. However, you'll need them both in the afternoon where you're not producing squares."

"And we've reduced inventory, because now we only need to hold eight parts total to be able to ship, rather than 12," said Phil.

"Absolutely correct," confirmed MacAllister. "Similarly, in the afternoon, you're using the extra squares to ship, and producing two extra triangles, which you will need to ship in the next morning shift. And you can go further, we can double shipments again."

181

C/O	Ship	C/O	Ship	C/O	Ship		Ship
Produce ■ ■ ■		■ ● ●		● ● ▲		▲ ▲ ▲	
Buffer ● ▲ ▲	3	■ ■ ▲	3	■ ■ ●	3	■ ● ●	3

"I think I got it," said Phil excitedly. "Now, we can still ship one set of square, circle, and triangle at each shipment, but we've got to hold six parts total in inventory. Now, let me try it with both more changeovers — let's say, six — and four shipments a day. I'd need a buffer in any case. Here goes:

C/O	C/O	Ship	C/O	Ship	C/O	C/O	Ship	C/O	Ship
Produce ■ ■	●		● ▲ ▲		■ ■	●		● ▲ ▲	
Buffer	▲	3	■	3	▲		3	■	3

"So, I can deliver a set of square, circle, and triangle four times a day with only four pieces in stock at any one time. Mind-blowing!" exclaimed Phil.

"Pretty good, um? Here's the breakdown:"

	Pieces in Stock Based on Deliveries per Day		
Changeovers	1 delivery	2 deliveries	4 deliveries
3	12	8	6
6	12	6	4
12	12	6	3

The conversation moved on to other matters, while Phil was poring intently over the piece of paper, and I swear you could hear his mental cogs turning. He redrew MacAllister's demonstration carefully, and suddenly said, "Okay, I understand pull. With this, we reduce inventory. But how is this going to help with waste reduction and getting costs down?"

My father and MacAllister stared at him, and shared an amused, tolerant smile.

"It's about rigor and discipline," said the professor. "Look, if you've got the entire day to ship, you can afford to lose some time in the morning with a problem or a breakdown, and then try to catch up before the evening shipment. We've already established that this sort of variation is precisely what hides all sorts of wasteful operations. But now, if you have to ship every two hours, you've got to solve problems much quicker, because —"

"I've got less stock!" exclaimed Phil, with an appreciative whistle. "The lake and the rocks!"

"Let me put it this way," jumped in Dad. "A few years ago, one of the factories in which we had implemented just-in-time was sold to another group. When the new management came in, they couldn't believe the pain we were putting ourselves through. We had very short production runs, which meant many tool changes, which they thought was silly because we were losing valuable production time. We used small plastic containers for parts, which was silly because we had materials handlers running back and forth carrying these small containers where it would have been more effective to take away one huge load at a time, and so on. So they went back to traditional 'economical' large batches.

"Now, this plant runs in three shifts. When we had a just-in-time system in place, if a machine had a problem during the night, the team leader called the production manager. Awakened at 2 a.m., he'd ask how much finished parts inventory they had ahead of themselves. Three hours, tops, they answered. So he'd kiss his wife good-bye, and in the middle on the night would drive to the plant to fix the problem, and problems got fixed! Now, with the large batch system, if they wake up the production manager because of a machine problem in the middle of the night, and he asks how much inventory they have, they'll answer about two or three days. So he asks, 'What the heck did you wake me up for? I'll be down there in the morning.'

"And so," Dad concluded, "the plant goes back to being lazy and fat."

"You make it sound so easy," I wondered. "Can people actually bear that kind of pressure?"

"My son the psychologist," snorted Dad. "But, I'll confess that the first time my own sensei explained this, it's exactly what I said: you can't run a production system like that, I argued. It's far too precise and demanding!

"'Very good!' my master replied. 'Very good. Now you understand the lake and the rocks,' and he draws the hateful lake as the batch size and the rocks as the inefficiencies, which are hidden by the inventory."

Which made MacAllister laugh, in a "good old days" kind of way.

"I remember an American manager working for a Toyota plant," he chuckled, "who told me the story of the three managers, a Frenchman, a Japanese, and an American who are building a production unit in Peru. They get taken hostage by guerrillas who tell them that since they are agents of capitalistic world domination through globalization, they will be shot. But since the guerrillas respect freedom of speech, they're allowed a last word. The Frenchman cries, '*Vive la France!*' and then is shot dead. The Japanese manager comes next and says, 'I'd like to talk to you about the lake and the rocks,' at which moment the American manager jumps forward and rips open his shirt, facing the guns, yelling, 'If I must hear about the lake and the rocks one more time, shoot me first!'"

"I'm the one," hooted my father in sudden peal of laughter. "That's me. If I have to hear one more time about the lake and the rocks, shoot me first. You've never told me that one before!"

"Now, you're taking it out on us, right, Dad?" I teased, still smarting from the "psychologist" remark. "So, it's all about solving problems as they appear."

"Indeed," agreed MacAllister. "There is a tendency outside of

Toyota to turn lean into a program, you know, a recipe, with all plants having to follow set and rigid steps. Of course, it never works. Lean is about developing people with a pragmatic attitude to resolving problems as they appear."

"First as a countermeasure," nodded Dad, "and then as root-cause problem solving."

"It's pretty impressive," muttered Phil. "I must say I find it somewhat awe-inspiring, not to mention overwhelming."

"It shouldn't be, at the end, it's all about —"

"People, yes. Come on guys, enough!" I complained. "We'd better join the ladies before we get into serious trouble."

"So, Bob," said Phil, standing over the Porsche's door as Charlene was getting into the car. "Thanks again for everything. If I understand Steve correctly, I now have to organize people running around that factory with small boxes of parts all the time, right?"

"Something like that, son. You also have to understand a lot more about pulling. Tell you what: when you've digested all of this, why don't you pop around the Yacht Club and we'll see where to take it."

Great, I thought. More weekends on heijunka and takt time.

"And bring that bright girl along," said Dad with a wink!

"What girl?" I heard Charlene ask Phil as he squeezed his bulk into his ridiculous orange roadster.

Way to go, Dad!

With one thing and another, we didn't get together until a few weeks later. I arrived late that morning, fresh from the barber. They were lounging over brunch on the Yacht Club deck. It was a misty morning, with a chill in the air, and from up here we could barely see the ocean. The harbor fills the end of a deep creek, and the pines on the other side faded in the mist like an ancient Chinese silk painting.

"Mickey! I see you've finally got rid of that damnable beard!"

"Yes, you look younger like this," giggled Amy. "Less serious."

"I'm on a sabbatical. No students to impress with my age and wisdom."

"We can tell you now, buddy," chipped in Philip. "It never looked good on you, only scruffy."

"Now he tells me. Have I come all this way to discuss facial hair?"

"We're going over the squares, circles, and triangles exercise again."

"Good luck!" I told him sitting down, glancing at the paper napkin he held on the table, crisscrossed with squares and circles. He was fumbling with his explanation to Amy, under the amused supervision of my father, who seemed to be enjoying his traditional breakfast. My mother would have had something to say about all that bacon and eggs if she'd been here!

"Oh, I get the idea," she said, "smaller batches, more frequent deliveries, less inventory. No sweat."

"Simple as pie," agreed Dad with a smile. I could tell he was enjoying himself, which came as something of a surprise.

"We need to work that out in practice," Phil said, with a worried frown. "Now that we're starting the new STR-X production."

"STR-X?"

"Yeah, we've finally worked our way through the backlog of STRs for our main customer, so they're asking us to slow down and stick to the original 50 a week, which we can now deliver. They've got a truck coming round to pick up 10 STRs daily. Fortunately, we've finally ironed out the kinks in the new STR-X breaker. It uses the same STR core capsules, but three mechanisms instead of four, so the mechanisms are slightly different. It's not as powerful as the STR, but it's cheaper and fine for certain applications. We've had a prospect interested in it for a while, but the development guys couldn't get the mechanism to work reliably."

"Hah!" huffed Amy. She didn't like the development team much.

"We've finally fixed that," pursued Phil with an aggrieved look. "I hope. And Matt clinched a deal for 40 STR-Xs a week with the customer. So we're going ahead with this."

"How are you building them?"

"At the moment, we've got Gloria and the veterans we've put in charge of building the DGs assembling them one at a time, so that we understand how the work flows. Originally, we wanted to create a special STR-X line, but Amy's been arguing to integrate it in the current STR production."

"Hey, I'm just following the logic," Amy said. "We're down to two lines right now, one that does STR mechanisms all day, and the other which alternates between QST-1 and QST-2, which they're getting the hang of — the two products are not too different."

"How do you work that out?"

"Well," Phil replied to Dad, "I've been working on this leveling concept of yours. I'm getting quite a lot of resistance from Gloria, who says it just confuses the operators if they have to switch from QST-1 to QST-2 all the time. At the moment, we've broken down the week demand in days, so 11 QST-1 and 10 QST-2, which amounts to 74 mechanisms to build per day, roughly a takt time of six minutes. At the moment, they've agreed to produce QST-1s in the morning and QST-2s in the afternoon."

"You're producing each product within the shift then, which is a good start," said Dad. "But, you could level more!"

"I know what you're saying," answered Amy. "At the extreme, I could be alternating a QST-1 mechanism with a QST-2, but I can't seem to make enough of a case to convince them!"

"How long does it take them to switch from one to the other?"

"At the moment, about 10 minutes. They've got jigs to replace and parts to move around, but I'm sure they could reduce it to almost nothing."

"How?" I wondered, curious. This relentless drive for improvement always bothered me, somehow. I'd always assumed that the real world had to have limits sooner or later.

"We could have all the parts needed for both QST-1 and QST-2 right there on the workstation. I haven't achieved that yet because it would mean even smaller containers, but at the moment they have to replace the QST-1 parts containers with QST-2 parts containers to switch production, which is time-consuming and, yes —" she raised her hands with a smile to ward off Dad's objection, "wasteful."

"Wasn't going to say anything, miss," Dad said with a quick grin.

"I'm not confident about forcing the issue just quite yet," she concluded. "Should I?"

"Not necessarily," answered Dad, helping himself to another pancake and liberally spreading maple syrup over it. "But you're going to have to do it at some point."

"I understand the general idea," muttered Phil, trying to get the waitress' attention for a coffee refill, "but in our specific case, I'm not sure why."

"The point is that the longer your production run is, if you're using the same resources for another product, you need to stock-up the other products because you'll be withdrawing them eventually. This is typically waste of overproduction: producing too much or too soon."

"And if the withdrawal is not regular, we need even bigger inventories to make sure that we haven't got missing parts," said Amy with a low, slow whistle. "No wonder we've got parts coming out of our ears."

"You got it. All the MRP does is apply a magical formula to calculate when an upstream activity needs to produce another batch on top of what's in stock and avoid missing parts. So if you help yourself to huge, unpredictable quantities in your stock, the MRP is going to be on an erratic replenishment orders, and you end up with massive inventories."

"A multiplier," concluded Phil.

"Yes, Philip. A variation multiplier."

"I hear what you're saying," Phil said after a long silence while they were both trying to work out the implications. "But that doesn't answer the changeover problem. Yes, I know you're going to tell us to reduce the changeover time and all, that's still a problem right now."

"Stop assuming I'm going to say this, or that," grumbled Dad. "I was about to acknowledge that changeover time has to be taken into account. The Toyota rule is to invest 10% of production time in flexibility."

"Meaning production changes?" checked Amy.

"Yes, say 10% of your available time goes to changeovers. The faster they are, the more of them you can make until you reach zero changeover time and one-piece flow." He let that settle, before continuing, "Which means that your production batch size is going to be 10 times the amount you make during the time needed for a changeover. Arguably, of course, you'd want your changeover time down to close to a minute, so you'd spend a lot less time on changeovers, but we can use this rule of thumb to start with before we go into more complex calculations."

"Why should the batch be 10 times the changeover time?"

"In actual fact, there's some sort of formula," answered Dad, pulling a face and grabbing Phil's notebook. "Here: you take all the available production time during an interval (say a week), and subtract from that all the required run time (parts cycle time multiplied by average demand). The remaining time (ignoring downtime and scrap) is available for changeovers. As a rule of thumb, you want about 10–15% of your available time going to changeovers. This leads you to far more changeovers than an EOQ calculation. It reduces inventory and puts the onus on the operators to reduce changeover time further and increase availability on the machine."

"Right," said Amy, shaking her head dubiously. "So, in our case, 10 times 10 minutes, we should have production runs of 100 minutes? That's 14 mechanisms apiece. 14 QST-1, then 14 QST-2, and so on?"

"Precisely. You'll have the minimal inventory while not wasting too much time in changeovers. Now, if your production changeover time came down to five minutes ..."

"We'd be halving our batch!" she exclaimed.

"Exactly. Which also means reducing your overall QST inventory."

"It's all completely theoretical in any case," sighed Phil, staring at Dad's scribbles on his pad, "since the downstream customer, the conveyor, is not leveled by a far cry."

"Not yet," replied Amy with a thin, determined smile.

"Yeah, dream on. Imagine what we need to explain to —"

"Exactly, Philip," cut in Dad. "That's your challenge. The next step is to get a real pull system in place."

"How can we do this?" protested Phil. "I thought that the whole point of a pull system was to only produce what is being picked up by the customer. But you can't do it in our place, we're delivering to our customers when we please, or when they shout loud enough. On top of it, you never quite know when they want the parts. Most of them ask us to keep a consignment stock so that we carry the inventory for them."

"Well, that's got to change! Remember what the Toyota people had me do? Although their truck came every two weeks to pick up parts, we had to place parts in the shipping lane on a two-hour basis. That's what we have to do now, so we can later put a proper kanban system in place."

"A supermarket for the entire plant, right?" Amy said. "A finished goods supermarket for completed units. We need to designate dedicated locations for each of the products, which we fill up regularly, regardless of when customers actually ask us to deliver. That's what the stock should be, a supermarket aisle."

"Yep. I call it creating a *perfect customer* within the factory. This finished product stock will help us to simulate a regular pull on the entire production system."

"A regular pull, how?"

"Virtual trucks," Dad answered with a wink. "We know that real delivery is not regular, but we still want to pull as levelly as we can from the conveyor. So, we imagine that if our customers *were* perfect, they'd come and pick up parts just-in-time: small quantities on regular schedules, like four times a day. We then end up by splitting our finished goods inventory in two distinct physical locations. In the conveyor area after testing and packing we have half the goods. And we have the other finished goods inventory in a truck preparation area where we build up the real delivery trucks progressively."

"You've lost me there," I complained. "Doesn't that mean more useless movement of crates? Why two locations? Isn't that muda?"

"You're right," chuckled Dad. "It is muda, but in this case we're fighting unevenness, or mura. Oh, come on, don't look at me like that! Let me explain. On the one hand, we can't control exactly when the trucks pick up. On the other, we need to have a smooth pull on the conveyor. So we'll separate the two issues."

"I get it!" cried Amy. "The conveyor supermarket controls the conveyor, so we pull on it regularly and smoothly, and take the crates to the truck preparation areas where we deal with variation in pickup times!"

"Exactly, provided we're not dealing with volume variations as well, but we'll look into that later."

"Which means, in any case," concluded Phil, "that to start with we need to clean out the mess at the shipping dock. We're going to need Dave's help on this one, because he handles it more or less himself."

"Yeah, yeah, before we start knocking Dave again," scolded Dad, coming unexpectedly to Dave's defense, "we'd better be clear about what we want to do here. So, do we all understand about supermarkets?"

"I think so," Amy answered quickly. "The idea is to locate a supermarket of the items finished by each process, at the end of each process, including final assembly. Is that right?"

"How do you see it working for the mechanism line?" I asked, to stay in the game.

"We need some sort of flow rack at the end of the mechanism line, right?" conjectured Phil.

"How would it look?" I continued.

"An aisle for each product, I guess, with small containers," noted Amy. "It would have to work first-in first-out as well. Just like with the burgers, essentially. They have a slide for each kind, and as we supply them from the kitchen they slide down to the counter."

"Good," said Dad with an encouraging tone. "That's a replenishment pull, mind you, and it doesn't work in all cases. But, here, yep, that's the idea. You want a supermarket of finished parts at the end of each process."

"So that the operators of the following process can come and help themselves?" I said in a brave attempt to keep track of it all.

"That would create variation in their work cycle," disagreed Phil.

"Someone comes and picks it up for them, then!"

"I think I'm fine with the mechanism supermarket," said Amy. "And we need to apply the same thinking to a finished-product supermarket at the end of the conveyor."

"Yeah," agreed Phil, "but I'm still fuzzy about this 'truck preparation area.'"

"That's to absorb customer variation!" I announced, beginning to feel that I was putting the pieces together.

"Delivery variation, yes," agreed Dad. "The trick is to try to minimize the impact of variation on our operations. If customers were perfect, they would come and pick up parts regularly, in order to feed their own needs regularly and not create inventory. But they're not, for whatever reasons. And if we don't pick regularly on a supermarket, then eventually upstream production should stop."

"So we need to pick up regularly from the supermarket as if we were the customer," surmised Phil, working it out carefully.

"A *perfect customer*, that's right. The trick is in clearing out an area near shipping where you prepare the truck for the next load. How many trucks leave your factory every week?"

Amy thought this over while Phil was adding it all up.

"All together," he said, "we can simplify things by saying that we see two trucks per day. We still ship 20 STRs to Richmond every day on their milk run, but that's going to go down to 10 next week. Then, once a week we deliver shipments of 20 QST-1s to Sacramento, 15 to Pittsburgh, and 20 more go to Ontario. Twenty QST-2s go next door to Oakland and 30 to Farmington, and the remaining 20 DGs go in single units all over the place. So that's five big shipments for STRs, three for QST-1s, and two for QST-2s. That adds up to about 10 big truck shipments a week, plus occasional pickups of individual DGs."

"Each truck goes to just one customer?"

"Not really. Sacramento, Pittsburgh, and Farmington are facilities of the same firm, and they build equipment using a mix of breakers. In actual fact there are cabinet differences in the QSTs according to who and where we ship them. The STRs only go to Richmond, which comes to pick them up daily with their own transport."

"It's not that simple, Phil," Amy pointed out. "Not all QSTs are actually the same. We have at least three variants of QST-1, and two variants of QST-2."

"Ah, yes, I guess you're right. The mechanisms are the same, but the surrounding cabinet and the instrument panel are customer-specific. We should really talk about QST-1A, QST-1B, and QST-1C, and same for the two QST-2X and QST-2Y. As for DGs, no two are the same. Pittsburgh, for instance, requires some QST-1A, QST-1C, and QST-2Y."

"In your case the delivery is pretty firm, yes?"

"Pretty much so," said Phil. "Most of our customers work on a project basis, so we know well in advance where we need to deliver the stuff. And in any case, they pretty much take what we give them. So the more regular we are, the happier they are."

"Excellent. In this case, imagine that we clear the shipping area of the plant, and we now draw on the floor six preparation zones, one for each type of shipment.

"Now you need to pull regularly from your supermarket and bring the crates to the proper truck preparation area," my father explained.

"You're saying we need seven lanes in our finished-goods supermarket at the end of the conveyor."

"Let's see," said Dad, thoughtfully. "We need lanes for STR, STR-X, QST-1A, QST-1B, QST-1C, QST-2X, QST-2Y. That's seven, all right. Eight, in fact, if we need a DG lane as well. Think back to the supermarket. Branded bread and private-label bread might be very close to the same product, but you're still going to find them in different locations on the shelves. With the exception of the DGs, which can all go into the same lane, obviously since no two are alike. But there's few of them."

"Fine," said Phil, who was looking away, working this problem out in his mind. "Eight lanes. Then, at shipping we have these six truck preparation areas, if I ignore DGs. And then a material handler comes and helps herself in the supermarket and then delivers to the truck preparation area all through the week, despite the fact that the truck only leaves once a week. That sounds really weird!"

"You'd be moving the crates in any case," pointed out my father. "When the truck arrives, I bet there's a panic to find the right crates and to get them on the truck. If we do that, when the truck arrives, all the products are there, and we can load without drama and off it goes."

"The advantage I can see right away," said Phil enthusiastically, "is that if we're late on a shipment, we'll know immediately. Let's say we pick the crates once a day for the QST-1B going to Pittsburgh, where they always give us grief on missed deliveries. We ship every Thursday. We're saying we're going to place two crates of QST-1B on the truck preparation area on Friday, two more on Monday, two on Tuesday, two on Wednesday, and the last two on Thursday to complete the 10, and the truck goes. If we haven't got six crates there on Wednesday morning, we know we're in trouble already! It's brilliant."

"Congratulations, you've just discovered visual management," commented Dad with a grin.

"There's just too much to this!" Amy exclaimed in sudden exasperation.

"It's not that hard, darn it," scolded Dad. "Instead of moving all the crates at once because the truck is waiting, you level it regularly through the week. How complicated is that?"

"Fine. I understand the logic," she replied with a tight smile. "How often should we pick on the supermarket?"

"Answer your own question!"

"Takt time, I guess."

"Obviously. That's what a perfect customer would do. They'd come and pick on the supermarket at takt time. Now, sometimes it's not practical, so you can take a number of crates together, and have longer picking rhythms. Toyota originally had us pick at two hours, but we soon went down to 20 minutes."

"In our case," said Amy, "there's not much point in stacking the crates up on the forklifts. It's inefficient *and* dangerous."

"So, we get a material handler to pick up a crated breaker every 10 minutes from the finished-goods supermarket and bring it to the truck preparation area."

"That's going to change their way of working, I can tell you that!"

"No joke!" she said with a sudden low laugh.

"More work!" sighed Phil.

"More arms to twist," said Amy, to herself as much as to the rest of us.

"One thing I meant to ask you, Bob, if you don't mind," started Phil cautiously. Dad raised an eyebrow.

"How do you always seem to know exactly what we have to do next? I mean, why do we have to move to pull now? Can't it wait? We've already done a great deal. Don't you think we should let people rest for a while?"

"It's your plant, son, so it's your call. As far as I can see, you've still got these inventory heaps all over the place, so the cash situation can't have changed all that much."

"Ouch. You've got a point there."

"Listen, Philip. It's still all about this damnable lake and rocks thing. As long as you haven't got a pull system in place, you haven't got the human machinery in place to make sure improvements will keep happening instead of the whole system sliding back down where you started. It's about people, remember? Not parts!"

Phil nodded, pulled off his glasses, and rubbed his face wearily.

"And as to how I know what to do? The answer is straightforward enough. I'm walking you exactly through what the Toyota people had me do all those years ago, and which I've repeated in countless factories since. And as long as people are willing to try it, believe it or not, it works. It's more or less always the same sequence:

One, you sort out as many of the quality problems as you can, as well as downtime and other instability problems, and you get the engineers to worry seriously about internal scrap.

Two, you make sure the flow of parts through the system is as continuous as possible, which involves setting up the U-cells and making some market locations, avoiding variations in the operators' work cycle, and so on.

Three, you drive in the notion of standardized work and make sure the pace of work stabilizes through the various processes.

Four, you start pulling, so that no parts or materials move forward until they're called for. Which is what we've got to get to right now, and it involves setting up your perfect customer, looking at the production scheduling, and eventually replacing production weekly or even daily orders with some type of frequent signal, like kanban cards.

Five, you even out the production flow by reducing batch sizes, increasing the rhythm of internal deliveries, and leveling your internal demand.

Six, you work at it day and night with kaizen and quality circles. And when it finally works perfectly, you're ready for an 'Oh No!'

number. You pull resources out and start again."

"And that never fails?" I wondered cynically.

"The method? No. Why should it? It only fails when people give in and choose the path of least resistance. It's like an exercise regime: no will, no results."

"Yeah, no pain, no gain!" grunted Phil. He doodled on his pad while Amy stretched in the deck chair, showing off her pretty legs, apparently unfazed. But a closer look suggested that the past month of kicking that factory into shape had taken a toll. Her eyes were closed and her chin held high, but even so she looked tired.

"I know you said you wouldn't do it," said Phil finally, having resolved his internal debate. "But I think we really need you back in the factory if we want to move forward."

Dad stared at him, glowering, but didn't protest outright.

"From what I understand, much of this has to do with production planning and scheduling. Then you've just mentioned kanban. Now, I've heard about it, but I don't know of anyone who actually knows how to make that work. Our consultants certainly did not. Oh they could talk about it well enough, but when it came to actual implementation —"

"Philip, I've told you that —"

"If," interrupted Phil, holding his hand up, "if I get Dave to see some sense and to agree to work with us on this, would you be ready to give it another shot?"

Dad said nothing, just kept frowning in a way that had discouraged more than one hardy soul.

"If he's not, I'm ready to fire him over it," said Phil tersely. "I'm convinced this is the way forward, and I don't ever want to find myself back in the panic of the last couple of months. I'm going to fight the design people over the quality issues, so I need production straightened out, and I am ready to go all the way with this."

I looked at my friend in wonder. Was that the easygoing, conflict-avoidant Philip I'd known all these years? He sounded different. He even looked different, grim, decided. In a flash, I realized he had exactly that same harsh look of stubborn defiance I'd seen on Dad's face all these years, and it gave me a chill. Hadn't I brought up the leadership issue in the first place? I half regretted those hasty words now, as one always does in my line of work.

"No call for that, son," answered my father in a soothing tone. "Your man Dave is probably in over his head, that's all. You need him for his experience, so if he's ready to play ball, I'll give it a second try. I tell you what, you sort out a supermarket for your finished product and, when you have, you give me a shout and I'll come have a look at it."

"That's a relief," sighed Amy, curling up in her seat. "You mean I won't be the only one fighting the inertia of that place! I like the sound of that."

"Oh no, Ms. Cruz. Don't get any ideas. I do the talking, but you do the fighting!" said Dad with a genuine, heartfelt laugh.

Chapter Seven

KANBAN RULES

It couldn't have been more than a couple months since my father had first stormed out of the plant, but the place was hardly recognizable. Even to my inexperienced eye, I could see the effects of a vigorous 5S campaign, up to the new coat of white paint, which still left a rather overpowering smell.

"We thought that if the vacuum core plant could look like a science lab," explained Phil, "so could this plant. What do you think of the 5S?"

"They call us 'the witches' behind our back," Amy chuckled, talking about the ironhanded trio she had formed with Gloria and Ester Ramirez, the new team leader of the final assembly area, a matronly Mexican-American woman who'd been working on the conveyor line for years. "The *brujas*! I now conduct a 5S audit every other week in which each cell gets graded."

"Remember how we didn't know what to do beyond the first three Ss?" added Phil. "Well, now she's got me signing off every time a cell is ready to move from one S level to the next!"

"It shows that you care, boss *darling*," she countered. "It's hard to believe how seriously people take it now, I sometimes feel I terrify them."

"Well, you terrify me!" I kidded.

"You should see me on the shop floor," she bantered back. "I expected a lot more resistance from the workers after the Jake Rogers episode, but in fact they've been quite sweet about it. We've even started some kaizen projects with the older guys. As long as you don't ask them to write anything down, they've got plenty of really good ideas. Here we are."

The mechanisms assembly area was transformed. They had moved the entire assembly process all the way up the plant, right behind the conveyor. Then they'd transformed the four mechanism lines into two lines, barely recognizable. They were compact and each operator had a small amount of materials in front of his or her workstation. "We try to keep this supply of materials as small as possible," Amy said, "and so we replenish it on a regular basis, refilling only what is needed."

Separating the two lines was a wide aisle, which, I guessed, allowed the operators to be supplied without interruption.

"How does that work?" I asked.

"With a double-bin system," she answered. "Each component is on the shelves in front of the operators. They help themselves from one small plastic box for each part, with a spare box right behind it. When they finish the container, they slide it underneath through the opening, which is a signal for it to be replaced from outside the cell."

"Who handles the supplying?" asked my father.

"Logistics should," she answered, with a quick frown. "However, we've not got the system working perfectly yet, so Gloria often takes care of it. Thankfully, although each operator needs many small components, which forced us to have very small containers, they assemble at takt time, which is between seven and 10 minutes, so one bin doesn't need resupplying for a good while."

"That's a lot to do for Gloria," objected Dad, "if she also deals with rework."

"We know that," she said crossly. "We're trying to obtain hourly deliveries from logistics, but —"

"Remind me to talk to you about that before I go," cut in Dad, and moved on.

A single empty space separated each station and there was an opening to shunt the parts needing rework off the line. I could finally see what Dad meant by putting the operator first. Everything was organized to simplify the operator's job, with the main priority given to the workstations, and all the logistics arranged around it.

"As you can see," Amy said pointing to a whiteboard, "we've set up a production board for each of the lines and each line has a five-minute meeting first thing in the morning. They track hourly objectives of the previous shift, if they have one, and try to anticipate the problems they will have and explain the why of the shortfall, if they have one. At the end of the day, Gloria debriefs with each of the team leaders and notes down all the problems; and she often deals with other departments and engineers so that these problems don't come up again."

"I see you're also tracking the number of accident-free days," remarked Dad approvingly.

"Yes, something else I remembered from frying burgers."

"Safety first. Excellent."

"Really, all of this is going quite well. Where I'm having serious difficulties," she said, suddenly looking discouraged, "is with those stinking engineers. Except for Josh, who actually gets his hands dirty, there's no way the others will come to the production line to see how you need to be a contortionist to build their idiot designs. They're always too busy to attend the workshops. They look down their noses at you. Jerks!"

I had to grin, and she smiled back, with an edge.

"The new STR-X start of production was a nightmare. We were chucking every other part in the red bins, and thank God for Joshua, who worked night and day to get the process to flow. Precious little help he got from his colleagues as well. Phil and I have been reviewing the annual appraisal system; they're in for a surprise, I tell you!"

"Ah, real HR work, at last," I kidded.

"Silly," she said, giving me a glancing blow. "Now, here we go: our mechanisms supermarket."

"Would you look at that!" exclaimed Dad as we reached the conveyor area.

Right before final assembly was an actual supermarket with containers of mechanisms on the rack lanes. In contrast with the shelves at my neighborhood supermarket, the contraption was impressively deep. In fact the sloping racks reached all the way back to where the two mechanism lines were producing, side by side. At the end of each line, a flow rack started, conveying boxes of mechanisms directly to the conveyor. The mechanisms arrived right at the station where operators were assembling them into the circuit breaker. All they had to do was help themselves from the requisite container on the rack behind them and carry it a few steps to their workstation. I thought Dad was going to give them hell for all the unnecessary movements, the turning around, the carrying of parts, the walking, and I was expecting another spiel on transforming motion into work, but he didn't. He couldn't seem to get over the size of the thing they'd built.

"Look at that," he said. "Why d'you make it so big?"

Amy and Phil just shook their heads while Dave Koslowsky stared at him, with an expression of studious interest carefully groomed on his features. He'd kept very quiet in a pugnacious kind of way, but didn't seem outwardly hostile. Phil continued to think highly of the man despite his obvious struggle with new ideas. He was a hard worker, and truly dedicated to the plant and its people. His resistance came more from the natural reluctance of a practical man, once bitten, twice shy, than any permanent rigidity, and Phil was confident that if lean made sense, it should be possible to convince Dave, in his own terms.

"I mean, it's good, but it's huge! The shelves must be longer than a football field," Dad persisted.

Gloria, however, who'd just joined our little group, with Ester Ramirez from the conveyor area, was now looking seriously put out. Amy was urgently whispering in her ear.

"Do you realize the work we put into this," said Phil exasperated. "Just getting Matt to approve the plastic containers!"

"Yeah, it's great," Dad agreed. "But why so big?"

"You know why," Amy bristled. "Because we carry too much stock."

"I'll say that for it," said Dave, trying to make nice. "It works really well, and all things being equal, there's about half the WIP in there that we used to have. And the mechanisms roll directly from mechanism assembly to final assembly so the, um, nonvalue-added time from moving the mechanisms has been reduced, as you'd say. It has to count for something, surely?"

"All right, all right," answered Dad impatiently. "But why not make it smaller?"

"Because we're still not good about the leveling of the conveyor, there," snapped Amy. I could smell exasperation in the air.

"Hey, where's that positive spirit, miss? And," added Dad with a frown, "considering what I've seen back there with the cabinet assembly. Your presses —"

"What about the presses?" grated Dave, ready to be goaded into another explosion, as Philip laid a calming hand on his arm. Dear God, did Dad have a way with people.

"Listen, Bob," replied Amy, sounding distinctly miffed. "I understand our aim is single-piece flow, so that we should be able to build the mechanism in direct sequence with the conveyor and get rid of this flow rack entirely. But, we need to get there one step at a time. That's what you taught us anyhow. No customer risk! Delivery first, so really, it's a big supermarket."

"Yeah, it's there. You've done it, congratulations, you get a pat on the back" conceded Dad. "Now we're gonna have to figure how to reduce it!"

Amy let out a loud, exasperated huff, but didn't say a word.

"All right, all right. Take me through it one step at a time. How do you fill that thing?" asked Dad to Gloria.

"Originally," she said tersely, "we thought that one container should hold all the mechanisms for one breaker, but it turned out to be too heavy to lift easily. So we've switched to smaller, plastic trays that each hold one mechanism. Whenever each new mechanism is finished testing, the operator puts it on a tray and places the tray on the flow rack in the right corridor. See, we've labeled them. It then queues, waiting for a conveyor operator to pick up a tray on the other side of the flow rack, right by the working station, and so on."

"I can see that. It's great. And how do the operators know which mechanism to build?"

"As we always did," Gloria shrugged. "We get a production schedule from production control, unless Dave tells us different. We agreed to try and build each product each day, so we build STR mechanisms in the morning on line 1, and STR-X in the afternoon. Then we do QST-1 and QST-2 on line 2. The DGs we build one-by-one on a bench, according to what we need."

"Essentially, you're pushing."

"Are we?" asked Amy, looking puzzled. "The operators on the conveyor are pulling parts, like shoppers at the supermarket."

"Yes, they are, but you still don't reproduce what's being consumed in the same order, right?"

"Could you repeat that?" I interrupted. "That was a bit fast for me."

"Just-in-time," Dad said irritably. "Produce what has been consumed in the same quantity and *the same order*. Look, although the conveyor operators are *pulling* on the mechanism supermarket, the line is still *pushing* mechanisms on the supermarket. You must have huge variations in the lanes."

"We do," confirmed Gloria. "Which is why we need it to be so large."

"I see your point," agreed Amy, frowning. "We're following production planning instructions, instead of replenishing what has just been consumed. Ideally, every time a mechanism is assembled in a circuit breaker, we should somehow be producing one."

"That's right."

"Is this finally where the kanban comes in?" wondered Phil.

"Yeah," Dad replied. "This is about kanban. The question is: How? Follow your intuition."

"Well," pursued Phil. "If we want to produce a new mechanism every time one has been consumed, we need some sort of signal from the conveyor back to mechanism production to tell them what they've just taken from the supermarket. Like a computer message or —"

Dad just gave him the look.

Phil stopped completely for a moment, reflected, and then added, "Okay, think like a Japanese farmer, forget the computer. Hmm. I don't know, a signal of some kind," he concluded lamely.

"Amy? Gloria?"

Puzzled silence.

"Well, come on, people! All you need is a tag of any kind. It could be a bit of plastic or cardboard, anything that identifies the part, which you stick on the boxes of mechanisms. When a final assembly operator picks up a box, you create a way to take the tag off the box and send it back to the mechanism assembly line, and put it in a queue there. Period."

"So we have waiting lines of tags that tell us how to exactly reproduce that which has just been consumed by the conveyor," reasoned Gloria. "Smart. Why didn't we think of something like that?"

"You'd be surprised how hard it can be to arrive at common sense," said Dad. "We usually use cards, which is pretty straightforward. Create one, describing the part and the number that go in the container (which in this case is one), then place them in a queue."

"Don't look at me, Gloria," Phil joked. "I'm far too highly trained to think of anything that practical."

"Hang on," said Amy when the giggles had subsided. "This assumes that we build the mechanisms in units of four."

"Yeah, I know," grinned my father. "You want to build, say, 20 STRs in a row because you don't want the hassle of changing from one model every time. So just bunch the cards until you have a large enough batch."

"Bunch the cards?" asked Gloria, her eyes narrowed in concentration.

"Designate one box to hold STR cards and another for STR-X cards as they come back from the conveyor. If your batch size is 20 STR mechanisms, then, when you get 20 cards back, clip them together and put the clip on the waiting file. Simple."

"Let me see if I get this straight," said Gloria slowly. "The conveyor guy takes a tray from the supermarket, with, say, an STR mechanism on it. He pulls the card off the tray and puts it in the 'STR cards box.' When I see 20 cards in the box, I clip them together and take them to the mechanism line, and place the clip in the queue?"

"Yes, so when they get to the clip the mechanism operators know they've got 20 STRs to do now."

"Sounds pretty simple when you say it like that," agreed Gloria.

"Tell you what," said Dad with a kind smile. "We can do it even easier. You can build the 'STR card box' as a stack of 20 small slots, so you can immediately see when 20 cards have come back which need to be brought to the mechanism line waiting list."

"God, it's annoying!" burst out Amy, to Dad's amused raised eyebrow.

"I mean," she stammered, "it's so obvious!"

"I know. I used to get equally frustrated with hindsight. We just don't think that way, that's all."

"I'm still missing something," protested Phil. "You're saying we always make a fixed number of mechanisms of one type."

"Yes, we're working on a fixed batch size of 10 times the change-over time," said Amy, tugging at her hair thoughtfully. "I think we had calculated something like 15 mechanisms in a batch."

"Okay. But doesn't that create a problem?" asked Phil. "We're installing four STR mechanisms in each STR cabinet, but only three STR-X mechanisms in the STR-X cabinets. From what you're saying, if we build batches of 15 of each, we're going to build far more STR-X than we really need!"

"Not the case," replied Gloria immediately. "It just means that the clips of 15 STR cards are going to come back more frequently than those of STR-X. So we might find, say, two clips of STR on the waiting file for every clip of STR-X, am I right?"

"Absolutely," agreed Dad. "We're assuming that the STR and STR-X mechanisms take the same time to assemble, which is why both batches produce the same number of mechanisms. You're totally correct. Although you're batching, which distorts the consumption signal from the conveyor, the order of the batches appearing on your waiting list will reflect the order of the mechanism consumption on the conveyor. There you go, Philip, there's your kanban."

"It sounds too simple! The consultants always seemed to go on about really complex stuff. Is that all there is to it?"

"If you're not trying to justify outrageous consulting fees, yes, that's really all there is," added my father with a thin smile. "You may need to write all sorts of stuff on the cards, such as the part name and number, and how many parts in a container and how many containers in a batch and how many cards in the loop and so on, but basically, it is that simple. There are other sorts of kanban to deal with machined parts or supplier components and so on. But the fundamental logic is the same. The first principle of kanban is that the latter process goes to the earlier process to pick up the parts needed."

"Is there a second principle?"

"Well, yes, which is that the earlier process only produces the amount the latter process has withdrawn. That's the trouble you're currently having with your mechanism supermarket, and that's precisely what the kanban should facilitate."

"Okay," summed up Phil. "We need to try to smooth the flow of breakers on the conveyor by alternating the types and leveling the schedule."

"And we've got to move from push to pull with the kanban telling us what to make on the mechanism line," Amy concluded with a nod to Gloria.

"And reduce this monster rack," concluded Dad. "It's great to see a supermarket in this plant, but one that large is, I don't know, offensive somehow."

"Yessir. We'll try."

"So, let's see what you're doing with the perfect customer then," continued my father, walking away from the mechanisms toward the end of the conveyor with a thoughtful frown. I could see Dave tense up immediately, a slight flush creeping up on his ruddy cheeks, but he kept quiet. At the end of the final assembly conveyor, right after testing and packing, they'd organized a large area with 10 lanes of heavy metal rollers on which they placed the packed crates. Large printed signs were hanging from the ceiling identifying each product lane. As we walked there, an operator finished sticking a label on one crate, and placed it on the end of a lane, pushing all the other crates forward. A couple of lanes were empty, while another had crates stacked on top of each other.

"I understand what you want us to do," started Dave. "But it's not working. This overflows regularly, and we still have to stockpile finished breakers over there against the wall and then, sometimes, you can see right now that the lane is empty."

"I can see that," replied Dad dryly.

"Well, these three lanes we put in extra," said Phil defensively, "in case we develop more new products."

"Sure, son, but look at this one. It's crammed with an overflow of STR, isn't it?"

They fidgeted, while Amy kept unusually quiet. I suspected that they'd already had a number of arguments on that issue.

"How does the picking work from here?"

"We've done what you suggested over there," continued Dave,

showing us the area close to the open dock where seven rectangles had been painted on the floor, most of them empty.

"Here's the truck preparation area, one per customer site."

"Why are they all empty, then?" asked Dad.

Dave shrugged. Gloria and Ester exchanged silent looks. If they knew what was going on, they weren't about to tell. Ester stayed slightly behind the larger woman, slightly out of the line of fire.

"The material handlers don't see the point in moving crates throughout the day if the truck only leaves once a week," said Amy tightly.

"The material handlers? That's their opinion?" asked Dad, raising his eyebrows in mock astonishment.

"Logistics, actually," said Dave. "They work for Kev Morgan, not me. And I haven't been able to come up with a solid reason."

"I keep telling —" Amy blurted out, sounding very annoyed.

"Take it easy, Amy," said Dad surprisingly gently. "None of this is obvious to anyone at first." He looked directly at Dave: "Do you see the logic, though?"

"I'll be straight with you. I understand what you want to do. But, first, I don't know that it will help. It would just mean more comings and goings, and, second, in any case, I don't know how to organize it in practice."

"That's all right. Let's take things one at a time," said my father with uncustomary patience. "However," he added with a frown toward Phil, "don't expect me to fight your battles with logistics for you. You're going to have to handle this yourself."

Phil nodded gloomily.

"First, do you see why you're having trouble with the supermarket?"

"Because there is no level pull!" jumped in Amy, looking impatiently at Dave, probably an ongoing argument.

"If you withdraw large quantities irregularly," confirmed Dad slowly, "you won't be able to keep an orderly supermarket. It's as if I need to stock up for 500 friends who have suddenly lost all their food and supplies, so I go to the local supermarket. I'll just empty the shelves all at once, and they'll have all the trouble in the world to stock up again."

"I understand that," said Dave with a contentious tone. "But that's like what you said about mixing the breakers we assemble on the conveyor. Sure, if you can do it, I understand your point about lowering the inventories, but still, it's going to cost me more in assembly. Every one knows that what pays in this game is volume!"

After letting the following silence drag a bit, my father replied: "Have you ever wondered why a soda costs twice as much at a holiday resort as in your local store?"

"What's that got to do with it?" replied Dave sourly. But then he added, "Because they can get away with it, I reckon."

"Partly, but mostly because they only work half the year, so they have to recoup their fixed costs over the holiday season. What you're saying is that the cost of assembly goes down with volume, and I'd agree with that. But that's not the cost of the product. Just assembly."

Dave looked at him perplexed, but listening.

"Every time you create a peak and then a valley in demand, you create inventory, do we agree with that?"

"I guess."

"You need to hold enough inventory to be able to deliver at peak demand. The rest of the time, there's low demand, but you never know when the next peak is going to come, so you hold the inventory ready just in case."

"Yeah, I get that. And if you're forced to lower your inventory," he added with a meaningful look to Phil, "when the order finally arrives you're out of stock."

"Sure. However, you also have to add the cost of holding this inventory to the price of your parts."

"To some extent, one might say that."

"And then, because you're dealing with peaks and valleys, you're creating the same ups and downs at your suppliers' as well who, consequently, will also have to hold inventories. In practice, this is a phantom productivity gain since you're not building to customer demand, you're just adding inventory, which raises costs."

Dave didn't actually acquiesce, but I could see he looked troubled. Dad had won a point.

"You want us to pick up a breaker every 10 minutes from the finished-goods supermarket and place it in the truck preparation area, is that right?" Dave said at last, wearily.

"As if you were a perfect customer," agreed Dad. "You pick up products at the same rhythm your customer uses them on his own line."

"Regardless of how we actually ship them."

"That's correct. You fill up the truck preparation area little by little at the takt time, to smooth the peaks and valleys in your own flow. Think about it. If you're only shipping once a week, you're creating a huge peak of demand on the delivery date and a valley the rest of the time. In this manner, we gradually even out the demand on production."

"It sounds unnatural, but hey, I'm ready to give it a try," Dave said with a shrug. "If I can convince the logistics people."

"I'll push," said Phil firmly.

"You mean, you'll pull," corrected Amy with an impish smile.

"Still, I can't figure out how to tell the material mover which crate to lift," Dave conceded, frowning.

"You shouldn't have to," replied Dad. "That's the point. The material mover needs to know exactly what he picks up and when. We're going to use kanban again."

"Like the previous kanban?" wondered Amy. "I don't see how that applies."

"Ah, well, those are *production* kanban. Here, we need to use *withdrawal* kanban."

"You mean there's more than one kind?" I asked, aghast.

"Yeah, Mickey, at least two. Think you'll cope?" he jabbed, and then turned back toward Dave.

"To start with, let's consider the product range you have here. If I understand corrrectly what Philip has told me, you've got two product families, STR and QST, but they're customized for each customer."

"Each of our customers requires a different instrument panel and the cabinet size varies to a small extent," Dave explained. "At the moment we regularly produce seven different finished units of STRs and QSTs, and every DG is different. Overall, if we group our customer by delivery points, our daily plan breaks down into 10 STRs, eight STR-Xs, five QST-1As, two QST-1Bs, four QST-1Cs, four QST-2Xs, six QST-2Ys, and a variety of DGs."

"Lets forget the DGs for the moment and start with the most common products. Amy, how would you work the perfect customer?"

"Something like that, look: if we have truck preparation areas over there, what we need is just one guy who keeps doing a circuit with the forklift from the truck preparation area to the finished-product supermarket, crate by crate, on and on again. Is that it?"

"How long would that take?" I wondered.

"I don't know," answered Dave looking at Amy, who just shook her head, "two to five minutes."

"Well, there you go, then. Now the question is, how does he or she know what to pick up from the supermarket?"

"Kanban cards?" suggested Phil uncertainly.

"Bingo. Hand me your pad. Let's say that every half hour, the material handler has to get the information to pick up one specific product and move it into the truck preparation area. We start by constructing a box, which we'll call a heijunka, or leveling box, with a slot for every pick-up. If we say every half hour, we make 16 slots to cover the day. We create rows for the seven products lines like so:

Products	8:30	9:00	9:30	10:00	10:45	11:15	11:45	12:15	13:45	14:15	14:45	15:15	16:00	16:30	17:00	17:30
STR																
STR-X																
QST-1A																
QST-1B																
QSR-1C																
QST-2X																
QST-2Y																

"What about the DGs?" wondered Amy.

"They're exotics, we'll deal with them separately. Now, consider that a card travels with each product. Given your demand, we can place the cards as evenly as possible to smooth the load, like this:

Products	8:30	9:00	9:30	10:00	10:45	11:15	11:45	12:15	13:45	14:15	14:45	15:15	16:00	16:30	17:00	17:30
STR		／		／	／		／	／		／	／		／			／
STR-X	／		／		／		／		／		／		／		／	
QST-1A	／					／			／			／				／
QST-1B				／							／					
QSR-1C		／				／			／				／			
QST-2X			／					／			／				／	
QST-2Y	／			／			／		／			／				／

"Which tells the material movers what they have to pick up from the supermarket every 30 minutes."

"You mean that at 8:30, they have to pick up one STR-X, one QST-1A, and one QST-2Y?" checked Amy.

"And at 9:00, one STR-X, one QST-1C," continued Phil. "And they pick up two or three crates each turn."

"Obviously. What can be simpler than that? They take the cards, and withdraw products from the finished-unit supermarket, and move the crates to the corresponding truck preparation area. Surely even your logistics people can handle that?"

"If they choose to, no question," replied Amy, with a frown that spoke volumes, while Dave raised his eyes to high heaven, opening and closing his hands in displaced frustration.

"Remember, they're doing the work anyhow. They have to make the trip at some point if you want to load your trucks," Dad insisted, irritated. "And doing it this way should avoid the usual loading panics when the truck is waiting you can't find an available forklift or you haven't got a clue where the units are to be found in the plant!"

"Sounds like every Monday," grinned Phil.

"We get them to follow a standardized circuit!" suddenly clicked Amy, "which should help us with logistics' productivity!"

"Precisely," agreed Dad. "That's a side benefit of leveling. Chances are you have twice as many material handlers as you really need!"

"No way," grated Dave. "There's never one when you need them!"

"Yes, Dave," continued Amy cheerfully. "Think about it. If they have to follow a standard circuit, we know exactly where they are and when."

"And how does he know where to take the crates?" I pointed out.

"There's a pick list by truck," answered Dad simply. "Overall, that's all there is to it. The heijunka box drives the material handler's job. At any given time, he or she can see what products need to be picked up from the supermarket next and brought to the truck preparation area."

"That's just it! What you suggest tells us how to organize work for the finished-goods material handler, paced to customer demand," objected Amy. "But it doesn't tell us how to organize the production on the conveyor."

"Doesn't it? Think about it."

"I see that we should produce on the conveyor in the same order that finished goods are picked, in order to replenish our finished-goods supermarket," she answered without batting an eye, as if it was perfectly obvious. "What I don't see is how to do it in practice."

"How do you do it now?" Dad asked Dave, who shifted uneasily.

"I've been trying to apply some of your approach, so I break down our weekly demand by day, and draw out a loading schedule for the conveyor, which I then give to Ester and she tries to apply it. Amy and I have discussed it, and I try to do like you said, every type of cabinet every day. But that's as far as it goes; we still build the 10 STRs in a row, then the QSTs, and so on. I haven't tried to go beyond that."

"Well, that's a start. Does it work?" Dad asked Ester, who thought carefully before answering, looking from Dave to Amy.

"So-so. We have problems with missing parts so I have to fiddle with it," she said slowly. "Then there are panics when some finished units are missing for a delivery, and we have to build those first."

"I'll say this for the truck preparation area," threw in Dave. "We now see problems coming up beforehand, which we didn't use to. So we can correct earlier, and have fewer missed deliveries."

"That's true," remarked Phil. "I don't hear from Pittsburgh as much these days."

Dad thought about it a long while, and then took a deep breath.

"All right, I'm not sure you're ready for it, but I can explain to you how you'd reproduce on the conveyor the order of withdrawal on the finished-breaker supermarket, which, in the end, is the only way to stabilize your supermarket and have no more than the minimal number of parts on it. Where do we start?"

"Final assembly?" I suggested, which triggered a look of resigned contempt from both Phil and Amy.

"Truck preparation!" Amy corrected, giving me a "you idiot" look.

"Customer first, as always," agreed Dad with a brief grin.

He ripped a page from Phil's pad he was still holding and folded it in four.

"Now, I'm at the heijunka box, and I've got a kanban card which tells me that I have to pick up a crate of STR," he said, walking to the STR lane on the supermarket with his paper in hand.

"I take this away. But somehow, I'm going to have to send a production instruction to the conveyor saying that they should build another STR to replace the one I just withdrew, right?"

"Okay," said Phil. "No problem so far."

"How do I do that then?"

"Production instruction — the other type, right?" said Phil carefully. "One way or another, we should send another card back to the conveyor."

"And that's exactly what we'll do," agreed Dad. "We'll place a kanban card on the crate as it is moved to finished goods. Then, this second card will be returned to production at the point the crate is moved to the shipping lanes."

Using Phil's pen, he made a large cross on another sheet from Phil's pad, and folded it so that the cross was clearly visible. He placed this new piece of paper on top of the STR crate while giving the original folded paper to Dave, saying, "Hold this."

"Now, I'm a material handler," Dad explained, walking back toward Dave and taking the piece of paper from him. "I take the kanban from the heijunka box in shipping, and so I've got my withdrawal kanban in hand," he said, waving the paper in the air. "This tells me which crate I have to pick up from the finished-goods supermarket. I get to the crate and put it on the forklift," he continued, mimicking the move. "I now take off the production kanban, which is tagged to the crate," he said, walking back to the roller lanes and picking up the crossed paper on the crate, "and replace it with the withdrawal kanban I brought with me. Is that clear?" he asked, switching the two papers.

"Then you place the production kanban card in the waiting queue to be produced!" exclaimed Amy. "It works!"

"Sure, the kanban card goes to one point, let's call it a collection post, and then it can be collected by the material handler and brought to production to be replenished."

"What about the withdrawal kanban? What happens to it?"

"The withdrawal kanban goes off with the container to the next process, in this case to the truck preparation area, to make sure the areas get filled properly."

"Fine, I think I'm getting this," said Phil. It's consistent with the kanban principles you mentioned. First, the downstream process goes to the upstream process to pick up parts. Second, the upstream process is only allowed to produce exactly what has been withdrawn, and in the same order. Any more?"

"Well, Ohno had six kanban rules, which we can progressively implement. To make the two preceding rules work you have to make sure that nothing is ever produced, or picked up, without a kanban. Which also means that every part or container in your plant should have a kanban attached to it. Of course, to make that work, you must have only good parts in the containers, since defects will screw the whole thing up. Finally, you need to progressively reduce the number of cards in the loop to increase the process' sensitivity. Now, obviously, you don't need to apply all the rules at once to get started."

"Here goes," summed up Amy cheerfully. "The rules are:

Uno, the following process comes to withdraw from the previous process.

Dos, the previous process only produces what has been withdrawn.

Tres, production or withdrawal only happens with corresponding kanban cards.

Quatro, no parts are allowed around the place without a kanban attached to them.

Cinco, zero defects in the parts delivered by the upstream process.

Seis, reduce the number of kanban over time."

"You heard the lady," said Phil, looking at each of them straight in the eye. "Let's get to it!"

A few weeks later, we'd agreed to get together again at the Yacht Club, even though it was a workday. I hadn't heard from Phil, so I assumed all was going well, and indeed he seemed quite upbeat when he unfolded himself out of his Porsche. Dad was already settled on the porch, in animated conversation with Amy and, of all people, Harry. The big man wore his yachtsman's outfit, complete with the navy cap at a rakish angle. The faint scent of booze in the morning didn't help his image either.

"So," he said loudly when Phil and I joined them at the table. "It looks like you managed to save your hide?"

"We're making a lot of progress in the plant, where we've made incredible gains that have allowed us to increase production with the same number of operators," said Phil proudly. "So we've caught up on our backlog, which has brought in enough additional cash to keep us afloat, and we're shipping new products."

"Hey!" cried Amy. "We've done more than just that. What have I been busting myself on the floor for? We've organized the mechanisms area in cells, increasing their productivity by a third and doubling their quality. We moved them close to the conveyor, which they're now supplying FIFO. And we've set up a finished-goods supermarket at the end of final assembly."

"But what about inventory reduction?" pressed Harry.

"We're having trouble with the kanban," admitted Amy with frustration. "And with logistics!" she added, pulling a face.

"Oh?"

"No joke. The logistics manager doesn't want to hear about regular pickups from the finished-unit supermarket — or anywhere else. He says he's not about to increase his logistics cost by tripling the amount of work the material handlers have!"

Harry and Dad exchanged a glance and laughed, although I, for one, could not tell what was so funny about what Amy was saying.

"And he says he knows all about kanban and is working on it," she added, flushing with anger. I couldn't help but think that she looked good when she flushed with anger.

"What a jerk!" she concluded, reclining in her chair and pulling her sunglasses down over her flashing eyes. Amy had the fastest temper I'd ever come across. Strong emotions came and went so fast that sometimes you could barely catch them flit across her face before they'd be replaced by her usual good humor.

"Business as usual, huh, Bob?" chortled Harry.

"Yup. But this time it's not my fight," answered Dad levelly.

"Actually, I know I shouldn't ask," started Phil cautiously, looking carefully at my father, "but we'd really appreciate if you could come around once more and tell us what we're doing wrong."

"I don't mean to be rude," answered Dad with a deep scowl, "but which part of 'no' don't you understand? How many times do I have to tell you I've had it with production plants? I'm not going back to the factory. Again."

"I understand how you feel, but we really need your input," insisted Phil.

I was surprised to see him so persistent. Clearly, as my father had pointed out, he was not taking "no" for an answer. Maybe he had more of the entrepreneur in him than I ever gave him credit for. Amy hid behind her shades and we shared a quick grin.

"Whatever. Well, in any case, not today. Harry and I are going fishing."

"Don't be such as spoilsport!" exclaimed Harry, coming unexpectedly to Phil's defense. "I'd like to see what you're doing with those boys — and lady," he added with a nod toward Amy, who looked impassively back. "C'mon, it'd be like old times!"

"No it wouldn't," glowered Dad. "And there was nothing so great about old times anyhow."

"Come on, Phil, I'm sure you'd like to show me your plant!" Harry said to him.

"Absolutely."

"You don't know what you're getting into, son," Dad reminded

Phil, for once sounding a bit avuncular. "Harry used to eat bigger plants than yours for breakfast."

"Ah, don't be such an old lady, Bobby. It'll be fun. Come on, just a quick walk around the shop!"

"What about fishing?"

"We'll still go. In and out. And then we worry about the fishies. Not like we catch anything anyhow."

"Please, Bob. We're really stuck with the kanban. We need your help."

"All right, Philip," Dad accepted grudgingly, "but you asked for it."

That sounded rather ominous for just a factory visit.

"So what seems to be the problem?"

We'd driven straight to the plant and were now back in front of the mechanism supermarket. Gloria wasn't there, but Ester Ramirez had joined us while Harry was getting the guided tour around the plant, shepherded by Kevin Morgan, the logistics manager. Ester had none of Gloria's flamboyance. She was a low-key, stocky woman who didn't say much, with careworn eyes, short dark hair and a serious expression. She reserved a smile for Amy, who patted her arm affectionately.

"It's like this, no matter how hard we try, we can't seem to hold to the smoothed program," conceded Dave ruefully. "It's not like the kanban doesn't work. We've not yet reached an agreement with the material handlers, but I've been using the heijunka box idea to mix the production program for final assembly as much as I can, and some days it works fine, in fact helping to stabilize the supermarket of finished units. It's just that we can't seem to hold it."

"Why not?"

"Mostly, missing parts. So what do you want us to do, stop the conveyor?"

"Yes," concurred Ester, pointing toward the stack of metal boxes, which were being fitted on the hanging frames of the conveyor one by one. "The cabinets, they don't come like you want them. Sometimes we have plenty of one type, and none of the other. And some of the other parts also, for the circuit boards."

Dad just looked at the conveyor, saying nothing.

"So if we can't build one type, we continue with the one we've got until the parts for the new model are found," added Dave.

"Which, in turn, plays hell with whatever kanban we're trying to install on the mechanism lines," concluded Amy. "My guess is the missing parts from the press screw up the leveled program at the conveyor and then pass on the variation to the mechanism supermarket."

"I think you're right, Amy," agreed Dave. "That's how I see it, anyhow. I mean, if I'm out of cabinets, what am I supposed to do? I'm gonna continue building whatever I have parts for, right? Actually we're working on a kanban to pull the cabinets from the stamping and welding area."

"Well, it sounds to me you've figured out the problem," said Dad slowly. "I still don't see what you need me here for, other than to hold your hand."

"But," insisted Ester, "it's not just missing cabinets. We also get missing parts from purchased components."

"What's going on here, Phil?" said Dad, suspiciously. "You told me you'd solved that issue a while back."

"I thought we had," agreed Phil, a bit peeved. "Dave? What's the score on missing parts? I haven't heard anything about that."

"Yeah, well you'd do better to talk to logistics about it, then, wouldn't you!" Dave said bitterly.

"Meaning?"

"Morgan again," sighed Amy.

"What's going on here, guys?" asked Phil again, aggrieved.

"It's not my turf, so I won't go there!" balked Dave.

"Amy? What gives?"

"What I heard is," Amy started cautiously, "that since there's such a pressure on inventory, Matt has given Kev really tough objectives on the purchased parts inventory. But I haven't looked into it, so I don't know for sure."

"So they squeeze inventory and now you have missing parts," guffawed Dad. "Classic. All right, before we start knocking logistics, we'd better sweep our own doorstep, so we need to have a look at cabinet assembly. That's nothing to do with procurement. What are y'all standing here for?" he asked brusquely in his inimitable style. "The action is over there, not here, so, let's go and see how you build them cabinets!"

"You should!" barged in Harry loudly, arriving back from his tour with a diffident Kevin Morgan in tow. A youngish man, Morgan had a narrow pinched face and short reddish hair. He was one of the new management team, hired to replace the old crowd Phil and Matt had fired after the purchase. A protégé of Gary Pellman, apparently, a numbers man. He dealt with logistics in the two plants as well as some purchasing and procurement. I seemed to remember that his official title was an important-sounding role such as "supply chain manager."

"You won't regret the sight," Harry bumbled on with a mischievous glint in his eyes, looking rambunctious as ever. "And Bobby boy, have you lost your touch, or what? Have you been back there? Where they make these boxes! What a mess! And their machines, holy smoke!"

"What d'you mean about the machines?" asked Dave, tensing up.

"They are an absolute mess. Oil, rags, haven't you guys ever heard of 5S? What has Bob been telling you?"

"We did 5S in that area!" Amy replied angrily.

"Around the machines, sure, for all the good it'll do to production. What about *in* the machines? Where it counts! No wonder you can't keep up with the smoothed schedule. I'd be surprised if the presses are up half the time!"

"Now, wait a minute, mister," started Dave, now furious and red in the face.

"And have you seen their inventory of pressed parts? They've got entire walls of the stuff. Containers up to high heaven. Bob, I'd never have accepted these guys as a supplier. I thought you said that you've been working with them!"

Strangely enough, this got no reaction whatsoever out of my Dad. He just looked on placidly, neither agreeing nor disagreeing.

"You see what I've been saying about downtime?" suddenly snapped Morgan, shoving a prim finger in Dave's face. "If your presses weren't in such terrible shape, we could stick to the production schedule!"

"And if your schedules weren't always so damn tight, we could at least have parts to produce something!" replied Dave hotly, as Amy and Ester exchanged knowing looks.

"Listen, I've been scheduling just-in-time all along! I've reduced inventory by 10%. I've calculated economic order quantities on the basis of all customer orders and we've stopped the cash drainage from over-ordering parts that was drowning this company," said Morgan, ticking off his achievements on his fingers. "I've now got our suppliers delivering just-in-time as well, so don't give me any grief over the production programs. It isn't my fault if production can't ever come up to scratch!"

"You little know-it-all!" erupted Dave. "It's precisely your stupid programs that are dragging us down. With all the work we've done we can finally produce what's needed, you understand? But you've been squeezing us at both ends — no materials coming in, none going out! I can't produce anything if I've got missing parts all day. Can't you ever get that straight in that bean-counting head of yours?"

"Hey, pal, it's never your fault, is it? I don't see what you're doing about this. And you can't fault suppliers if you don't respect your own programs, now that I've implemented supplier kanban! Fat lot of help you've been with that."

"Kanban?" asked Dad.

"Listen up, Bobby, that's the good bit," said Harry, as if the others weren't there.

"Kanban my foot," Dave was yelling, beside himself. "We've never had so many missing parts. Just so you'd make your bonus, you — "

"I don't have to take this!" Morgan shouted back.

"Hang on, son, calm down, we need to understand this," said Dad with a tone so unnaturally calm I knew, from years of experience, that trouble lay ahead. About the only person who seemed remotely comfortable in the midst of this tumult was Harry, who looked about as gleeful as a kid at a monster truck rally.

"First, how did you manage to get the purchased-parts inventory down so fast?" asked Dad.

Kevin Morgan glared back, but said nothing.

"He told me he lowered the buffer stocks in the MRP calculations," Harry cut in, ever the agitator.

"You *what?*" gasped Phil.

"We're trying to reduce inventory aren't we?" sputtered Morgan defensively. "So I checked all the buffer stocks in the MRP and they were incredibly high compared to normal. So I took it all down."

"And you didn't worry about creating missing parts?"

"No, why should there be? I'm telling you, we had an outrageous high days of parts inventory."

"Average days, isn't it?"

"Obviously," he answered with a smirk.

"And it never occurred to you that average inventory could still mean too many of some parts and none at all of others?" yelled Dave, hopping mad. "You only need one missing part to screw up assembly!"

Morgan didn't say anything, just stared at Dave with a superior air.

"What was that about supplier kanban?" asked my father quietly.

"Ah, see, on critical parts, the MRP calculates a daily demand and sends an electronic kanban message to the supplier who now delivers just-in-time to the factory."

Unexpectedly, Harry laughed out loud.

"How come you've never told me about this?" Amy asked with cold steel in her voice.

"I'm not finished yet," he answered back defensively. "Anyhow, it's a logistics issue, not HR."

That went down well! She said nothing but her thin lips and narrowed eyes spoke for themselves. Ester was now urgently whispering to Dave, probably trying to calm him down.

"And you don't get any missing parts on these items, of course?" Dad continued.

"I haven't checked specifically," Morgan answered uncertainly, "but I've done it before. I've set up supplier kanban, in my previous company. I was trained as a black belt and we were taught just-in-time. In fact, I tried to apply this when I arrived here but no one would listen."

"And, of course," Harry insisted theatrically, "you make sure that the procurement message you send to suppliers is perfectly level. No surprises, they have to send the same number of parts at regular intervals."

"Why should they?" stammered Morgan, now uncertain. "The whole point of just-in-time is that they have to respond to our needs. Right?"

"How do you work that out?" asked Dad very quietly.

"As I said, I calculate our weekly consumption of components from the MRP and then send an order, which they have three days to deliver, except of course for the long-distance parts."

"And this weekly order you give them is the same from week to week?"

"Of course not," replied Morgan with a puzzled frown. "Because Dave here can't seem to produce evenly, the orders vary significantly from one week to the next, that's why the supplier has to react just in time!"

"But every week you send them a couple of months' forecast of what you aim to build in this period?"

"How could I? Whatever I forecast, Dave builds what he pleases."

Dad and Harry exchanged a look.

"And you don't get missing parts?"

"I guess we might get some," conceded Morgan. "But it's the

supplier's responsibility to deliver, so I ask them to keep a stock of components if they're not flexible enough. Or use special shipments, whatever. It's their problem, not mine."

"And don't you think the cost of the stock or the expediting will find its way in the price you pay for the components?" asked Harry.

"Or that the only way for the supplier to be able to deliver what you ask him day to day with a huge variation is to keep a massive inventory on his site?" threw in Dad.

"That's his problem, surely?" the logistics man insisted.

"And you think he's not going to charge you for it?" Harry said, accusing as much as asking him.

"Or that, if he chooses not to hold that inventory, the resulting missing parts would not screw up everything we're trying to do here on the shop floor?" added Amy crossly.

"Hey, what are you all saying? That I should do everyone's job for them?" exploded Morgan, stammering with anger. "I was told to get the inventory down, so I did. My job is to program production with the MRP, and I can guarantee, *guarantee*, that my production schedules work! Now what can I do if the supplier doesn't respect his commitments, or if Dave's people on the shop floor don't put the right data in the system, or if production can't keep to a schedule and keeps changing things around all the time? Is it my job? Is it? No one can fault my planning, that's my job, and I just would like the delivery teams to deliver, for a change."

"Phil, take my advice, and fire this idiot before he does any more damage," Harry said, almost matter-of-factly. "Believe me, you've got enough trouble in this plant as it is without suffering fools, and he's going to have to go sooner or later, take my word for it!"

We all stared at Harry with disbelief while Kevin Morgan turned bright red, gaping wordlessly, wondering whether he'd heard correctly.

"Of all the ... ," he croaked, as Harry looked at us disingenuously.

"What?" he asked spreading his hands in mock innocence. "He's screwing up your relationships with your suppliers by forcing them to hold unnecessary inventory and make special shipments. This in turn causes endless missing parts in the plant. Then he dreams up this fantasy kanban without even bothering to look at the impact on the shop floor. All without a hint of doubt. Bob, you know the truth of it. And Phil, frankly, you should too. The longer that man stays here, the more damage he'll do."

To my amazement, Dad just sighed sadly. "Nothing is ever set for sure, Harry, you know that. Not with people!"

Kevin Morgan looked at each one of us in turn, going crimson and then white as the blood drained from his face. Astonishingly, no one, not even Phil, came to his defense. He just stood there, spitting mad, opening and closing his mouth like a landed fish, looking from Phil to Dave to Amy, who avoided his eye in turn. In one jerky move, he turned around and walked away at a fast, mechanical pace, pounding his rage into the concrete floor of the plant. I realized with a start that I'd been holding my breath and my chest felt tight.

"That was uncalled for!" burst out Amy.

"I didn't hear you sticking up for him," answered Harry.

"I agree with Dave that the guy definitely needs an attitude adjustment, but he didn't deserve that kind of humiliation."

"Hey, lady," shrugged Harry, "if you can't stand the heat stay out of the kitchen." He then turned as if nothing had just happened and cheerily asked Dad, "Well, Bob, since you're not doing anything useful here, aren't we going fishing?"

We all turned toward Dad, expecting him to blow his top, but he simply stood there, fiddling with his cap, the very image of mildness.

"You're right," he finally said. "Let's go fishing."

"As for you, my boy," said Harry as he left to Phil, "take my advice. Against stupidity, the gods themselves contend in vain, as they say, and you've got enough problems without having to deal with idiots in your management team."

Phil just stared, at a loss for words.

"By the way. Your presses are a god-awful mess," Harry shared as a parting shot to Dave. Dad gave us all a quick glance, shrugged once more, and followed Harry out without a further word. And then before we had caught our collective breath, they were gone. Around us, the plant continued operating, working, breathing, living in mechanical unconcern. A few people were looking at us from afar. I imagined that, as in any ship, scuttlebutt would have the incident around the place by the evening, and there'd be hell to pay in the morning. Fishing!

"That was something!" let out Dave, drawing a deep breath, still in shock.

"I'll go back to my work, if you don't mind," blurted out Ester, looking distinctively ill at ease. Amy gave her a quick, reassuring smile and a whispered catch-you-later.

"Why do they have to act so ... tough?" she almost screamed.

"Maybe they just *are* that tough," I thought out loud. I still felt queasy from reverberated aggression. "From what I've heard, Harry used to be Attila the Hun, before he got religion."

"Big-shot automotive purchasing VP. What do we expect?" agreed Phil, looking ill. "Of course he's tough. The question is, 'Is he right?'"

"And you, you, " Amy stammered angrily at Phil. "Couldn't you at least say something! Anything!"

"Should I have?" Phil snapped back. "That's rich, coming from you! You, of all people, should be agreeing with Harry. How many times have I heard you say that the only way to explain Kevin's stubbornness is the bone between his ears?"

She flushed darkly, eyes blazing back at Dave, who looked at her questioningly.

"We all know it. Kevin hasn't got a clue beyond his precious MRP, and he rubs everyone the wrong way. But what about the man!" she almost screamed. "Forget about kanban, for a sec. You've just seen one of your management team humiliated in public, and you don't care!"

Philip looked at her slowly, and thought carefully before

answering. "You're always telling me I'm not tough enough when it comes to management decisions. Maybe I'm learning."

"What, you're going to fire him?" she asked, incredulous.

"Not on Harry's say-so, of course. But he'd better get with the program, because the writing is on the wall."

Dave wasn't saying anything, but he looked frazzled. My bet was that he was suddenly realizing just how much his defensive attitude might have cost him. "Well," he added with a self-deprecating chuckle, "I'd better go and look at those presses."

I wasn't feeling happy either. How many times had I heard Dad bitch at home about management? He never blamed the workers, but he had a litany of complaints about management. How often had I endured his rants and raves to my mother about the people he wanted out but didn't have the clout to fire? Well, I was finally seeing it for real, and glad that I was in a job that didn't require any such decisions of me. Me? I found it difficult enough to fail a student in my class.

"So what do we do now?" wondered Phil.

"What did you think you were doing?" Amy asked accusingly the second my father opened the door to let her in. "What was that all about?"

It had taken a while for the dust to settle. It seemed that Kevin Morgan hadn't even gone back to his office, but straight out to his car and driven away, leaving his jacket and briefcase behind. Then Phil got an earful from Gary Pellman, who'd heard it from someone else, and so on. In the end, I'd agreed to take both Amy and Phil back to my parents in the evening to try to talk to Dad, not quite sure of the kind of reception we would get, but feeling that today's episode needed resolution.

"You had it planned! I bet you did." She continued heatedly. "Was it more of the good-cop, bad-cop routine?"

I'd had similar suspicions myself and wondered what Dad would have to say about it. He had been unusually accommodating when we said we'd like to talk to him in the evening, and we'd all ended up in the kitchen while he was grilling a fish he'd caught this afternoon with Harry.

"It wasn't. We'd not talked about it."

"You didn't look very surprised though," I pointed out.

"No. I guess not. I know what Harry's like. He's done this before."

"Do you realize the kind of fuss this is going to stir?" Amy railed, looking at Phil, who just looked concerned and thoughtful. Like most people she'd got Phil completely wrong, confusing his aversion for conflict for weakness. Phil hated conflict. In fact, as far back as I could remember, Phil tended to freeze in the face of emotional intensity. But that didn't mean he backed down. I remembered him as a teenager, resisting the most hardened bullies in tongue-tied silence and awkward inaction, through sheer size and force of inertia. I had never seen Phil moved to violence. I'd never seen him run away either.

"Don't confuse your enemy, miss," snapped my father. "And don't underestimate Harry. Don't be fooled by his manner. He used to be one of more powerful purchasing czars around, and he knows what he's talking about."

"What was that all about, then?" Phil asked, echoing Amy.

Dad sighed, and concentrated on cooking the fish for a while.

"First, your man Morgan *is* a problem, and *will* continue to be a problem, mark my words. Second, Harry was really just having a go at me."

"At you?" wondered Phil, surprised.

"Yes, son, at me. You see, he thinks I should either not have gotten involved at all, or that I have to actually make sure you get out of the deep water. Right now, according to him, I've only muddied the situation."

"He's got a strange way to make his points," quipped Amy.

"Harry doesn't make points, Amy," answered Dad quietly. "He makes things happen. In effect he's more or less bullied me into getting more involved, given me a lesson about forgetting about the *gemba*, and, brutally, I admit, opened the door to deal with logistics. Not all is always as it seems."

"Gemba?" I wondered out loud.

"Yeah, gemba. A Japanese term meaning the 'real place.' Where things really happen. I've tried to help you out from a distance, removed from the gemba and, I have to admit, that's not enough."

"What's that got to do with Kevin Morgan?" asked Amy, not yet ready to be mollified.

"Quite a lot, actually. It has to do with the attitude you need to get a kanban to work, not just the technique."

"What do you mean by that?"

"Well, making this work is not just about kanban per se. It's about a pragmatic approach to getting things done. What really annoyed Harry was that this guy was so focused on his own narrow perspective that he wasn't interested in the practical, shop-floor impact of his job, and, worse, he was blaming everyone else for the problems he was creating in the first place."

"This whole thing about reducing buffer stocks," said Amy, thinking aloud.

"Yeah, I thought that one through," agreed Phil. "Buffers are there to mask some sort of variation, so if you reduce the buffer arbitrarily without reducing the causes of variation, all you get is missing parts. That's exactly what is happening. We would build up the purchased parts inventories precisely because we didn't understand the variations, but our main objective was no missing parts on the shop floor. Now on a whim, Kevin's changed all that without telling anyone. So *presto*: missing parts."

"Not just on a whim," pointed out Amy. "I'm sure Gary Pellman put him up to it."

"Whatever," replied Phil uncomfortably, "but what about this supplier kanban thing?"

"Same problem. Let's take this step-by-step. What's the point about using kanban?"

"Produce only what has been consumed."

"That's not all."

Deep concentration from the home team, but no further suggestions.

"Produce what has been consumed *in the right order*."

"Damn it!" Amy swore. "I knew that."

"Uh-huh. Why is it so important?"

"Because if I'm producing one item," said Phil, "I'm not producing another that has to go on the same line or equipment, of course, we're back to leveling."

"Yes. You have to figure that production time of one item is nonproduction time of all other items. Now if I calculate my immediate needs for parts and just send this order to the supplier saying, 'bring them to me,' what am I doing?"

"Unless my production schedule is totally leveled," answered Amy cautiously, "I send him parts orders that will vary from one day to the next."

"And if, in order to maximize the use of transport, I batch my orders in economic order quantities, what's likely to happen then?"

"Rather than get a variable order every day, the suppliers get a fixed order in terms of number of parts, but which comes at a variable interval, unpredictably."

"What tends to happen is both. The upshot is that the supplier never quite knows when the orders are arriving and for how many. The only way he can deliver right away is if he permanently keeps an inventory for the maximum order possible in his factory, which of course, he never does."

"So what happens?"

"Well, when the order arrives, he ships what he's got on hand, and then schedules the rest of the order for later according to his own production schedule, which might take a while. And —"

"Missing parts for us," concluded Amy.

"Yep, but if you're not careful, you can be doing exactly the same thing in your factory, with this sort of botched kanban."

"How come?"

"Remember, we discussed that returning kanban cards have to be placed in a queue or a file, a system that specifies the order in which they've returned."

"So that our production runs reproduce the same order in which the parts have been consumed, isn't it?" Phil checked.

"Yep. However, in many cases, people set up a kanban board so that they stack up the returning cards from the customer process. So let's say we've got a pile of cards for STR cabinets, one for STR-X, one for QST-1, one for QST-2, and so forth … Then, on the board, we draw three zones: green, orange, and red."

"I get it," chimed in Amy, quick as ever with this stuff. "Each card that comes back is a cabinet being consumed by the conveyor, right? So if the cards are still in the green zone, few cards on the board means still plenty of cards on the cabinets lineside, and we don't need to produce any more. If the cards move up into the orange, we have to worry about it, and if the cards pile up and reach the red zone, we're in a panic because it means that we've got all the cards here and the conveyor is out of this type of cabinet, and we need to produce some more in a hurry. Is that it?"

"I think I visualize it," I mumbled, groping with the idea. "But what happens if all different kinds are in the red at the same time?"

"Actually, that's a good intuition, Junior," said Dad. "It can and does happen. Back in the early days when we discovered this the hard way, we called it the French kanban," joked my father.

"Why on earth?"

"Because if you don't level, your stacks of cards go up and down, up and down. You know, like French cancan," he explained with a grin, making dancing steps with his fingers.

"More seriously, it's all about …"

"Leveling!" we said in unison.

"Yeah, of course, but in this case, it was more *people* I had in mind."

We looked at each other and burst out laughing. Somehow, I doubted we'd ever be getting any of this right.

"Autonomy, in fact. In order to be truly autonomous, operators in the cell should always know what they have to do next."

"Which is what the kanban file does, really," said Amy.

"Which is exactly what the kanban file does, if you have a file. As long as it works smoothly, the cell can function as an autonomous team because they have their work sequence laid out for them. But that's not the case with a kanban board. The board with the green-orange-red zones doesn't specify the order of production. There are decisions that people need to make."

"You mean someone has to look at the board and decide which batch of cards they're going to produce next?"

"Absolutely," agreed Dad with his thin smile, "and how many cards they decide to produce in one go as well, which is precisely the kind of decisions operators can't make meaningfully when they haven't got the knowledge about what is going on elsewhere in the plant. So typically the supervisor hangs around and keeps making the calls."

"And we've not achieved much," concluded Phil, "beyond replacing MRP instructions with cards."

"We had a consultant once do a time-and-motion study of what supervisors actually do. It came down to two things: They run around looking for missing parts, and they make decisions about which production to run next."

"Awesome," said Amy, sounding truly impressed. "With the proper kanban queue, you resolve both problems. Components are pulled into the cell by kanban, and the cell operators always know what production they have to do next by kanban. Cool stuff."

"As long as your kanban system specifies the *order* in which parts have to be produced as well as their quantity," Dad explained. "The trick is that the operator has to know without a doubt what his next production will be and how many parts it has to be."

"No wonder supervisors resist it," I remarked. "There goes their job from what you're saying."

"In no way. It just changes, and gets more interesting. What they now have to do is work on standardized work and kaizen."

"Jeez," swore Phil. "The more you put it all together, the more impressive it gets. Amy's right. That sounds awesome."

"But," said Dad, pointing a finger in the air, "you can only do that if the kanban works. And that means delivering good parts!"

"And if we have the kind of supervisors who can work well with operators on kaizen," frowned Amy. "I'm not too worried about Gloria or Ester, but imagine if Jake was still there!"

"Never easy," agreed my father quietly. "Always the same story, you tend to need more supervisors and team leaders, and rarely the ones you've already got. It's never easy, because it's all about people."

"It's pretty daunting," muttered Amy with a soft sigh. "Every time you look at something, there's so much more to do."

After a surprisingly good meal we had gravitated to my parents' porch, where we now watched the stars appear over the hill with coffees and brandy, greatly mellowed. Even Amy had thawed and was edging back to her usual vivacity. The evening was quiet and cool, without being cold, and the cicadas where chirping. My mother's cat had mysteriously appeared and jumped up into Amy's lap, where it was now purring happily under her caresses.

"Amy, don't you start having doubts!" teased Phil with a grin. "Worrying about never getting there is my department. But I agree with you, it sometimes seems like two steps forward, one step back."

"Oh, come on. What makes you say that?" asked Dad.

"Well, like today. I think we now understand how the kanban works, or at least in theory. But it only delivers if we have zero defects on the one hand, and no missing parts on the other. Our reality just isn't so ideal yet. Hell, Harry was right about our presses. They seem to be down every other day, and on some days they continue to make bad parts. On top of it, it's hard enough getting Dave on board. Now imagine us trying to explain all of that to that fool Morgan. Especially after today's showdown," he concluded with a pointed stare at my Dad, who stared back, unmoved.

"I believe you've got it the wrong way around, Phil. Kanban isn't supposed to work in a perfect world. It's supposed to help you get to a perfect world. Look, if you've got too many kanban cards lined up at a process, it means that production has been delayed. And of course it happens. Reality fights back, so you get machine breakdowns, shortages of every kind, from materials to capacity to human, quality problems, and so on. Kanban makes you visualize the work so you're constantly aware of it and do something about problems instead of just whining. And if the other case is a production stoppage because you're out of kanban cards, which means you're ahead of schedule and then you should seriously think about your capacity excess, either people or equipment. Maybe, in the end, you'll find out you don't need that many presses!"

"That'd be the day!"

"Ultimately, kanban is a kaizen tool, and not the other way around. By reducing the number of kanban in a loop, you force more inefficiency to the surface. Problems that used to be covered up become clear, so you can work the continuous-improvement magic. Don't you see, it's all about people. How many times do I have to say it! People! The kanban system focuses them on sorting out problems rather than hiding them and suffering. And now, if your logistics guy can't take it, well it's not his money at the end of the day. It's yours!"

"Yeah. Of course, you're right. And don't think I'm not listening, that I'm ungrateful. I just get discouraged by the number of things we've got to do. Presses. What do I know about presses!"

After letting Phil stew for a bit, Dad finally relented.

"Is the plant working tomorrow, Saturday?" he asked wearily.

"No, thankfully, no. We're still working occasionally on weekends, but not tomorrow."

"Good, we don't need another drama, so this is what we'll do. It's not as effective as going there when the plant is operating, but we'll go and have a look at your presses tomorrow morning, and we'll talk some more about gemba."

"Thanks, Bob, I really appreciate this. I owe you."

"Forget it. Harry was right. I got you halfway there, I might as well try to pull you through."

"Another weekend at the plant!" Amy exclaimed with exaggerated enthusiasm, "and me wondering how I was going to fill my time tomorrow. Fine, guys, it's late, and I'm off. See y'all tomorrow morning."

I watched her say a polite good night to my Mother and walk out of the door. Watching Phil give Mother a warm goodbye, it dawned on me that there might be a hint of cunning in his constant whining. It was irritating, sure, but in the final event, he had managed to wheedle more advice out of my father than I'd thought likely at the outset. Phil, manipulative? Now that was an eye-opener, and no mistake.

"So that's the Amy I'm hearing so much about?" said Mother as I was helping her clear up. "She looks sweet."

"Sweet? I wouldn't call her sweet. She's hard as nails in her own cheerful way."

"Your dad says she's quite the bright cookie. He's very impressed."

"Yeah, she probably has kanban rolling through her mind at nights. She's got an intuitive grasp of all this stuff that completely baffles Phil and me. And it's not like she's studied it before, she's from HR."

"So your dad tells me. He says she gets concepts right that took him years to understand. He also said you like her," she added with a sly look.

"Oh come on, Mother, not again. She's just this woman who works for Phil."

"Well, I find her sweet," she added conclusively. "That deep voice of hers. She should be in radio."

Just what I needed, I thought despondently. Not only am I spending my weekends at the factory, but my Mother is now trying to sell me on a budding production expert. How low can it get? And my own book not getting written for that matter, as my sabbatical was running out. Just-in-time indeed!

My Dad walked us back to our cars, our feet crunching loudly on the gravel. As Phil was squeezing his bulk in his orange toy, Dad rapped him lightly on the head with his cap. "And what's even better than kanban?" he asked with an amused grin.

Phil glanced up, looking twice his age in the yellow glare of the front-door spotlight, his eyes strangely obscured by the reflection on his lenses. He shook his head resignedly.

"I give in."

"No kanban! Obviously," laughed Dad.

A slow grin spread on Phil's tired features. "I get it! Continuous one-piece flow, of course, you don't need kanban for that!"

"That's right," said Dad good-naturedly. "There's hope for you yet."

"Okay. That gives us something to look forward to," Phil chuckled. "Kanban rules!"

"Yeah," I snorted back, shutting the door on him. "Kanban rules."

Chapter Eight

GEMBA ATTITUDE

Phil was already there when I arrived the next morning. I joined him where he waited, leaning back on his flashy excuse for a car, facing the empty lot lost in thought, and Amy found us reminiscing about the bad old days of high school when she arrived. She looked tired. Definitely overworked, I thought, and less than her usual lively self. She perched herself next to me without a word and gave me a friendly squeeze for a greeting. We were quietly sunning ourselves when my father's pick-up pulled in.

"Gimme a hand," he shouted, not bothering with morning chitchat. He climbed into the back of his truck and pulled out folded garden chairs, which he passed down to us, without a word of explanation. So, in we went, our feet clattering in the empty corridors of the plant's offices. The deserted offices had an eerie air of end-of-the-world catastrophe, of abandoned cups of coffee, and piles of paper left to rot.

The feeling of desolation was even stronger in the factory. No metal stamping, no honking forklifts, no harassed engineers, no galley rowers chained to their benches. The metal and oil tang mixed uneasily with the lingering paint smell from the recent 5S drive. We walked silently past the conveyor and the mechanism line, past the stack of metal crates and gutless breaker cabinet stack, and into the back area where the metal boxes themselves were assembled.

"The flow here is fairly messy," Phil said quietly, although his voice sounded suddenly very loud in the silence of the factory's uneasy sleep.

"Metal sheets are cut into shape and punched here on this CNC puncher. One sheet is turned into two panel sides for the cabinets.

239

Then the panels are either moved directly to forming over there where they're bent, or moved to the storeroom we just passed. After bending, they're welded together way over there. The instrument panel and doors are, as you've seen, fitted, on the conveyor."

"That sounds pretty straightforward," I remarked.

"Yeah, but there's the door panels as well. See, the doors need special forming so that we can fit the customers' instrument panels on, so they go through this old forming press, here, before going to bending as well. And whereas the side panels need on average one bend each, the doors need at least four bends."

"Then they get fitted at welding?" asked Dad.

"That's it, we assemble the cabinets, and then all the rest of the stuff gets added on the conveyor, at final assembly."

I tried to visualize the flow and imagine operators moving parts from one station to the next, but all I could see was a couple of large greenish machines and a jumble of wire-mesh crates filled with metal parts.

"So, what's with the chairs?" asked Amy gamely. I found once more that her natural high spirits tended somehow to dispel my morning gloom. There was something humorous about her relentless perkiness, which just cheered me up. And she didn't take crap from anyone, not even the Woods, father or son.

"I was once part of a benchmarking group touring industrial facilities," said Dad. "We got lucky inasmuch as the organizers had managed to set up a tour of one of the first Japanese transplants in the U.K. with one of the surviving Total Quality gurus of the time, a very old man by then."

He slowly unfolded his chair, and placed it right in the middle of the shop floor, among the crates and the machines, with no apparent purpose.

"One of the plant's engineers had, cap in hand, embarrassingly confessed they could not think of any improvements to the line, which, to be fair, was pretty impressive. One of the most productive car manufacturing operations in the world at the time, and certainly one step above anything else we'd seen in Europe. To everyone's puzzlement, the old master didn't say anything directly but asked for chairs to be brought to the shop floor. He had all of us sit down in silence without pen or paper right in the middle of the stamping presses, huge, noisy monsters. We were not to get up, he said through his apologetic translator, until someone came up with a fundamental improvement idea."

"How long did you stay there?" asked Amy, with a quick low laugh.

"Four hours, and believe me, we were getting stiff and sore, not to say hungry. It looked really good. We just couldn't see anything obvious until the old guru finally pointed out that the line was waiting for a crane to help change over a machine and parts were not moving. By pulling that string, they completely reorganized their setup method, and reduced batch size by 30% more. It was incredible."

"We're not likely to see much with everything stopped," I said, still feeling rather put out for being told I now had to sit for hours in silence in a deserted factory rather than, ah, I suppose, sit for hours in silence in front of my computer and unfinished manuscript.

"You're right. We'd see a lot more if the plant was running," agreed my father overlooking my attempt at biting irony, "but after yesterday's drama, I doubt they'd take very well to us staring at them while they work. In any case, there's plenty to see right now."

"You really sat for four hours?" wondered Phil as he settled down on his chair and started glancing around, not quite certain of what he was supposed to look for.

"Oh, yeah. There's a long tradition of this in the lean movement. My own teacher claimed that Ohno himself trained him by drawing a chalk circle on the ground in front of a machine and asking him to stand there until he had an improvement to suggest."

"No joke!" exclaimed Amy, laughing heartily. "I'd like to do that to Kevin Morgan next! Or Gary Pellman for that matter." This drew a reluctant smile from Phil.

"It sounds like Japanese teaching myths, you know, *Karate Kid* style. 'Wax on, wax off!'" she added in a gruff tone.

"Sand floor!" replied Phil with sudden mirth.

"Win, lose, no matter. Make good fight. Earn respect," I replied, joining the fun.

"Good film," agreed Dad, surprising us all. "What? You think I don't remember you and Philip watching that movie over and over again when you were teenagers?"

Amy chortled, giving us a pitying look.

"And yes, there is some cultural element to it. And a lesson for us. At some point, the old guy diagnoses the kid's problem as an 'attitude' problem. The bad guys have 'wrong attitude,' correct?"

"Yeah, I remember that bit," recalled Phil. "Something about that there are no bad students, only bad teachers."

"Yep. Wrong attitude from the teacher. This is exactly what we're here to work out this morning. Yesterday evening, you asked me why Harry came down so hard on your logistics guy, and told you to fire him."

Phil squirmed uneasily, remembering yesterday's scene.

"I didn't answer you right away, but this is what we're going to find out today. It's an *attitude* issue."

"What do you mean by that?" asked Amy.

"First, watch. Look around and tell me what you see. Then we'll discuss it."

Hai, I thought. Yes, *sensei*.

We sat there for about 10 minutes in silence until Dad asked us again: "What do you *see*?"

"It's a mess," said Phil.

"In what way."

"No flow, for starters."

"I agree," concurred Amy. "And there are in-process stocks all over the place. Look at those crates of blanks."

"Not just that," pursued Phil, "but think about it. They punch the blanks, then either leave them here or move them all the way to the storeroom. Then they come back to the press over there. Then back to the store, and back again for welding."

"Same story all over again."

"Absolutely," agreed my father. "Just like the mechanisms. Start with what you did there."

"A cell," Amy remarked. "We organized a cell to spot the variation in the standardized work and move them to takt time."

"Yeah, one-piece flow," agreed Phil. "But it doesn't make much sense here."

"Why not?" I wondered.

"Well, the CNC puncher cuts a blank into two side panels in about a minute; then, to do another two panels, you have to change the cutting program which takes one or two minutes to load, so the guys typically cut 100 of one side panel, then 100 of the other, and so on, which explains why we have crates of panels over here."

"A hundred of one side?" exclaimed Amy in mock outrage. "That's two weeks' worth of cabinets! No wonder we've got crates of the stuff."

"Probably worse," conceded Phil ruefully. "Remember that we've got about eight variants of cabinets, so that means we're cutting 48 different panels. Even if we cut them two by two, we get about 24 different runs of 100 parts at a time."

"So, at the minimum, you've got 2,400 panels lying about," chuckled Dad, "which is potential for 400 cabinets, although you build 200 circuit breakers a week. Nice going."

"Okay, okay," conceded Phil irritably. "I've got it, but what else can we do? On top of it, every sixth panel has to be formed, which takes 20 seconds because of the two press passes, and — don't even say anything," he admonished quickly, "since the tool changeover on the press takes forever, we do half-a-day runs of these."

"That's 600 parts runs of doors on eight variants?" protested Amy. "So we're keeping 4,800 formed doors around. *Dios mio*, that's 24 weeks of doors!"

"I told you not to say anything," muttered Phil. "I've got it. I see now why we have all these metal parts lying all over the place. But what can we do? All these machines run from 20 seconds to a minute, and then welding takes about 20 minutes to assemble a cabinet. The time-scales are completely different, and the changeover hassle is endless."

"Philip, Philip," repeated my father reprovingly. "Stick to the principles. Where do we start from?"

"Standardized work?"

"Before that."

"Customer!" exclaimed Amy. "Takt time. Of course."

"Yes. How many times do I have to say this? Always start with the customer. So what's the takt time for breaker cabinets?"

"At the moment, we're shipping 50 STRs a week, 40 STR-Xs, 55 QST-1s, 50 QST-2s, and about 20 DGs, so that's 215 boxes of various shapes a week — 43 per day."

"At 450 minutes of open time a day," Amy continued, "we have a total takt time of a little under 11 minutes."

"Let's say 11. You can work out the exact figures later," Dad said. He paused, taking a moment to think. "Now what we're saying is that, just for the door panels, you keep months of panels in stock although you only build a cabinet every 11 minutes."

Phil did not reply, but scribbled calculations on his pad.

"And that's the best case," continued Dad relentlessly. "I somehow doubt they're going to change the tool every half-day. I'd not be surprised if we found years worth of door panels in the storeroom!"

"Come, on. It can't be true!" erupted Phil. "We must talk to Dave. We must be getting this completely wrong."

"It doesn't matter. You can check the specifics later, but the reasoning is sound. And not particularly surprising."

"Why don't we outsource these parts then?" Amy suggested. "It has to be cheaper to do externally."

"We thought about it," replied Phil, "but we figured we didn't want the added aggravation of dealing with yet one more supplier — clean blueprints, late deliveries, and so on. In any case, these machines were depreciated long before we took over the company."

"Don't confuse book value with economic value," nagged Dad. "The worth of a machine is its resale value, which, in this case, I agree, is not likely to be much. In any case, don't get distracted, stick to the reasoning for the moment. How does it work with the press brake?"

"Same thing. We need about six or seven bends per cabinet. Let's say seven. Plus the four for each door panel. One box will require 11 times 25 seconds, which is about four and a half minutes. We'll do 43 in a little more than three hours."

"If I get this right," checked Amy. "To achieve daily demand, we'd have to use the press brake three hours a day."

"Sounds about right."

"Now, welding the cabinet together takes 20 minutes. Can someone add all this up?"

We stared at the press in front of us in silence. I didn't bother to try. I kept myself amused by betting silently that Amy would come up with something fast.

"We can still flow," she said enthusiastically. Bet won, I thought. Too easy. "It's not like we're using the presses for anything else. We can still flow them!"

"What do you mean?" asked Phil with a deep, puzzled frown.

"Let's work it backward. Takt time of 10 minutes. Let's be optimistic and keep welding somewhere under 20 minutes, that means two operators, with time to spare, right?"

"Yes, but what about —"

"Wait a sec. We're cutting two panels a minute, so three minutes for an entire cabinet, then 11 bends, so five more minutes, and the door panel goes through the forming press, that's 25 seconds. If we add it all up, I'm still under 10 minutes. So, if we're clever about it, one operator can do the entire kit under 10 minutes, and then pass it on to the welders. They do 10 minutes each, and there you go, we're flowing!"

"But the press would run so slow!" objected Phil. "One hit every 10 minutes?"

"So what? They'd actually cycle at regular speed, they just don't start again until needed. It's not like they have anything else to do. They're sitting idle most of the time."

"And then we'd lose two minutes for every one at the CNC puncher. Every time he does a different blank, he needs to reload the program."

"So," answered my father. "If we have the puncher right in front of the press brake, he could use the loading time to do four bends, that's an entire door. The actual cutting time could be used to do the bends on the other cabinet sides."

"Could that really work?" asked Phil uncertainly.

"I don't see why not. Amy is right; you're not doing anything else with the machines. The forming press hitting only every 10 minutes is not particularly shocking, since it does nothing else. It's already standing idle most of the time in any case. In my old industry, it wouldn't have made any sense because the plastic injection presses were always a bottleneck, and huge investment, so we did everything we could to keep them operating as much as we could."

"Makes sense, with a capacity investment," agreed Phil.

"You bet!" Dad snorted. "I remember one plant where they had actually applied the flow dogma to such extremes that they had linked a 1,500-ton press to the assembly cycle. I tried to tell them that to be lean, the first thing they had to do was to keep the press running as fast as it could to maximize the press capacity, so that one press could service many assembly lines rather than one, but they looked at me as if I was crazy."

"How does that work out?"

"Heck, in most injection presses, you've got at least one operator working with each press to check the parts and pack them into boxes. Since the press is quite fast, the operator doesn't have time to do any real value-added work. But still, you've got one operator per press. Six presses, six operators. We were also dealing with small parts, and smaller presses. The operators were kept busy by wrapping the parts in cellophane and other such nonvalue-added work. What we did was organize a conveyor so that each of the six presses dropped its finished parts on the conveyor lane. The parts all came to a cell where three operators sorted the different parts coming down, and stacked them in special containers and straight into the supermarket. We reduced the number of small press operators by half."

"Way to go," blurted out Phil.

"Oh, we didn't stop there. We realized that the six presses were never fully loaded, because of breakdowns and slowdowns or simply because the workload was erratic. We worked like mad to make sure that the presses ran continuously without a hitch — seriously tough job, I'll tell you — and then to make sure our changeovers were under 10 minutes so that we could run all the production of the six presses on five. So, in the end, we saved an entire press, which we sent to another factory of the group that was ready to invest into an additional press. We must have saved at least $2 million that had been tied up in that press. Not bad for a year's work at TPM."

"TPM?"

"*Total productive maintenance.* I'll get to that later. The point is that you are in the opposite situation: you have no capacity constraints. These old warhorses have been paid for. You're not about to supply anyone else with pressed parts, so who cares whether you spread their utilization in one go or throughout the day."

"But you just said that in your plant, you disconnected the press from the flow," I retorted.

"Haven't you been listening?" he scolded. "In that case, equipment capacity and investment were the problems. In our case they aren't. Flow is the problem, and avoiding stockpiling months of parts — which is just plain silly. Lean is pragmatic first and foremost. You reason it out, and you figure out what you want to do! There is no set solution, it's just try it and see!"

"Okay, I get your point," agreed Phil thoughtfully. "In our case, we could have a cell producing cabinets."

"With a supermarket," Amy suggested, "on which the final assembly process would come to help itself in cabinets."

"The issue of the die exchange remains, though," countered Phil. "If we're saying we're going to stick to the leveled flow of the container, it means we should produce a different box every time. In fact, you'd have to add an hour changeover time to the second operation itself. It's plain silly."

"It may look silly, perhaps. But the important thing is flowing cabinets to the conveyor, right?" argued Dad. "Who cares if all the operators here strip and work in the nude, as long as we supply the conveyor just-in-time?"

"Spare me," laughed Amy. "Although that'd be a sight to see, I'd rather miss it."

"I take your point. It wouldn't be particularly shocking to have a long tool change and a short punch run as long as we're within takt time. Which means getting the die exchange down under 10 minutes. Hell, this is really looking at it upside down!"

"Still, if you spend so long to change tools, it would be wasted work, *motion* — which is operator time that could be used more productively elsewhere adding value. It's not a matter of how it looks, but of reason," reminded my Dad. "Now, say we can get the tool changes down to 20 minutes, we can still batch the cabinets."

"Okay, 20-minute changeovers, with your rule of thumb, would make for a 200-minute production run. Which means a batch of 10 boxes of one type. That's close to a day's production of most of what we've got. That could work."

"Actually, you should aim for doing just that," agreed my father. "One of lean's immediate aims is producing EPES, *every part every shift*. This is a simple, specific goal to achieve."

"We've still got to get our tool changeover down to 20 minutes," remarked Phil. "I've heard you mention SMED, how does that work?"

"SMED means *single minute exchange of die*, and it is as straightforward as it gets."

"Single minute exchange of die," repeated Phil.

"The target is to get your tool changeovers to under 10 minutes."

This made Phil laugh.

"I'll tell this to the guy in charge of the presses. I can't wait to watch his face," he chortled.

"Well, it's clear that you don't move from here to there in one single leap. Under 10 minutes is the usual benchmark. The workshop procedure in itself is simple as pie. The only thing to beware of is to make sure every one realizes that the issue is not the 'changeover' time in itself, but the elapsed time from last good part to first good part."

"Last good part to first good part," repeated Phil dutifully.

"Yes. Now, the key to SMED is to separate internal work that can only be done when the machine is down from external work that can be done to get ready while the machine is still running. There are six steps:

First: Measure total changeover time in the current state.

Second: Identify and measure the internal work elements versus the external ones.

Third: Move the external elements and execute them before the machine stops.

Fourth: Standardize, reduce, and eliminate the internal work, especially adjustments.

Fifth: Standardize, reduce, and eliminate the external work to the extent possible.

And sixth: Standardize the entire procedure and improve.

"It's pretty straightforward," my Dad said. "It's also methodical, hard work."

"I'll tell you straight, Phil," Amy said pointedly. "I'm not getting involved in any of in this. Tool changeover sounds way out of my court."

"Don't fret over it. There's plenty of specialist consultants who do that very well," replied my Dad. "Today is about gemba."

"Okay then, let's see if I got the big picture right," said Amy. "As an immediate goal, we want cabinet building organized as a cell, producing every type every day, is that it? That's going to be another huge change."

"Only in their minds, Amy. The machine doesn't care one way

or the other. You've already done this successfully with the mechanism; it's exactly the same here. First you organize a cell and get them to understand value, then you get them to flow the parts, and finally, you pull."

"Okay, you're right," agreed Phil. "We've done this already, and we should be able to pull if we can achieve leveling on the conveyor — then it's a matter of running a kanban from there to here. Damn," he added with heartfelt frustration, "I just don't see it!"

"Don't sweat it, Philip," said Dad quietly. "Work the numbers. Amy's right. As long as you know that the working content fits, it's a matter of organization, so work at it backward:

- You want to produce cabinets for the conveyor, one every 11 minutes, and at least every eight variants every day.
- Right behind the shop stock, you've got your two welders assembling the cabinets. It takes them 20 minutes each, which means that one cabinet gets pushed onto the shop stock every 10 minutes.
- For the welders to assemble the cabinets, we need all the cabinet parts to arrive in position every 20 minutes for each welder, coming from part forming.
- So visualize an extra jig on which you can place all the parts, so that the welder can simply grab it and start to work."

"What they do now in any case," interjected Amy, "except they lose a lot of time finding the right panels and fitting them on the jigs and so on."

"Exactly," pursued Dad, "so, ideally, these jigs arrive fully loaded to the welders so they can work without variation. Let's continue:

- The six cabinet sides need to be cut.
- Five of them need to be bent.
- The fifth, a door, needs special forming and more bends.

"From our estimates, all of this should fit within 10 minutes, but now you've got to organize it so that one operator can easily move from the CNC puncher to the press brake and the forming press, and place the finished panels on a jig, which then goes to the welder. Once you've sorted that out, you can start worrying about organizing the kanban signal from the conveyor. Easy!"

"I wish it were," complained Phil. "But I get the idea. If we work the numbers and get our heads around it, we should be able to do it!"

"That's the spirit," said my father approvingly. "But lets put aside all these flow issues for the moment. This is not the central point I want to make today. You keep telling me what you want to do, how you visualize the flow and so on, but you're not giving me anything on what you're actually seeing. Here. Now, in front of your very eyes; look around. What do you see?"

"The area is quite clear. We've done some 5S."

"Don't try to anticipate what I'd like to hear, Amy. Watch. See. Tell me."

We sat there in silence, getting increasingly frustrated and sore.

"I don't know what you expect from us, Dad," I complained. "I don't know anything about any of these machines. I can't figure anything out beyond the fact that their color is ugly and that the paint is flaking."

"Excellent, Mickey," he responded unexpectedly. "There's hope for you yet. Keep going."

"Well, there's oil on the floor under the casing over there."

"Yeah, actually there's even some sand over there to absorb the oil," added Phil. "And there's a stack of blanks on a piece of cardboard at the left of the machine. What are they doing there?"

"I can see a rag around a pipe from here," contributed Amy, getting into the spirit of the thing.

"And look inside the press itself. It doesn't look too clean either. Look at the oil tracks!"

"Hey, they're old ladies."

"All the more reason to keep them spotlessly clean," Dad replied.

"Is that what Harry got so worked up about?" asked Amy. "We've done some 5S, but we haven't pursued it *into* the machine, so to speak."

"Partly, yes, as a start. But it goes farther than this. What this tells me is that no one really takes care of this equipment."

"That's harsh."

"Well, can you tell me how it runs?"

"Not like this, no."

"So, if you can't see it charted on the machine itself, it's because no one here really cares."

"Dave complains a lot about the machines being down often," agreed Phil. "And Matt and I have been fighting endless requests to purchase new ones, both from Dave and engineering. We keep telling them that we haven't got the cash, but —"

"For crying out loud!" exclaimed Dad with a whiff of exasperation. "How many times do we have to go through this? Invest in people, not equipment. At this stage, zero investment in this plant should be obvious to all. You're teetering at the brink of not paying vendors and they still want you to buy presses! Darn, it's always the same thing."

Phil just looked at him blankly.

"Listen, get this straight. We can spend a little on gimmicks to keep these machines operational, but you can get them operating 100% without *any major investment*. Do you read me?"

"I'd like to, sure," said Phil. "But this sounds about as magical as Kevin's MRP formula. What can I do? To start with, I don't know anything about presses. And Amy even less, right?"

She gave him a supporting nod.

"Well, I don't either, son. I used to work with injection molding machines that haven't got much in common with these things. But I can tell you that this press here is not cleaned properly. Why is cleaning important? It removes dust and metal shavings, which cause friction, clogging, leaking, and electrical defects, and they ruin moving parts.

"Also, sand and oil on the floor, plus look at that reservoir there, with all its grime and sludge. When did they last check the oil? Without proper lubrication how do you expect this equipment to do its job? And if it's leaking oil, it means that the whole circuit is not reliable.

"Now, what can you see right in front of your nose, just at the foot of the press, in the sludge? Yes, right there."

"I can't see anything," said Phil, who then corrected himself. "Ah yes, a small bolt. Jeez."

"Precisely. I hope its something the last maintenance guy dropped from his pocket, because if it's not, this press is not going to be a happy press for much longer! A single loose bolt can bring this huge machine to a dead stop. It can increase shaking, which in turns loosens other bolts, and creates even more vibration and so on, until you get a breakdown.

"Do you see my point, Philip? I don't need to know anything about presses to tell you something is not right here!"

"You're talking about more 5S?" asked Amy.

"To start with, but it's not just a matter of cleanliness. Do you remember what we said about 5S?"

"Of course. Sort through what's around and get rid of what's unnecessary. Then find a place for each thing and make sure it stays there, or goes back after use. Then clean, and so on."

"Well, you're going to have to do this more rigorously here. For instance, you need to figure out where all the special tools for the machine are kept, and create spaces around the machine to store them, in plain sight, so that they're accessible, but also so that we can see in what working order they're kept. Now, about seiso, clean or 'shine,' as some say, in this case, you're going to have to it work out with the operators and maintenance people exactly:

– what needs to be cleaned regularly,

– how to clean it safely,

– who will do the cleaning and when, and

– how clean is clean."

"I hear what you're saying," said Phil. "It's a far more demanding approach to 5S than what we've done up to now."

253

"And that's only the start. There's a lot more about TPM than in-depth 5S, but it's a good place as any to start."

"TPM again?" asked Amy.

"Yeah, total productive maintenance," answered Dad with a sigh. "We could spend days on this, but I'm only going to share a bit of background. The 'total' in TPM actually stands for three totals. The first means total effectiveness. The second is total involvement, as we were discussing. Operators clean the machine daily and monitor the dials like anyone does for their own car. The people in maintenance repair and eliminate problems; and the engineers follow up with root-cause analysis and fundamental machine-reliability improvement. The third total is total life cycle: tending to the long-term demands of the machine as it changes over time and use. Just like taking care of a human over a life cycle, actually. Most intensive at birth, and then again in our old age.

"When they started developing all these tools, Japanese engineers grasped a fundamental insight. Any piece of machinery functions well if it is placed in optimal conditions. TPM is actually aimed at creating optimal conditions for a machine to produce with zero defects and zero breakdowns. At its minimum the goal is to ensure that every machine is always able to perform its required tasks."

"One could argue it applies with people as well," chirped in Amy.

"Trust an HR manager to confuse people and machines," I teased her.

"Very funny," she said, kicking the leg of my chair.

"Yeah, well, I don't know about people, but it sure works with machines. Unfortunately, few people are ever interested in whether everyday 'normal' working conditions of machines are optimal or not."

"What we're looking at right now, I certainly wouldn't call optimal," commented Phil, nodding toward the press.

"That's the point. Everyone here operates the press in this mess without realizing it. They spend a lot of time 'fixing problems,' but that's like digging a hole in the sand. The more you dig, the more you find. Human nature being what it is, confronted with any problem, people tend to stop at the first possible cause of failure and act upon it, regardless of whether it's the root cause or not."

"It's easier to look for the key under the lamplight rather than grope in the dark," I remarked.

"Something like that. In fact, the very first contact I had with the Toyota system was about maintenance. I was production manager at the time, and, as part of a benchmarking program, I visited a supplier, who was our direct competitor at the time and whom we'd identified as a benchmark. I didn't understand most of what I was seeing back then, but one thing I came back with was TPM.

"We were supplying plastic parts, so we had a lot of problems with our molding machines, which accumulated a lot of downtime. Since we had overcapacity, we did not worry unduly about it, but I realized during the visit how much more effective they were in terms of capital utilization. We had 11 presses, which were down from 15% to 20% of the time due to a variety of causes, and I calculated that we were wasting the equivalent of a full press in stoppages. That figure got my CEO's attention real quick, and eventually we started a Total Productive Management initiative, which I must confess now, was something of a joke. But we tried hard."

"Didn't work?"

"I wouldn't say that. We obtained results and better utilization of our capacity investment in molding machines, but nothing to the order of liberating a full press. In the end it didn't seem to matter because the management was happy in investing more machines, which cost the company a fortune."

"What's so hard about maintenance then?" asked Phil, puzzled.

"Nothing hard about maintenance, son, it's total productive maintenance that's hard. At the end of the day, with complex machinery, you can only detect one effect at a time, which means you have to test various hypotheses carefully and systematically. Most engineers jump in the moment they see a possible cause. Trouble is they invest a lot of energy solving problems that aren't really that important, and in the process they miss the real ones. So to do this properly, we have to carefully validate every hypothesis before trying to solve it."

"This process must be owned by the operators," Dad continued. "We want the operator to know the machine well enough to recognize when something is going wrong well before an actual breakdown. Like anyone else, maintenance people tend to stop at the first obvious symptom. If the fuse blows, they'll replace the fuse and not look much further. So part of the difficulty is getting them to search for root causes."

"So, don't stop at symptoms, look for root causes," repeated Phil.

"That's right. I was telling you how I first got involved with all this lean approach by trying to implement TPM where I was working at that time. Well, I was with manufacturing engineering in those days. In the early 1980s, we'd never heard about Japanese industry, but we received a couple of Japanese engineers who were trying to replicate one of our machines to produce similar parts. It was a bilateral deal of some sort. We didn't take these guys very seriously, but we showed them around, and let them fiddle with the machines. Now, imagine this Styrofoam cup is the machined part," he said, picking up a discarded coffee cup lying next to his feet. So much for 5S, I thought to myself.

"See the line here on the side of the cup? We'll say it's a defect on the product. So the Japanese engineers ask us: 'Do you see that line? How do you do it?' We were a bit embarrassed, and had to tell them we didn't intend to produce that line, it was a defect. '*Hai!*' they answered. 'We understand, but how do you do it?' These guys are idiots or so we think, so we say louder that we didn't intend to make the line, it just happens, it's a defect in the process.

"Now, as part of the exchange, I get sent to Japan with a colleague. The same engineers are very pleased to see us, and they've built a replica of our machine," he said, pointing at the line on the stained Styrofoam. "'Look,' they say, 'we've replicated the line.' I still remember looking at my colleague thinking these guys must be even dumber than I thought. But when we looked at the production from the machine, none of the finished parts showed any line whatsoever. They'd resolved the problem and sorted it out!"

"Wait!" said Phil, putting his pen down. "I think I've figured it out. A defect has to be built into the process right? It doesn't appear by magic, it has to be actively worked into the product at some stage."

"Yes," continued Amy. "So they explored the machine's settings until it could replicate the defect at will, so they could set the machine *not to* produce the line!"

"Exactly. They didn't stop at an analysis of the symptoms, as we'd done. They went looking for the root cause. They asked a different question. How does this machine build the defect into the product? Once they could replicate it, they could eradicate it!"

"Talk about rigor!" said Amy, looking doubtfully at the used Styrofoam cup.

"This is where another lean technique comes handy. Have you heard of the 'Five Whys?'"

"Another five?" I remarked smartly. "What's this with five? Japanese superstition? Good luck number?"

"Could be," Dad answered with a rare show of humor. "Five tends to crop up a lot in lean tools. In any case, the idea is that, when confronted with a failure, we should look beyond the obvious to discover the root cause of the failure and eradicate the possibility of failure once and for all. There is a famous Ohno example with a fuse blowing repeatedly:

First why: Why did the machine stop? Because the fuse blew due to an overload.

Second why: Why was there an overload? Because the bearing lubrication was inadequate.

Third why: Why was the lubrication inadequate? Because the lubrication pump was not functioning right.

Fourth why: Why wasn't the lubrication pump working right?

Because the pump shaft was worn out.

Fifth why: Why was the shaft worn out? Because there was no strainer attached where it should be, letting metal-cutting chips in.

"By asking why until you reach the root cause you can find a sustainable solution, such as attaching a strainer to the lubricating pump."

"That's brilliant!" exclaimed Phil. "Ask 'why?' five times!"

"More workshops," sighed Amy. "I hope that's it for maintenance!"

"Unfortunately not," grumbled Dad. "TPM is one of the hardest tools to master, and there's more to it than I can probably say. The 'five why' approach sounds simple, but in actual fact is not so easy."

"Sounds pretty straightforward to me," I ventured. "Ask why five times."

"Yeah. But if you're not careful, the answers you get will be pure fantasy. The 'five why' works only if each answer is properly validated."

"Same thing you were saying about failure analysis?" she asked. "Have you got another 'five why?' example?"

"Let me think. Yeah, here's a good one. In one plant, when we started supplying Toyota, they continuously increased the number of trucks coming in to pick up parts daily. As a result we found ourselves with a growing congestion of trucks and crates in the expeditions bays. At the first 'why?' it soon became apparent that we didn't have enough loading docks to accommodate the number of trucks coming and going, which created waiting times and gridlock in the yard. We could have stopped there and invested in more docks, but we continued to ask 'why?' and realized the problem was not so much the number of docks, but the time each truck spent at the dock."

"I get it, one truck waiting at the dock is the next in the queue waiting in the yard."

"Correct. Then we figured out that trucks were waiting at the dock because their load wasn't ready on time, so loading time was compounded with finding the stuff and moving it to the loading area. In the end, we created a designated truck loading area, which had to be ready before the truck came in. This not only minimized the time spent at the dock, but also helped us to better control delivery flow. So we solved the problem without investment. In fact, if we had built more docks we would simply have compounded the problem by moving the pile-up from the courtyard to the docks themselves."

"No joke!" swore Amy. "It's all about leveling again. It's the perfect customer idea."

Dad nodded, "Which is how we finally understood why Toyota insisted on truck preparation areas — which we'd never paid any real attention to before. More fuel to Mike's theory that people only see what they expect to see. Unless we encountered the problem and resolved it ourselves, we never knew we'd been shown the solutions right away."

"I guess it's not always obvious to identify the immediate answer to the 'why?' question," Phil wondered out loud.

"Precisely. In general, you get a number of potential causes. If we go back to machine failures, in some cases, several causes combine to produce a breakage. So at some point we're going to have to take a more systematic approach. The thing is that most maintenance engineers tend to think like firemen. They know the machines. They fix the problem. But many of their fixes are just glorified gut feels, which sometimes work and sometimes don't. We need a more structured approach."

"Back to measurements?" asked Amy.

"Afraid so, no way around it. If only to make sure that the engineers speak with facts rather than impressions. Sooner or later you need complex analysis and rigorous methods. And there's the rub. People risk getting so involved in the paperwork that they lose track of the core problem: stopping machine breakdowns."

"As you say: gemba?"

"Yep. You have to always stay focused on what really matters.

I certainly learned this from experience. We had developed a comprehensive program to reduce press downtime. It was designed with consultants, and full of sophisticated tests and measures. Then we get a new product from Toyota, and our production goes to hell. For all our efforts to fix the tools and the presses, quality is hopeless, we have constant tooling problems and so on."

"Something must have been wrong with your hypothesis testing, as you said," I surmised. "Did Toyota ask you to do more detailed analysis?"

"Ah, no. It was really embarrassing. They sent a couple of technical experts who just stood there in front of the machines doing nothing but observing and taking notes, for hours on end. At first we thought they were just dumb, and eventually plain crazy. That is, until they started showing us how our own use of the equipment had created the problems."

"Is this gemba again?" asked Amy.

"You bet," said Dad. "Humbling, let me tell you. I had to learn to actually watch a machine cycle over and over until I could actually *see* the connection between the use of the machine and what was going wrong."

"It sounds pretty obvious," I said naively. "Why hadn't you done that before?"

Dad just laughed out loud. "Oh we had all kinds of reasons. My boss insisted we didn't have enough resources to waste technicians' time just standing stupidly watching the machines. The only 'problem-solving' time that was considered valuable by management — and the consultants for that matter — was time spent in offices and meeting rooms."

"But I thought gemba is about how people and machines work on the shop floor," Phil said.

"Ah," said Dad. "There's hope for you yet."

"TPM is not the main lesson here, on the shop floor," he continued, straightening up and folding his garden chair. I followed suit gratefully, wishing fervently that we were done for the day. Phil stayed seated, working furiously on his notes.

"What is it then?" asked Amy pertly.

"You tell me."

"Something about attitudes," I suggested. "We were talking about *Karate Kid* and you mentioned attitudes." That's my field, after all.

"Yes. And why Harry thinks Morgan should be fired."

"Amy, let's not go there again!" reproached Phil. She was still brooding over the incident. I couldn't blame her. Even the day after, I still felt the poor chump's public rout. Harry had dismissed him so out of hand that even if the incident ever was forgotten, his self-esteem must have taken a serious blow. Surely, there must be a better way to disagree with people!

"What do I keep harping about?" asked Dad.

How about everything? I thought.

"People," answered Amy. "It's all about people."

"So what's the underlying theme to all we discussed this morning?"

We looked around in silence.

"What Mike was saying earlier?" suggested Phil tentatively, flipping over his notes. "That we don't see what we don't expect to see?"

"Close enough. Learning to see. What did we see this morning?"

"That you don't have to be a mechanical engineer to realize that something's not well with this press," answered Amy. "And that the problem is a *human* one, not a mechanical one."

"People spend practically more time in this factory than they do at home, and still they don't see that anything could be wrong. Management in particular."

"Yeah, we're far too focused on reports and numbers," agreed Phil, who hated that side of his job.

"Seeing can't be taken for granted," Dad insisted. "It's an attitude. It's a commitment to go to the 'real place' — the gemba — and figure out what is happening for *real* and not be content with what sounds likely. When in doubt, go and see what is really going on."

"We never do it enough, I agree," confirmed Phil.

"Which is the problem with Kevin, right?" asked Amy thoughtfully.

"A caricature," agreed Dad. "He's operating in his own little world of computer calculations with absolutely no interest in what happens in real life on the shop floor, and when things don't turn out as the numbers say, it's somebody else's fault. And on top of it all, when challenged, he goes in to total denial. The man's dangerous."

"Why dangerous?" aasked Phil. "He's harmless. Annoying at worse."

"Don't you see? He's going to continuously come up with perfect-on-paper schemes that never work out for real, at the gemba. He'll continue to lose credibility with operators every time as a result. Furthermore, he's going to surround himself with like-minded people. Gemba is not just a fact, it's an attitude. It's a deep emotional commitment from management that the only important place in the plant is at the operator's station, where we're actually *working* for the customer. All else is support. Nothing more."

"And you'd fire someone over a perceived attitude issue?" questioned Amy, obviously disapproving.

"Over what else?" answered Dad with a sad shake of the head. "Hear me out. I've never liked firing people. As long as I've known Harry, he's always given me a hard time on how slow I was to act, and he was, and is, right about one point. When it was an attitude problem, sooner or later, they had to go. Often it was later, and we'd discover only after the fact the kind of internal damage they'd done. Remember, all of this is about people, and their attitudes to work. We've got far too many managers out there who believe in numbers more than they do in flesh-and-bone, or nuts-and-bolts, for that matter."

"That doesn't make it right," I protested. "Doesn't everybody have the right to a second chance?"

"Come on, Mike!" he replied gruffly. "By the time it comes to that, how many second chances have people had, d'you think? You of all people should know that attitudes hardly ever change, unless people work like heck at it. More importantly, you've got him in place, and don't have another lean logistics expert to replace him with. As a manager, you haven't got much of a choice. Either you change what's in people's heads, or you replace the people. Guess what's easier."

"Gee, that's hard, though."

"When you get to my age, Amy, you'll see it's a survival war. Most lean programs I've seen in other companies failed because of this. You can acquire the vocabulary, the tools, even the experts. But if you don't have a gemba attitude, you've got no chance."

Dad looked around the workplace and continued. "Gemba attitude means that you make every decision based on the principle that real improvement only takes place through a shop-floor focus based on direct observation. So if you don't spend enough hours yourself on the shop floor you can't understand the important details, and won't be able to challenge the people to come up with better solutions. Even managers must understand the need to prioritize investment in direct supervision. A Big Three line might have one supervisor and 50 to 80 people in the area. On the other hand, Toyota will have a team leader for every five to seven people on average, and a group leader for every three team leaders. Toyota has more supervision on the floor than a traditional workplace, and it's proved to be far more efficient.

"Amy, since you've taken on this job, how long do you spend in your office?"

She thought for a few seconds before answering. "A couple of hours. One hour when I arrive in the morning; one before leaving at night; and if I'm not conducting a workshop, one at noon. I see what you're driving at."

"Don't kid yourself, Philip," warned Dad. "At this stage, what you've achieved rests on Amy alone. And the time she spends working at the gemba. Do you realize that? She leaves, it all disappears in less time than it needs to say so."

"Ah, but she's not going to leave, is she?" said Phil, trying to joke his way out of a conversation that had suddenly taken a very uneasy turn.

Amy gave him a dazzling smile but, I noticed, did not answer.

"Mike? Listen, I'm sorry for phoning so late, but can I talk to you for a minute?"

"Amy? Sure, what's up?"

"What else," she said disgustedly. "There's been a big bust up between Matt and Phil, and I think it's my fault. I feel really bad about it!"

"What happened?"

"I was trying to implement that supply-train idea of your father's to deliver materials and components throughout the plant when —"

"Hang on, back track a bit, I must have missed that part."

"Sorry. You know how your dad keeps saying delivery first, then reduce inventory, then worry about cost, yes?"

"I'm with you."

"Okay, we've got the finished-goods delivery right, more or less. Now with this leveling business and the kanban and all, inventories are coming down."

"Good."

"I was trying to solve the problem of supplying the mechanisms line with purchased components, and Gloria and I decided to draw up a regular supply circuit, like a train running throughout the factory every hour or so, putting the entire factory on the double-bin supply system."

"Hold on, let me think. One guy runs a train of carts pulled by some kind of motorized tugger, picks up the empty containers at each station, goes back to the store, replaces by full bins, and does the circuit again replacing the empty with the full. Makes sense!"

"And then does it again! A delivery circuit. But then Morgan starts complaining that we have apparently increased the workload of material handlers with moving parts all over the factory all the time. You know, lots of small containers being moved at regular, specified times."

"He's got a point, hasn't he?"

"No way. In fact, I believe that if we had established circuits for material movers, we'd find out that we have actually reduced the workload, with the supermarkets both at the mechanism and finished-product ends. Now Phil and I have got Dave more or less on board, and he's helping us work the system. But then we had another run-in with Morgan. He's arguing that it doesn't make any sense to pull from the finished-unit supermarket to the truck preparation area, that's simply unnecessary movement, and we've had a lecture from him about waste, work, and motion, believe it or not. So here we have the MRP jockey explaining logistics efficiency all over again, with economic quantities for material handling and what not. The gemba thing."

"Right."

"Anyway, Phil is not there. I try to explain to the jerk that all this 'moving small containers around' is what keeps the WIP inventories down, but what do I know? I'm just a girl, right?"

"Hmm."

"So he goes away and I start working on the train idea, which leads me into applying standardized work to all the material handling that goes on in the factory. It turns out that these guys are all over the place with their forklifts but totally inefficient, since they spend more time looking for parts than delivering them."

"You'll have to explain this to me."

"Well, I figure, why shouldn't every material movement be inscribed in a regular circuit? Like a postman's run. Not cowboys running every which way every time someone needs something. Since we've cleaned up the streams so much, it's quite easy to do."

"You mean a circuit for each of the material handlers so that they always do the same pickups and deliveries."

"Yeah, you know, standardized work, but for material handling. Which is why we're not increasing the material handling cost, but, in practice, decreasing it by making it more efficient."

"I think I understand. Where's the problem?"

"No problem. I calculate my stuff and the bottom line is that, as I guessed, we employ about twice as many materials handlers as we need."

"You're joking!"

"No joke. I might be a bit optimistic, but it's exactly like the productivity improvements we had on the mechanisms line right at the beginning with your dad. If you standardize the circuits, even though we're moving stuff around all the time, we can really rationalize the whole thing and seriously cut logistics costs."

"That's good, right?"

"I thought so. So I write it in a memo and e-mail it to Phil, who, by this time, is away visiting a customer in Chicago. He reads it, forwards it to Matt, and somehow it ends up on Morgan's desk. He talks it over with Pellman."

"The engineering head you've been giving so much grief to about the shoddy design work his people come up with, when it comes to manufacturability?"

"Yes, him. They go and see Matt. Then Phil comes back, and there's this big argument and nobody talks to me anymore and it all sucks."

"When did all that happen?"

"Right now, today, this evening. It's all about me being a woman and they can't stand it."

Uh-oh.

"Has Phil said anything about it?"

"Oh, he's sweet, but he can be such a wimp sometimes. He said not to worry, it will blow away!"

"And how do you feel about that?"

"I feel real low. I mean, I feel better for talking to you, and all, but I'm still really angry."

"Will it blow away?"

"Maybe. I don't know what happened with Phil and Matt, and, at the end of the day, they're the bosses."

"Listen, Amy, for what it's worth, Phil's never told a fib in his life, except to cover up for my pranks when we were kids, and we always got caught because he was so bad at it. He's been partners with Matt for longer than I can remember, so if he says it will blow away, you can trust him on it."

"I know, I guess. But it's just so hard, you know, working so hard to get this place moving and having these stupid managers breathing down your neck and screwing things up for you."

"Yeah, can't be easy."

"That's the breaks, huh? Goes with the territory, I guess. I wanted the job, like Harry said, so I have to learn to take the heat."

"Harry said that? Harry and my Dad, you know, you shouldn't take their act too seriously."

She didn't answer right away.

"Do you want to meet up somewhere for a drink?" I suggested.

"Oh, I'd love to, but I really feel washed out. I think I'll just go to bed and cry myself to sleep."

"Will you be okay, though? You're all right?"

"Yeah, thanks for letting me get it off my chest. I just didn't know who to call who would understand any of that. Every time I complain to my parents they think I should come back home and get married!"

"Is that right? Not very helpful."

"You can say that again. Thanks again for listening."

"No problem. Call again if you feel like talking."

"That's sweet. And I'll take a rain check on that drink. You're really easy to talk to, you know?"

Real easy to talk to, sure. Fine. I put the phone down and stepped onto the balcony to smell the sweet, wet evening air. The neighborhood was full of music and firecrackers tonight, a real local evening. I was thinking about Amy again. Not my type, I kept telling myself, but still, I thought about her. What was it about that girl?

It did blow away in the end, but not in the way I'd thought, and not before blowing up first. We'd seen it coming. One day, as I was finally getting some writing done, I got a call from Dad. Dave had run into trouble with reducing the changeover time on the presses, and Phil had called Dad for help. He'd agreed to come and have a chat with Dave, but, holding me to the letter of our agreement, asked me to drive him up to the plant. I was already feeling fairly disgruntled and was further disappointed to find out that Amy was away at some conference. We got welcoming smiles from both Gloria and Ester, who rushed to my Dad to show him their production boards and discuss some incomprehensible point about how to organize operators with the mechanism assembly on the conveyor. Dave and Dad finally moved on toward the press area, where two guys were discussing the blanking press, which was wide open, exposing its innards to the world.

"We've followed the method," explained Dave. "We've listed all the operations we have to do to change the die, and separated the internal from the external setup."

"What?" I blurted out, as Dad just sighed.

"External activities are those we can do while the press is still running. Internal are all those we need to stop the press for. Previously, we used to stop the press first, since it runs so little, and then do it all. But this way, we can considerably reduce the changeover time."

"Tell me, what have you got under external?" asked my father.

"Preparing the jigs and the dies. The tools. Also preparing the workbench and clearing a place to store the parts we remove."

"Sounds all right. Internal?"

"Mostly replacing the die, centering, and adjusting."

"That's good, so, what's your problem?"

"To tell the truth," said Dave, scratching his mass of gray curls, slightly embarrassed, "the guys and I are not quite sure of how to organize ourselves to go faster, beyond externalizing what we can."

"Right. Well, the first point is, at first, not to do it alone. You must seriously think about how you can spread operations between two people. If you actually make sure both are working usefully all the time, you're cutting the internal time by half."

"Makes sense," said Billy Larson, a gruff old boy with handlebar mustache and thinning long hair pulled back in a ponytail.

"And then you ask yourself common-sense questions, such as:
– Do we have a checklist of all the elements that need to be prepared beforehand?
– What tools need to be on hand?
– Are the jigs, dies, and tools ready and in good order when we start?

"That sort of thing, nothing more."

"A checklist," agreed Dave. "Yup, that would come in handy."

"Listen, start with that, and then keep track of where you have difficulties when you set up the tool. Typically nuts and bolts, cables, tubes, anything which needs to be connected and disconnected. And then ask maintenance to work on each of these things so that they attach more easily. Color coding works well with wires and —"

"There you are," said Phil joining up. "How are they doing?"

"Well enough. Now it's a matter of perseverance."

"I'm glad you're here. I'm trying to convince Dave that we should move the machines into a production cell."

Dave looked decidedly uneasy, shifting his weight from one foot to the other. His attitude seemed to have changed considerably since the last time we'd seen him. Gone was much of the defensiveness, as if he no longer saw Dad's abrupt criticisms as a personal attack.

"Have you discussed it with these gentlemen?" asked my father.

"Yeah, we've talked it over," said Billy. "We've done all the time measurements with Amy, er, Ms. Cruz, that is."

"And?"

"It's like this. We see what you want. ..."

"But?"

"Aw, it would mean being back on the chain, that's what."

Dad didn't say anything and let the silence stretch while the poor man looked for support from the maintenance guy who was now fascinated by his own shoes.

"The way it is, Mr. Jenkinson," he said, sticking his chin out and widening his chest, "is that we talk to the guys on the mechanism line. Now that they've reorganized, they do work a lot faster."

"Harder, d'you think?" asked Phil worriedly. We'd had a long discussion with Amy about whether the operators worked harder on the mechanism lines now that standardized work and kaizen was beginning to be for real. She claimed that the operators worked faster, yes, but not harder, as operations were being systematically simplified. Accidents on the line had certainly gone down. But she'd also said that operators who where not part of the cells were swapping rumors of increased hardship caused by the productivity hikes on the mechanism lines. Phil, to his credit, was very sensitive on this topic, but, never at ease with people, didn't quite know how to address it.

"I haven't said that. That's not what they say either, but, you know," he said cautiously, looking at Dave, "we don't see so much of them now, like for a smoke or a cup of coffee."

"That's because they're not running after parts all the time any more," answered Dave, slowly going red in the face again. Good thing that the man was generally respected, because his people-management skills were appalling. Between Phil's reticence and Dave's short fuse, they made some management team.

"Yeah. That's what they say, that the work is getting easier to get into because there's less distraction. I don't know if I'd like that, but ..."

Phil was about to say something, but Dad discreetly motioned him to keep quiet while Billy chose his words.

"The way it is, work is work, and I'm not afraid of hard work. None of my buddies are. So we're willing, if what Ms. Cruz says about no more layoffs is true. With the improvements, I mean."

Phil took a deep breath, and looked relieved. So that was the lay of the land!

"You know I can't promise anything, it completely depends on how the company is doing. But as long as we're doing good work I don't see why we should let anybody go. In any case, it's not signed yet, but it looks like we're going to get new contracts for next quarter — so we'll need everybody on board. It also means bigger bonuses if we show a profit at year-end."

"The crew will be happy to hear it. So if we've got your word on this, Mr. Jenkinson, I'm ready to give it a try, although we'll look like idiots if we changed tools every part, like Dave said you wanted."

"What about producing every part at least once a day?"

Billy nodded his head sideways, undecided. He looked at the other man, who just shrugged.

"If we have to," he finally answered, "why the hell not?"

Right then I wondered what kind of deal had been brokered. I suddenly realized that Phil was now shouldering the responsibility of all these people as well. Not that I didn't know it, but I'd never actually appreciated it as a real-life fact. It made me shiver just considering it. I'd hate having to bear a load like that. No wonder so many managers became such callous bastards. I didn't think Phil ever would, but one had to wonder what that kind of responsibility did to you over time.

"Well," said my father. "If we'd be creating a cell, how would you place the machines? You'd have to load the puncher, start it, go and load the press brake, start it, unload the puncher, change the program, and then go back to unload the brake and pass the part to welding. Then you need to fit in forming the doors as well. Remember, we want to make inventories disappear."

"Yeah, we've looked into all of that. We'd need to move the machines right close to welding then," suggested Billy.

"And have them real close together if I keep moving from one to the other."

"You could have one facing the other, like so," Dad suggested, motioning with his hands.

"Kind of what we figured," said Billy. "It might work. We figured that if we had the puncher right in front of the brake, with the forming press a bit back in the middle, it could work. This whole business of doing parts one at a time sounds damn unnatural, but if that's what you want, we could move from puncher to bend, and then for the door panels, from puncher to press to brake for the bending, and then onto the welding jig. It'll look weird, but it can be done."

"Right. What are we waiting for, then?"

They all looked at him bewildered, not quite believing he really meant it. Dave's flush had deepened to a bright crimson now, but he didn't raise a protest.

"No time like now, if we all agree, let's move the darn things," insisted Dad. "Let's do it!"

"But, but, we can't do that —" Billy said. He'd seen a lot in his day, but this, apparently, was heresy.

"Why not? You've done the time measurements. You've talked it over. You know where you want the machines. I'm sure you've got a forklift large enough somewhere in the plant!"

"We don't. But the power station next door has massive ones," suggested Dave, playing along. "Maybe we could borrow one for a couple of hours."

"Let's go and ask them," said Phil with uncharacteristic decisiveness. Since we were kids I'd always get so annoyed at his general wishy-washiness that I kept forgetting that once his mind was made up, he could act swift and hard, like when he decided to sign on with Matt, or right now.

"Good, then," said Dad forcefully. "We'd better start by clearing the area around the welding stations. Let's get to it."

Which is pretty much how we found ourselves moving these presses around the shop floor one Tuesday afternoon. I confess that I was terrified. I had my stomach in my shoes all the time the press brake teetered on the massive forklift the guys next door had kindly provided. I was convinced some disaster would happen when they started lifting the press brake, and had visions of crushed bones and torn flesh, not to say destroyed machinery. But the people from the power station said they were used to moving rather fragile, very large parts in their station's operation, and my father spent a long time with them making sure they could move the machine safely. He then cleared the area in the path of the forklift and made sure no one was anywhere near the destination, which he had Dave highlight with tape on the floor.

For all that I was impressed with it, the station people seemed to know exactly what they were doing, and obviously thought it was quite a lark. They turned out to be friendly and easygoing, meticulous in their work, and surprisingly curious of why we wanted the machine moved, obviously interested in this "flow" concept.

"Good guys," said Dave when they left with thanks and the promise of a case of something good from Phil, which summed it up, really.

"You realize this is not ideal," Dad said to Phil as they slowly withdrew the supporting struts from under the press, at its new location.

"What, moving machines on the spur of the moment? I'm sure it's not."

"Oh, that? No. To start with, at any rate, you just got to go to it. And believe me, you'd better be ready to move them again, and again, until we get it right. Kaizen, right?"

Phil shook his head in dismay. "What's not ideal then?"

"Well, we've positioned the puncher in front of the press brake with the old forming press at the back forming a U, which is fine. Although they're still way too far apart — look at how many steps the poor man will have to move parts from one to the other."

"We had to put them there!" replied Phil. "With all the electrical, hydraulic, and pneumatic cables and all. You yourself said that we were incredibly lucky to have had the machine at this very position all those years ago, so we could move it back and simply plug it back in. We can always put rollers or a convey —"

"I know what I said," replied Dad irritably. "And you might want to think just why they used to have the machine there when they purchased it, and why they moved it to the other part of the plant later. In any case, it was miraculous to find hookups so close to the welding. Anyhow, forget the conveyor; just move the machines closer next month, when you've had a chance to prepare the area. No, that's not the real problem. Look at welding."

"What's wrong? We've got two parallel stations that fit right with takt time, since the operation is 20 minutes long, and we've got a 10-minute takt? We've got the movable jigs in between, so we get one-piece flow. The guy at the presses can only fill one jig at a time, and the jigs rotate back and forth to the welder."

I'll confess I couldn't see anything wrong either.

"That's the problem. How can you expect to kaizen them?"

"Kaizen?"

"Yeah. You've got two welders assembling an entire cabinet on each bench in parallel. How do you expect to do further kaizen?"

Dad was about to launch into another lecture about kaizen when we heard someone calling out. "There y'all are," yelled Matt, who approached, leading a delegation of white collars. Morgan, I recognized. I assumed from Amy's description the third man was Gary Pellman, the engineering head.

"What the? What are you doing? Moving the presses?" he asked, as if he couldn't make sense of the scene in front of him. "Are you sure that's safe?" he blustered at Phil.

"Almost done now anyhow," Phil answered levelly. Matt didn't look happy. The plastic smile had slipped and he appeared, if anything, burned out. His usually well-groomed hair was visibly mussed. His perfect shirt was hanging out over his patent-leather belt. Morgan looked smugly at Phil, which didn't bode well. Pellman could not hide a hint of anticipation. These two had probably concocted something, having confused Phil's conflict avoidance for weakness, or worse, lack of intelligence. Phil was not one to hold a grudge, but he had an outstanding memory. In his case, it wasn't ever a case of forgive and forget, but more a case of "I'd be happy to forgive if I could forget."

"Here we go," muttered Dad under his breath.

"Mr. Woods, I'm glad to see you. I've heard you've done wonders," Matt said, the smarmy smile pasted back tightly in place. "Excellent advice you've given us." Dave was now scowling openly, but I missed the subtext.

"You were producing 30 circuit breakers a day before we started, you're now at more than 40 on the same resources. That's a 30% productivity improvement without any additional investment," noted Matt.

"In my book, I'd say Philip, Dave, and Ms. Cruz have done a splendid job, yes," answered my father deadpan with his usual sense of *à propos*. Dad's blunt answer threw Matt out of his stride for a second.

"Yes. That's excellent, actually, and we're very grateful. But we've been having something of an argument with Phil and Dave, here."

"Oh?" asked Dad noncommittally, raising an eyebrow over his notorious glare. From Phil's clouded face, I had a gut feeling that the argument Amy had stirred was somehow bigger than I'd expected. Matt usually left the running of the plant to Phil, and God knows what had had happened for him to risk his designer loafers in the plant. I shouldn't have dismissed Amy's concerns so lightly.

"Yes. Kevin tells me you want to have the material handlers running around all day moving crates. He's calculated the added investment in terms of necessary forklifts and people if we only halve the size of the current containers, and I'm afraid it's just impractical in our current situation."

To everyone's surprise, my father put his head back and laughed, a long low laugh. Phil looked askance, but I could only spread my hands in total bewilderment.

"Added investment? In forklifts? Is that what he's asking," said Dad. Morgan was bright red again, and Matt was smiling, trying to smooth things over. Pellman seemed slightly discomfited, but essentially unreadable.

"Forklifts. Right. Gentlemen, if you will follow me I suggest a tour through the plant counting a) parked forklifts and b) forklifts running empty, without cargo. Let's start with the stock of blanks and cabinets, shall we?"

Throughout his life, Dad had managed to remain tall and thin, unlike me, already squidgy around the edges. These days he walked around with a slight stoop, but when he straightened up, he still made a rather fearsome figure, which seemed to trigger an automatic compliance instinct in the chimp part of our ancestral brains. I'd learned to fight it over the years (or so I liked to believe). But as he turned and walked toward the storeroom without a further word, full of righteous ire, everyone followed suit without further argument.

"Of course, my so-called 'constant running around with containers' would, in all likelihood, make this wall of idle parts disappear," snarled Dad. "Which you'd really miss, wouldn't you? Considering your cash situation and all."

Matt winced, and had the grace to concede the point. "I can count pretty well. I can tell cash lying around when I see it."

"But we're here for the forklifts, right? Well I count two stationed over there, by the logistics plant office."

By the end of Dad's tour we had counted no fewer than four forklifts parked haphazardly, and of the four others we'd seen operating in the plant, only two were loaded with parts, while the two others were running on empty. Phil and Matt had now trailed behind our little group and were arguing furiously *sotto vocce*. Dave strode next to me, trying hard not to gloat, but failing. We ended up outside the plant by the shipping bay, watching a truck being loaded with crated breakers. Morgan looked as though he was about to be sick.

"Unless I'm very mistaken," concluded Dad, "my running around with containers can be achieved with the four forklifts we've seen actually running. The other four can go straight back to the leaser. As for people, well ... ," he let his words trail, looked fixedly at Kevin Morgan, making his point without a further word. The silence stretched as Morgan went paler and paler, in the warm light of the setting sun. Finally Pellman stirred and cleared his voice.

"How would that work?" he asked.

"Well, use forklifts to move heavy stuff like finished breakers or crates of metal parts, and handcarts for anything lighter. You need one forklift running from the finished-goods supermarket, and then from the truck preparation to loading the trucks themselves with time to spare. Then you'll need another to move steel cabinets from the cell we're creating now to the conveyor, and that's about it. Let's count a third one extra, just in case. The fourth, I'd convert to pulling carts to deliver components to the mechanism line and conveyor area."

"Okay. We may not have been open enough to a new setup," Pellman conceded quietly.

"Damn right," Matt said, now staring at Morgan. "Kevin, I expect you to have these forklifts off our books by month's end, and to have done everything Mr. Woods says to make this work."

Morgan just nodded, robbed of speech, miserable.

"Phil!" said Matt. "We need to talk. We need to have a second look at the budget," he added darkly with an evil glance at Morgan.

"Sure," said Phil casually, but I could tell he sounded relieved.

"Mr. Woods," carried on Matt, turning his highest voltage smile on my father. "We can't thank you enough for your help. We need to think about how to express it more concretely, but, you have my gratitude for your support."

"Uh-huh," grunted Dad in his own unique style, and left for the car without another word as I hurried behind him to catch up.

Dad looked old and drawn as I drove him back into the hills, dark purple in the dying day. Behind us, a bar of pure gold shone blindingly in my rear view mirror.

After a long silence, he sighed heavily. "That went rather well, don't you think?"

"We spoiled Kevin's evening, for sure."

"They don't ever learn, do they?"

We drove on as I meditated that last cryptic remark.

"Can they deliver on that promise?"

"The forklifts? Huh, sure. Amy's started organizing regular pickups from and to the supermarkets. From what I've seen she's progressed with the internal parts withdrawal loop. They've got plenty of transportation. It's just a matter of standardized work. If each forklift is on a planned tour, then instead of running around erratically refilling containers with parts, they can rationalize the materials handling. I'd also like her to get everything on the floor as soon as possible and take the wall racks down, to avoid unnecessary lifting. They'll be fine with fewer forklifts, even if they might have to find something else to run the supply train. No sweat."

I thought that over, adding up what Amy had told me over the phone the other night.

"But did you see how the engineering head turned his coat, right then and there? Smooth operator that one," said Dad.

I wouldn't have put it that starkly, but I saw what he meant.

"The cheek of the man! I can't stand those corporate politicos," he fumed on. "I always hated it, Mike. I still do. I told you I wouldn't deal with any of this crap anymore, and look, it's happening again. Can't they see what's in front of their own eyes? It's not like it's a religion or something. It's just being rational."

"I'm starting to agree with you. It's the gemba attitude. They either have it or they don't. People don't see what's not important to them. Just as we can watch a movie with Mom, but not see half the things she goes on about afterwards."

"I guess you're right. Matt at least sees money, bless his greedy heart. He didn't understand any of it, but he can add."

"So can Phil. Look, gemba is not the way he was trained, but he's trying hard."

"I'll give you that, he hasn't cracked yet. But it's not over, by far. I thought I was done with all of this!"

"But you're so good at it!" I protested.

"Doesn't mean I enjoy it," he answered gruffly. "Particularly when you have to deal with sitcom dramas like today. What a terrible waste of people. And of my time."

We drove in silence the rest of the way back to my parents' house. At the end of the day, for all the perverse fun of it, I hadn't much enjoyed the humiliation of Kevin Morgan either. I wondered whether Amy was aware of the dust-up she'd triggered. Thank God she'd not been there. On the other hand, moving the machines had been an exhilarating experience, and I'm sure she would have enjoyed that as much as I did, or probably more. Just do it! Something that had sat there for so long, and suddenly, lo! Just move it.

As I drove back home after dropping off my father, I wondered about the spirit of transformation. Since we left the caves, most of what surrounds us, from cathedrals to cars, from the green revolution to jury trials, from epidemics to microwave ovens has been created by people for people, and yet we treat things as if they were immutable and set in stone. Morgan assumed that more regular trips meant more people. The shop floor assumed that once the machine was put down, there it would stay.

And yet, Dad didn't see it that way. He had somehow acquired a certitude that anything in front of his eyes could and would change, which obviously gave him the confidence that he could make things happen himself. Grudgingly, I gradually understood more of his frustration with all the foot-dragging and politicking. "Solve the problem!" was a simple practical statement to Dad, whereas it was a recipe for blame setting for most other people. "Fix the problem, don't fix the blame," Dad kept saying.

His take is that problem solving is a core attitude in TPS. He often said that in most companies, people are ashamed of being linked to problems. In Toyota, it's a learning opportunity with your boss or mentor. In my small way, I'd started unconsciously to apply lean concepts in everyday life and was becoming not only more aware of the amount of waste we casually generate — waste of energy, waste of time, and worse, waste of people — but I could also see practical possibilities to improve, well, value and flow. Yet, to my dismay, whenever I suggested any improvements, I was met with the sullen incomprehension my father had faced all his working life, and I didn't like that feeling any more than he did.

In any case, I now had a better feel for what my father had called a gemba attitude. Amy had it in spades. Phil didn't, but was working hard at acquiring it. As for me, well, it slowly dawned on me how the absence of such a gemba orientation was a widespread ill, the cause of untold damage in many more places than the factory shop floor. We certainly could do with some gemba thinking at the Social Sciences Department, back at the ranch. There you go, I thought as I let myself into my lonely, empty, waiting apartment. There you go, wisdom in unlikely places. Well, we'd survived this crisis. When could we expect the next?

Chapter Nine

THE HEIJUNKA WAY

The next crisis wasn't long in coming, but it didn't concern Amy this time. I'd had a drink with Phil a couple of days later and asked how she was coping with the political heat she had generated, but he'd dismissed the whole thing out of hand. "She's pushy and she's right. So they all hate her guts," he laughed. "But she's doing a super job. She'll be all right."

Are you telling her that? I wondered, but let it be. Later on that week, Dad had suggested Phil and I meet up again at his place. He hadn't mentioned anything specific, so I steeled myself for more lean talk, but as I arrived home, my mother gave me a quick warning gesture and pointed toward the patio where Dad and Phil were having drinks.

Phil was crumpled on the bench, looking thoroughly dejected, while Dad was scowling in his best supercilious manner.

"I agreed to help you out, Philip. Not to run this place for you!

"Ah, Mickey. I was telling Philip that I'd rather not go back to the factory."

I was completely taken by surprise!

"Why?" I asked grabbing a drink on the tray, "I thought you did well out there."

"That's not the point," he growled. "I'd sworn never to set foot in one plant again, and, well, the heart of the matter is I'm done with manufacturing and all that jazz."

"But you're helping us so much!" complained Phil, with a whine in his voice. "And we still need your help more than ever, now that we've caught all the low-hanging fruit. We're just getting the inventory under control and ..." his voice trailed away in the night. Somewhere out there, the cicadas were having a ball. "Maybe it's a matter of compensation? Matt and I have agreed all along that you shouldn't be working for free."

"Now, don't insult me, son. I've been helping out because Mike asked me to and because I've known you since you were a kid. As for money, praise the Almighty, I've got more than I need."

"Then, what is it, Dad?"

He swirled his glass a while, before taking a long swallow.

"Well, like I said, I'm feeling my age. I really don't want to get drawn back into all those corporate battles. I've done my time, and I've earned my retirement. It's just time to quit, to stand down, you understand?"

I nodded, quietly. We'd never talked about any of this and I did not know quite how to react, but there was a vulnerability there I'd not glimpsed before in a man I still resented for his tyranny during my teenage years. There had never been any give in Dad, no matter what the opposition was, which is, I guess, why his colleagues respected him as much as my brother and I resented him. Had he finally learned to back down from a fight?

"Besides, Philip is missing the point. He's got to learn to do it himself, that's the whole thing. You can't ever delegate running your business. That's the lesson. Every other executive tries, and it always fails. Running a business is about running a business, period."

Phil's head shot up. "Then you'd agree to continue advising me? If it didn't involve actual factory work? Just talks like we started?" he asked, full of hope. At times, there was something so endearing in Phil's earnestness, him being such a big guy and all, that I couldn't help but smile.

"Talk?" wondered Dad, mulling it over. "Sure. Why not?"

"Brilliant. Then, about the presses ..."

And they were off again.

I left them to it and walked idly around the pool, which shone eerily with its lights turned on in the dark of the night, and thought about how Dad continued to surprise me. I had naturally assumed that he would be pleased and excited to get his hands back onto a factory to shape up. But then I'd also seen him relaxed and at ease with his boat and his buddies at the Yacht Club, and I realized I'd known the man all my life, and never figured out what made him tick. He wasn't easy to get along with, that's for sure. My brother who was trying to make it as a scriptwriter down in Hollywood hardly ever came by, but with this Phil business, I'd been spending more time up here than I had in years, and had to adjust many of my long-held attitudes as a result. The way Amy really took to him, for instance, was a surprise, as was. ... Ah, too much soul-searching for one night, I thought as I watched the silver fingernail of a young moon rise over the hill.

"Okay, so having two welding stations in parallel is not a good idea because you can't work on kaizen and you can't be flexible if the takt time changes," Phil was saying, looking chagrined as usual. It took me a while to understand what they were going on about until I realized they were continuing the conversation about the welding stations, which had been interrupted by the Morgan drama.

"So we should cut the welding work content in half and spread it over the two guys. And eventually, as we improve the work involved in tool changeover at the blanking press and forming brake, we should aim to move from three people to two. Is that it?"

"At your current takt time, yes. But if what you tell me of Matt bringing more business in is true, takt will go down, and you'll need more people!"

"Aargh! I'm not sure I can take anymore!" grumbled Phil. "Too many dimensions to deal with at the same time. It's just too much!"

"Here, have another drink. Take a deep breath. It's not that hard, you've got to keep up with a few principles, and then think 'gemba!'"

"Easy for you to say, Dad," I said, putting in my two cents' worth. "But you know these principles, Phil doesn't."

"I can't help it if he's slow," was the true-to-form answer. "I keep going on and on about them."

"Mike's right, Bob. Would you mind spelling the principles out for me?"

My father seemed hesitant for a second, then he harrumphed loudly.

"These are *my* lean principles, all right? The Toyota people I've met tend to be real cagey about anything abstract. What I mean is, for all I know, they might have formulated some general principles. Probably they do, considering how consistent their system is. But that's the point. If they do, they never told me. So here are mine."

He seemed to be marshaling his thoughts and I couldn't help but be amused by Dad's casual advice to apply principles he didn't actually know existed for certain. Sometimes I had the sneaking suspicion he was making up half of it as he went along.

"My personal description of lean," started Dad slowly, "would be: *customer satisfaction with lean manufacturing*. In that sense, customer satisfaction is definitely the first principle, and whenever you have a doubt about what you're doing, go back to your understanding of customer satisfaction."

"Delivery first, as we discussed right when we started."

"That's one aspect of it, but customer satisfaction extends to product performance, service, and cost as well," replied my father.

"Then, I'd say, *flexibility in mix and volume*. The entire lean approach was built on the need to produce variety from limited equipment at a cost that could rival high-volume mass production. So the trick is to maximize flexibility while keeping capital spend under control, which requires a bit of creative thinking, but works wonders in the long run. Kanban is a gemba manifestation of this principle.

"Third, a *gemba attitude*, as we discussed. Go and look, rather than talk about it. To the real place, with the real people and the real thing. Don't lose yourself in generalities and abstract thinking. Ohno used to rail against university-trained engineers who had been spoiled by the western 'dekansho' method."

"Dekansho? Doesn't sound very western to me."

"Descartes, Kant, Schoppenhauer."

"Oh, come on, get out!"

"I'm not pulling your leg! He wrote about it. But that's the point, cultivating a gemba attitude as opposed to letting your mind get in the way."

"Thinking like Japanese peasants," joked Phil. "It doesn't come easy, but I'm trying."

"Yeah, we know, as you keep reminding us, you've been far to highly trained to come up with anything practical," I kidded him.

"Fourth, but some might argue that it comes first, and I am sometimes inclined to think likewise, *produce people before you produce parts.* Your people are assets, not costs. It's all about people, and it's all about knowledge. So you really need to focus on what people know and —"

"How involved they are. Okay, I'm with you."

"Finally, last but not least, *never bypass a problem*, and then kaizen. Developing knowledge does not happen through training or theory. It happens because people get involved with continuous improvement, which leads them to learn a lot of detailed things about their own processes. The first thing a young engineer is asked to do at Toyota is an improvement project. I don't think of kaizen as a source of monetary savings, although it clearly is also that. I see kaizen as a way to develop people so they understand more about the first three principles and deliver results, and hence economic performance. There. You asked. But remember that lean is more a practice than philosophy."

"Okay, that's quite a handful. But I concede that you've been discussing these issues from the start. It's just so hard to fit it all together."

Phil reflected on this for a while, and readied himself to go. "Thanks for all this, Bob. And I can call you, right? If I run into more difficulties?"

"I'll be here, Philip, just don't ask me to be back there every other morning. Remember the gemba! You're going to have to embrace that yourself if you want to move forward. And don't rely too much on Amy. She's got plenty of drive, but it's your factory. Not hers."

"Gemba, okay, 'night!"

Dad walked him back to the front door, and I wandered outside. The pool lights had switched off and the night was darker than dark. I stood on the hard stone and looked up to the stars. The thin moon was already disappearing over the range, a wink from space. Despite myself, I wondered what I had learned from ferrying my father back and forth to Phil's plant. Heijunka definitely didn't talk to me, at least not yet. But I was starting to see about takt time. For instance, I'd started wondering why we only did exams and teacher evaluations at the end of a course, precisely when nothing could be done. Surely this was not very leveled.

Right now, draped in the sweet smell of the bush at night, and under the twirl of galaxies, I reflected upon two things that had been bugging me for some time now. First, although I'd listened to my father preach about waste without paying attention, adopting a gemba attitude slowly made me realize that for every value-adding step, we tend to do five wasteful ones, which is a scary thought. "An opportunity for improvement" would be Amy's phrasing. Second, I realized that after teaching all these years, I hadn't confidence in my student's ability to resolve anything.

Amazingly, Dad, for all his poor opinion of most people, expected anybody to be able to resolve any problem. Understand the flow, see the waste, solve the problems, and start all over again. Most of my academic education had been about how humanity's problems were essentially unsolvable, a strange reflection, I now realized, of some original sin. But it wasn't true. Locally, at least, we'd solved famine, banned slavery, and no two democracies have ever gone to war. To a professional critical thinker, there was something profoundly disturbing in my Dad's simple belief in his team's ability to solve just about anything. Define value, understand the flow, see the waste, solve the issues, and start over again. Confusedly, I felt there was hope in that low-key search for perfection. Standing there on the cold, hard ground, I was reminded of Oscar Wilde's quip that we are all in the gutter, but some of us are looking at the stars, and, tonight, they didn't seem quite so distant.

"Have you heard they fired Kevin Morgan?" Amy asked as she settled in the beat-up leather sofa, plunking her tray of salad and mineral water on the table in front of us.

"Phil told me he resigned."

"Resigned, hah!" she sniffed crossly. "That snake Pellman. After the showdown at the OK Corral the other day, he dropped his boy like an old sock. Pellman knows how to adjust to Matt's every mood. He gives me the creeps."

"How do you feel? Relieved?"

"Guilty, more like it. I should have made more of an effort to get him to buy into lean, even if he was an arrogant jerk. He certainly didn't deserve to be treated that way. You see, Pellman encouraged him to stand up to Phil for his own reasons, until he saw the wind turn, and then, bye-bye, baby."

I had spent the morning at the university catching up on the paperwork, which had overtaken my desk in the department, and she'd phoned to join me for lunch. The restaurant was straight across from the campus and full of lounging students, the hip and the disaffected, the boisterous and the listless. Amy looked younger, surrounded with people closer to her own age. She kicked off her shoes and folded her legs under her on the couch, attacking her salad as I munched on my sandwich. No one would call her beautiful, nor even conventionally pretty, but she undeniably had a natural unaffected grace, a lightness of spirit, I thought.

"Did your dad really move those two presses?" she asked with one of her bright smiles.

"With his own bare hands."

"Too bad I missed that," she laughed. "Just to see Dave's face."

"And how is it working out?"

"Oh, fine, as far as I can tell. They've got so much inventory to work out of the system that we won't know for a while yet. I think that the nail in Morgan's coffin was when we actually looked at the inventory in the incoming parts stores and found crates of parts from products we haven't built since the factory changed hands."

"Ouch."

"As your dad would say, gemba. The sad loser never put his nose in that storeroom, and the parts didn't show up on his precious MRP, so he didn't know any better. Dave's a changed man. Ever since Morgan's disgrace, he's turned into a lean fanatic!"

"So it's all going well?"

"I don't know," she shrugged, looking thoughtfully at the water she was pouring in her glass. "It's changed. Not as much fun, really."

"What d'you mean?"

"At first, it was just a lark. But now, they're doing this in earnest. The good thing is that Dave's really getting into all that stuff, and Phil spends a lot more time on the shop floor, so I've had time to catch up on the HR work I'd left hanging. But it's a lot tenser now."

"In what way?"

"I don't know how to describe it," she bit her lip, looking at me. "The company was teetering on the brink of bankruptcy, but everyone in management was quite friendly, really. I mean that they got on well together in a vague kind of way, everyone doing their own stuff. But now, Phil's running a tighter ship. He expects answers, and wants problems resolved, which is surfacing a lot of underlying conflicts between departments. If people don't have a good grasp of the problem, Phil says 'let's go to the gemba!' and takes them to the shop floor and gives them a hard time until they get to see the real issue. The atmosphere has changed."

"That doesn't sound much like Phil."

"Oh, he's changing, all right. Less approachable, I'd say. He's driving everyone much harder."

Phil? I was surprised. I'd been invited to Phil's house for lunch over the weekend, and both he and Charlene had seemed more relaxed than I'd seen them in a long time. Phil had resolved to be home by six, come rain or shine to spend more time with the kids. "What was the point about being the boss if I can't come home early?" he'd said. All in all, he looked far more settled than he had for months. On the other hand, having argued for Phil to face up to his responsibilities, I could hardly be surprised if doing exactly that would change him, somehow, and not necessarily for the better.

"It's all probably for the best, I guess." She went on, mirroring my train of thought. "I mean, if he continues to surface all the stupid things this company does, he'll finally ask himself the right questions about the people there."

"You don't sound too sure."

"Oh, I am. Some of the staff are ready to be awakened again, and itching to improve things, particularly with admin processes. Others won't take the pressure. My problem is that, at the moment, many blame me for the change in style, particularly the office staff. And it's not easy. I'm a woman, and a lot younger than most."

"No complaints on both counts!" I kidded her.

"You're sweet, but if it ever comes to personnel spring cleaning, guess who'll have to take care of it? The part of HR I hate. So I'm not looking forward to this."

"Sounds depressing."

"No, no. That's not what I meant. It's great to see an actual turnaround as opposed to hear about it. And the factory stuff is brilliant. I'd never think I'd have so much fun in brick-and-mortar after working in the dotcom environment. It's just tough, that's all. But it's all good. And we've only scratched the surface of lean."

"Hold on, hold on. Please don't tell me you came all this way to discuss the plant with me. You've got the wrong Woods in any case. Me, I'm a psychologist, remember?"

"What else?" she asked, surprised.

"I don't know," I answered, taken aback. "I'm sure we can talk about something else."

"Like what?"

"I don't know. What about that book you were reading, *Cien años de soledad*. What did you think of it?"

"Not much. Never got around to finishing it. I'm not even sure why I even bothered trying in the first place."

"Ah ..."

Lunch with Amy had left me strangely exhausted, and I didn't feel like returning to my pad and all the unfinished writing lurking there, so I drove lazily into the hills to my folk's place, curious to discuss the latest developments with my Dad. He was on the phone in his office as I walked in, and he motioned me brusquely to sit down as he put the loudspeaker on.

"Philip, Mike's just come in, so you're on the speaker."

"Hi. I'm here with Alan, who's taking over for Kevin. The team here had understood that just-in-time meant replicating in the plant the exact customer demand, so they recalculate all the MRP whenever there's a new order and pass the changed fabrication instructions on to Dave."

"I bet he likes that."

"Yeah, he keeps complaining that logistics change their mind all the time and that creates a mess on the shop floor. Now, from our last discussion, I understand that he's not altogether wrong."

"I keep telling you that the MRP is not the issue! We don't need the MRP to run the plant, we need it to plan ahead and calculate what we ask from suppliers, according to the bill of materials. There's no need for the MRP in the factory, no need to waste operator time in nonvalue-adding activities like plugging numbers into a computer, and no reconciliation issues, it's all muda!"

"I know, Bob, I know. I'm aware of that, but even if we run the entire flow with kanban and no instructions from the MRP, we still need to know what to build every day, and what to order from suppliers. I'm right here with these guys now, what should I tell them?"

"Explain how they do this right now."

"We have overall contracts with customers specifying how many circuit breakers they need, but then they send us e-mails or faxes to tell us when they want them. So, basically, when we receive an order, which is a demand for a number of breakers for a particular site, we put the number in the MRP, which then issues all the relevant production instructions."

"You put the information in the computer, which then tells Dave what to produce?" Dad asked Phil.

"It's not quite that simple because we also have to calculate our parts needs according to the current contracts we have, to order from suppliers and so on, but that's what we do."

"And it never struck you that you might be giving widely irregular information to Dave? What if a customer uses 10 breakers a day but he only wants them delivered once a month? Do you plug in 200 breakers for next week in the computer and see what happens?"

Lots of muffled discussion on the other side of the line.

Finally Phil came back and said, "It's not that straightforward, but I'm afraid that's more or less what we do."

"Oh Lord! Okay, let's forget the MRP for a second, and ask ourselves the question the other way round. What does Dave absolutely need to know?"

"What he's supposed to be building next week."

"But if you give him a lot of garbage he's going to make his own calculations, correct?"

More talk in the background.

"Yes, that's what he does."

Dad pressed on. "So, ideally, what information do we need in order to know what to build next week?"

"A forecast?"

"More than that. We need to know what our customer's plan is. Listen, you don't have that many customers. It should be someone's job to obtain weekly or monthly production plans direct from the customers rather than waiting for shipping orders to arrive."

"But what if they don't respect that plan?"

"It doesn't matter. If I know they intend to build 50 machines with STR breakers in them over next week, then I can average it out over five days and produce 10 STR breakers a day."

"But they never respect that," protested an unknown voice from the group.

"The point is that they will, eventually. They'll do anything to catch up in order to avoid delivering late to their own customers. So if they only ask for 40 STR breakers this week, you can bet that they'll ask for 60 next week! We might as well build 50 this week and hold 10, and then build 50 again next week, add the 10, and ship 60."

"But you're building to inventory!" the voice sounded outraged.

"In any case we are. If Dave knows from experience that customers might suddenly ask for 60 breakers one week, he'll make sure he's got at least 10 extra in inventory just in case. So he's going to hold an inventory of 10 breakers every week to avoid being caught with his pants down if the order comes — which is totally the right thing to do. Now, if we level our load we can lower the inventory considerably. Think about it."

More muffled discussions.

"We're not following, Bob. Can you explain this again?"

"Right, imagine that the customer has planned to build 200 machines in the next month. First week, all goes well and he has asked for 50 breakers. Second week, he's also asked for 50, but he's had problems, missed deliveries, and has only managed to build 40. So, in order not to keep inventory, in week #3 he only orders 40 breakers, right, since he's got 10 leftover from last week. But in week #4 he has to catch up the lost production, and build 60 machines. So he orders 60 breakers to catch up."

"Okay. We're with you."

"Now, all you know, is that sometimes he asks for 40, and sometimes for 60, how do you make sure you can always deliver?"

"Keep 10 extra in inventory on top of the 50 you intend to produce, just in case."

"Correct, that's the only way. But it means that at month end you've still only sold 200 STRs, so you're left with your 10 extra breakers in stock."

"Gotcha," agreed Phil. "And that's an extra day of production."

"So," said the other voice now sounding very distant, "you're saying that by keeping exactly to what the customer orders, we're creating inventory? How is that possible?"

"It's not the schedule. It's the fact that Dave cannot suddenly change his own production schedule without major problems, that's all. Now, on the other hand, if you realize that the customer will work very hard to stick to his original building plan, by only building 50 per week, all you carry is 10 extra breakers on week #3, but your turns are 20% higher than what you'd have if you keep the extra 10 throughout the month."

"But what if he asks suddenly for 70 breakers?" wondered the voice.

"Why would he?" answered Dad, getting irritated. "If he can't build 50 widgets a week, it's unlikely that he's going to start building 70 all of a sudden. Unless he's only built 30 at some point, and then you know it and you've got the parts. In any case, you can run an analysis of the usual variation in your customer's demand against the average demand, and build up a buffer stock accordingly."

"But what if his production program increases?"

"Then it's totally another matter, and you need to address that differently. Remember that you need to find out what he intends to build in advance, rather than wait for the orders to fall."

"And what if we have our own problems? Like a breaker failing to pass testing or something?" wondered Phil.

"Again, that's another problem," answered my father testily. "If you need safety stock to cover your own problems, well, create some.

If, on average, you screw up assembly of one breaker in 100, then it means every other week when you thought you had produced 50, then you only have 49 shippable breakers. In this case, you still need to assume you're going to ship 50. So, keep a safety stock level of one extra breaker and plan to produce 51 breakers every second week rather than 50. Fine, in total, and if nothing goes wrong at production, you end up at month end with an inventory of two extra breakers. It's still a lot less than 10!"

"So, we average the customer demand over four weeks, add a buffer to be sure we won't disappoint the customer, and then use that to schedule production?"

"Taking care to maintain a finished-goods inventory made up of average demand, a demand variation buffer to protect you from spikes in customer demand, and a safety stock (to protect your customer from failures in your process). And you can then level it further by dividing your week by five production days, so 50 a week gives you 10 per day. And then breakdown the day to takt time, which is building a breaker every 46 minutes, and so on. Got that?"

"Sounds clear. I don't know if we can do it, but I think I understand."

"Good. Any more questions?"

Long intense discussion in the background at the other end of the line.

"Not on this point as yet, Bob. But I've got a separate concern."

"Shoot."

"Hang on, let me wrap up the meeting."

More noises.

"There, they're gone. To be honest, I'm getting a bit overwhelmed here. We're starting actions all over the plant. Now I'm getting into logistics as well. Amy is overworked, and I'm losing my bearings."

My father swung slowly in his chair, but didn't say anything, and we stared at the phone's speaker as Phil searched for words.

"I know what you say about gemba, but I need some way to keep a broader picture. To know where I'm going with this. I also realize that the information flow is just as important as the fabrication process, but it's all mixing up in my mind. I know that it sounds like a very general question, but do you know of anything that would help?"

"Maybe I do, Philip, maybe I do. Tell you what, I'm going fishing again on Saturday, so if you want to meet at the Yacht Club early on, we can discuss your problem."

"Yes, sir," said Phil's voice, sounding enthusiastic. "Thank you, sir."

"And bring Amy along. You need someone with brains there!"

"Will do!"

I arrived late that morning. The Yacht Club looked deserted, and I parked next to my Dad's truck, Philip's pumpkin Porsche, and Amy's convertible. The day had started hazy, and a light fog was hanging in lazy ribbons around the ponderosas, rolling out toward the sea. They weren't at the bar, and I found them all in the *Felicity*'s cockpit in animated debate with Harry. Even Amy seemed to have overcome her dislike of the big man and was now heartily laughing at something he'd said.

"So, have you finally done something about all that inventory?" Harry was asking Phil as I clambered on board. He was looking as incongruous as ever with his impressive beer gut and scrawny legs, wrapped into an impeccable navy polo shirt and khaki shorts, still the perfect yachtsman. At least he'd lost the cap.

"Mike," said Harry loudly as I climbed on board, "have I ever told you how I met your dad? I was a purchasing VP in Detroit, and had just sent a letter to all my suppliers telling them we would now require consignment stocks. And this madman, who I'd never met, barged into my office and proceeded to tell me in no uncertain terms what I could do with that letter. He went on to lecture me about lean and the idiocy of creating extra stocks that would be no one person's responsibility."

"It wasn't quite like that," Dad protested with a grin.

"You're right. It was worse! At any rate, you were so convincing that you sold me on the total evil of inventory." He then turned his gaze directly to Phil and asked, "So, have you done something about all that inventory?"

"It looks like it. We think we'll have cut down our inventory by half by the end of the quarter."

"And did you turn around your cash crisis?"

"Touch and go, but we've pulled through," said Phil. "It's still too early to tell in the long run, but we have increased production, started a new contract, and Matt's about to sign yet another new customer. Our cash intake is better. Also, as you'd suggested, we're looking hard at how to get rid of the old product lines. I'm a lot more confident it will work out," he said resolutely.

"Don't sound so glum," scolded Amy. "What about that huge credit extension we got from the bank last week?"

"Sure. We may have more credit available, but it's always at a cost!"

"Maybe, but the point is the presentation we made on our factory improvements really impressed them. It even impressed Matt. Have you noticed how he's listening to us now that the bankers are interested?"

Phil laughed, pushing back his glasses. "Yeah, Amy, you're right, we did win some breathing space. And Matt's been more open-minded since, well, recent developments," he added lamely with a quick side-glance at Harry.

"How about the operators? What's the feeling on the shop floor?" asked Harry.

"It's hard to say, but I have two strong impressions," answered Amy. "First, I think they are starting to realize why the company has been in such bad trouble. From their point of view the gains of productivity and space we've made are hard to dismiss, so no one is arguing anymore that there was a problem. Second, I think they're slowly starting to trust us on the fact that we really want to improve things all around, and not simply screw them one more time. Since we're talking about trust, what about this rumor that the management team is going to get a 20% raise while the salaries are blocked for the rest of the plant?" she asked pointedly at Phil.

"Okay," he squirmed. "It won't happen, but let's say some of the top guys need money so the idea was floated about."

"You must be joking!" I sputtered, as Harry and Dad just chortled.

"Well, son, someone in your management doesn't quite trust your efforts," said Dad.

"Yep," added Harry, "the rats are starting to feel it's time to pump all the dough they can out of the ship before it sinks."

"You're not serious?" asked Phil, looking genuinely outraged.

"Grow up, kid!" answered Harry, his narrow black eyes twinkling with amusement behind his bulbous nose, making him look like an overgrown, mischievous pixie. "Happens all the time. Look around you. The management knows the company is in trouble, gives it a face lift, asks for money in loans or any other cash influx, paying people in stock options and such, and pays themselves huge bonuses for a job well done. If the company goes into liquidation, they're laughing, they've got their honey pot."

"We're not like that!" disagreed Phil stubbornly.

"Of course not," said Harry with undisguised mirth. "No one ever is!"

"Relax," chuckled Harry. "I'm hearing some real progress on the shop floor, and some cash improvement, right? Well done. Of course, you know what's going to happen next?"

"What now?"

"Think about it, kid, you said your company was profitable but with a bad cash crisis, right?"

"Yes, we would have shown a profit, but for a while there, we were not sure whether we could pay our employees," Phil recalled with a shudder.

"Now, you've brought your inventories down and improved your profitability, so your cash flow has increased and the cash crisis eased up, am I right?"

"Absolutely. It's happening."

"Have you thought about how that's affecting your short-term profitability?"

"Oh, damn, I just assumed it would follow suit," moaned Phil, after a moment's hard thinking, taking off his glasses and rubbing his hand over his face. "If we include the inventory discrepancy in our production costs, we've apparently increased our production cost rather than reduced it, is that it?"

"Yeah. Let's count your cost of goods sold over a period, we have:
– start-of-period inventory,
– plus cost of materials,
– plus cost of direct labor,
– plus indirect production costs, and then
– minus your end of period inventory.

"Which rounds off your production costs, yes?"

"Yeah," Phil nodded along unhappily, although Amy and I were still completely in the dark. I glanced at Dad, who was busy splicing a cable and appeared totally unconcerned.

"Then, let's say that although your inventory is real high and it's murdering your cash flow, it is stable during the period and you end up with as much of it at the end of the period as you had at first. It cancels itself out in the production costs. All you have to account for is cost of materials, direct labor, and indirect production costs to offset sales."

"Yes. I see where you're coming from. But if I have halved my inventory in the period?"

"Assuming all your other costs remain equal, the end-of-period inventory you're going to subtract is half as much as what the start-of-period was, so you have an increase in your production costs to the level of your inventory reduction. I guess you didn't tell him about it, Bob. What have you been teaching these kids?"

"Well, Harry, I figured he had enough on his plate as it is. Anyway, this only happens in the first period, after that, your inventories balance out again, and you're fine. And don't worry, remember you've increased sales, so you're probably still profitable."

"Doesn't it ever stop?" Phil complained miserably.

"Hey, come on, kid," Harry jeered cheerfully, getting up noisily. "Anybody want some hooch? That's the fun and games. If just anybody could do it, everybody would."

"You wanted to discuss keeping an overall vision of the improvements, right?"

"I sure could use some help there," nodded Phil. "We seem to be doing so many things at the same time, I find it real hard to see the whole picture"

Dad scrounged around for a piece of paper and started sketching on the back of a worn pad, until Phil slid his notebook over to him. "Let me share a technique Toyota taught us: material and information flow analysis. These days it's often known as value-stream mapping. You were saying you're having trouble to see the big picture? It gets like that, doesn't it? The trees hiding the forest."

"You're right. I just don't know how to keep the proper focus."

"Helicopter view. You need to be able to switch from the big picture to gemba-level detail, and back. Here's the big secret: the treasure map to your gold mine. Something the Toyota engineers only showed us when we were well advanced with all of this," said Dad, when he came back with a refill. "As I said, they called it a MIFA, a materials and information flow analysis."

"Sounds ghastly," I muttered, totally ignored.

"This flow analysis helps you to see the big picture."

Amy came down from the roof where she had been lounging and squeezed in next to me as we crowded around Dad into the cockpit to watch what he was sketching.

"In a way, you want to represent your entire value stream on a map to figure out where your gold is getting stuck, and where you have to get it moving. For instance, we can draw the original state of your factory when we started.

"First was your product flow, then the heaps of inventory you held between processes, and finally —"

"You're only looking at STR?" interrupted Amy.

"Yes. It's a value-stream map. We're mapping the way gold flows through the gold mine, stream by stream, one product family among many, so I only worry about STR at this stage. Draw them one at a time. So later we can do STR-X and QST."

"Okay, that's the product flow."

"Now, the important thing is also to add the information flow. How you know what you have to produce when."

"Production orders, calculated by the MRP," said Phil.

"Right, so let's draw them in."

"Now don't forget to add the presses and the cabinets to your maps, you also need those to build the completed unit."

"See, that's what your STR stream looked like when we first started. (*See map on back inside cover.*) As you go on, you can add all sorts of quantitative data to make the map more accurate, such as:

– people,
– cycle time,
– inventory,
– scrap rate,
– changeover time, and so forth."

"I get it," agreed Phil.

"Good, now you can draw a new MIFA map with all the improvements you've made to the stream."

"You mean with the supermarkets and kanban?"

"Exactly."

They worked on it for a while, and came up with a quite different picture.

"What do you see on this new map?"

"Well, we've done good, but there's still this massive stack around the presses we've got to sort out."

"That's it. That's how you know how you keep the high view: draw a map. If you draw this map regularly, you can see how you're making changes and how you're progressing!"

"That's absolutely brilliant, Bob! Why on earth didn't you tell us about this right from the start?" exclaimed Phil enthusiastically.

Dad just shrugged.

"And then I can extend this to include what's happening with my suppliers, right?" continued Phil brightly. So I can map my entire supply chain!"

"You can, son, you can. Eventually. But you'd better start with your own processes before moving on to grander things. And don't forget, it's only a map."

"And the map is not the territory, just as the word is not the thing, and the word cat does not scratch," I remarked, and they all looked at me blankly. "Elementary semantics!" I explained defensively as they poked fun at me.

"Now, the important thing about this map is not just what's happening to your product flow, but the understanding of how the information flow controls the material flow."

"As in how the MRP creates inventory?" Amy asked.

"Precisely. Essentially, all the MRP does is compute the magic formula: production needed equals customer order minus inventory plus safety stock.

"This formula aggregates up to calculate the economic order quantity, and then it sends the results continuously to all the computers you've got in the plant, which determine what operators are supposed to produce when Dave's not countermanding it," Dad explained as he marked the information links from logistics into the plant.

"Okay. Now we know that doesn't work too well," said Philip. "I guess the computer never knows exactly what is in inventory. After all, it only knows what we put in. Garbage in, garbage out."

"Good gemba thinking. That's part of it. The other thing which tends to happen is that if somehow the customer order dips into what the computer thinks is the safety stock, it will send an order for stock replenishment adding on top of it what needs to refill the safety level all in one go."

"So we suddenly get a massive production order. I see now why you want to scrap the MRP and work with kanban."

"Not so fast, Philip," replied Dad. "You do not want to scrap your MRP. I certainly never suggested that. We need the MRP to calculate production and purchased parts needs. MRP remains essential for producing forecasts for personnel planning and your suppliers. We just don't want it to compute the production program or issue production orders, because it wasn't designed to handle leveling. But that's not the only issue —"

"Yep, gemba," said Phil, who took one lesson at a time but worried at it like a terrier with a bone. "The cards keep us close to the gemba, so we can see what goes on and whether we're ahead or late. If it's all in the computer, we haven't got a clue."

"There's hope for you yet," agreed Dad, with a satisfied smile.

"Is he done yet?" shouted Harry from the dock, coming back from the clubhouse with a six-pack in each hand.

"Almost!" Dad yelled back. "Now, don't forget to track the whole lead time at the bottom of the map, as well as identifying value-added time. That's what tells you if you're making any progress. Remember that all that is nonvalue-added is ultimately waste, and it shows up in the total lead time."

"As in when we used to take the parts all the way from blanking to the storeroom to bring them back for forming."

"Yes, miss. If you don't do that any more, you considerably reduce nonvalue-added time, and so increase your reactivity. Ultimately, the reason we hold inventory is that our production response time is far slower than the customer's purchasing loop. If I could produce instantly on demand, with a lead time close to nil, I wouldn't need to keep any inventory at all."

"I hadn't thought about it this way," laughed Amy. "But of course. And if we get sudden huge orders, we find it even harder to deliver right away, so we need to keep a larger inventory!"

"Yup, do you remember the argument we had over what message you send to suppliers?"

"I'd rather not!" she said with a disapproving frown, which only made my Dad smile.

"Well, I once visited a truck factory we were trying to sell parts to. As I arrived on the site, the first thing I saw was row after row of trucks in the courtyard parked there without any tires. I asked the production manager what had happened, and he launched into a diatribe against suppliers who couldn't deliver on time. I guess he was also trying to soften me up, but I suggested talking to the person who actually passed the orders for tires. Now, he got curious and we finally tracked down the assistant whose job was to send a fax to the tire supplier with the ordered quantity. Over time, their orders per day were 0, 0, 0, 0, 0, 160, 0, 0, 0, 0, 0, 160, 0, 0, 0, and so on."

"You mean, that although trucks were built at a given rate, the tires were ordered in large, irregular batches?" pondered Amy.

"Precisely. When we asked the assistant who passed the order faxes how she worked, she said she received a weekly ordering schedule coming straight from the MRP. The only way the supplier could have delivered the tires would have been keeping a huge inventory just in case."

"I'm sure we do that as well," muttered Phil.

"Very probably. Everything we do starts with the customer. Consequently, to start your MIFA, you have to prepare a spreadsheet with all you need to know about your customer demand, such as product, customer, weekly mean demand, daily mean demand, number of deliveries, quantity per container, and so on. Then you can do the same at each production step, such as welding for instance, with product, customer, weekly demand, daily demand, working content, takt time, cycle time, changeover time, and so forth. Then you can identify all the stocks in the process and evaluate them in time. Finally, don't forget to estimate transport, in terms of the frequency of transport, the hours of the trucks and how many trucks you get in a period, and how many trucks you count between a demand and its answer."

"That gets terribly specific," commented Phil.

"That's the whole point," replied Harry, popping a can open. "It gets you to know your process in every intimate detail."

"And the same goes for information flows. First you can distinguish provisional information from firm information. You have to write down the frequency at which you get the info, the date and time at which it arrives, as well as its time horizon."

"I bet logistics hasn't got a clue about any of this," chuckled Amy.

"They'd better find out," echoed Phil resolutely. *Had* he changed?

"Don't give them too much of a hard time over it. No one would've asked them for anything that detailed before. But that's the opportunity to understand exactly how the information flows. Most companies assume it just does, and don't bother to find out more."

"It's like kanban in a way," remarked Phil. "Ohno's kanban rules, I was thinking. You know, that every container in the factory should have a kanban attached. We need to know exactly where the parts are, where they come from, where they go to, and with what frequency. That's the same with information."

"It's the same. You can't specify one without the other."

"Another way to look at it is that companies tend to be very highly coupled," added Dad, introspectively. "Because information flies around the place all the time, whenever you touch something it affects everything else, in very weird ways. A side effect is that every decision becomes very political. The information links, however, are very loose. Information gets transmitted at the coffee machine, or by a phone call, and so on. What we're trying to do here is to tighten the information flow: the fax is sent once a week on the Tuesday at 10 a.m. and the forecast is valid for eight weeks. That's really specific. Now, if we do that, we can also start uncoupling operations and have more local reactivity as opposed to everything climbing the pass-the-bucket ladder and ending up on the boss's desk. In essence, we can create a system that is more reflexive."

"Amen to that," said Phil with real feeling.

"Heijunka is not just a technique, Philip," said Dad, sketching another page. "It's a way of thinking!"

"What do you mean?" asked Phil, uneasy as always with large statements.

"Obviously," chipped in Amy, "if we want to be able to level our production flows, we need to level the information flow. Is that it?"

"Yep. There's no way we can level the production flow if we keep getting last-minute scoops from logistics or sales. We need to find the earliest reliable information source at the customer and build it into our production planning process, our own information flow."

"How do we do that?"

"We talked about it already on the phone, Philip. The customer knows his production plan, and it's not a state secret. Just ask for it. Ideally, you need two kinds of information: forecast and firm. If you ask them, your customers will give you a forecast. Their plants will also send you firm shipping orders. From the forecasts, you can build a high-level plan over the next couple of months. You're saying you're anticipating a new contract, all well and good. When is Dave going to hear about it?"

Amy burst out laughing, while Phil mumbled something about Dave being kept in the loop.

"You're right," he conceded. "We're supposed to do regular planning meetings, but they never happen on time, and they're a mess anyhow."

"Well, say you're producing 1,000 circuit breakers a month, and the new contract brings you to 1,200. How do you know whether your plant can cope? Your lucky inasmuch as you don't have any capacity constraints on presses or such."

"We've got the ovens for the vacuum capsules," pointed out Phil.

"There you go then. Can you absorb the 200 extra breakers next month? And you rely on the existing number of skilled operators. Can they make it? Same thing for key suppliers."

"Okay, okay, I get your point."

"Ideally, you need to start thinking about producing a weekly forecast with a horizon of about two months, and a firm program for the week, every week. Now, the paradox about leveling is that on one hand producing smaller and smaller batches more frequently makes us more flexible, and on the other we want to avoid variations if we can. Or if variation comes, we want to absorb it slowly."

"How's that?" asked Phil.

"Well, moving from 1,000 to 1,200 is a big jump, a 20% hike. You're lowering your takt time from nine minutes down to seven and a half minutes. Could you do it right away?"

"I'm not sure," answered Amy with a quick frown. "That is quite a step-change."

"However, if we start right now by averaging the increase from one month at 1,000 and the next at 1,200 to two months at 1,100, which is a takt time of eight minutes or so, that's far less of a step."

"But the information is not certain yet! And we'd be building up inventory!"

"I'm not telling you to do it, son. Just to think about it. Following the heijunka way is about avoiding peaks and valleys. It's a two-pronged approach: first you level your production to avoid a peak of one component, and then a valley. Second, you try to smooth out large-scale market variations to make them more palatable, or at least easier to absorb. D'you follow?"

"I guess so," muttered Phil uncertainly, scribbling furiously on his pad. "However, if you do this you can see that a lot of our problems come from what our customers tell us. If only they'd give us clear reliable forecasts —"

"Reliable forecasts?" Harry repeated sarcastically. "Safer to believe in the tooth fairy. There's only two ways to go about this. Either you believe it's your customer's or supplier's fault that you are in a mess, and you try to do anything in your power to force them to accommodate you."

"Like what Kevin was trying to do with our vendors," muttered Amy.

"Or," countered Dad, "you fix yourself and lead others by your example. Choose your camp!"

"That's pretty deep, actually," I acknowledged, surprised.

"What do you mean?" asked Phil looking properly abashed.

"Well, as I psychologist, I believe there are two fundamental attitudes in people. One kind of person blames every one around them for what happens to them and tends to become a professional victim — or a bully. The other kind believes that whatever happens, it's up to them to improve themselves to cope better with the new circumstances. These are very deep attitudes to the world, which, I'll agree with Dad on this one —"

"Hear, hear," laughed Amy.

"Divide people into two camps."

"Discipline others vs. improve yourself, I like that!" said Dad.

"Enough!" barked Harry. "We're going fishing! No more philosophy."

"You heard the man, kids," growled Dad. "Off the ship!"

"Hey, guys," asked Amy, "can I come with you?"

They both looked at her with a mixture of surprise and suspicion. Phil and I just gawked.

"Fishing?"

"In my case, sunbathing."

"No shop talk?"

"I swear. I mean it. It's a lovely morning. I won't get in your way. I'll be in the front getting a tan. Pretty please?"

Harry was killing himself with contained mirth. Dad just shrugged and got up to start his engine as we stepped off the boat in disbelief.

"Let that be a lesson to you, young'uns," said Harry, gloating. "Women choose experience over callow youth any time."

We stood on the pier as Dad untied the hawsers and steered the *Felicity* out, as Amy waved at us cheerfully from the bow.

Phil and I returned to the Club's bar, where we bought a couple of sandwiches. From up there we could see the *Felicity* slowly making her way out of the harbor's sheltered access and into the swell. The sun was mild, the air was fresh, so we walked back down among the boats, and sat on the wooden pier, legs dangling over the water. Kids again, for a jiffy, watching the waves pool, merge, and break on the wooden pillars at our feet.

"So, did you ask her out?"

"I beg your pardon?"

"Amy. Did you ask her out?"

"What makes you think ...?"

"You obviously like her, and she doesn't seem to mind. Come on, isn't it time —"

"— to mind your own business?" I snapped.

"Take it easy. I was just asking."

"Anyway, bright ambitious girl like that, what would she want with a bookworm on the rebound like me?"

"Beats me," agreed Phil. "But you won't know till you ask her."

Ah. I had to admit he had a point there.

"How 'bout you?" I asked, desperate to change the subject. "What shape are you in these days?"

He took another deep bite on his sandwich and munched thoughtfully.

"Good, I'd say, all things considered. We still have huge debts, but the pending crisis seems to have blown over. Our inventory turns have increased from 10 to 17, so everyone is pleased. Your dad has triggered a true revolution in the shop floor, and Amy is bullying everyone into making it happen. Even Dave is starting to say good things about it."

"And at home?"

"You saw for yourself. Charly is busier then ever, the baby is teething, and the twins beat me at every computer game they've got." He took a long sip of his beer, and continued. "A strange opportunity came up, actually. One of our customers was visiting the plant the other day, and they were really impressed with the work we've done. They approached Matt with a discreet offer. We think they might want to buy the plant, and pay a good price for it."

"Did they? What did Matt think?"

"Matt? You know him. He figured that if they were that interested, the company was worth double, so we'd better stick to our guns and go for public ownership."

"And what did you think about it yourself?"

"To be honest, I'm not sure. It's been so much pressure, so much stress. And we still have a lot of debt. Sometimes I wish I could get back to lab work, at least it was simple then. But if we sold out now, I'm not sure of what I'd want to do." He hesitated, looking out toward the open sea. "Also, I'll say that for all that lean stuff your dad is teaching us, I'm really curious to know how far it can take us, now that I've seen what immediate results we could achieve. But now that he's put himself out of the loop. ... I don't know."

"How far can it go?" I'd asked Dad the same question a few weeks ago. He had chuckled at the question, before answering, "about as far as they want. Don't worry, they'll stop before they run out of improvements. Sooner or later they'll tire, or hit a snag they won't be willing to tackle." Something to look forward to, I thought grimly.

Chapter Ten

KAIZEN FOREVER

"Can you believe it!" said Philip angrily as he climbed into the back of the car. "She's left! She quit!"

"I know," I said quietly.

"How d'you —?" he started, staring at me suspiciously.

"Because I told him," said Dad as he gunned the engine and drove out, taking me off the hook. "Amy asked me if I could serve as a reference."

"And you …?"

"What do you think?" he said. Dad actually stopped the car and turned to stare at Phil for added emphasis before resuming. "I like that girl. She's been headhunted by a consultancy trying to build up a lean production practice. They're doubling her salary, Philip."

"But," he said, clearly at a loss, "she was the driving force behind all we've done back at the plant. I would have thought that …"

"Let's face it, it didn't earn her many thanks," I pointed out, not very kindly.

"What do you mean?" he shot back to me.

"Did you realize how much flack she was getting for all her efforts? How much she resented the way the top managers patronized her or dismissed her? Had you noticed how tired she looked recently?"

"We're all under pressure," he answered quietly. I could feel him lapsing into one of his sulks.

We drove in silence for a while, reaching the highway.

"What am I going to do without her?" he asked, in such a plaintive tone that I suddenly flashed back to that rainy night not so long ago when Phil appeared at my door in drunken despair. I knew that Phil was a brilliant scientist, the head of a technologically sophisticated company, and that scores of people counted on him for their livelihood. Yet at the moment he was my old schoolhood chum, feeling hurt and betrayed that one of his other friends had gone to play for the other dodgeball team.

"Aw, stop whining for God's sake!" barked Dad, brimming with his usual empathy. "You still don't get it. Grow up!"

"Get what?" bit back Phil.

"That's your job. You run that place. People come, people go. Your responsibility is to keep it ticking. That *is* the job."

"And how the hell do I do that? I'm a physicist at heart for crying out loud."

"Not if you take on a business. You're either a leader, or you're history," replied my father. I stared straight ahead, silently getting equally riled at both, Phil for his refusal to acknowledge he was going to have to own up to his responsibilities one day, and Dad for his usual lack of compromise, not to mention tact.

"I am starting to come to grips with it," Phil finally said in a quieter voice. "But it's like the lean work. I simply don't know how to do it."

"Well," Dad answered, mollified. "In that particular respect, I use the three-squares model."

"Three squares?"

"Yes, think of every employee on your payroll and ask yourself two questions:

– Where should I move them next?

– Who do I move in their place?"

"The three boxes are current role, future role, and who's doing the replacement, right?"

"Yep. Think about it. Where would Amy go from here? Is there a place in senior management in your company for someone as young as she is and with her qualifications, no matter how much of a natural she turned out to be at operations?"

"I guess you've got a point," agreed Phil with bad grace. "But in the meantime she leaves me in a lurch."

"Well, son, that's the second key problem of leadership. You always lose the good ones because they get poached or they get bored. Part of your job is to constantly think of ways to retain them."

"What's the first problem?" I asked, curious.

"Have a system in place. Something that doesn't depend on having to exercise control every day. Something that tempers down the arbitrariness of management."

"Like the *Toyota Production System?*"

"Or navy procedures, yes: a system which makes people function together as a fighting unit. Like, standard answers to typical problems or situations. Leadership is about turning that into some sort of *esprit de corps*, some feeling of togetherness."

"You keep mentioning that, what exactly do you mean by *esprit de corps?*"

"I couldn't define it precisely, but it's the collective will of the people to make the system work, rather than work against it, and the pride they get out of it."

"Like what Gloria gets out of the operators working the mechanisms cells with the 5S?" wondered Phil.

"Exactly. They work hard, they develop self-discipline, and they're proud of what they do. That's it."

"But how do you obtain that?" I insisted.

"Part of the problem," he added with a quick side-glance at Phil in the rear-view mirror, "is that you've got to keep them long enough for the team spirit to happen. To grow, the *esprit de corps* needs a fairly stable team to develop. After a while, although they'll argue and bicker as they chew over problems, they'll stay because they talk the same language, enjoy the same challenges, and generally have a ball. Amy left because, at the end of the day, she was let down."

"How d'you mean?" Phil retorted sulkily. "I backed her every time!"

"Still, she felt she was fighting alone against all and sundry. She wasn't part of a team. One lone star will never do the trick. One leader is not enough. You need to develop a leadership team to see that *esprit de corps* happens. You need them to feel that the grass is not greener elsewhere, that they won't ever find again a place where they can work with the same atmosphere, within the same set of values."

"And how do I do that?"

"That's the second problem," Dad chuckled. "See, the first problem is to have a system. The second is to find people who will lead this system. Find them, push them, lose them. Find some more. Ongoing headache. It's like in wartime. Every time you develop a leader, they, well, lead their troops into battle, and they get shot up, so you have to find another brave soul who'll do the same. Obviously, the longer you keep them, the better it will all come together. But you must be prepared to lose them also, and not lose everything you've built. It's a tough call, but the alternative is worse."

"Yeah, the alternative is rear-guard generals," agreed Phil, "and we know how well that works!"

"Yep. The great generals are the leaders who've been lucky enough to survive the cannon fire. The point is that as a general your role is to look endlessly for talent, recognize it, push it forward, and make them work together."

"Sounds like the movie industry." I suggested, thinking about my brother.

"Same problem."

"Are you saying I was overreliant on Amy?"

"Not 'over,' son. I'm saying you should start thinking as a general. She's gone, good luck to her. Who have you got lined up to replace her?"

"No one yet!"

"Well, it's high time to start thinking about that."

"And about what you're going to do about your rear-guard generals," I added for good measure.

He didn't respond, lost in his thought, looking out through his open window as the miles swept by. In our part of the world, we get three kinds of weather: blue skies, rain, or fog. Today was hot and muggy, with a dark storm hovering over the bay. Rain was next. With my father's dislike of air conditioning, we had the windows down, drowning the car in damp air. Unexpectedly, Dad chortled and Phil threw him a sour look.

"What?" I asked.

"I once had a very interesting discussion with the HR manager of the Toyota plant we used to supply, when they started up their U.S. transplants. He was telling me that by and large the employees, team members as they called them, were satisfied with the 'give us your 100% and we'll take good care of you' Toyota deal. Those who coped less well were management. No perks, no overtime, and working round the clock. On top of it, managers complained that HR actually coddled operators and generally sided with them in disputes. They lost many managers to the resume upgrade of having worked for Toyota, which is exactly what Amy's done. So if she found a job, it might mean that someone out there believes you've actually made some progress!"

Dad laughed at his own wit, and kept grinning as Phil sunk even lower in his seat, disconsolately.

"Tell us about this guy we're going to meet at the airport?" I asked to break the tension.

My father had traded his truck for my mother's smart sedan, and had even spruced himself up, wearing a neat blazer, pressed chinos, a starch denim shirt, and, oh wonder, a thin black knitted tie.

"Tanaka-san is a rather old gentleman, and he's going to be tired and jet-lagged from the flight, so I expect you boys to be on your best behavior. He's coming to speak at a conference later this week, but since we've known each other for years, he accepted, as a favor to me, to come and have a look at your plant, Phil. Make no mistake, this is a great honor."

Honor? Favors? What had we got into now?

Tanaka-san was a sparse, small man with a shock of brittle white hair. He wore a drab, crumpled gray suit, and walked with the exaggerated deliberateness of the old, taking slow, measured steps toward us as soon as he saw my father waiting at the security barrier, his wrinkled face lighting up with a wide smile. They seemed genuinely pleased to meet each other, with an odd mix of double-handed handshakes and bows. I felt like a complete fool when my Dad introduced Phil and they exchanged business cards, realizing that mine never left the plastic box in the top drawer of my desk at the university. Tanaka-san didn't seem to mind, and sounded very glad to meet 'Professor Woods,' as Dad had introduced me. He continued for a while in Japanese, and I asked my father what he was saying from the corner of my mouth.

"That he's pleased to meet you," was the terse answer.

"I didn't realize you spoke Japanese that well!" I exclaimed, bemused.

"I don't," he answered edgily. "I don't catch more than a word here and then. Tanaka-san always insists that we talk Japanese together, he says that it's good for me!"

Tanaka laughed, and harangued my father in Japanese until he turned toward us and, switching smoothly to English, which he spoke fluently, explained to Phil and me that anyone foolhardy enough to try to learn Japanese should be encouraged in his efforts, which drew an unexpected laugh from Dad. While Phil and I sat in the back of the car, feeling like kids again, Tanaka and my father swapped gossip and friendly banter, mostly exchanging news about who was doing what in the small, select community of lean experts in the United States. Something in the way my father had presented the man had made me expect a fearful dragon, but his engaging, easygoing attitude did much to allay my apprehensions.

All of which changed radically as we reached the plant. Tanaka's face closed up in a look of intense concentration, a mask of aloof focus with nary a smile or a wink. He ignored any attempt Phil made to explain what the plant produced or how it worked, but went straight to the workstations. The factory was transformed. They'd cordoned off about a third of the plant, which now stood totally empty and meticulously scrubbed. At the start of the conveyor, they'd placed another supermarket for the cabinets. They'd also moved the cabinet cell right next to the conveyor on the other side of the mechanism lines, and the machines were now spotless. In front of each cell we could see a whiteboard with the day's hourly objectives, a kanban queue, and a few indicators being tracked. The clutter of blank parts crates had disappeared, and although a few bins remained in the storeroom, they stood on the floor, and the racks along the wall were visibly empty.

None of which seemed to interest Tanaka much. He went from operator to operator in the mechanism assembly line, picking up parts, staring at the operators working. Walking slowly up the assembly line, he looked long and hard at the mechanism supermarket (which had been reduced by half since our last visit), and spent a long time pushing containers up the rollers and watching them roll back down toward the conveyor operators. More of the same at the conveyor, where he stood and watched in silence, station by station. He walked more quickly through the cabinet assembly cell, unexpectedly beaming at the sight of the old press, and muttered something unintelligible to my Dad.

"He's fond of old machines," Dad repeated in a stage whisper. "He says they make him feel young."

After about an hour of his silent visit, Tanaka-san approached Phil, who, by now looked clearly worried.

"Do you not care about quality?" he asked distinctly.

"I'm sorry?" stammered Phil, completely thrown.

"Your managers," he said slowly and precisely, "they don't care about quality."

"What?" more and more bewildered.

"Your operators, they don't care about quality either. Or if they do, no one has bothered to ask them."

"I'm sorry, sir, I don't understand. Of course we pay attention to quality. We have 100% inspection of our products."

"You can't inspect quality into the product," answered Tanaka cuttingly. "You must build quality *into* the product," he emphasized, pointing at an assembly station.

Phil sent a helpless glance at my father, who stared back impassively.

"This line, does it stop?" continued Tanaka-san.

"No, not anymore. We've done a lot of work with standardized work and now the line runs very smoothly."

"It doesn't stop enough. You have too much inventory!"

Phil looked at me aghast. I could hardly see any inventory left in the plant beyond what was in the shop stocks and the odd pallet against a wall."

"You must ask Bob-san to explain lake and rocks!"

He bobbed his head at Dad and motioned him to follow him a few steps away where they had an intense muted conversation with Tanaka, pointing to things here and there in the factory and Dad nodding conscientiously. Finally, they walked back to where Phil still stood agape.

"Thank you very much for your welcome, Phil-san," he said, smiling and bowing. "You have done very well with this plant, and I think it will become a model plant in U.S., yes?"

"Don't be an ass. Thank Tanaka-san," Dad whispered fiercely in Phil's ear, and while Phil smiled and bowed, Dad took me aside and said quickly: "I'll explain later. I'm driving him to his hotel and taking him for an early dinner. Why don't you boys come around the house for a drink later this evening?"

And they were gone without a further word of explanation. Phil stood totally baffled, absently polishing his glasses against the edge of his shirt, with the hollow look his eyes had without his lenses. His bewilderment was so comical I had to fight back a smile. Wait 'til Amy hears about this, I thought, amused. It'll have her in stitches.

"Some visit!" blurted out Phil, dripping with rain, as soon as my father had the door open.

"Hmm, Tanaka-san has definitely mellowed with age."

Mellowed? Dad picked his martini up and nodded toward the stairs. I extricated myself grudgingly from the movie I'd started watching with Mom, while Phil pulled a couple of beers out of the fridge. The downpour had started as I'd reached the house, so rather than take our usual station on the porch, we climbed to Dad's study, leaving my mother to watch her latest movie in peace.

"Tanaka-san was my first lean mentor," Dad explained. "Back then, I was managing a plant that supplied Toyota, and we were part of their supplier development program. He's the guy who, on his first visit, told me that I had to throw away my large metal containers and replace them with small plastic ones, cut my changeover time in half to do more changeovers, and, although the Toyota truck only came to pick up the parts twice a week, I'd have to have a material handler supplying the truck preparation area every two hours. I threw him out of the plant," said Dad with a chuckle.

"I can see why," said Phil with feeling, pushing his glasses back repeatedly.

"But he was very patient about it. I mulled over it for a while, and then asked him to come back. He repeated exactly the same thing. Fine, says I. How do we do it? And we've worked exceedingly well together from that point onward."

"He didn't seemed particularly mellow to me," I chuckled.

"You haven't seen him in action. Some time after he retired, he came back stateside to talk at some conference or other. He doesn't like public speaking, so his entire presentation was made up of 'before' and 'after' photos. They so impressed the CEO of a large industrial group that he went straight up to him as he was leaving the podium to ask him to come and consult with his company. Tanaka said he was retired and declined. But the CEO would not take no for an answer, and finally managed to invite Tanaka to dinner. He took him to the best restaurant in town, but as soon as they'd ordered, he pulled out a plan of his main factory, and showed him all the lean workshops he had in mind. Tanaka glanced at it briefly and said something like 'Wrong, wrong, and wrong.' The CEO then begged him to come to the plant one more time.

"Finally, exasperated, Tanaka-san agreed that if he'd shut up about it and let him enjoy his dinner, he'd accept to have a quick look at the shop floor after the meal. One condition, though. Whatever he said, they'd do — no arguments."

So that's whom he gets it from, I smiled to myself.

"They ended up at the plant around midnight; Tanaka-san cast a quick look around, and asked the CEO whether he had a night maintenance crew. "No argument," he reminded him, or if not he was straight back to his hotel. In the end, the night shift spent the night moving machines around creating flow, and they cut the lead time by something absurd like 80%.

"When the CEO needed someone to drive the lean transformation in-house, Tanaka-san gave him my name, and that's how I ended up Manufacturing VP."

"What did he mean by 'my managers don't care about quality?'" huffed Phil, regaining some of his outrage.

"Just that. Do your managers care about quality?"

"Of course they do," he stammered. "You know that, we do everything we can to test every single product."

"Is that another of these gemba questions?" I ventured.

"Shrewd guess. It is."

"I don't follow," Phil griped.

"Well, son, do you remember me talking about the skipper who is on deck to anticipate problems, as opposed to the one who's below with the reports, his ship on the rocks, but knowing exactly why?"

"Vaguely, but I fail to see —"

"How long has a skipper got to react if he spots a problem?"

"Not long, I guess."

"How long has a manager got to react if a quality problem arises?"

"Ah, I see your point."

"How long?"

"I don't know. A few hours?"

"More specifically, how long?"

"Until the situation arises again?" This stuff was starting to rub off on me.

"Precisely. Before the operators start their cycle anew."

"One operator cycle?" Phil repeated, dumbfounded.

"Of course. Think about it. That's the only time available until you start producing dross."

"But no one can react that fast," he protested.

"Not if they're sitting in their office, they can't."

"But we can't be all the time on the shop floor?"

"When I was running a lean plant, I'd spend about 10 hours a day at the factory, and only two or three of those in my office. The rest of time I was on the shop floor!"

"Doing what?" exclaimed Phil.

"Figuring out how to improve things, mostly. Looking out for quality issues. Challenging the supervisors on anomalies, nitpicking on their proposed counter-measures. That sort of thing. Kept me busy, believe it."

"But what about the other stuff? You know, all the paperwork I have to deal with."

"A lot disappeared, mostly because I caught problems before they reached my office. Some I simply didn't do, such as the overreporting that the head office was always asking for. As for the rest, well two hours of solid work is a lot of time."

"And meetings?"

"No meetings. Hated meetings. Waste of time most of them."

"Tanaka-san made four broad points today," said Dad. "The first one is that if there's a problem, the plant's management has no way to know about it and has to wait for a report — by which time it's usually very late. Second, you've worked very hard on flowing, but less on quality — which is largely my fault because I have not talked to you much about that beyond the red bins. To keep to our analogy, you're flowing gold faster in the process, but still losing far too much of it. Third, operators have no procedures to correct defects automatically, and are not asked for suggestions, which is why he surmised that 'operators did not care about quality.' Finally, your flow now runs too smoothly, so you're not surfacing problems any longer. If you reduce inventory some more, problems will appear, which will stop the line, but that's all right, because it means they'll be resolved."

"Oh. Is that all? Why didn't he just say so?" Phil complained with a tired smile.

"That's exactly what he did, Philip," answered my father.

"There's an entire aspect of the Toyota Production System that I have not touched upon," my father explained with a long, drawn-out sigh. "Their system rests on two main pillars. One is just-in-time, where, visibly, you've made some real progress. The other is called *jidoka*. The core idea is that, as you know, the downstream process comes and picks up from the upstream process. However, the upstream process has to agree never to deliver defective parts."

"Zero defects."

"Yeah," concurred Phil. "We discussed that about the red bins. You said that it meant zero defects accepted."

"Close enough. If I'm in charge of a process, I take on the responsibility of delivering only good parts. Now there are two ways of doing that. The first is of course —"

"Inspection."

"Correct. And I'll work inspection all the way to the operators who will be expected to inspect their own work."

"How do you do that?" I wondered. I couldn't imagine how you would realistically hold people to inspecting their own work. It goes against the grain.

"Checklists, mostly," he answered. "With each operation comes a checklist of points to inspect, from a couple to seven or eight. And operators are trained to follow a visual circuit to make sure they do check them all."

"Standardized work again!"

"To some extent, but don't try to bring it all under one single concept. However, that's not nearly enough. The fundamental point is that you can't inspect quality into the product. You've got to build it in. There's an old Toyota family tradition on this issue, since Sakichi himself, the Toyoda founding father who invented automatic looms at the turn of the 20th century had an epiphany. The key to building quality in the product, he reasoned, was to have the process stop every time nonquality was identified. Consequently, he had his looms stop automatically every time a thread broke — which had lots of people running to fix it and figure out why it broke and so on."

"Which is precisely what my engineers don't do because they don't even know something went wrong until much later. And in any case, they seldom consider it their problem," Phil admitted ruefully. "Then again, if we'd completely stop the chain every time an operator hits an assembly difficulty and get the engineers down there, they'd feel a lot more concerned."

"Aha, I can just picture you," I kidded Phil. "'Go to the gemba and see for yourself!' I'd love to hear you tell that to that guy Pellman."

"Don't think I won't at the next opportunity," he answered deadpan.

"This is one aspect of lean to take on simple faith," continued Dad. "Experience shows that if you invest resources in resolving problems when they appear, your overall costs will go down, including labor."

"That's going to take some work to persuade the management team," complained Phil. My father just shrugged.

"As with just-in-time, jidoka is a multifaceted concept. It all revolves around building quality into the product by stopping nonquality from happening, but it has led to a number of systematic developments. The most visible one at Toyota is *andon boards*, massive electrical boards with numbers corresponding to working stations. When an operator hits a snag on the line, he pushes a button, which lights up his station's number on the board. The team leader and supervisor come running because they've now got the time of one work cycle to fix the problem before the line stops."

"How long is that?"

"Well, it depends on the takt time, but they churn out about a car a minute. So it's not long."

"Do you think we should get one of those for our factory?"

"It'd look mighty silly," guffawed Dad. "That would be heavy artillery for a small shop like yours. Besides, your cycle times are a lot longer, you've got the whole of 10 minutes to react. You need to figure out some way the operators can visually flag problems when they come across one. It could be red flags for all I know. Just some big sign, which says, 'Come over here, there's a bug.'"

Red flag, Phil underlined on his pad.

"Flagging the problem is only half of it, remember. You must also have a rule that if the problem isn't solved in one cycle, everything stops. Period."

"Until you've resolved it?" I asked.

"Of course not. Only until you've found a countermeasure to make sure you're not producing rubbish. Then you have to figure out what caused the problem in the first place, which can be a complex analysis and take far longer. But you're still stopping the line until you've got a quick fix."

"That'll put the pressure on, for sure," agreed Phil, sounding impressed.

"You'd better believe it. I've lived through some hairy line stops, but at least everyone involved focuses on solving the problem. Do this for 10 years, and you get far fewer problems."

"What about machines?"

"Same thing. No difference. They call it *autonomation*. Basically, they've done a lot of work to make sure that their machines can spot defects, and stop. Then a big red light comes on, and people rush to the rescue. One of the advantages of this is that it liberates people from babysitting machines in case they break down. One person can handle a number of automatic machines and intervene only in case of failure or for loading and unloading. It's been in their thinking since the looms."

"A meme!" I exclaimed, thinking out loud.

"Pardon?"

"Memes. That's like a gene applied to concepts. A meme is a core idea, which gets transmitted over generations, mutating along the way. Like the self-stopping loom, which becomes a number of techniques a century down the line. Same meme. Different mutations."

"TPS is full of those," Dad agreed, to my surprise. I usually get a lot of ribbing when I come out with something from my own area. Maybe he was mellowing as well. Not likely!

"Let me see," checked Phil. "I've got to build quality in my products. To do so, I need first to make sure no defects are passed down the line. So one, the operators check for defects as well as the machines themselves whenever possible. Two, when there's a defect they call for help. Three, if no solution can be found in the current cycle, everything stops. Dave's gonna love that one!"

"Indeed, it's not in your culture. On the other hand, a team leader who never stops his line is either hiding quality problems or not seeing them. Plus, remember, the operators themselves push the button that will stop the line at the end of the cycle. If the button is not pushed again by the team leader because they've found some quick fix, the line then stops."

"That's quite a responsibility for operators, isn't it?"

"It's involvement," he replied.

"That's still a lot to ask of operators. Hell, if I was doing the same thing over and over again, I'd find it hard to stay focused on spotting quality problems."

"I agree with Phil, Dad. I find it hard enough to switch the lights out when I leave a room."

"True, that's why they need to be helped."

"Helped to do what?"

"To avoid making mistakes of course," Dad answered irritably. "Obviously you're right. It's a lot to ask people to both produce and constantly double-check for mistakes. The idea is to build devices in their work environment that will help them avoid making the mistake in the first place. Toyota calls it *poka-yoke*. It's often translated as mistake-proofing, or error-avoidance."

"Like what?"

"Well, your own circuit breakers, for instance. What are they for?"

"I see what you mean. If there's an electrical overload, they break the circuit before the equipment fries. Are you talking about things like child-proof caps for medication?"

"Exactly. Or different width of nozzles at a gas station to avoid pumping diesel into gas-powered vehicles. First you will color code, to make sure that people are less tempted to make the mistake, and then you find some way of stopping the operators if they've got missing parts, or are not assembling right, or the equipment is not doing it's job properly."

"Do you have specific examples?"

"Hard to say like this, we'd have to be at the gemba. But in general, true poka-yoke stop you from performing the operation incorrectly. If you can't do that, there are all sorts of signals you can set up with sensors. Not as good, but there are plenty of cheap sensors on the market now that you can use to make sure the parts you're punching are the right shape, or that you've drilled the right holes, etc."

"Where would it work for us?"

"I don't know, Philip. You're going to have to think it out for yourself. But look at mechanism assembly. They have a lot of small parts to fit into those mechanisms. How can you make sure that none are overlooked? Talk it over with the operators, you'll find some ideas.

Or welding. You could have a counter that counts the number of spot welds trigger a signal if some welds are missing at the end of the cycle. Figure it out!"

"Where's Amy when I need her," muttered Phil, scribbling furiously in the dim light of Dad's office. "I thought we were getting there, what with the plans to start a new line in the space we've cleared from the improvements."

"That's why it's called continuous improvement," quipped Dad dryly. "You're never done. Which was Tanaka-san's last point. If your line is running too smoothly, take some in-process inventory out, and all sorts of problems will appear, so you can resolve them. It's the same with the poka-yoke. They make it clear where you have some problems so you can kaizen them away."

"Lower the water in the lakes and the rocks appear, right?" I remarked.

"Yup. You will learn to hate that image. Until you do, Philip, you've not tried hard enough."

"I'm still puzzled about something, Dad. From a social point of view, how do you maintain the momentum? How do you keep people on the lookout for problems all the time?"

"That's pretty much a leadership issue. For instance when I was running the plant I was tracking the number of suggestions per person daily."

"You mentioned something about a suggestion program."

"I did. Tanaka-san said your operators were not interested in quality. In fact, you're not making them interested in quality. You're not interested in their opinion."

"I am," Phil replied, sounding hurt.

"If you are, you're not asking. Not formally anyhow."

"I've heard of suggestion programs," I objected. "They never work. At least at the university they don't."

"And why don't they?"

"I don't know. Because people don't take them seriously, I suppose."

"And why don't they?"

"Are we doing 'five why?'"

"Just follow your intuition, darn it."

"Because, because, it doesn't ever have any effect. People ask you just for show. You could have the best suggestion in the world, but you still would never see anything done about it, so why bother."

"Precisely. The only way suggestions work is that you react to them right away and you discuss them with the operators. Quickly."

"How quickly."

"Well, within the week. Beyond that, they've moved on."

"Forget it. I'll never get my quality department to answer suggestions within one week. Or maintenance!"

"Gemba first, Philip. I'm telling you, it's an attitude problem. Remember that you want the quality guys to resolve problems on the line during one working cycle — that's within takt time!"

Deep sigh.

"It's not that bad. No one needs a definitive answer that fast. What they really need is for you to go and talk to them about it. That's all. From where you stand, it feels like you see everybody all the time. But to them, you're still the boss, so when you talk to them it's a big thing. Think about how Ester and Gloria are eager to show you what they've done. You've got to commit to your gemba and your people, Philip, or you won't get them to commit to you."

"Okay, okay. I'm doing it. It's just that, you know. Time just flies!"

"You haven't got that many people in that plant. All you have to do is discuss suggestions daily with each of your supervisors. You'll see, they'll surprise you."

"Yeah, okay. Produce people before you produce parts."

"And kaizen," I added. "And gemba. But you're right. It's an attitude thing as much as anything else. I take your point about having to be rigorous about measurements and analysis and so on, but fundamentally you're talking about an attitude change. A people attitude, and a kaizen attitude. And a gemba attitude, isn't it? And take it from a professional psychologist, changing people's attitudes isn't easily done."

"Which is why you have to be so careful of who you work with. The truth is, I've always felt that may be 50% analysis, but it's also 50% emotional, if not more. You have to want to do things better, in your gut. If not, go home. Don't bother. How did you feel about Tanaka-san's visit?"

"To be honest," answered Phil with a frown, "I felt mortified. I felt angry and offended. I felt he'd made me for a complete fool."

"Did he now?" asked Dad with a knowing grin.

"Sitting here, in your study, with a drink and pen and paper, I can see he was simply giving a lesson. But out there on the shop floor, I didn't take it so well. I felt I was being belittled in front of my own people."

"Yup, he used to rub me the wrong way every time at first," confessed Dad, laughing. "Until I realized that I was the one with the attitude problem, not him. Ultimately, I've come to believe it's the principal hindrance to kaizen. We have a cultural difficulty to challenge what we've done. Hey, it's hard enough to build the darned things in the first place, so what more do you expect, right?"

"I take your point, it sounds just like the engineers who resent Josh because of all the quality issues he feeds back to them," agreed Phil. "It's hard enough to design the breakers, one of them had the gall — "

"Or naivety —" I interjected.

"Yeah, or naivety to tell me when I was asking him to resolve one of Josh's issues, *pronto*."

"Nobody likes to be criticized. Particularly in our feel-good culture, negative feedback is a big no-no. It wasn't quite as bad in my time. But yes, that's a problem. I've long suspected that the legitimacy of criticism was part and parcel of Toyota's enduring success. Kaizen will only happen if people are ready to challenge what they've just done, and fix what's not satisfactory."

"All well and good. But how do you get them there?"

"Well, there ain't too many ways of going about it. At the end of each activity, you've got to take a break and ask yourself how it went. Do a post-mortem, of sorts. And fix what went wrong."

"That's pretty vague!" I protested.

"Not if you've got standardized work. Then it becomes specific quickly."

"That's good for shop-floor operations, but what about the rest?"

"Same thing. Standardized work becomes checklists, that's all."

"How come?"

"Are you boys slow, or what!" griped my father. "It's all the same, haven't you figured out what kaizen is yet, whatever the activity?"

We looked at him blankly. I wish he would not make us feel so dumb all the time, Japanese teaching technique or not.

"Standardized work is the beginning and the end of continuous improvement. You can have all the best problem-solving approaches in the world, but if you don't start with standardized work you'll be disappointed by the results. And standardized work is nothing more than a very specific checklist. Checklists. What a difficult concept to grasp!" he added, rubbing it in. "If you want to improve any activity, start by drawing up a checklist!"

"Such as what?"

"Anything. Everything. The key points you need to remember in order to get it right. What do you have to do to have a successful class?"

Pray that the students turn up in a good mood, was the first thing that came to mind.

"Let's see. I need to have a clear list of the points I want to make during the class. I need to have the support material with me. I need to bring corrected papers if I've got any because grades are the only thing they care about. I need to start by asking them what they remember from last class. I need to continuously fish for reactions. I need to try to get them to link what I'm saying to their personal experience because if not it goes in one ear and out by the other. And I need to tell them what they've got to do for the next. That's about it. Then I've got to teach the class and hope for the best. Ah, yes, I always forget. Administrative information."

"There you go, write the checklist."

"Here, hand over the pad:

– main points,

– support material,

– graded papers,

– admin,

– roundtable on what they remember from last class,

– challenge them to ask questions,

– get them to relate key points to their personal experience, and

– give homework."

"Now, after each class, you can ask yourself how well you did on each of these points."

"Ow. That'd be pretty painful. Particularly the point about challenging them, it's all touchy-feely stuff."

"Still, you either succeed, or you don't. Something in what you say and or do must make a difference!"

Yeah, sure. We're talking about students here!

"Fine, admitting that I do a review at the end of every class, then what?"

"You identify inefficiencies on each of the steps, or points where you think you could do better. You try them out, and if it works, include them into the checklist. On and on again. With industrial processes, it's mostly about knowing what is value for the customer, and then identifying waste. Basically, anything that does not deliver value is waste. Then you have to find ways to eliminate waste, and, if it works, you include it back into the checklist."

"All things being equal," I agreed cautiously, "it might apply just as well to teaching. If we define value to students as increased knowledge, much of what teachers do in class has little impact on actual knowledge intake. Mostly, they just deliver information, which is probably one of the least efficient ways to get anyone to learn. On top of which, we all tend to bore students to death, which ensures that they turn off their brains the moment they sit in the classroom."

"Surely they ask questions?"

"Oh, trust me, they soon learn to do that on automatic pilot. My point is that if we applied the kaizen cycle rigorously to teaching, we'd probably find out a thing or two. As one of my colleagues keeps saying, ultimately, teaching is not about filling a vessel, but lighting a fire."

"Okay, so the kaizen cycle is:
– checklist or standardized work,
– identify waste,
– figure out how to remove the waste, and
– if it works, update the checklist or standardized work."

"Is it really that simple?"

"Simple, yes," assured Dad. "Easy, never. But if you do this on and on for a decade, then you certainly end up with a very different process, if only because you've learned a lot. The difficulty lies in maintaining it."

"And that's as much attitude as technique," I stressed.

"That's right. If you want to, you'll try it; if you try to, you're already doing it!"

"Kaizen forever," concluded Phil.

"Kaizen forever."

The storm had moved on as I drove down the hill, and the rain had stopped. The air was warm and thick with smells of soil and flowers, as if the very earth had opened, giving up its fruit all at once. I drove slowly, with the window open, lazing my way down the dark, winding roads. Strangely enough, Tanaka's shotgun visit had got to me too, in a very different way. To Phil, it had just been the cold shower of raised expectations when he expected a pat on the back. But his achievements were real enough, having turned his plant around in record time, saved himself and his company from financial failure, ultimately transforming himself in the process.

Phil had filled out, these days, in some ineffable sense. He'd gained an edge he never had. It seemed to me that he had somehow come around to using the dogged mental powers that had made him so good at esoteric physics to every other problem the plant threw at him, process- or people-wise. And he was also learning to do so through other people. Altogether, it didn't necessarily make him a nicer man, but his natural placidity now seemed more like poise and less like indecisiveness. I had, on instinct, advised him to focus on solving the plant's problems rather than wallow in introspection, and never expected it could have an effect on his very character.

The experience of the plant had crystallized a real concern over my own work, which had been lurking in the dark recesses of my mind the past few weeks. My basic argument, in the book I was having such a hard time writing, was that our minds didn't evolve to reason. They evolved to believe, which is a pretty neat trick. If I start running up a tree because I got fooled into believing there's a predator behind the bush, and I turned out to be wrong, well, at most, I look stupid. Conversely, if I reason there couldn't be a predator behind the bush, and I get it wrong, I get eaten. Evolution would favor belief over reason any time. Obviously, we do reason, but my take on this was that reasoning is actually a social skill, not necessarily an implicit human one. Science, for instance, is a great reasoning achievement, but it's slow and painful, and in the end, not particularly rational, inasmuch as people get hung up on all sorts of crazy ideas and, at the end of the day, scientific thinking progresses one funeral at a time. But it's also about people first, then practical, narrowly defined topics, and finally constant research. People, gemba, kaizen.

In the final analysis, here I was writing a book on all the instances of people not being rational, even within the scientific community.

Why? Mostly because we're individually too lazy to bother with rational procedure, such as define problems, explore alternatives, measure effects, test solutions, generalize successes, challenge results, and so on. And yet increasingly, it appeared that what I thought to be an organizational system was in fact an individual learning system. The more I thought about what I'd learned from following the lean track, the less I was concerned with the mechanics of kanban or leveling, but the more I was impressed with the amount of specific knowledge Amy and Phil had gained in such a short time. They'd learned to be rational, to systematically recognize problems, attack them through detailed observation, investigate options, and resolve them one after the other: precisely what I was saying we're not supposed to be good at. At the end of the day, all they'd done was resolve one problem after the next, until the waste in the system was slowly rolled back. I'd not recognized the plant each time I returned there — but they didn't share that experience at all. They felt nothing much was happening and it all took so long and that they met with endless resistance.

The truth of the matter, I now believed, was that rationality did not lay in higher reasoning powers, in visionary schemes, but in the ability to narrow down problems until one reached the nitty-gritty level at which one could actually do something about them. The rest is philosophy. And indeed, I was reaching the conclusion that vision was a philosophical problem, but rationality is in the details. All in all, in my research on irrationality, maybe I had been studying the wrong field all along, which was a very scary thought.

"Poor Phil," she said when she'd finished laughing. "Especially as he'd done so well. It must have been a serious downer. I'm sorry I wasn't there."

"Any regrets?" I'd been uneasy to learn Amy was moving on to greener pastures. I could see that it was a positive move for her, but felt torn in my loyalty to Phil, and had seen firsthand how badly her defection had shaken his confidence in his ability to pursue the turnaround. She turned her soft, round face toward me and flashed one of her quick bright smiles.

"Are you joking? This consultancy is paying me tons of money, and they've even agreed to finance a part-time MBA. Seeing different companies is also going to be good experience. I feel sorry for Phil, nonetheless, I really left him up the creek."

"Without the proverbial paddle. You could ask him for a raise, he's a generous guy and I've never known him to hold a grudge."

"After I argued against management pay increases? No way. In any case, it's not just the money. It was just getting to be too much, trying to motivate everybody all the time. And so many of them blamed me for rocking their sinking little boat. You know, arguing the leak was on the other side, so not their problem. It was wearing me down."

"To think that Harry got you this consultancy job!"

"Not exactly," she corrected. "He mentioned to the headhunter that the company was best practice in lean implementation. Which is why they came looking for me."

"Still, small world."

"Yeah, who would've thought! Remember when your dad stormed out that first time! He terrified me then."

"He terrifies me still," I replied out of habit.

"Give it up," she smiled. "He's a sweet guy."

"Whatever. But the good thing is that you made it! You've turned that factory around. How does it feel?"

"Good, I guess. Clearing out that section of the plant to prepare for the new line was really exciting — a real team effort. But if you'd seen the monstrosity the engineers have dreamed up for the new line. It makes you wonder!"

She thought about it a while, and then she smiled wistfully.

"I don't know," she sighed. "It feels too much like unfinished work, to be honest. And from what you're telling me of Master Yoda's visit, it sounds like I only read half the book after all. What was that all about? Jidoka?"

"Do you really want to talk about the plant?"

"I want to know. Tell me!"

"Well, Dad made a great case of what this Tanaka-san character said, about building quality in the product."

"As opposed to inspecting it out?"

"I suppose. Then he talked about systems to flag problems as soon as they appear on the shop floor, to make sure that management reacts immediately to flow disruptions as opposed to the usual paperwork."

"Gemba!"

"Gemba indeed," I said. "Then they discussed different ways of helping operators avoid mistakes by using clever error-avoidance devices on the working station, but if you want to know more about that, you're going to have to ask my Dad."

"You think I can?"

"I don't see why not. Finally, we got into this big discussion about kaizen, which kind of freaked me because we applied it to teaching and I suddenly realized how little I knew about students' learning process. And I'm a cog-sci expert, so think about the rest of my colleagues out there!"

"Does it apply?"

"If push comes to shove, I'd have to say, 'Yes.' We've never defined value. And we haven't considered teaching standards, although to be fair, in some universities there are real discussions about curriculums, such as what is knowledge, and what is valid pedagogy, but it generally remains very woozy. None of this reflecting systematically on each class and comparing what you did against a checklist."

"On the shop floor it's soon clear that without standardized work to start from, there's no real way to do continuous improvement. At the best you have random change."

"And, oh, yes, Dad mentioned you've managed to miss all the real HR work in lean implementation!"

"What did he have in mind?"

"Suggestion programs, mainly."

"Makes sense. Gemba. Kaizen. *People*. I guess I've still got a lot to learn about this lean stuff!"

"You could always go back!"

She laughed again, but her dark eyes remained thoughtful.

"You mean, forget the pay raise, and the two-week break I get before starting the new job? Not likely."

I thought not. But I also thought she'd soon miss the hands on work in a real company, with real people. Consultancy sounded like a lot of talk, and very little walk.

"And have you finally decided what to do with all that free time?"

"Not yet. Any ideas?"

EPILOGUE

Capabilities can be extended indefinitely when everyone begins to think.
– Taiichi Ohno

I once heard an anecdote about Winston Churchill, one that is probably apocryphal but instructive nonetheless. In his waning years, the grand old man had accepted a speaking engagement at a boys' school to tell the young gentlemen something about moral fiber. The pupils had been duly briefed by their teachers to pay great attention to both form and meaning. Here was the world's greatest speechmaker and a Nobel Prize recipient in literature. Churchill arrived, gave his young audience his best bulldog gaze, said, *"Never, never, never give up!"* and sat down. The lecture was over.

I find the story too good to be true, although it sounds Churchillian enough. Yet it captures marvelously the essence of what I have discovered in following Philip through the thick and thin of his industrial adventures, as the Boswell to his Johnson, the Watson to his Holmes. And as an observer on the trail of my father, whom I have come to see in a different light and with much greater respect, not to say understanding. The lake and the rocks indeed! Strangely enough, according to Dad, never giving up seems to be a feature of the Toyota system as a whole. He claims he could have gotten rich collecting a dollar every time he heard someone say that Toyota was "moving away from just-in-time because it was not flexible enough," or "automating the system to keep up with the industry," or whatever new nonsense business pundits came up with. He says that, to him, the most extraordinary achievement of Toyota's people is they never gave up. They stuck to their ideas, and continuously adapted them as the competitive environment turned and changed around them, never letting go of the core insights of lean and pull system and kaizen and fighting muda — waste. There you go: I am speaking Toyota-ese as well.

Phil has taken up sailing, to the extent that he will go and spend every other weekend with my father polishing wood on the *Felicity*'s deck, or adding yet another coat of paint. I hear that they sometimes even take it out to sea. He's told me he was considering joining the Yacht Club and, more surprisingly, that Charlene really liked the place and the atmosphere. She was already contemplating how to rearrange it all, as well as exotic sailing holidays for the family in the West Indies. What do you know? Phil and Matt have offered Dad a place on their board, which he has reluctantly accepted on the condition he would not have to do any work, but I can tell he's secretly delighted. I occasionally accompany Phil and my father on their weekend outings, when the weather is mild, and the sea calm. Of course, they talk shop. How many hours can one spend discussing the intricacies of lean and the inequities of management? Last time, Phil was slowly working through people issues again.

"I understand it's all about people," he was saying, "but how can I pick the right people?"

"Tricky," answered Dad, steering the *Felicity* toward the ocean swell. "Experience, I guess. And one still gets it wrong. In my last job, we used to have this system where four of us would interview a candidate separately, and then we'd debrief together. The rule was that if anyone vetoed the guy, we wouldn't hire him or her, period. And I had no special privileges for being the boss. In the end, we were not after stars, but winners, people who'd perform consistently over time and would fit within the team. We lost some brilliant guys, and made a few errors, but by and large, it worked out well for us."

He kept quiet for a while, focused on handling the ship as we hit the first waves, and I foolishly hoped that would be it for the day, but then he picked up again, musing aloud.

"I used to think that people have two fundamental dimensions. Are they good at their job? And can they help me work the system in place."

"More lists?" I quipped, moving out of the sudden spray. "A list, B list, C list, right?"

I had them both glaring at me now.

"Something like that," admitted Dad. "People good at what they did and ready to help me run the system would obviously be pushed for further leadership roles, and asked to show their mettle, no big worries there. Those who are neither have to be gotten rid of fast. The problems arise with the question marks."

"Someone good at what they do, but poor at working with the system?"

"Yes, a cowboy. They deliver results, but don't ask them how, and how many corners they cut. Conversely, there are the good boys and girls who do exactly what you say, but don't deliver the results."

I could recognize the types in some of my students all right.

"At first, I tended to be indulgent of the cowboys. Heck, I'd done it myself enough times. But then I realized there was more to getting the job done. If I wanted to develop *esprit de corps* I had to defend such positive values as were embedded in the system."

"Such as making it work, rather than the opposite?" asked Phil.

"Yes. Right first time, zero defects accepted, and so forth. Doing things the right way, not cutting corners for the sake of immediate results. So I changed my policy and fired the cowboys and gave a second chance to those who could work with the system but weren't pushing hard enough. At first I thought they lacked some fundamental grit, and some do, but many just need experience, and they can shape up into splendid leaders. Alternatively, they can also become high-level experts who won't have to manage people so much."

Philip has come a long way, to the point of exerting far more authority around him, not necessarily an endearing feature, but such are the ways of power. After the Kevin Morgan drama and Amy's departure, he started promoting younger talent in earnest. The company is doing well, to the point that Matt is already angling for another bigger, better deal. The venture capitalist who backed them in acquiring the second factory is so impressed with their turnaround results that he asked Phil and Matt to take care of an ailing group of industrial companies he's got on his books and that hovers on the brink of bankruptcy, dangling as bait a large management fee and share options. I guess they really have the gold flowing now! Will they go for it? Bigger bucks, bigger responsibilities, bigger headaches, but hey, as Matt says, in business if you're not growing, you're dying.

My sabbatical is almost over, and I am girding myself to meet another batch of hapless students to educate and enlighten. My book on "casual irrationality" is nowhere near finished, but my list of practical examples grows longer by the minute. Instead, I've written this account of lean transformation, which, one never knows, might be of greater use to more people in the end. If not, never mind. For one thing, this strange year has reminded me how full of surprises life can be and how mysteriously the lines of our lives get woven together. I even find I enjoy sailing these days — at least with blue skies, calm seas, and sunny weather —— so there's hope for me yet, as my old man would say. Dad and Phil have entered the *Felicity* in an overnight race down the coast over the weekend. Believe it or not, I'd be out with them right now but Amy is preparing a presentation on "supervisors, team leaders, and the team" for a big conference in Michigan next week, and she's all stressed out. So I'll be busy taking special care of my favorite lean expert this weekend.

For Further Reading

The authors have focused this book on the human story of one lean turnaround, only explaining the technical details of lean practice to a degree sufficient to tell the story. There are several key publications that offer rich lessons for lean students and practitioners seeking to learn more about how to put these ideas into practice. We recommend the following titles:

Harris, Rick, Chris Harris, and Earl Wilson. 2003. *Making Materials Flow: A Lean Material Handling Guide for Operations, Production Control, and Engineering Professionals*. Brookline, MA: Lean Enterprise Institute. This hands-on workbook teaches how to create continuous flow by supplying purchased parts to the value stream in an optimal manner. This guide would come in handy to Phil and Amy as they try to sort out logistics toward the end of this story and address the new challenges exposed by the successes the company has realized.

Liker, Jeffrey. 2004. *The Toyota Way: 14 Management Principles from the World's Greatest Manufacturer*. New York, NY: McGraw-Hill. An excellent, detailed, and rich book that combines a thorough reporting of Toyota's practice with an insightful codification of the company's principles. Liker's deep knowledge of Toyota's practice over the past 20 years brings extra rigor to his explanation of the principles. This book answers Phil's questions about the core principles of TPS with a slightly different focus than that of Bob Woods.

Marchwinski, Chet, and John Shook, compilers. 2004. *Lean Lexicon: A Graphical Glossary for Lean Thinkers*. Brookline, MA: Lean Enterprise Institute. A pithy guide to the key terms and ideas of lean. Comprised of clear definitions and helpful examples and illustrations, this guide creates excellent working definitions of the essentials.

Monden, Yasuhiro. 1993. *Toyota Production System: An Integrated Approach to Just-in-Time.* Norcross, GA: Engineering & Management Press. Monden, a professor of managerial accounting at the University of Tsukuba, was given the opportunity by Taiichi Ohno to study every last detail of Toyota's production system. For better and worse, he managed to do so. His dense and massive manual is an essential resource for anyone who wants to master the technical aspects of lean. Whereas Bob Woods often uses a rule-of-thumb approach, Monden's work is the most comprehensive reference for readers who want to know how to calculate matters such as the number of cards in a kanban loop or batch size in fixed lot production.

Ohno, Taiichi. 1988. *The Toyota Production System: Beyond Large-Scale Production.* Portland, OR: Productivity Press. After retiring from Toyota, Ohno wrote this appealing series of essays that give a high-level explication of Toyota's famed system. While this book doesn't give readers a set of actions to put into practice on Monday morning, Ohno provides fascinating insights on topics such as how Toyota developed the system in response to its post-World War II resources and abilities and what it consciously adapted from Henry Ford. While many of the "Ohno stories" that Bob Woods tells may be apocryphal, they are often told and retold in the lean community for teaching purposes. This delightful book clarifies many core TPS concepts, and gives an insight into Ohno's character and outlook.

Rother, Mike, and John Shook. 1998. *Learning To See: Value Stream Mapping to Add Value and Eliminate Muda.* Brookline, MA: Lean Enterprise Institute. An excellent introduction to value-stream mapping. This detailed workbook shares both the principles and the practice of diagramming every step involved in the material and information flows needed to bring a product from order to delivery. Bob Woods only introduces the notion of value-stream mapping after he has determined that Phil and Amy have developed a gemba attitude. For readers looking to figure out where the gold is being held up in their processes, this workbook is the best place to start.

Rother, Mike, and Rick Harris. 2001. *Creating Continuous Flow: An Action Guide for Managers, Engineers, and Production Associates.* Brookline, MA: Lean Enterprise Institute. This workbook explains, in simple step-by-step terms, how to introduce and sustain lean flows in pacemaker cells and lines. A sequel to *Learning to See*, this workbook shows how to move from seeing how work and materials are organized to setting a production rhythm and applying the principles of continuous flow. An essential guide for the type of work that Amy and Phil tackle when redesigning the production cells and lines.

Smalley, Art. 2004. *Creating Level Pull: A Lean Production-System Improvement Guide for Production-Control, Operations, and Engineering Professionals.* Brookline, MA: Lean Enterprise Institute. An excellent and robust workbook showing how to continue the lean transformation from a handful of isolated improvements to an entire level, pull-based system. Those who implement these ideas — beyond point optimization and flow in just one value stream — are conducting *system* kaizen to create a lean production control system that ties together the flows of information and materials supporting every product family in a facility. Even Bob Woods tends to focus only on one of Phil's products when explaining pull, although he mentions other elements of the system. This guide works through the details of facilitywide pull systems in an instructive manner and clearly addresses the thorny issues of leveling in mix and volume.

Womack, James, and Daniel Jones. 1996. *Lean Thinking.* New York: Simon & Schuster. The book that popularized the principles of lean production to a broad audience. Spanning companies in different industries and countries, the authors draw from elaborate research to extract a handful of powerful principles that define lean practice. The first, and still the definitive, book on lean practice. Extremely useful, especially to hold up against the definition of lean as proposed by Woods senior.

Womack, James, and Daniel Jones. 1990. *The Machine that Changed the World.* New York: Rawson Associates. The first book to introduce the phrase "lean production" to the world, this exhaustive study of manufacturing practices among global automobile companies identified the profound benefits that could be realized from a fundamentally different production approach, which the book labeled "lean."

Womack, James, and Daniel Jones, 2002. *Seeing the Whole: Mapping the Extended Value Stream*, 2002. Brookline, MA: Lean Enterprise Institute. Learning to see, and to map, value streams, represents a powerful step in identifying and removing waste. This comprehensive guide teaches users of value-stream mapping how to extend this field of view beyond the facility level to see all the steps and time needed to bring a typical product from raw materials to finished goods. Now that Phil has begun to see the flow of value, this workbook would prove handy as he continues to pursue lean with customers and suppliers.

Also by Michael Ballé and Freddy Ballé
The Lean Manager